TALES OF AN ELDRITCH WASTELAND

C.T. PHIPPS

"You are going to get yourself killed, Abdul Alhazared, and everyone will remember you as a madman," my uncle, Abbas, said.

The sun was beating down on our heads and we'd been riding our horses for hours. We were well provisioned and had just left a camp of Banu Ua nomads when their questions about where we were going had grown too close to the mark. It was said that they murdered anyone who attempted to loot the ruins of the Rub'al Khali or "The Empty Quarter." I did not consider myself a looter but a man of philosophy.

Nevertheless, I'd pushed us to an unhealthy degree and wondered if I was putting our lives at risk. It was not yet eleven in the morning, and when we reached noon, I did not know if I could stop myself from pressing further. If it was not for worry that our horses might pass out and strand us there to die alone and forgotten, I'm certain I would not have stopped.

I snorted and looked over at Abbas. "They already consider me to be a madman, Uncle."

"You are not helping your case," he said. "I have indulged you far too much over the years. Your obsession with the idolaters of the past has blinded you to what is important in life. You should be putting your third child into a second wife's belly."

I shook my head. Women had never interested me, or boys for that matter, but I had long been cursed with a temperament unsuitable to the rest of the Caliphate. I had questioned everything my tutors taught me and my father.

CONTENTS

ACKNOWLEDGMENTS

Special thanks to David Niall Wilson, David Dodd, Matthew Davenport, David Hambling, David J. West, Andrea Pearson, Seth Skorkowsky, Bobby Derie, Ruthanna Emrys, Anne M. Pillsworth, and Tim Mendees. You're all people who helped make me appreciate Lovecraft and his works.

Also, HP Lovecraft, Robert E. Howard, Stephen King, and Brian Lumley because you're better authors than I'll ever be.

FOREWORD

Ia Cthulhu!

I had a strange start to my love of the Cthulhu Mythos as I didn't begin with HP Lovecraft. Instead, I first became familiar with the Mythos through the works of Brian Lumley when he created the Titus Crow novels. These followed a far pulpier hero than Lovecraft's usual ones in Titus' adventures against a wholly evil pantheon of Great Old Ones. Very binary good versus evil (even if that's not how I like my Mythos). That led me to the *Call of Cthulhu*, *Arkham Horror*, and various video games. Eventually, I did read all of HP Lovecraft's writings and loved their fantastical vision of scientific horror combined with occult monstrosity.

Many years later, when I decided to set down and become a writer, I was inspired to combine my love of the Cthulhu Mythos with my love of post-apocalypse fiction. *Cthulhu Armageddon* was created as much from *Fallout*, *Mad Max*, Stephen King's *The Dark Tower*, and *The Stand* as it was HPL's world. I threw in a bit of Conan the Barbarian as well since John is a much more Robert E. Howard hero than Howard Phillips.

However, the *Cthulhu Armageddon* novels and its sequels aren't the only writing I've done in the Cthulhu Mythos. Indeed, they aren't even the only material I've written for the *Cthulhu Armageddon* world. The Cthulhu Mythos is such a fertile and fascinating world for exploration that I've been inspired many times to return to it.

Here, you will find stories set in the distant past, the present, and the post-apocalyptic future. The Cthulhu Mythos was created primarily in short fiction and that is something that I've dabbled in primarily with the Books of Cthulhu series. Indeed, most of these stories, albeit not all, are found in that series. However, now you can enjoy them all in one handy volume. I've also included notes about each story at their beginning to provide some context for the works and what I was thinking writing them.

Fans of my writing may be surprised at the variance in the stories' tones. Some of them are post-apocalypse adventures, others more firmly horror, and a few of them drift into outright fantasy or science fiction. That's because the Cthulhu Mythos can tell all these stories and none. It is an unknowable mishmash of multiple genres and I feel that it works best when it zigs when the audience expects it to zag.

I hope you'll all enjoy.

"The Skull on the Desk" is the opening fiction I wrote for Tales of the Al-Azif. *Basically, a collection of short stories written about the* Necronomicon. *We needed a story that would link them all together thematically and I came up with the idea of the 'origin story', so to speak, for Abdul Alhazred. Who was the so-called Mad Arab, why did he do what he did, and where did he learn what drove him to write the world's most infamous book? I had a lot of fun subverting the traditional hero's narrative here as the protagonist is not what he seems.*

THE SKULL ON THE DESK

"Y ou are going to get yourself killed, Abdul Alhazred, and everyone will remember you as a madman," my uncle, Abbas, said.

The sun was beating down on our heads and we'd been riding our horses for hours. We were well provisioned and had just left a camp of Banu Ua nomads when their questions about where we were going had grown too close to the mark. It was said that they murdered anyone who attempted to loot the ruins of the Rub'al Khali or "The Empty Quarter." I did not consider myself a looter but a man of philosophy.

Nevertheless, I'd pushed us to an unhealthy degree and wondered if I was putting our lives at risk. It was not yet eleven in the morning, and when we reached noon, I did not know if I could stop myself from pressing further. If it was not for worry that our horses might pass out and strand us there to die alone and forgotten, I'm certain I would not have stopped.

I snorted and looked over at Abbas. "They already consider me to be a madman, Uncle."

"You are not helping your case," he said. "I have indulged you far too much over the years. Your obsession with the idolaters of the past has blinded you to what is important in life. You should be putting your third child into a second wife's belly."

I shook my head. Women had never interested me, or boys for that matter, but I had long been cursed with a temperament unsuitable to the rest of the Caliphate. I had questioned everything my tutors taught me and my father. I dare not ask Allah to bless his soul given my blasphemies, and had been smart enough to beat prudence into me when they'd claimed I was an atheist. I was not, I just did not believe in the gods they did. I did not share the faith of my countrymen and could not believe in a benevolent all-powerful being who looked over our world. I *did* believe there was something beyond this crude physical matter, though, and that it was the duty of all righteous men to seek its secrets the way the ancient Greeks had. Had Socrates not believed in an Unknown God that was better and more interesting than the naked stone statues his people had prayed to?

"You do not indulge me," I said, more amused at my uncle's chidings than annoyed. "My father left his entire fortune to me. You live off my largess."

Money was unimportant in the grand scheme of things, a belief my father and uncle had continually bemoaned. What good was currency when the universe was vaster and more exciting than anything that could be bought with gold or silver? What purpose was the gathering of wealth when we would all die one day and be food for insects? Better to devote oneself to unlocking the secrets of the world than fretting over petty things like the price of rugs. Ironically, though, it was the wealth my father had gained haggling over every coin that allowed me to pursue my research.

Abbas snorted, unhappily. "I may have a habit of overindulging in ways that are not forbidden, but at least I do not waste a vast merchant empire's funds on pottery, clay tablets, and scrolls."

My uncle did not believe and that was a good thing. Well, perhaps it was better to say he believed in the common ways of the locals. His dreams were not filled with stories of ancient Dagon and the city of R'lyeh where he dwelled with Dread Koo'toolu or of the idiot god Azazel-Thoth who lived at the center of the universe (if such a place existed). No, his dreams were untroubled by dark, unseemly shapes that flapped wings on invisible winds while whispering of worlds beyond this one.

Half of my father's employees had abandoned me, forcing me to buy slaves to replace them, and I'd had to whip one to death after he'd sought to exorcise me with a cat. I still remember how I'd slept peacefully for a week thanks to his savage's prayer to Allah, Bast, Nodens, and a host of other strange deities. Most would have appreciated such a thing, but I lived for my strange mind-bending dreams.

"I have retrieved relics and wonders from the ruins of Babylon, spoken with the mystics beneath Memphis, and learned long-forgotten languages," I said, defending my studies. "Thrice I have been invited to speak with the wizards at the Umayyad court."

I did not mention that I was now banished from the court on pain of death. The old vizier, a Greek Christian heretic hated by all but the Caliph, was thought to have been dragged off to hell when tricked into walking onto an Elder Sign claimed to be given to the new Caliph by an angel. The new Caliph, despite his learning, believed more like Abbas and said that I was a damned fool who had sold his soul to Iblis'Nyarlathotep. As if I would be wasting my time with fools like him if I could garner that being's attention!

"And what has it gotten you?" Abbas asked.

"I just said—"

"They burned down our warehouse in Baghdad," Abbas said, shaking his head. "I tried to arrange three marriages for you and each family turned me down when I said it was for you. Our reputation is worse in every town we visit. Only Christians, Jews, and heathens from Cathay will deal with us in some places."

I frowned. I didn't want to admit to my uncle that there had been material cost to my actions beyond even what he knew. The family fortune had been halved by my actions and halved again. This might consume the whole of my remaining funds. If we found nothing here, then I might be forced into the streets. "They are fools."

I would do anything to continue my research. I would find a way.

"You are not a wazir, Abdul," Abbas said.

"What?"

"A wise man, a wizard, a sorcerer, whatever you want to call it," Abbas said, shaking his head. "I know what you have been chasing this entire time and it does not exist."

I turned around and snarled at him. "You know nothing."

Indeed, if he knew my true purpose here, he would not only turn back, but run screaming from house to house that I was an enemy of God.

He'd have been right to.

"You talk of speaking with wizards and the courts, but I know a man who can pull a snake from his mouth as well as make a camel disappear, none of which actually uses real power. There is no such thing," Abbas said, clearly disgusted. "You have been chasing children's fantasies and ghost stories for your entire adult life and it is time for you to grow up."

I could not tolerate his words, they were too close to the truth because I was chasing real magic out here in the desert. The power of the real gods, not the ones prayed to my countrymen. Beings I hated and envied in equal measure.

My hand moved down to my scimitar. "Apologize now or—"

"What? You'll kill me? Your own flesh and blood? We are alone in the desert and almost to the point we need to turn around! Let go of this madness!"

I spit three curses at him and galloped off.

The endless dunes confused and frustrated me, and the Nameless City was no closer than it had been hours before. The heat, and my abusive treatment toward the horse, who had trusted me to get us both through the journey safely, seemed likely to be my undoing. I, who had raised natural forces like the heat and the weather, above any theology or god, was threatened with dehydration and exhaustion, with none of the water I had expected to find in sight.

I proved to be a greater fool than my uncle. The heat got to me, and my horse collapsed, leaving us both exposed to the noonday sun. I had devoted so much of my time to the study of ancient civilizations and languages that I had never learned the proper way of surviving in the desert. In the end, my horse died before me and I was left to a slow, lingering death under the burning heat of the sun.

Perhaps that would have been a fitting end for me in my desire to prove Allah false and the universe ruled by more unforgiving forces. I'd made the mistake of believing this made my quest righteous when truth had no favorites. The universe did not care if the insects or humans (was there a difference?) knew what gods ruled over its physical laws. It simply was and the whole of humanity was an infection growing in the wound that was life on Earth. I would have laughed but my lips were cracked, and my throat was far too dry.

I only lasted the night before I fell to unconsciousness and expected death. My dreams, at least, were still a place of refuge and I saw things that enticed the imagination even as my upbringing made me recoil. I saw the obsidian-skinned face of the Black Pharaoh in the stars above, looking out over a vast kingdom of a million celestial spheres. I saw men shaped like beetles, worms, gnats, fish, and slime praying to things I could only make out the indistinct hideous shadows of.

I saw the early Earth receive falling stars containing these monstrous things—beings that were miles-tall and half as wide—shaping reality with thought. There were no humans in this world, and for a moment I believed that the tales of my faith would prove true. These were the jinn and efreeti, creatures created long before man. They were nothing like us, though, and as far superior to us as I was to a locust. I saw these beings war with flower-headed fleshy things and each other, destroying the world multiple times until they went into a terrible slumber.

Dead but dreaming.

Why are you showing me this? I begged the Black Pharaoh.

The Black Pharaoh did not give me an answer, though, instead gesturing to another sphere. Many other spheres in fact. I saw races on dying worlds drawn to the Earth. Fungus from Yuggoth, goatmen from Leng, shapeshifting centaurs from Kastro'vaal, and hive-minded insects from Callisto. They came to pay homage to these great old beings that settled on our world. It sickened me to realize that we were a destination for a pilgrimage by the universe's other races. Religion and truth were not enemies and the only thing different for enlightened beings was what forces one humbled oneself before.

Do you still wish to know the truth? The Black Pharaoh finally spoke to me. *Even though the truth will bring you nothing but misery, despair, and madness?*

Its voice was like a lion's claws on my soul, tearing away my sanity with each syllable. As a child I had often torn the wings off of insects to amuse myself. It reminded me of how I felt realizing that as such a mighty being had deigned to notice me.

"Yes!" I shouted, suddenly feeling like my throat was healed. "There is nothing man was not meant to know, no truths that I fear, and no greater thing than to know the unknowable! If madness be my punishment, then let it be the madness of the enlightened among the ignorant!"

One of my tutors had told me of the scholar Plato among the Greeks. My tutor, an obese debauched man named Duhat, had believed them to be the greatest civilization of all time. I had ignored most of what he tried to teach me, but one story remained stuck in my head. Plato had spoken of a cave where all of humanity was imprisoned, and the only things the prisoners knew of the outside world were shadows cast upon a wall. Then one poor soul had wandered out of the cave and been exposed to the beautiful, yet terrible, world beyond. When he returned and tried to enlighten his fellows, they had ostracized and killed him. I did not know if the latter part was an invention of Duhat's or not, but I preferred to be the man who had seen the true world than the disgusting fools in the cave.

Is the madman the one who denies the truth or the one who proclaims himself the sole holder of it? Does any of it matter since truth is a concept of humans? Nothing in life matters except to those beings who recognize facts and interpret how they make them feel.

Silence! I snapped, only to reel back in horror at the realization I'd addressed a god with such insolence.

Instead, Iblis'Nyarlathotep just laughed. *You address only yourself.*

I pondered those words and interpreted their meaning. *Yes, I am a god or, at least, their prophet. I must write my own holy book to guide the feeble masses from Plato's cave. Madman or genius, I will be the father of a new religion.*

Or many. You will find the answers you seek in the Al-Azif.

The Book of the Insect?

The Book of Lies, the Black Pharaoh said. **The remnants of a dead civilization that sought to save itself but could only shift its fate to another damned, doomed race. Despite the fate of its authors, that book contains the names of many Great Old Ones and true gods, or at least true as any such being worshiped by mortals may be.**

Show me this book! I will do anything! I must know!

I promise you, Abdul, you will know more about everything than any other man of your race has ever learned. It will merely cost you knowing yourself.

That was when I awoke.

Air entered my lungs and I felt like a new man. I soon found this to be literally true. I turned to see my corpse lying beside me on a stone slab. The two of us were in a pyramid-shaped chamber with multiple stone slabs, like altars. Light was provided by organic crystals growing along the walls and bathing us in an unnatural blue-green light. I was relieved to find that I was intact, with two hands, two feet, and smooth brown skin. My manhood was intact, apparently even my circumcision undone. The Abdul Al'Hazred beside me looked like he'd died of dehydration, however, and was little more than a skeleton.

I felt, given the circumstances, my next actions were quite reasonable.

I screamed.

A woman entered the chamber, but not like any woman I had ever seen. She was dressed in a shockingly immodest style with only wrap around her breasts and a loincloth. Her hair hung down past her shoulders and her skin was black like the Pharaoh's, yet her eyes were of the clearest blue. There was a vague sense of the old Egyptians about her, but I also sensed that she was something else. Whatever soul, if such a thing existed, emanated behind that gaze did not feel in any way human. It was as if a pagan goddess was gazing upon me or one of the creatures I'd seen in my vision.

"Away woman, with your nakedness!" I said, covering myself.

The woman seemed annoyed rather than apologetic. *You will find no one here believes or shares your social values, Abdul Al'Hazred. I suppose you are not as enlightened as you think you are.*

I heard her voice in my mind. It was melodious but inhuman, sounding like a choir of pipes rather than an utterance of words.

"What are you?" I asked, stunned. "How do you know my name?"

We are the Yith, the woman said. *We read your memories while transferring your mind to a clone. You are an important historical personage of this reality's time period.*

"A c...lone?" I asked, trying to understand. I felt like a foolish, ignorant child compared to her.

You would call it a homunculus. We took samples of your essential salts and used them to grow you a new body before transferring your soul into it. That is the closest approximation I can make of the science involved to your frame of knowledge.

Her words angered me. "I can learn anything you can teach me."

Why would we do that? the woman asked.

I had no answer for that. Why indeed? Most beings were motivated solely by their own self-interest. It was one of the reasons I hated my fellow man. "Why save me in the first place?"

You are a source of information we are collecting about humanity's extinction.

I blinked and stood, no longer caring about my nakedness. "Extinction? What do you mean?"

Humankind is not the first intelligent species to have evolved or existed on Ketra'goo'an, what humans call Earth. The Yith, my species, inhabited it sixty-five million years ago before an extinction-level event forced us to move our consciousnesses to the far future. As part of our efforts to gather and preserve knowledge, we have charted and catalogued the period between those two times. I am wearing the body of a woman of this time period while her consciousness is safely stored in the past. Many of your greatest scientists, philosophers, or thinkers were either my race or beings who learned from them.

I found myself stunned and fascinated. Here was proof positive of the Earth being far older than so many theologians claimed, yet a part of me had enough lingering loyalty to my species to be appalled. "Is there no way to stop the death of my race?"

The woman stared at me with her empty, ancient eyes. *Your race has already died. Time is not a progression. All that is happening, has happened, and will happen at once. Consciousness is a movement along a pre-arranged set of events. Events may change based upon which reality in the quantum frequency you are inhabiting but—*

I felt like my head was going to explode.

I am distressing you. I shall stop.

"No!" I shouted, raising my hands in the air. "You mustn't! I must know more! This is why I have come to the Nameless City! To discover the secrets of the worshipers of Acheron, Baalzebel, and the Lords of Locusts!"

I had lied to my uncle, who I expected to be either dead or safely on his way back to Baghdad in order to loot my fortune. I had told Abbas my goal here was to investigate a city consumed by a sandstorm in order to find a cache of gold that had been hidden away by the pagan idolaters who once inhabited it. I'd used golden fish I'd bartered from the cult of Dagon along Egypt's shoreline to convince him or at least incite his greed. Abbas had insisted on melting down the sacred relics of the ugly, foul-smelling people in order to make coins, but I'd convinced him to help me. He never would have agreed to come if he'd known my true purpose.

The *Al-Azif*. The Book of the Insect.

It had been ages since the oceans had drunk Atlantis and the rise of the sons of Aryas. The ancient times had passed with the Israelites putting to sword the Canaanites, Stygians, Philistines, and worshipers of Set-Yig. True magic was a thing of the past and I'd been able to find only a few scattered fragments of the *Book of Eibon* that served as humanity's sole insight into not only the truth of reality, but the art of manipulating it. It was said that the *Al Azif* was the last relic of unfathomable power to be had by those brave and deranged enough to read the secrets of devils.

The woman looked at me curiously. *The mutated humans who inhabited this world, possessed by brain parasites containing Callisto consciousnesses, have been purged. The advanced life-forms of their world worshiped Yog-Sothoth, the collective consciousness of space-time, and do not respect the proper flow of history. They were attempting to alter the flow of events in order to guarantee their ascension in this planet's future. They would replace both my race and the hybridized offshoots of humanity's future evolution with their own descendants.*

I barely registered anything she said after her first sentence. "The Nameless Ones are all dead?"

It was like a blow to the chest and I almost murdered the woman where she stood. This had been my last chance of discovering the secrets of the universe. The Nameless Ones were said to be walking corpses full of scarabs that knew the true names of the wind, fire, earth, and water.

I did not believe in superstition, but I'd seen a fakir put a scarab it claimed to be from the Nameless City into a child's mouth and the boy then speak great wisdom about magic, gods, science, and the future. I had sat down at the feet of the hybrid being and learned of countless fascinating things, including the location of this city. The price had been high, at least for the boy, with the scarab eating its brain after a few hours but I felt it well worth it. Sadly, the scarab died not long after I slit the throat of its owner in my attempt to acquire it.

So, the woman replied. *You wish to see the Al-Azif? Your mind practically screams in lust for it.*

My gaze met hers. I wondered if she knew how much I was willing to do to achieve greater knowledge. She'd dangled a carrot in front of me and there was only one response. "Yes. Take me to it. Now."

The *Al-Azif* hovered in the air at the center of a chamber that had been a temple for once-human creatures. It was a towering pyramidal edifice built around a single central chamber that seemed infused with unearthly alien power.

The chamber had no seats, but dozens of rows of black stones were arranged in a circle around the blue nimbus engulfing the *Al-Azif*. My mind briefly conjured the image of hideous desiccated corpses, riddled with otherworldly vermin, shambling forward to offer prayers to the unholy thing. The *Al-Azif* itself appeared as a vellum book very similar to the kind produced by the Caliph's scholars. I had expected it to look much older but a part of me realized that it was not a book made of pages and ink. Instead, somehow, it appeared thus to me to aid my understanding but was more like an information source incarnate.

"Beautiful," I whispered, walking forward. The Yith woman had provided me with a robe and sandals that lent me a false sense of decency and modesty as I approached the object of my search. "It is everything I could have imagined it to be."

The Al-Azif has been a plague upon your race since its arrival on your world sixteen million years ago, the Yith woman spoke. *The Ixtol, as they called themselves, devoted themselves heavily to the worship of the Great Old Ones and constructed machines to channel the power of the mind. They derived the secrets of Azathoth, Nyarlathotep, Yog-Sothoth, and the Sleeping Ones.*

"They were wise," I said, slowly approaching the book.

They were fools, the Yith woman said. *They conjured things that they could not put down and warped themselves trying to become more than they were. Eventually, the planet Ixtol, that you know as Callisto, was scoured of all life. Their Priest-God sought to preserve himself and his people. He poured their consciousness into an artifact that he believed would eventually possess lesser beings.*

"So, he sought to do exactly what your race did," I said, not afraid to show my contempt. I was right outside the nimbus of blue light now.

Yes, the Yith woman did not deny it. *But they wished to destroy a sentient species to do so. Your species. Which is unforgivable.*

I did not see the difference between what she said the Nameless Ones had planned for humanity and what her people had done to the residents of this city. The Yith had, indeed, purged the city of all life. I could find no trace of the Nameless Ones as we passed through courtyards, streets, and palaces on our way to the *Al-Azif*'s location. There were no signs of men, women, or children (if the Nameless Ones could be said to have any). Instead, they were empty, but curiously alive with lights, and strange metallic sounds that emanated from each building. I did not see any other Yith, but statues made of living metal shaped as animals or hovering cones moved about the place.

I tried to touch the book, but my hand was shocked when I reached for it, causing me to pull back. "Sorcery!"

Science, the Yith woman replied. *Though the two words are merely variations on the method of using the will to create an effect.*

"You say the Nameless Ones tried to alter time?" I asked, unable to comprehend such a thing, no matter how I tried.

Yes, the Yith woman said, walking beside me. *They provided advanced knowledge to species unprepared for its use. The so-called Sorcerer Kings and mutant civilizations of the past owe much to their influence. Not all of them, though, because the other species of humanoids on your world, like the Deep Ones or Ghouls, have their own origins. Indeed, it was the Deep Ones who destroyed the early civilization on your island of Crete to prevent the extinction of mankind. In time, the* Al-Azif *will be used as the basis for your book—*

"I must read it," I said, looking at her. "Now."

That is not how it should happen. We have done our best to repair how events are meant to flow in order to facilitate an optimal timeline for our—

I grabbed her by the throat with both hands then threw her against the blue nimbus, causing her to utter an involuntary cry of pain. I gripped her and slammed her head into the nimbus repeatedly. After the first few blows, there was a sickening crunch. I threw her lifeless corpse to one side.

Good, the *Al-Azif* spoke in my mind. ***You are worthy.***

I looked at the book and reached for it. "Yes, I am. Are you...are you the Black Pharaoh?"

A mocking, hideous laughter answered me and I closed my fist tightly at the mockery. The fist passed through the blue nimbus without difficulty.

"What is so funny?" I asked, my voice taking on a dangerous edge.

I am Vhourvath, the voice spoke. *First and last among the Ixtol.*

"So you're not Nameless Ones after all," I said, grabbing hold of the book.

What followed was an agonizing sensation, like fire burning through my body and brain. It felt like I was burning, inside and out, but I saw no wounds or flames. Falling to my knees, I clutched the *Al-Azif* to my body despite the fact it was the source of my agony.

Your mind is a black, swirling storm of chaos. I cannot take your body, Vhourvath spoke to me.

"What?" I called out, sweating from every pore. "You wanted to *steal* my body?"

I didn't know why the thought was so shocking to me. I had always admired the glorious amorality of the races I'd read about. How they were wild and free, unshackled by notions of good or evil. Yet, it was *offensive* that they dared treat me with the same disdain they treated other humans.

The Yith or something else has blocked my passage. You are useless to us.

I felt another burning sensation across my body and realized the Nameless Ones were trying to kill me with pure pain. Dropping the book had no effect and I thrashed on the ground and held my head with both hands. "I can help you! I can give you bodies! Worshipers! Whatever you desire!"

The pain stopped.

What do you want in return? Vhourvath asked, sounding almost human in its suspicions. *Your species evolved to be as selfish as any other.*

I needed several breaths to calm down before I answered. "Knowledge."

Power it is.

With Vourvath's assistance, I made my way through a strange series of portals that carried me across the desert back to civilized space. What followed was close to a decade of studying the *Al-Azif* and bartering with its deranged occupants. I was forced to flee from the cities I dwelt in many times, the missing children and dead priests inevitably creating a panic among the foolish locals who did not understand the importance of my work.

My uncle abandoned me, having informed on me to imams and wazirs both, and causing the Caliph to call for my head. There was a substantial price on my life throughout all the lands the Prophet had united through his faith. Many times I was forced to fake my death or use the powers now at my disposal to protect myself. Whole villages ended up carried away by byakhee or swallowed up by blood-drinking Cthonian horrors. I could not control the terrible things the book allowed me to conjure, but I could summon them and sometimes even turn them against my long-dead insectoid patrons.

I lived thus until I completed my life's work, the *Necronomicon*. I compiled it from secrets I learned from the lips of mummified skulls, from eaten brains, and from drug-induced visions. The *Al-Azif* had aided me in my work, but was not the sole source of my knowledge. Indeed, by the year 730 of the Christian Calendar, I had surpassed Vhourvath and created a text that had been copied hundreds of times by my followers. It was the new Quran in my mind, and would usher in an age of horror and wonder once all mankind had embraced it. My book's existence caused certain challenges, though, that needed to be dealt with.

You are a fool, Abdul Al'Hazred, to believe you can simply tuck me away in a chest, Vhourvath whispered as I carried the book through the underground tunnels my followers had dug beneath Damascus.

"You have become…inconvenient," I said, thinking about the near miss I'd had in Samarra. Hundreds of my scarab-eyed slaves had been blasted to dust by a wizard who had conjured the power of a golden-eyed god named Kthanid.

Many of my followers, from the fallen Byzantine knight Lord Wilfred Whiteley to the debased medusa Marcia, had been slain by these cults of the Elder Gods. They had the means to track the beings I had helped the book to "rebirth" in the bodies of my former race. I had no loyalty to the Nameless Ones, any more than they had loyalty to me, but they had become useful servitors. Most of them were all but mindless without their master and obeyed whomever claimed to represent their eldritch gods. I had better servants now. Humans who believed I was a true mouthpiece of the gods and were pledged to live for great Cthulhu the way other fools did for 'Īsā ibn Maryam or the Prophet.

You think you can simply hand me over to the dogmen and I will disappear from your life? You are as much a fool as the zealots you claim will be spared when the Great Old Ones rise.

The ghouls underneath Damascus were a nation unto themselves and had agreed to bargain with the *Al-Azif* for more of its secrets. I was growing older, and while not even as old as my uncle Abbas had been when he'd first joined me on my quests for forbidden lore, I was already pondering the means to escape my impending death. I did not trust the immortality of the Nameless Ones, who promised much but simply moved around one's corpse like a beetle did its shell.

"It is my destiny to live forever," I said, simply. "You who act as a superior species have had millennia to destroy my race. Instead, all you have done is create a few failed civilizations and vermin-oriented cults. I am done with you. When people think of the texts that answer the questions of the cosmos, they will think of my book, not yours."

You still think with your pedestrian human mind. It hurts to even lower myself to speak with you as if you were an equal rather than a slave-tool made by Elder Things to supplement their shoggoths. What have I devoted to your race? Twenty thousand years? It is a pittance of time to manipulate your species to become slightly more useful for the hour of mine's rebirth. You are nothing more than cattle we have husbanded as food.

I had gotten used to Vhourvath's delusions of grandeur. I had once thought the Nameless Ones to be a superior species, but years of exposure had made me realize that both species were equally pathetic and insignificant. The Nameless Ones were but one of a million races in this star cluster alone, and the universe would not mourn their loss any more than it did my race.

"My race is still alive," I said, feeling strangely defensive about a species I'd long held in contempt. "Yours is but copied information in a reliquary. You're not even the real Vhourvath, just his memories and personality stored along with those of his servants."

Reality and dream are one. When you learn this, you will truly be dangerous. But the hour of your end is almost upon you.

I ignored him. I would live forever, no matter the cost. I saw that the end of the cave contained a half-dozen dead ghouls. The furred, wolfen-faced beasts had been shot with Cathay crossbow bolts and their throats cut with scimitars. Dozens of smooth stones were spread around their bodies, each etched with a heinous Elder Sign. I could not see beyond their bodies for a moment, because I had to avert my eyes from that twisted star. It seemed to contain all that I despised in the universe, despite being nothing more than lines carved in rock.

I held tight to the *Al-Azif* as my vision cleared, seeing four masked men in robes, the Elder Sign hanging from their necks on leather cords with weapons drawn. Their eyes were crystal blue and contained an inhuman intelligence. They were not what surprised me the most, however. There, looking like a sheep in a pack of wolves, was my uncle, Abbas.

Time had not been good to the once overfed and healthy man. Most of Abbas' hair had fallen out and his face was gaunt. There were deep wrinkles under his eyes. Liver spots dotted his neck and he'd lost perhaps forty pounds. He was sixty years old but now seemed like a man approaching eighty. There was none of the warmth or faith in his eyes, either, but instead the paranoid look of a man who'd been exposed to the horrors beyond, and without the strength to embrace their gifts. He held a copy of the Quran indicating that he still clung to the beliefs he'd tried to instill upon me, but his expression was one of dread and hopelessness.

I fell back a step and lifted my right hand, making a pair of horns with my fingers. "You! You cannot have my book!"

It was a ridiculous statement and I wondered why I made it. If the Yith desired to retrieve the book, they were welcome to have it. I had bargained, manipulated, and tricked every secret I possibly could from Vhourvath. Indeed, I had exceeded him as both a magician and master of the arcane.

You are a primitive creature with an ape's mind. You cannot begin to know the secrets of the Ixtol.

I scoffed at his taunts, focused instead on the assassins before me. They were not moving forward but instead keeping their distance. This gave me hope I might conjure flame, lightning, or a host of flesh-eating bugs against them. The real magic, imposing one's will upon the universe through dreaming, was not simple. Every syllable of the inhuman tongues I'd learned to mangle the words of seemed banished from my lips. The Elder Signs prevented my speaking, the words lodging in my throat as if the sun was burning away my saliva.

"You have done terrible things, my nephew," Abbas said, his voice weak and broken. "You have consorted with devils and sent many souls to hell. I have followed you and your cult, trying to help those who would unmake this hideous religion you have created, but it is too large. Slaves and sultans worship your evil gods. I beg of you, surrender, and let us try to make right what you have done before both of us are judged."

My uncle advanced, but it was not with weapons or even his fists. Not that he looked like he could wrestle a girl fresh into maidenhood. Instead, there was only love and pity in his eyes. I saw that he blamed himself for not steering me from my path, and had genuinely tried to make amends for what he perceived as my moral failure. I rewarded him for this by bashing his head in with the *Al-Azif*, splattering the book with blood and brain matter. It was as heavy as a stone tablet in that moment, then light as a dream the next.

The four Yith came at me, but I hurled the book toward them and ran in the opposite direction. I did not know if they were a species that would take revenge for one of their number being murdered, but did not wish to risk it. Instead, I simply ran in a crooked path underneath Damascus' busiest streets. I knew these paths well and had used them to visit my acolytes. Many a second or third son, sometimes a female babe, had been offered up for the favor of Cthulhu's Chosen.

Climbing up a rickety wooden ladder, I exited into the back of a lamp shop and pushed through the crowding shoppers into the broad daylight of an open market. That was when I saw dozens of blue-eyed Yith staring at me through those eerie eyes. They had known where I was going to be!

I hissed and cursed before raising my hands in the air. "Ph'nglui mglw'nafh Cthulhu R'lyeh wgah'nagl fhtagn." *In His House at R'lyeh dead Cthulhu waits dreaming.* None of the insects around me understood what I said, but I then began to chant their doom. I called across space and time for the dark things to come forth and kill every man, woman, as well as child in the city. The Yith inhabited the bodies of men, regardless of their true nature, and would die confronted by a creature that ate consciousnesses as well as flesh.

I laughed.

Right up until a small boy deposited a rock covered with an Elder Sign at my feet.

The thing that ate me before a horrified crowd of onlookers was both invisible and uninterested in the other residents of Damascus.

It also took over an hour to finish.

Death was not a release.

I was disappointed that oblivion did not greet me. I felt caterpillars crawl in and out of my eye sockets while flies flew around inside my brain cavity. I was trapped inside a bleached yellow skull, the flesh of my body having been eaten away by the centuries that had passed. One of my followers had retrieved some of my remains, and then used my own principles of sorcery to bind what lesser men would call a soul.

Yet, in my followers' stupidity, they did not copy it precisely. Imbeciles like Baron Randolf of Dunwich, John Dee, Lady Johanna De la Poer, and the blood-drinkers Solomonari of Romania introduced errors where I had created perfection. Hundreds of variants of the *Necronomicon* spread throughout the world, their truths watered down and poisoned with the religions or suppositions of fools. The cult of Cthulhu spread, turning science into religion, and became the hidden faith of millions, in defiance of my wishes, but I could do little. I had become a toy for whatever wizard used me to consult with them or their descendants, and who knew me as a mere curiosity.

Despite my wretched state I remained aware of two facts. One, the *Al-Azif* was still out there and had not remained with the Yith for long. I maintained some small connection to the accursed tome due to my long use of it and felt whenever a mortal of enough will or knowledge tried to harness its secrets. Two, the Great Old Ones would eventually arise and destroy the world that the Nameless Ones sought to colonize.

It was a petty revenge, unworthy of a great wazir such as myself, but one had to make do with what one had. The Yith had tricked me. They had seen how the *Al-Azif* would interfere with their preferred timeline while knowing it had always been my destiny to bring horror to the world through forbidden knowledge. They had sent their enemy down a path to his doom (or was it our doom?) by giving me a silver key to open the door to hell. I knew my own fate as well as that of the human race's, but it would be centuries before I could divine that of the artifact. No wizard or priest would lend me their power to learn the truth, even if they craved the book for themselves.

Instead, one writer in the New World was the answer to my last desire. The storyteller had a mind with a strong will as well as powerful abilities as a dreamer. Sitting on his desk as a gift from Aleister Crowley, who knew his wife Sonia, I was able to briefly steal his potential while inspiring him with tales of the weird as well as macabre. I used him to peer into the future as well as the past to know what fate met the *Al-Azif* after it left my hands. I could not see all its past, mostly the last century before and after my time, but what I glimpsed amused me terribly.

Tales I will now share.

"The Last Page" is a story from Tales of Al-Azif *where we find out how the book that inspired the Necronomicon ended up in the hands of John and Mercury. It takes place after the events of* The Tower of Zhaal *and is fairly important for establishing that Mercury regained her sanity after seeing Cthulhu and their life in New Ulthar. I hadn't intended to make a full sequel to that book at this point, so it was actually serving as an epilogue for the characters. John serving as a small-town sheriff and Mercury as the local madame/doctor (like Doc Holiday) seemed appropriate for its pseudo-Western style. Plus, we get the pseudo-return of an old Lovecraftian villain.*

THE LAST PAGE

A *Cthulhu Armageddon* Adventure

"So, you have a magic book?" I said, leaning back in my wooden stool and looking at my cards.

Two aces, two eights.

All black.

The Dead Man's Hand.

Well, there was also a Queen of Hearts, but no one knew what the last card held by Wild Bill Hickok had been when he was shot in the back by Jack McCall. It was a story that wasn't really told anymore. Not many people had much to say about the Wild West of the 19th century since humanity had largely ended in the 21st.

The previous twenty thousand years of human history seemed like a distant dream, a fanciful lie told to children. No one could even conceive of a time before the Rising, when the Great Old Ones stalked the Earth and mankind were the insects that crawled on the surface of its face.

My name was John Henry Booth and I was a survivor living on a dying world. I wasn't human, not anymore, and I was considered insane by the standards of my own shapeshifting twisted race. I preferred to live as a human being, wearing their form like a suit of clothes, than give into the alien timeless inhumanity that was my birthright. It was a constant daily struggle, though, that ate away at my consciousness. Eventually, I knew the monster inside me would win and I'd fly off to distant stars with the human I'd been as immaterial as a forgotten dream. In the meantime, though, I owned a bar that doubled as the town brothel. I was also the local sheriff.

"Not just *a* magic book," Owen Jones said, his face flush with drink and his breath smelling of rotting flesh. He was a Wastelander with weathered leathery features, bad teeth, and stringy white hair. He wasn't a local and apparently had made a lengthy journey from Canada's irradiated ice lands to the New England deserts. *The* magic book, the *Al-Azif*. That may not make much sense to you—"

"It's the book the *Necronomicon* was created from. Supposedly, the Mad Arab had a vision of the book and copied its contents out into his more famous work," I interrupted, throwing in half my pot on this hand. The cards weren't especially good, but Owen couldn't afford it and I was ready to end tonight.

I'd pegged Owen as trouble as soon as he'd come in here hours ago, accompanied by a young slave girl. New Ulthar was a free town but no one was willing to raise their guns to him either. The girl also didn't seem ready to abandon the man either. Life was hellish enough that some accepted life as property if it meant surviving another day. There was also an aura of the unnatural about Owen, even more so than most Wastelanders, that made me think he was a threat to my people. It looked like I was right. I was glad I'd lured him into this card game as it meant I'd kept him out of whatever trouble he might have otherwise caused.

Owen narrowed his eyes. "You know a lot for a local."

"You have no idea," I said, giving a bitter chuckle.

Owen huffed then looked back at his cards. "Nice establishment you got here."

"It's a hellhole but it's my hellhole," I said, simply.

The Wages of Sin catered to travelers between Kingston, the University, and New Arkham. I'd killed the man who'd previously owned the place and taken over the business. Property rights weren't a thing people cared too much about in this corner of the Wasteland, and the man I'd killed was an asshole. Really, people had been more concerned at the possibility of the place shutting its doors than anything else.

The Wages of Sin wasn't particularly different from other similar establishments in this corner of the world. It had a piano in one corner, a bar, tables, and a second story where the women, and one man, conducted their business. I also owned the hotel next door, or more precisely, my wife did, since Mercury was far savvier at business. Generally, the rougher sorts plied their trades here and the more genteel customers availed themselves of theirs. It wasn't a great retirement for a man who'd literally saved the world, but I supposed I'd only delayed the inevitable.

"It seems I'm a little short," Owen said, frowning. "I'm still willing to play, though."

"Do you have anything I'd want?" I asked, deliberately proving him.

Owen looked upstairs. "Your madam took my slave girl up to her quarters. I think that's worth something since you're using my property."

Owen assumed Mercury, my wife, had taken his slave to bed. Instead, Mercury was finding out everything she could about him. His girl didn't seem to want to go with our earlier, hidden, questions but that might not be the case once her options were explained to her. Either way, I didn't like slavers and was happy to put two bullets in the back of his head to get his property's freedom.

"What's her name?" I asked.

"Asenath," Owen said, as if the name was somehow offensive to him. "She comes from around here. I never did find out how she got all the way up in Canada but she's the reason I'm on this crazy mission."

"Really?" I asked.

I had to wonder at the sort of circumstances that could compel a young woman to depart across the hostile New England Wasteland to the equally horrifying desolate Canadian Badlands. When I was a New Arkham Ranger, I'd once made the perilous journey but it had taken an entire year. I'd lost two of my team during the trek as well.

"Yeah," Owen grinned. "But the rest of the story requires you covering the bet. What was your name, Booth?"

Owen poured himself another whiskey, coughing hideously and only covering his mouth after he'd sprayed a few droplets of blood and blackish phlegm onto the table. He could have spit on the floor. It irritated me he was belittling me, but I'd dealt with far worse in my time. When you faced down a rampaging shoggoth with nothing more than a pair of magic pistols, humans became an annoyance at worst.

"My friends call me John," I said, holding my cards close. I'd pegged him for trouble the moment he'd come in. Most trouble the locals could deal with—if it was human. The alternative? Not so much. In this world, you came to deal with the supernatural the same way you did famine or flood—you did your best to survive it and move on. I had additional advantages being not entirely human myself.

I took a moment to look at my "guest" more closely, taking in elements I hadn't properly considered before. Owen looked about seventy with a long white beard and a bald head. He wore a thick pair of denim overalls over a cotton shirt, his arms had a fetid green tinge. Sometimes, I saw movement inside his jeans when he breathed, as if something was swimming inside him.

The warm human face he wore seemed oddly placed, as if he'd somehow sewn it on. No one else had noticed that he probably wasn't entirely human, either, but I knew that creatures who wanted to fit in had ways of making sure their prey didn't notice. It was more reason to make sure he didn't leave my little town alive.

"I see, John," Owen said, misunderstanding my meaning.

"I didn't say we were friends," I said, pulling out a cigar from my pocket and lightning it. Tobacco was rare these days but there were lots of strange plants you could smoke if you weren't too concerned about your sanity. I'd sacrificed that on the altar of truth a long time back.

Owen narrowed his eyes and reached down to his pocket, possibly going for his gun. Despite the fact he was more corpse than man, he'd drunk hard liquor all night. "I have some emergency gold but I'd rather not touch it. Still—"

I chose my next words carefully. I wasn't interested in gold or silver and his words about the *Al-Azif* were probably bragging but, if true, made him infinitely more dangerous than just another slaver. Inhuman or not. "Why don't you tell me your story and show me the book. I'll consider that covering the bet."

Owen paused, and I knew I had him. He was human enough to still love the inherent dance of lies and greed that was gambling. "Alright."

He moved his hand from his pocket to the bag on the ground by his foot and picked up a book that, to my human eyes, looked like an old leather-bound volume with paper pages. If it had been written during the heyday of Medieval Arab culture, it would have been composed of different materials than the modernized thing in his hands. Luckily I could see with more than the fleshy orbs I'd been born with.

My 'Eyes of Yog-Sothoth' saw that the volume was a living piece of the Dreamlands. It was a glowing collection of thoughts and ideas that was more akin to a rift in the fabric of time than a mere book. It shone and whispered to anyone with the Sight, issuing promises and seeking a way in—a way to possess. The powers behind it trying to enter a mortal mind was a bit like an atomic bomb being used to remove a stump. It was a thing beyond the pathetic lifeforms that had evolved on this third rock from the sun.

"Interesting," I said, understating matters. "Two pair."

"Three of a kind," Owen said. "I guess we'll be continuing to play."

"For now," I said. "You still owe me a tale."

"How do you figure?" Owen asked, looking ready to get while the getting was good. He'd picked up on the fact I wasn't another Wastelander and he'd perhaps said too much about his prize.

"Your luck is changing, and you don't want me to leave," I said, guessing he was as addicted to talking about himself as playing cards. Either would work, though. "Long journeys need cash and supplies."

"Deal the cards and I'll tell you everything," Owen said. "Centuries ago, my slave's ancestor, Andrew Doran, was a fool who actually thought he could fight the horrors beyond. Foolishness, I know, because I understand that the humans are the aberration, not the monsters. He discovered that this volume was actually a reliquary, all that remained of an insectoid race called the Nameless Ones."

"The Nameless Ones?" I asked, dealing the next hand.

"They don't speak English, jackass," Owen said, sounding more than a little drunk. Which surprised me. I had thought that he was probably a walking corpse, animated by something eldritch, or some remnant of old magic, rather than a man. "The Nameless Ones were things born in the darkness of space from the same fungus that spawned the dreaded Mi-Go from Yuggoth. The two races split long ago and came to worship different gods. The Yuggoth worshiped Yog-Sothoth and science, while the Nameless Ones venerated Nyarlathotep and the debased cults of great Kai-too-loo. The Yuggoth took refuge on Pluto and the asteroid belt past it. The Ixtol, as close as their name for themselves could be pronounced by human mouths, settled on what we call Callisto."

"Not very nameless then, are they?"

"Do you want to hear the story or not?"

"So, the Yuggoths were the Catholics and the Ixtol the Protestants."

I personally didn't see the need to differentiate religion like that. Yog-Sothoth, Cthulhu, and Nyarlathtotep were all real, and existed in the physical world. Debating the worship between them was a bit like choosing to worship gravity or space. I wasn't about to tell him to shut up, though, since this was potentially worthwhile information.

Assuming he wasn't making it all up.

"If you want to humanize them that way. Personally, I've got enough of them in me to know they're monsters through and through."

"You might want to keep your voice down," I said, tossing in my bet. "There's places where saying things like that will get you burned alive. Places like this one."

In fact, the citizens of New Ulthar were surprisingly tolerant of the strange and unusual as long as they kept it to themselves. There were Deep Ones, glamoured ghouls, cultists, Catholics, Jews, psychics, and sorcerers among its modest population. Hidden temples, unnatural ancestry, and foul rituals were all things kept indoors. I'd been invited to two orgies and a cannibal feast in the last month, the latter's hosts insisting it had been arranged without innocent deaths.

"Right," Owen said, looking bored with my warning. "Eventually, the Nameless Ones encountered a malignant being, the spawn of Yog-

Sothoth with a mortal, that destroyed their civilization. Their immortal prophet-god, a wizard king named Vhourvath, summoned all the peoples of Callisto, and then devoured them. They became this book, which hurtled itself into space and eventually landed on Earth. It has sought the time and means to release its people into this world ever since."

"It picked a poor planet to avoid being eaten on," I said, dryly. "You'd also think it would have succeeded by now if it was a real threat."

Despite my attitude I was interested in hearing what he had to say. There were more weird tales in this world than even a quasi-immortal like myself could ever hear. That didn't mean I didn't want to hear as many of them as I could, though. It was, ironically, one of the ways I kept myself human.

Owen shrugged and raised his bet. "Supposedly, it almost did during the 1940s."

"What happened then?"

"Andrew Doran killed Vhourvath. Shot him dead."

I laughed then matched his bet. "So, the millions of years-old monster's plan to preserve themselves was a failure because of a human with a gun?"

I'd heard of Andrew Doran from the files in New Arkham's military base. He'd been something of an adventurer archaeologist and occult detective back in an age before humanity had learned that the supernatural was real—the hard way. No one knew what had happened to him past the Second Great War, which seemed a silly name for it, but there were legends that he'd fought Jack Parsons and the Selfosophy cult in the Fifties before ascending to another dimension. It was hardly the strangest fate I'd heard for a wizard but a somewhat anticlimactic end for a man who'd stood up to Dagon and lived.

"A bit," Owen admitted. "Vhourvath had to teach much of humanity the secrets of the occult to create the glyphs, wards, and science necessary to resurrect his kind. Without Vhourvath's consciousness to direct the hive-mind of the Nameless Ones. However, they were a shadow of themselves. Barely more powerful than humans, even if they were still immortal. The book's magic became wild and unpredictable. It got stolen from Miskatonic University by another cult sometime in the late 20th century. Apparently, that was a problem in those days. The TDS or Terra Defense Service, a dreadful secret society, researched ways to destroy it, and discovered a way, but only when the stars aligned properly."

"When was that supposed to happen?"

"After the end of the world."

I hadn't heard of the TDS but there had been many people who had tried to fight the Mythos before the Rising, with varying results. Some of them like the late Elizabeth Dee, had left their journals behind, while most had simply died or gone insane with little to show for their efforts. Maybe they had delayed the Rising for a time or maybe it had appeared on time when the stars were right, as impossible to oppose as the seasons. That didn't mean their struggle hadn't meaning but it did mean it was an existential one. To fight the chaos of the universe was a choice made knowing it was impossible like Sisyphus rolling his boulder up the hills of Hades, knowing it would roll back down immediately after it reached the top.

"So now." I looked at my cards. It was another Dead Man's Hand with clubs instead of spades, which made me wonder if the deck was stacked.

"Yes."

"The TDS were a nasty group of people," Owen admitted. "Wanted to wipe out everything nonhuman, which would have included you and me."

"I don't know what you're talking about," I said, looking at him.

"Sure, you don't," Owen said. "In any case, I might not look it but I'm over a century old. I was born before the Rising."

"Who told you that you don't look it?" I asked, being more insulting than I had to be.

Thankfully, Owen let the jibe slide and just smiled. "I was an occult book dealer before the end of the world. I knew enough to prepare for the end. While others stocked up on canned goods and ammunition, I took the book away from one of the TDS' last members, a gibbering-insane lunatic living in a Southern Gothic mansion untouched by the apocalypse. I used its power to live like a king. Perhaps you've heard of the Golden City of Halifax?"

"They say everyone there is immortal, beautiful, and that there are no children born or living."

Owen didn't respond to that. "Yes, well, we all make mistakes."

I didn't discard any of my cards. "So, what are you doing with the book now?"

Owen's eyes went blurry as he seemed to disappear into his own thoughts. Eventually, he spoke. "For the longest time, I did not think there was any evil act I could not perform in the name of pleasure and power. The book was a hungry god and I fed it many lives. There were, however, things even I would not do to fulfill its needs, and now I am going to destroy it. My slave and I are going to take it to Sentinel Hill where it can be fed to The Thing That Waits."

"You could give it a name, like Bob or something," I said.

Owen glared at me. "Call."

I laid my cards on the table.

Owen had nothing and growled, before pushing the chips across to me. "I think I'm done playing poker. I'll just fetch my slave and get going."

I guessed it was as good a time as any to shoot the man and rob him of the *Al-Azif* but, I admitted, I didn't want to. Slaver or not, the man had traveled all the way down here in order to destroy an evil that had imperiled the world. I decided I would kill him quickly rather than drawing it out as I did with most slavers. I was tempted to even give him a chance to leave peacefully. The thing was I didn't trust anyone to destroy objects of power like that but me. Even if I hadn't known about its existence nearby until a few minutes prior.

"She's a bit occupied right now," I said, looking up to the second story.

I'd caught a glimpse of Asenath earlier. She was pretty as a picture and seemed a lot sharper than her owner. I would have liked to have consulted Mercury to get a bit more information but, instead, moved my hand underneath the table toward my gun. I hoped whatever gods Owen believed in would be more merciful to him than I was about to be.

"That's not my problem," Owen hissed, right before his head exploded.

No exaggeration, Owen's head detonated like a watermelon struck by a shotgun blast. His skull shattered. I watched in fascination as his brain matter splattered across the table. It was alive with hundreds of disgusting, still-living alien insects that had formed a colony inside him. The thing was, I hadn't been the one to shoot him. No, the round that had ended him had come from another's hand.

That was unexpected.

I drew my gun and swung around, scanning the room. A tall man, maybe six foot nine, stood in the door. A heavy duster covered his clothes. He looked like a mummified corpse in dirty clothing. He had no eyes, but a pair of centipedes stuck out of the empty sockets, making screaming sounds at a volume their bodies should have been far too small to possess. Long stringy white hair clung to the back of his scalp. There was also a handcrafted rifle in his hands that was made from pipe and carved wood.

The sudden appearance of the supernatural and violence caused the expected reaction. Panic. Most humans had either learned to pray, or to run away from the monsters when they found them. Neither reaction helped, though those who ran tended to die tired. My clientele was not the usual mix. Instead of running, they opened fire, heading for windows and doors and throwing everything they had at the undead intruder as they went. Dozens of bullets struck the creature, but they had no more effect than if they'd been fired into a wooden post.

The thing ignored the attacks and headed straight for me. I saw he was going for the book. I was tempted to grab the thing and make a run for it but changed my mind. I grabbed Owen's bottle of whiskey, damn near hundred-proof, and hurled it against the creature's head. The tumbler shattered and soaked the creature good. I flicked my cigar at it, and the whiskey blazed, turning the thing into a walking torch.

That pissed it off.

Burning with no sign of pain or agony, it raised its rifle and aimed it at me. "You meddle with things you do not understand, Timeless One." It said in a dry, rattling voice.

"That I do," I said. I fired an orichalcum bullet into its head. Deep One gold was not of this Earth. It was often useful against trans-dimensional beings. It blew the creature to bits, splattering me with anti-climatic gore.

I blinked. "Huh."

That was when I saw a chocolate-skinned teenage girl grab the book and make a run for the swinging doors.

Asenath.

"Dammit!" I shouted.

I was out of my seat, across the floor, and out the door within seconds. I moved faster than a normal human, though it wasn't very impressive compared to some of the other things I could do.

"Get away from me!" Asenath said, turning around to punch me. She held a piece of broken glass in her hand, and it might have killed me, but I was faster. I grabbed her throat and squeezed, and her arm went limp.

"Owen is dead," I said, grabbing the book from her hands.

I almost immediately fell over. There was power in those pages and I didn't have to be a wizard or psychic to know it came from the Great Old Ones. Just holding it caused me to hear insects crawling on the surface of my consciousness, whispering the secrets of a dead world.

"Give that back!" Asenath shouted. "I'll call the sheriff!"

"I am the sheriff," I said, absently. "Mayor too. Mercury is the town doctor and brothel owner, like Doc Holliday."

"It was Wyatt Earp and his brother James who owned a brothel. Holliday was a dentist," Asenath growled.

I blinked, surprised at her knowledge. "Your owner said that you were taking this to Sentinel Hill to destroy it."

"That's not your concern!" Asenath hissed. "That book is dangerous! People are looking for it."

"People are a relative term," I said, my voice low and threatening. "Who is after them?"

Asenath stopped struggling. "The Cult of the Insect—"

"Stop," I said, letting her go. "You don't have to say any more."

The Cult of the Insect was one of the many religions, once secretive and kept underground that had emerged after the Rising to become the dominate faiths of humanity. I'd seen no sign of the Great Old Ones ever paying attention to the rites invoked in their name, but plenty of atrocities had been perpetrated by their followers. The Cult of the Insect was one of the worst, spreading disease and misery indiscriminately, because they believed they would be spared the wrath of the unfathomable aliens who ruled over the Earth. Crazy, but they were also possessed of real power. Real enough to send a man made of maggots after me. If they were linked to the *Al-Azif*, then that explained quite a few things. Mind you, I probably should have made that connection earlier.

"I need that book," Asenath said.

"You wouldn't get within ten miles of Sentinel Hill. It's across the Great Barrier Desert, past the Dunwych tribe, and through the Forest of Lies."

"Forest of Lies? Really?" Asenath asked, keeping her eyes squarely on the book.

"I didn't name it," I said, putting the book in the pocket of my shirt. "Nothing gets named anything normal anymore. I thought you were a local."

"I am," Asenath said. "Just not…recently."

"Uh huh," I said, trying to figure out what she meant by that.

"How are you holding the book?" Asenath asked.

"It's called a pocket."

"The book can't be held by humans," she said. "It burns the flesh of anyone not consecrated to the cult."

"I don't recall that from the legends I've heard of the book."

"Because I put that curse on it a few months ago in order to make it harder for the cult to retrieve it." Asenath spat on the ground. "It is evil, a thing of chaos. It warps and changes reality to better torture the living. If you're holding it, you're something less than human."

"Or more," I said.

Moments later, my partner, Mercury, came running down. She was dressed in a pair of denim jeans and a cotton shirt. There was a blood stain on her shirt and she was carrying a pistol.

"Asenath, I told you to stay put," Mercury said, looking at me. "What the hell happened?"

"I could ask the same."

"Cultists," Mercury said, making a sour face. "I managed to shoot two of them. The third collapsed into a bunch of bugs."

"Did you squish them?" I asked.

"I paid Gino the drunk to do it," Mercury said, shrugging. "He sang *La Cucaracha* the entire time as he danced on them in his boots."

Good ol' Gino.

"It's the Insect cultists," Asenath said, looking at Mercury. "Do you know this thing?"

I was really starting to dislike this girl.

"John is more or less human," Mercury said defensively.

"It's the less I'm worried about," Asenath said, looking disgusted. "I had to deal with that monster, the human kind, for months. I pretended to be his obedient slave, played on his insecurities, and convinced him he could find redemption by taking it to be destroyed. We're almost there. This could be the end of something terrible."

I looked down at her. "That's a lot of work for a young woman."

"I'm older than I look," Asenath said, simply. "Listen, I told my story to your friend. I trust her. She gave me the sign."

I raised an eyebrow. "The sign?"

"The sign of the University," Mercury said, simply. "She's one of their agents."

I grimaced, not at all happy with this revelation. Centuries ago, Miskatonic University had been the only place on Earth to do serious research on the occult horrors of the Great Old Ones. Some poor foolish souls had even tried to oppose them, though that was like trying to put out a forest fire with a teacup full of water. In the end, they'd failed to save the world and now existed as a depraved pseudo-religious sect that had made alliances with the Yith and with the Mi-Go. Sometimes they did things that benefited the world, and at others they poked things better left alone with an obvious stick.

"John, we have to help her destroy the *Al-Azif*," Mercury said, her tone brooking no argument.

"It's a book," I said, knowing in my heart that it was so much more. I heard it whisper that it could restore my humanity, make me stronger than any other man alive, or allow me to build a refuge for humanity in the Dreamlands. These were all reflections of my most heart-felt wishes. There was also something old, malevolent, and hungry in the book's pages—which weren't pages at all, but more of a mirage covering a pit of flesh-eating scarabs.

"The *Al-Azif* was injured by my ancestor," Asenath said, looking around the town to see if anyone was paying attention. She needn't have bothered. The people who lived in the tiny watering hole built around the Wages of Sin, charitably named New Ulthar, didn't care a lick about anyone but themselves. Really, the only thing they did seem to care about was no one hurt the ridiculous number of stray cats that lived around the town. One poor asshole had thrown a horseshoe at one that was eyeing his sandwich, only to end up flayed alive by something in the night. It was why I always bought a pitcher of milk for them every month.

"Injured?" I asked.

Asenath nodded. "Once it contained a whole race of aliens trying to survive. I don't know how but the book was like a whole other universe."

"Dreams are real and contain as much space as they need," Mercury said, as if this was some sort of profound statement. Then again, I'd physically visited the Dreamlands and seen friends killed in them. Witches had a different perspective on the world and Mercury knew the foul tongues of long dead races who could mold reality with their minds.

"My ancestor killed the wizard-god at the heart of it," Asenath said. "The people inside were consumed by the terrible things the Nameless

Ones summoned and bound to create their ark. What's left is a hungry vortex that is fueled by the deranged ramblings of an entire race's echo. A thing that, unleashed, would kill the whole of humanity with its dying scream."

I blinked. "Mercury, where would you put that on our scale of 'humanity-is-fucked o-meter'?"

"Five, five-and-a-half?" Mercury suggested.

"Sounds about right."

Asenath stared between us. "Are you not taking this seriously?"

"Lady, you have no idea the kind of unfathomable horrific shit we have been neck deep in for the past few years," I said, thinking about how unbearable the cost of trying to do some good in this world had been.

The most terrible truth I'd encountered as a New Arkham Ranger turned lawman was not that the world was a godless, soulless, place where humanity was an unimportant speck of bacteria. It was the world was a god-filled, soulful place, where humanity was an unimportant speck of bacteria. Mankind was not just insects buzzing against the face of beings infinitely their superior, but things those superior being's pets liked to eat.

Things like me.

"We'll help you," Mercury said, blinking. "One less relic of a dead world won't make a difference. Humanity is already going extinct. This might delay it for a few more days, weeks, or even centuries."

I thought, considering it was an object of power, that keeping it might save a portion of mankind, but I wasn't about to tell my partner that. Mercury and I disagreed on several things. One of them was the best way to try to make sure humanity's legacy didn't completely disappear. Mercury wanted to try and save humanity, as futile as that effort might be. We—no—-they were ill-equipped as a race to continue living in a world that Dread Cthulhu had terraformed into something closer to the primordial Earth his people found palatable.

Evolution had passed humanity by and the only way now to survive was to adapt. If mankind was to survive, then we had to become more like the Great Old Ones, wild, free, and immortal. My children and I could pass on our genetics and bond with mankind to create something new. To be as the race that was my genetic heritage and had sent their own ark to Earth to preserve—perhaps as fruitlessly as the creators of the *Al-Azif* had.

Instead of making that argument, I simply nodded. "You're right. The book has to be destroyed."

I wondered if, in a million years, the next race of Earth would look back on that moment and say, "*Yeah, that guy could have saved his mate's species, but ended up letting it be destroyed so he could continue to sleep with her. This is where Darwinism failed.*"

Asenath nodded. "Thank you, both of you. I guess I'll have to trust you."

"You really have no choice. You have no money, horse, car, or thing to barter. Any man or woman who wants to take you as a slave outside these borders would and could."

"I can take care of myself," Asenath said, dangerously.

Mercury punched her in the face.

Asenath hit the ground then felt her nose. "What the hell!?"

"Concise argument," I said, applauding her debate skills.

"Do what we say and stay behind us," Mercury said. "We've been across the New England Wasteland many times."

"I know the Dunwych," I said, not entirely happy to think about going back into their territory. "They aren't fond of me but they're not our enemies either. We'll have to keep the book secret if we want to make it to Sentinel Hill alive."

I was understating the difficulty. Sentinel Hill was one of the holy sites of tribal worshippers of the Great Old Ones. The Dunwych were descendants of a rural town and the refugees it had taken in that had degenerated into barbarism. They were among the most ruthless of all of humanity's survivors, and some of the most occult savvy. Not that humanity's knowledge of the truth of reality amounted to anything more than a thimble full of water from an ocean of madness.

"Then we should get going," Asenath said, her voice containing the barest hint of panic. "If the Cult of the Insect have found us, they'll stop at nothing to destroy us."

"We can handle—"

That was when the entirety of New Ulthar shook with an earthquake. The ground rumbled, and buildings began collapsing around us. People ran in every direction. It turned toward the Western edge of town, which was visible from the middle, and I saw a huge cloud of dirt flying into the air. A hideous, crawling thing emerged beneath it, rising above the buildings as if there was no end to its body.

The thing could not be fully perceived by human eyes or understood by human brains. They filled in images with something that resembled a dragon, a squid, and a centipede crossed together. My eyes were artificial, a product of my shapeshifting, but they still saw the horrible image of a monster. The rest of my vision, saw a thing that spanned six dimensions, time, and space.

The creature had been summoned through some foul sorcery I did not recognize. I knew, in some primordial genetic memory of the alien that sired me that it was an eater of worlds. The only thing preventing it from destroying the continent where I stood was its ability to manifest only the tip of its presence into this world. The fools in the Cult of the Insect had brought oblivion to the world in hopes of acquiring something that would allow them to do the same.

"A Tunneler!" Mercury shouted, misidentifying the creature as one of the primordial things that dwelled in the dark corners of the Earth. "John you need to kill it!"

I looked back at Mercury like she was insane.

"They can't be allowed to have the book!" Asenath said, missing that this was every bit as horrid a threat.

I realized we had no choice. It was seeking the *Al-Azif*, and the book pulsed like it had a heartbeat, craving to join itself to the monster. It wished to be devoured and merge its essence, to tear apart reality for a dozen galaxies width. The creature could resurrect its dead race across every micro-second of its life and have them live together in a chaos where nothing ever died but, at the same time did not exist. It offered that insane joy and peculiar immortality to humanity as well.

"No," I said, staring at it. "I'm not going to let you do that."

So, I opened the book and set my will against it.

That was a profoundly stupid idea.

I opened the *Al-Azif* and focused. I hoped that there was something inside the object powerful enough to beat back the Horror Below (as I'd instantly named the thing in a poetic flourish). Unfortunately, no sooner had I opened the book than my mind was assaulted by the THINGS inside.

The *Al-Azif* was not a book, any more than a Venus fly trap was a safe place for a bug to land. It was a device designed to absorb the consciousness and information of those poor souls who opened it, to tear the dream stuff that forged realities in other layers of reality, and then build a new home for a long-extinct race. The creatures within no longer had a central focusing consciousness but were a soup of a million lesser things. They were a mindless horde of hungry otherworldly consciousnesses lashing out and begging for release.

The thing was, I quickly realized, if you could provide the book with lives, you could use it for a little while before you were completely consumed. I recognized the trap at a glance. I felt the chaotic hungry creatures within reaching into my mind with invisible tendrils to plant their parasite. They would never be able to work as one but even one of their lesser castes could outthink a "mere" human and live again through their bodies. They thought I was a potential victim to replace the body of and give another of their race a form to live through.

This was a mistake.

If I was a human being, save perhaps one of those exceptional, deranged individuals like Randolph Carter or Titus Crow, I would have been obliterated outright. I was not, though, but a beast every bit as terrifying that chose to wear human skin. In that, I was every bit as insane as any human confronted with the unknowable horror of the unknown. It also meant my mind was not so easily obligated or cast aside. Instead, I reached into the book's pages, crossing five or six dimensional boundaries.

And I fed.

It was only as I tore at and feasted on the creature within that I remembered the billions of years my species has dominated their own corner of the galaxy. That the creatures around me, obscene and mammalian, ape-like things barely evolved from protoplasm, were nothing but mayflies unworthy of the least consideration. Breeding stock that I could create a newer, better, race from the ruins of.

NO!

I was not going to allow myself to go sane. To abandon the truth of the reality: that I was anything but a human being, a part of the terrible horrific things that dominated creation. I preferred to be a tiny immaterial thing for as long as I could manage it. I stopped feasting, having barely tasted the power within, and slammed the book shut. I turned; opened my mouth and unleashed a column of flame made of a hundred eldritch energies that tore into the Horror Below. It wailed, hissed, and thrashed before collapsing to the ground into a puddle of other-dimensional matter that should not exist in this reality but was real enough that it would probably kill whoever stepped on that spot for decades.

I'd have to put up a sign or something.

"John!" Mercury shouted, running to my side.

"What did you see?" I asked, hoping the spell remained.

Mercury was one of the few people who had ever seen the face of Great Cthulhu and lived. She'd also had her sanity completely shattered by the psychic backlash and been driven to catatonia. I'd erased her memory of the event, violating her mind in the process, then bound magics to make sure she could never see the true face of the horror about us. They translated, theoretically, into terrible but explicable monsters. A dragon could kill you, after all, but it would not leave you gibbering mad.

Ironically, the greatest effect of my betrayal was the fact that Mercury possessed the power to make invocations and spells to the Great Old Ones that had cost more experienced wizards their sanity. I'd seen her cast the winds of Ithaqua, summon tentacles of Zul'Cthonic, and speak words of Azathoth without any danger to her mind. Weirdly, her body too showed no signs of the strains that channeling energies of ancient foulnesses usually required. Looking past her, I saw fifteen dead and burning corpses of Insect cultists. They'd apparently not been content to leave my fate to the Horror

Below but had tried to ambush us as I used the book, only to be shredded by my lover's spells. This was turning into a bloody, bloody night.

"You throwing a fireball at the Tunneler," Mercury said, taking a deep breath. "What else?"

"I see."

"That's not what happened," Asenath said, coming up behind her. *"What are you?"*

"The person who is going to take you to Sentinel Hill."

Asenath looked at me with hate in her eyes. She clearly had enough sensitivity to know I wasn't human, was one of the things that threatened humanity by my very existence, but I didn't care.

"And if I refuse?" Asenath asked.

"Then I'll shoot you," Mercury said.

"Wait, what?" Asenath asked, doing a double take.

"This is a partnership, tenderfoot, and you helped lead a monster to our home," Mercury said, having already drawn her gun. "Just how many cultists are after us and how many more are we likely to encounter on the way to New Dunwych?"

Asenath looked down. "The Cult of the Insect has an entire city in Halifax."

"I like Canadians," Mercury muttered. "The kingdoms up there are pretty hardy."

"This is not a normal kingdom," Asenath said. "The Golden City's residents wear the skins of human beings and cover themselves with glamour but are nothing more than colonies of insects bound to human souls. It is a rebirth of the Nameless City cleansed by the Yith millennia ago. It was the original goal of the Ixtol, but without their leader, they are a shadow of what they once were. The residents depend on the *Al-Azif* to provide them with their immortality as well as power their dreadful machines."

"I thought Owen owned it."

"Owen is one of them or was one of them," Asenath corrected herself. "I can be most persuasive."

"Oh?" Mercury asked. "What did you do?"

"I cast a spell that warped his mind and made him think it was a good idea to destroy it," Asenath said.

"Ah," I said, nodding.

I thought of the irony of the Callisto people. They had sacrificed everything to create their dreadful artifact and now it was providing immortality to a bunch of depraved humans. The Cult of the Insect wasn't purely the creatures of Callisto if Owen was any indication but an unholy fusion of them with humans. Creatures like me.

"So, we're likely to face more of them," I muttered.

"Yes," Asenath said.

"Great," I said, looking over at Mercury. "I suppose we should get the hell out of town and try to divert their attention."

"So, you're robbing me and taking over my quest?" Asenath asked.

"Try and keep up," Mercury said, frowning. "Yes. Because, again, you brought this horror to our doorstep."

It occurred to me how ridiculous the coincidence must have been that she could come to our little town and find us out of all the survivors of humanity. That's when it clicked for me and I felt remarkably stupid.

"She's manipulating us, Mercury."

"What?" Mercury said, confused.

"She knew we were here. She directed Owen—"

"Balthazar," Asenath said. "His name was Balthazar. He was a horrible person but easily led about by his groin."

"So, you came here deliberately?" Mercury said. "Son of a bitch."

"I thought the famous witch here would help me," Asenath said, looking at Mercury. "I didn't know I'd also have to deal with her demon."

"Yes, well, if you're dealing with witches then you should be expecting to also deal with demons," Mercury said, dryly.

"Famous witch?" I asked, looking down at her.

"I do have a life beyond you," Mercury said, her voice lowering. "There's things I do not understand that I do not perceive the way other people do. I don't yet know what's happened to me, what makes me different, but there are things that I can do that you cannot."

I lowered my head. "True, Mercury. You are a powerful dreamer and that will benefit you. Still, I don't like being lied to or manipulated."

Asenath's eyes flashed a dangerous intelligence. "All I want is to destroy the book. When it is gone, there will be one less threat to the world. The Golden City will collapse, and its horde of ancient bug-ridden liches will vanish. That's all that matters."

Somehow, I doubted that. "Then I suggest we get moving."

"That's the first sensible thing you've said tonight," Mercury said, never taking her gun off Asenath, though she visibly relaxed.

Around us, the people of New Ulthar went back to their nightly routines. The deaths of probably a half-dozen townsfolk and the arrival of an enormous monster was not so uncommon as to mean a serious disruption in their evening.

I could not ride a horse; animals aside from cats could not stand me. We ended up piling into one of the few functioning motor vehicles in town. I'd purchased the ramshackle composite from a caravanner who wanted to leave the lifestyle of transporting goods from New Arkham to Kingsport. I didn't use it much and there had been a dozen attempts to steal the thing over the years, but the solar powered machine took us across the Great Barrier Desert past hordes of D'toan giant centipedes, each the size of houses, and the half-real Pyramids of Gah'nak.

Once humankind had held uncontested dominion over the Earth's surface, but their supremacy was an illusion even then. The ghouls had ruled the tunnels beneath their cities, and the Deep Ones had slumbered in dimensional pockets hidden within the ocean's many trenches. Cultists had venerated Great Cthulhu and the inner circles of many religions had been warped by secret worship of the Things Which Should Not Be. When the Rising had occurred, mad prophets and would-be despots had claimed the Gods Below would reward their faithful. If so, it had been only the reward of being eaten first and avoiding the horror to come. Even humanity's sister races like the Tcho-Tcho or satyr-like Leng had died in droves as their hidden fortresses were overwhelmed by the screams of the Great Old Ones awakening.

There were perhaps one in a hundred of the human beings left that had existed a century prior, and that estimation was generous. Many of the survivors of mankind were no longer strictly what could be referred to as human. I was on the far end of things, despite my delusion that I was as human as any other man, but even people like Mercury had elements wholly different from what existed before. Asenath's desire to destroy the Nameless Ones of Halifax made me wonder if she was driven by a desire to save humanity from another dangerous threat, or whether it was pure hatred of the Other. But what *was* the other when the mirror held only an enemy?

I had plenty of time for such thoughts during the eight-hour drive to New Dunwych. The Dunwych were a powerful tribal empire that stretched from the radioactive jungles of time lost Maine to the haunted rivers of Providence. They were a fierce and savage people who had fully embraced the insanity of the new world, which perhaps made them the only sane ones left.

"So, what is your story, Asenath?" I asked, looking back at the slave girl who seemed so familiar with things she should not know.

"I told you, I'm from Miskatonic University. I'm a descendant of the Doran line," Asenath said, giving a smile that did not quite reach her eyes. She was sitting in the back of our composite vehicle as a cloud of dust followed its exhaust.

"I don't recall Doran having any family," I said, keeping my eye on the rear-view mirror.

"Perhaps I'm the descendant of Harold Stubbs then, the famous London investigator, or Albert Wilmarth," Asenath said, dismissing us. "Maybe I'm just some poor waif they managed to pick up at one of the slaver's auctions. Does it matter? I lived, I learned, and I am here now."

There was something about her demeanor that put me in the mind of someone far older than her apparent nineteen years. The way she spoke was also more cultured than someone born in this savage age. Even Mercury, who had been educated as a doctor in a city state, had a coarser and more practical way of speaking. There was also something about her cold dead eyes that put me in mind of a snake. I could not see the interior of human's souls, though, and she seemed to have nothing of the Otherworld about her. Whatever she was, she was human.

Such as that was.

"Why all the questions, John? We're the ones who robbed her, after all," Mercury said, looking at Asenath with a longing gaze. She was an attractive girl and it seemed that her cover story of wanting to lie with her earlier hadn't entirely been a fiction.

"Clearly, I am in the wrong," I said, sarcastically before bringing the vehicle to a stop. It was not because of the conversation but because we had arrived.

Sentinel Hill was far into the territory of the Dunwych, surrounded by miles of dense forest that grew along the edge of the Great Barrier Desert. The Dunwych built their homes along the coast in tree-houses, cabins, and cottages nearby. The craggy peak was a place of religious worship for the tribals and had numerous stone temples surrounding it. The smoke from sacrifices accompanied the droning alien music of things not quite human summoned to pass their wisdom on to the natives. The Forest of Lies, as it was known, was full of traps and places of execution for the tribals' enemies.

"Do you think they're going to let us pass?" Mercury asked.

I shrugged. "Only one way to find out."

As I probably should have anticipated, Mercury, Asenath, and I were led to the sacrificial altar to die.

"Great job negotiating, John," Mercury said, her arms tied before her as she was pushed by a rifle-toting Dunwych.

The three of us were ascending the Path of Skulls, a rocky path up the side of Sentinel Hill. The road was lined with spears, each adorned with a human skull. So, it was an apropos name. The Dunwych wore white chalk on their faces and carried ancient but well-maintained weapons from before the Rising.

There were close to a hundred of them and they knew exactly who we were and what we carried. Unfortunately, they seemed to have very different ideas about what to do with the book than we did. We were all naked, our hands tied before us, the *Al-Azif* confiscated and held by a white-haired albino priestess with unnatural cat-like yellow eyes wearing only a loin cloth and bloody tattoos. It was like something out of a lurid Pre-Rising motion picture. I could rip free of normal bonds easily enough, but there were sorceries in the ropes that kept me from acting.

"Hey, we got here, didn't we?" I replied, less worried than I should have been.

"Yeah, that's a real comfort, John," Mercury muttered.

"I hate you all," Asenath said.

"They want the book's power," I said, looking at them. I spoke the Dunwych language and had been listening to them discuss it for the past half-hour.

"Can they take it?" Mercury asked.

"What do you think?" I asked, relying on her knowledge of the subject more than mine.

"No," Asenath said. "They do not know how to bind the energies within. They will unleash a horde of millions of hungry insects. They will devour this existence and leave only an empty dead world before turning on one another."

"How do you know that?" Mercury asked.

"I read," Asenath said. "It's why I deserve the book."

"What would you do with it?" I asked, trying to trip her up.

"Find a way off this rock," Asenath said, pausing. "If I wasn't destroying it, I mean."

"Of course," I said.

Our destination was the stone circle at the top of Sentinel Hill. It was eight stone pillars around a ninth rock that was stained with dried blood, viscera, and disgusting fluids excreted upon hundreds of deaths. We were forced to our knees before the high priestess and I debated transforming into something else. I wanted to wait until just the right moment, though.

"The blood of these humans will sanctify the book and provide us with the power of the Ones Above. Long ago, Abdul Al'Hazred was enlightened—" the priestess started a rather irritating speech that I had no interest in hearing. In her right hand was an obsidian dagger that glowed with unearthly power, though I was likely the only one to see it.

Before I could rip her head off, it exploded from a rifle shot and I hit the ground. Mercury forced Asenath down as well. The air filled with bullets as century-old jeeps that had been refurbished and reengineered so many times they barely resembled their own origins drove up the side of the hill. Insect cultists fired machine guns and rifles from their seats.

I tried to shift but found I could not, which made me realize my plan to get us here might not have been the best one. There was something woven into the rope that prevented the change.

Mercury grabbed the obsidian knife and cut my bonds before turning the dagger on her own.

"Help me!" hissed Asenath.

Mercury tossed her the knife and Asenath freed herself.

All around us, the Dunwych were getting massacred as the ground erupted with swarms of flesh-eating scarabs that stripped their bodies clean in seconds. Two D'toan giant centipedes emerged as well, throwing the Dunwych charge to the ground.

"Do your thing, John!" Mercury shouted. "I'll start the summoning!"

"You got…" I didn't get to respond because I was promptly stabbed in the side by Asenath.

The blade passed through my skin and into five or six dimensions, causing pain the like of which I hadn't experienced in a long time. The obsidian was not actually volcanic glass but the talon of something that bore some surface resemblance. I collapsed, feeling like I was being eaten away from the insides.

"Dammit," I muttered, clutching my side. "I should have seen that coming."

Asenath then punched Mercury in the face, grabbing the *Al-Azif* from the priestess' corpse. She spoke with a thicker, deeper voice that seemed to blend genders. "Thank you, John, Mercury, I couldn't have done it without you."

For a moment, I saw her glow. It looked like an amorphous sexless humanoid thing was puppeteering her body. Whoever Asenath was, she wasn't a nineteen-year-old girl. She was someone far older, perhaps a Deep One or human wizard, wearing their skin as you might a pair of clothes.

"I take it you're not actually Andrew Doran's descendant," I muttered, bleeding worse than any other time since I'd discovered I wasn't human. "Is Asenath even your name?"

"Oh, this body is and no, it's my daughter's name," Asenath said, her voice becoming an old man's. "She consulted with the ghosts that haunted Kingsport's oldest cemeteries and found me. It's not the first time I've worn a woman's body and I admit having grown comfortable with them. I'd recommend you try it if you weren't about to end with this wretched planet."

A swarm of flesh-eating beetles fell upon us, only for Mercury to make a Ward of the Elder Sign in the air, flames forming an inverted pentagram the size of a building that disintegrated the beetles in a shower of flame. It also bought us time, preventing the rest of the Cult of the Insect from reaching us. The symbol terrified me, and I and would have fled myself, if not for the fact I was badly wounded.

"What do you hope to accomplish?" I said, searching the ground for a weapon. I was injured but hoped Asenath, whatever her real name was, didn't realize I still had a monster's strength within me.

"I will summon the son of Yog-Sothoth, the brother of Wilbur Whateley, and bring back that which was banished here centuries ago. A creature that was meant to open the door and be both the key and the gate for his father."

"The apocalypse has already happened!" I snapped, angrily. "What possible good could that do?"

"As this world lays dying, I will use the *Al-Azif*'s energy to power a binding spell that will let me control the Monster of Sentinel Hill. It will carry me across the universes so that I may visit an Earth where the Old Ones never awoke or don't even exist! A place I can live a blessed life as a man or woman free from this miserable hellhole. I'll even settle for living a loop of the last hundred years of mankind."

"You'll destroy the world to escape to an alternate reality?" I asked, finding no weapon worth using.

"Yes!" Azenath shouted, a glowing circle of fire circling around her and preventing either of us from moving forward.

I'd heard some crazy over the years, but this took the cake. Then again, was it truly crazy or merely evil? Good and evil were things the Great Old Ones' ilk were beyond but I believed in them as a human concept. Yet, I found myself not able to judge her either. Not completely. This was a dying world and whatever man or woman chose to live on it was resigning themselves to oblivion. There were infinite worlds out there with infinite varieties of beings, I'd caught glimpse of them while traveling the Dreamlands.

Was it truly such a deranged idea to escape this shell of a world and seek out a place where human kindness was not so strange a concept? The answer was yes if the cost was unleashing the horror of an Outer Gods' spawn upon the rest of mankind. A mass murdering cultist was not going to be someone who could escape the Wasteland's horrors. No, they would simply bring it with them. It was why I could never leave this world. I was part of its nightmares now.

"Fuck you," I finally said.

Asenath shrugged and assumed a space next to the altar. "Goodbye. This is a mercy killing if that's any comfort."

It wasn't.

Asenath muttered words in an inhuman tongue that surrounded her in a glowing field that would serve as a barrier between humans and monsters both.

"Sorry, John, I'm a terrible judge of character," Mercury said, turning around and rushing to my side.

"You are," I said, feeling the life drain out of me.

Mercury turned around and started casting an invocation to Shub-Niggurath to heal my injuries. The agony of this was exquisite, but it drove the hideous otherworldly poison from my body. My blood was already on the ground, though and had joined with that of the dozens of Dunwych warriors now serving as bait to the hungry thing on the other side.

"Ia Vhourvath! Ia Hastur! Ia Cthugha! I invoke thee in the name of the Outer Gods! I compel thee to bring forth he who has been trapped in a moment of time in this place! I offer the spirits of Callisto to you! I offer thee beings so that you may feed and be free!" Asenath cackled. "I compel you to come and bind thee in the name of they father, in the name of the Crawling Chaos, and the name of Azathoth!"

It was all mumbo jumbo, but powerful mumbo jumbo. The words were not what was important but the will, the dreaming power of the mind behind them. Asenath was clearly a powerful sorceress, perhaps even more powerful than Mercury, and had a source of inexhaustible magic empowering her.

"Do not commit this insanity!" I shouted, helplessly. "This world still has people on it! Millions of lives who still matter."

"The only life that matters to me, is mine!" Asenath hissed. "I would not expect a brainwashed servitor of Yog-Sothoth to understand!"

The sky swirled and a thing that human eyes could not see but that my own could, began to descend. It was made of possibilities and ate time. Trust me when I say it was not something you wanted to comprehend. It was, however, a creature with a shared partial humanity. It had a mother, a brother, a grandfather, and a tie to this world that Miskatonic wizards had ignored. It was my kin.

So, I did something very stupid and asked for its help. "She is trying to kill this world! Your mother and brother's world! It is becoming a place where you can live freely but it will destroy everything here that matters! I will free you of your prison, friend, and let you sail through time. I ask you to rid me of this troublesome priestess, first."

The creature listened to my words and understood. I don't think Asenath ever considered it was born of this planet and human enough to care. It was, however, despite being trapped between dimensions.

Sentinel Hill shuddered and shook as the creature resisted the spell of the pitiful mind trying to bind it.

"I have the power!" Asenath called, holding up the book. "I am in control! The power of the *Al-Azif* compels you!"

Mercury shot it out of her hands with her revolver, the defensive spells the girl had cast not applying to the book itself.

Asenath looked horrified, and Wilbur Whately's brother promptly ate her. It then began to feast on the *Al-Azif*, devouring millions of souls and endless possibilities into itself. It became more solid and powerful, becoming a gestalt of the race that once had been, and might be again. The cultists outside Mercury's ward screamed and melted into the ground as their source of power evaporated.

Wilbur's brother escaped the prison he'd been placed in and vanished into the time stream, satisfied and now more akin to his father than the humans he'd left behind. Mercury invoked several powers to protect herself from possession by Asenath's ghost, but I suspected it was now part of something infinitely larger.

For a moment, I saw Wilbur's brother follow the timeline of the *Al-Azif* into the past. It set free the creature that Abdul Al'Hazred attempted to summon and followed the *Al-Azif* back to its homeworld of Callisto. I tried to send a message telepathically down through the timeline, linking my mind to the book, but only briefly was able to touch minds with those in the past. Ironically, including Andrew Doran. To my horror, I saw the planet and its peoples destroyed by the ever fatter and more powerful time-wyrm that had been born of a human woman giving birth to Yog-Sothoth's spawn. The Callisto people might have been able to use sorcery to save themselves but, ironically, had created a Mobius strip that guaranteed their own destruction. I'd been party to a genocide on a planetary scale but the monster inside me did not care and the human on the outside could not understand the whole. I simply shook away the image and turned back to join those still-living on this world.

"So, did we win?" Mercury asked.

"Yeah," I said, blinking. "I think we did."

"Good," Mercury said. "That damned book has caused way too much trouble over the years."

"The Laughing Skull" is the denouement for Tales of the Al-Azif *and basically shows Abdul Alhazred's reactions to all the stories that were included in that volume. John has destroyed the original tome but it's after humanity has long since been reduced to a shadow of its former self.*

The implication that H.P. Lovecraft was inspired to write his stories by Abdul's influence is clear but, honestly, I assume Randolph Carter is HPL's equivalent in-universe. Same with Robert E. Howard and Clark Ashton Smith being mentioned when they should have their own fictional substitutes. Chalk that one up to a continuity error. Yes, I worry about silly things like that.

THE LAUGHING SKULL

I was amused by the final fate of the *Al-Azif*, as well as disappointed. Even as I sat on the desk of my author, a half-finished story in his typewriter, I couldn't help but think the *Al-Azif*'s story was one of missed opportunities.

The source of unfathomable alien wisdom being destroyed did not surprise me. Vhourvath had been an arrogant fool and it had ultimately proved to be his undoing. Unfortunately, its history was not of spreading the glories of Great Cthulhu, Yog-Sothoth, and other beings across the Earth. It was not a legacy of bringing destruction to great empires and laying waste to the feeble excuse for civilization that mankind had constructed.

Instead, the history of the *Al-Azif* was nothing more than a series of adventurers like the kind Robert E. Howard and Clark Ashton Smith wrote about. Ignorant savages, including one who was an alien himself, struggling to protect humanity from a destiny that was impossible to avert.

In truth, the discovery that humanity survived the rise of the Great Old Ones left me disquieted. I had thought they would be annihilated by the time depicted in the final story, but they seemed to have eked out an existence in the shadow of eldritch gods. Perhaps they would eventually go extinct or give in to the wild magics I had helped foster in them, but it would not happen without self-styled adventurers like the kind I'd seen resisting it.

Pity.

The fact the *Al-Azif* had led to a stable time loop was something I decided I would ponder for the next couple of centuries. I had already decided I would educate my author in the secrets of the occult. Secrets far beyond the tidbits I'd placed in his dreams to excite the imagination and spread the glories of the Great Old Ones among the masses.

I would make him a sorcerer who would bring about an early rise of the monsters in his fantasies and thwart the future I'd seen. It would be my spite to the pathetic Yith who had set this bizarre story in motion. Perhaps I would even seize his body and wear it like a robe.

Yes, his latent talents would make that possible. I was tired of my cursed half-life and while it had taken centuries, I had fed from the dreams and wills of many users. There was another World War coming soon, and while human lives were like flickering candles, it would be a bonfire of death, more than enough to achieve my goals.

Howard walked into the room. "Sonia, I'm going to go for a walk. I must have fallen asleep on the couch. I had the most exciting dreams."

"More monsters?"

"More like people who fight them. I might actually let the humans win next time."

"Really?" a bemused female voice spoke from the other room.

"Nah," Howard said, laughing. "Who would want to read that?"

Howard grabbed his coat and passed by me without a second thought. I was already envisioning the terrible things I would make him do to his loved ones to break down his will when Sonia entered the room. There was something different about the Jewish woman and if I had lungs, I would have choked on my next breath.

Her eyes were now crystal blue.

A voice I hadn't heard in millennia spoke from her mind. *It is time to close the loop, Abdul.*

No, I have so much more to learn! I hissed, finding the words ridiculous even as they left my mind. Death cared for no man.

Not even me.

You have been permitted to know how the story ends, the Yith woman said. *It is only fair given how well you have served us.*

Could I have done differently? I asked, pondering how events might have achieved different results.

No, the Yith woman replied. *Then you would not have been you.*

I tried to think of some incantation, secret, or plea that would preserve my immortal life. Instead, I thought of the *Al-Azif* and all the terrible wonders it had opened my mind to. Then I laughed, letting mental peels of insane cackling fill the room.

The Yith woman then picked me up off the desk and hurled me into the wall. The last thing I heard before the shattering unmade my existence was the sound of buzzing insects. I didn't have time to fully ponder what that meant before darkness swallowed me.

Perhaps the ending was not so neatly writte—

"The True Name of God" is another story set in the Middle East, this time during the Third Crusade, and plays around with the concept of religion as well as what that means in a maltheistic world like the Cthulhu Mythos. Fans have asked me if I was inspired by the Assassin's Creed *games for this story but, no, I had the rough version of it written out long before I'd even heard of either it or HPL's writings.*

This story is a bit of an old-fashioned monster hunt and probably more influenced by my love of tabletop gaming. Especially as I'd come up with the rough concept in high school. It is also the origin of the "villain" that shows up throughout the anthology, Tales of Yog-Sothoth.

As for whether Yog-Sothoth is the god of certain real-life faiths in-universe, well, that's up to the reader. After all, many other less famous religions have had their gods collated with the Mythos by writers over the decades. What is Cthulhu but a god who will undergo a resurrection and pass judgement on the world? Sound familiar, my fellow believers?

Oh yeah, I'm going to Hell for that one.

THE TRUE NAME OF GOD

The assassin moved through the streets of Akka with a silent and deliberate speed, darting from alley to alley, rooftop to rooftop. His birth name was Ali ad Fariq but he considered his profession more important than his personal identity. He was Hashishin, one of the knives of Allah, and a holy slayer of the wicked.

Normally, Ali would have just travelled inconspicuously amongst the city's various midnight revelers, but such a disguise was suicide now. Their new sultan, Ṣalāḥ ad-Dīn had imposed a curfew. All those found wandering the streets after dark were to be flogged, a punishment which would likely kill him.

In the end, he came across the alley where he was to meet his contractor. Nestled between two potters' shops, it was a dark dead end. Pacing around in the middle of the shadow-filled alley, Ali caught a glimpse of the man he was to meet.

Rabbi Yosef ben Yosef looked spry for a man in his sixties, but careworn. A long, thick, white beard hung from his chin and a small, black cap rested on his head. He was dressed in a thick set of robes that marked both his people and station. There was something about the rabbi's stance, though, that told Ali there was something much worse afoot. He was shivering, shaken with fear, and his eyes darted around him every few seconds. The man's health also looked poor, with skin flaps telling Ali that he'd lost a large amount of weight recently, and a yellow pallor to his skin. Debilitating sickness was nothing surprising in any land, but if Ali was a superstitious man, he would have said the man had seen a ghost. He was not, though, and knew what monsters walked the night.

"I must be mad to be out here. Especially seeking..." Yosef muttered, rubbing his hands and looking everywhere but the entrance.

Normally, Ali liked to imagine just how easily he might kill his contractors. In the case of the rabbi, he discarded that thought. Ali bore no ill will to the Children of Isaac and there was no glory in slaying sickly old men. Still, he took some small pleasure in the knowledge his sudden appearance would startle the old man. He had not studied the arts of shadow for years to not indulge in the occasional bit of whimsy.

Stepping forward into the moonlight, Ali spoke, "Rabbi? You wish to speak with me?"

Yosef practically jumped out of his skin, needing a second to steady himself. "You've arrived," Yosef said, speaking in Arabic. "I am..."

"I know who you are," the assassin cut him off. The Old Man of the Mountain had once been injured during a secret meeting here in Akka, only to end up cared for by Yosef. The rabbi was entirely unaware of the event's significance, but there were debts to repay.

Yosef gulped. "I see."

"Why do you seek the Hashishin, Rabbi?" Ali stretched out a hand, hoping to calm him. He didn't need the man panicking when he was trying to do him a favor.

According to their contacts, Yosef had futilely stumbled around for days trying to contact their order. Upon hearing of it, Ali's superior had given the order for him to be given whatever assistance he required. If the rabbi wanted Ali to journey across the ocean and kill King Richard the Butcher, he would. The last Ali had heard, Richard the Butcher was still a prisoner in Austria and his captor demanding an outrageous sum of money for the English king's release. Ali hoped the man's brother never paid his ransom or, if he did, that it bankrupted their island. The war crimes of the crusaders were many, but their third attempt to take Jerusalem had been the worst in Ali's opinion. Maybe just because it had been the one that he'd lived through.

"Why does one seek ones known throughout the land for their proficiency at killing? He requires something slain." Yosef paused, staring down at the alleyway's dusty ground. He looked ready to throw up. Ali hoped he was merely feeling an overabundance of guilt for ordering a perfectly ordinary man's death. That would keep things simple, but there had been stories he'd heard about the goings on in the Jewish Quarter. Things that implied this would be no ordinary murder.

"I see," Ali replied. "I will hear you out. What do you know of our order?"

"Little," Yosef admitted. "Merely that you are amongst the most feared killers in the Holy Land. Some believe you to possess supernatural powers, the ability to appear and disappear at will, or to kill men with a glance."

Ali briefly mused about what other stories Yosef might have heard about their order. The Hashishin were a group which inspired all sorts of tales. Ali, himself, had heard quite a few interesting ones. That their leader, the Old Man of the Mountain, kidnapped young men and plied them with hash and sex. That he led his disciples through a hallucinatory death and rebirth ceremony, causing them to think they had visited heaven, so they had no fear of death.

Ali had even heard they were feared by Ṣalāḥ ad-Dīn himself, who had once led an army to their mountain fortress of Masyaf, only to turn around when a knife was found next to his pillow. That last story was true, for it had been Ali himself who had laid the weapon there. It was an honor he was proud to have been given.

"I wish that were the case." Ali shook his head. "We are merely well-trained in the arts of disguise and stealth, I fear."

That wasn't entirely true because the Hashishin once invited a wazir styling himself Abdul Alhazred the Second to dwell among them for a time. The false Abdul had conjured jinn, succubi, and gods of the idolatrous past to amuse his hosts. He had made great promises of power and immortality to those willing to pray to the Old Ones as well as gods from the Outer Dark.

In the end, the Old Man of the Mountain had ordered him killed in his sleep before the body was burned in the village square. Supposedly, the blasphemer's skull had escaped from the pyre and flew off into the air in the claws of a giant winged monster. Ali wouldn't have credited such a thing if not for the fact that dozens of witnesses were still living in Masyaf.

The Hashishin had chosen to keep some of the dead wazir's books, though. Some of the older assassins drank obnoxious potions and practiced dark arts to aid in the cause of the order. Ali had kept his soul clean of such things but knew a bit more about the monsters serving Iblis than most. He had hoped he would never have to call upon such things. Somehow, his instincts told him he would be required to do so now.

"A pity," Yosef said. "For such abilities would help you mightily with my request."

"Magic would help with many such requests." Ali smirked. "But the cost is too high."

"On that we agree, Muslim," Yosef muttered.

"Tell me of whom you need to meet his maker." Ali cut right to the point.

"I would not... seek you," Yosef looked as if he were struggling to find a way to put his request tactfully, "were not the situation desperate."

"Obviously," Ali said, a half-smile on his lips. "Do not be afraid, Rabbi. You have my word by Allah that no harm shall befall you tonight. The Hashishin owes a debt to you even if you do not remember it. Name this person and they will die."

"It is not a person... precisely," Yosef said, worried he would sound like a lunatic. "I need you to kill a monster. Something that is against all of the laws of God and man."

"Such a claim is easily bandied about in the Holy Land, Rabbi." Ali wrinkled his nose. During the war he'd often been called subhuman by

Franj soldiers. "It has been used by every side in this war. Arab, Christian, Turk, Templar, and Hashishin."

"I do not joke, Assassin." Yosef took a deep breath.

Ali nodded, unhappy that it was a literal thing of evil. "I understand. You mean a true monster."

"Yes," Yosef said, his voice cold and hesitant. "A creature unlike the demons I have cast out of children and madmen, but every bit as foul. It is made of flesh and blood like you and I but... not like us."

"Tell me everything," Ali spoke. It was still possible that Yosef was seeing the hand of God or Iblis in a normal series of events, but he had the look of a man who had dealt with a monster. That did not change the obligation of their order, though. Indeed, it increased it because such creatures could not be allowed to exist. The cults to the Nephilim, Old Ones, and other demons were insidious things that seemed to pop up every generation no matter how thoroughly the previous ones were exterminated. Christians, Muslims, Jews, and heathens all seemed equally vulnerable to the allure of black magic.

"Are you sure?" Yosef asked. "I would not blame you if you turned me away as a madman."

Ali didn't respond.

"Fine. It began two months ago, with a young woman of our community dying unexpectedly. She was in the prime of her health, young and beautiful," Yosef crossed his arms, staring at the ground. It was obviously a tale of great personal interest.

"Such things are not uncommon. Only God knows when He will call someone back to Him," the assassin said, leaning up against the wall of the alleyway and looking troubled.

Yosef looked up, obviously disliking being lectured on God by a hired killer. "I am aware of such things. If one woman were to die, I would say it was simply God's will. Were two to die, it would be a tragedy. Three, an uncommon work of misfortune. Four—"

"How many, Rabbi?" Ali interrupted. He wondered if he was just naturally rude after so many years of dealing with unruly contractors. Probably.

"Seven," Yosef said. "Each week, another perishes. Almost always on the Sabbath around the same time. Like an hourglass."

"The victims are always young women?" Ali asked.

"Yes, with one exception," Yosef said, looking thoughtful. "It would not be the first time Christians or Turks have targeted our people's women. I would assume them to blame where the women were torn to shreds with knives or stabbed or killed. They were not. Instead, each body was perfectly preserved like a statue, their bodies emptied of life with looks of absolute terror in their eyes. Breaking taboo, I had our community's barber open their bodies and each of them had their hearts missing."

The assassin nodded. There was little doubt that it was a creature of madness unless Yosef was lying, and that didn't seem likely. "Suspicious, indeed. You do have a supernatural killer stalking you. Is there anything else?"

Yosef looked hesitant. Whatever else had happened was close to his heart and perhaps the source of his haggard appearance. "There was a witness. A young woman carrying a child, newly married to one of my students." Yosef hesitated, as if debating saying more. Finally, he took a deep breath and continued, "My daughter, Rebecca. She asked for an amulet covered with the names of angels to ward off the demoness Lilith. I fear, even then, I was blind to the evil stalking us."

Ali's blood boiled at the thought of any woman carrying a child, no matter their faith, being assaulted. The fact it was by such an abomination as Yosef described only made it even more repulsive.

"She awoke when it came into her room and pressed the amulet against its face. Rebecca spoke of a creature resembling a walking corpse more than a man, its eyes sunken and its skin decayed as if it had been dead for two days. Its eyes burned like coals and it had a tongue more like a snake's than a man. There were other deformities I can scarcely describe, like things moving under its skin and bones. The amulet did nothing to drive it away, but she let out such a cry as to call her husband." Yosef paused, obviously in anguish.

"What happened?" the assassin asked.

"The creature killed him," Yosef whispered. "It tore out his throat with its hands and stalked off into the night, covered in my son-in-law's blood. We were unable to do anything about it, despite my daughter's screams."

"Such a beast is beyond the ability of anyone who is not a trained warrior." Ali tried to be reassuring. He suspected it would do little. Most men found Ali extremely threatening at the best of times. "What happened to your daughter?"

"She lost the baby," Yosef said. "It was a deformed mess with snakes for arms and legs. I burned it rather than bury it, infuriating my daughter. Afterward, her dreams were plagued of horrible things in a world where time and space were meaningless. I prayed over her and begged Yahweh to spare her, but she passed three days later. My own dreams have since taken on visions of this creature and the alien vistas she described in her dreams. I do not know if I am suffering a curse or being stalked by monsters, but death will claim me too soon."

Ali had no comforting words so he simply nodded.

Yosef added one final thing. "I hesitate to say this, because I do not know if you wish to involve yourself in such a thing, but my daughter says the killer wore the attire of a crusader, though its tabard was soiled and bloodstained. A Templar to be precise."

Ali pondered this before making his decision. "It will die, forever this time. You have the word of the Hashishin."

Yosef blinked, surprised by the man's agreement. "My people do not have much in the way of money but—"

"It will die," the assassin said, retreating into the shadows. "That is all you need to be assured of."

Disappearing through the streets of the city Arabs called Akka, Ali ad Fariq crossed from alleyway to alleyway until he snuck into the back of Karim ad Jaffar's home.

Karim was, publicly, a junk merchant, but was privately the overseer of the Hashishin in the region. Currently, they were the only two assassins in the city, but occasionally he hosted up to a dozen.

Karim was waiting for him, sitting down at a table in his simple kitchen, reading a Cathayan scroll by lamplight. The older assassin was middle-aged, no longer as fit as he'd been when he was a younger man, but still spry enough to kill three men half as well trained. Karim was dressed in a loose-fitting black robe and a pair of slippers, the former hiding no end of stains from when he'd messily eaten the day before. Table manners were a minor concern to the aged assassin and often ignored. Karim's eyes were glazed over, and the smell of incense mixed with hashish filled the air.

Karim was the sole reason that Ali knew anything of the Dark Arts and possessed abilities that could only have come from studying Abdul Alhazred the Second's books. While Karim possessed the Nizari Muslim faith, Ali doubted he took it very seriously. Karim regularly made sacrifices to beings he called angels like Jabrīl-Thotep, Mīkhā'īl-Kthanid, and Isrāfīl-Noddens. Ali knew that he simply equated older foreign gods with Allah's servants while calling upon them for power. It was blasphemous and worthy of damnation, but somehow Ali couldn't bring himself to condemn the old man for it.

Besides, I am going to need some of that unholy knowledge if I am ever to find this monster, Ali thought. *Who knows how long it will be before it starts stalking our people? Such a thing should not exist.*

"I trust your meeting with the Jew went well?" Karim said, raising his lamp to speak with his associate.

"It depends on your definition of well," Ali said, walking over to sit down across from him. "Rabbi ben Yosef claims that a serpent-tongued corpse is slaughtering the Jewesses of Akka."

Karim puckered his lips and picked up his lamp, going to the kitchen. "It would not be the first time."

Ali blinked, staring at the man. "What?"

"Allah has been known to curse those who defile his temples, mosques, and places. When the prophet Jesus was being crucified, some legends say God laid a curse upon on one of the soldiers who had tried to slay his representative. That soldier later made a pact with Iblis, becoming a creature who stalked the night. Other legends say that Qayin was cursed when he killed his brother Habil. My favorite story involves God cursing Absalom, David's most beloved son, to wander the Earth until he made restitution for his crimes."

"I do not think Allah creates monsters," Ali said, leaning on his table.

Ali knew Karim was patronizing him as he often made up religious justifications for the terrible things he studied, both to placate Ali's own faith as well as the Old Man. Ali caught a glimpse of the unrolled scroll on the table then turned away in disgust. While he could not make out the meaning of the marks that they used to record information, the author had illustrated some ghastly scenes in the margins. This scroll showed a woman abased by demons to birth some sort of horned giant and a cloud-demon. It was obscene.

"I do not claim to speak for Allah," Karim said, "but all things are his will, both good and bad. The creature you speak of is a *strigoi,* a half-human thing like the flesh-eating *ghuls* who live beneath the ground. I have heard of these undead spoken of by Teuton mercenaries, especially the ones close to the Balkans. You would not like the mercenaries, they are a strange people. I trust they knew of what they spoke, however."

Ali knew Karim often went out disguised as a Christian during the city's occupation by the crusaders. His ability to root out information from even the most tight-lipped souls was well-known in an order famed for it. Some whispered in Alamut that Karim did it because the Templars supposedly had their own secret cabals and unnatural secrets. It was another reason Ali believed Karim might be of help in this.

"How do I kill one of these strigoi?" Ali asked, troubled by the prospect. "I have slain a dozen men but the way the rabbi speaks of the monster, it is already dead. Furthermore, he speaks as if it is capable of tearing a man apart as if he were made of made of dry cloth."

"He is probably not exaggerating." Karim began preparing a plate of bread and leftover chicken for his ally. "Tell me what the rabbi told you and perhaps we may learn through logic. Do you remember the writings of the philosopher Aristotle?"

"Yes," Ali said, hating those lessons. The Old Man forced every one of his students to receive a classical education. "Unfortunately."

"Do not mock wisdom, even when it comes from heathen sources, *especially* if it comes from heathen sources," Karim said. "The legends I have heard say these creatures can be driven away by cloves of garlic, sesame seeds, as well as the smoke of burning Bastian oil from Ulthar. Thankfully, I have some of the latter here. I do not know if it is the truth, but it is best we rely on what is not superstition if we are truly to kill this thing for a second time. I will consult my most proven and tried sources to learn more about this creature."

"You mean summoning demons," Ali said, disgusted.

"Dream creatures," Karim said. "Call them demons, jinn, spirits, or gods—"

"There is no God but—"

"Yes, yes," Karim interrupted. "Finish up your story."

Ali hated when Karim treated him like a child but reiterated the rabbi's words exactly, finishing his story by saying, "I know you are no friend to Jews, Karim, but no one should die that way. Particularly a woman."

"I dislike everyone," Karim said. "That does not mean that I wish them dead. Your friend's story reveals some of our quarry's weaknesses, however."

"It does?" Ali said, surprised. "The amulet failed to drive it off."

Karim looked bemused, carrying over a plate of food to his friend and shaking his head. "The creature stalks the streets at night. This may mean it is nocturnal and is weaker during the day. Likewise, the creature feeds on a schedule, which indicates that it needs sustenance. The snake tongue ties it to Yig-Seth of the Ancient Egyptian pantheon. The fact that it chose to flee shows that there was something that scared it off. Enough so that it fled into the night from a helpless, waddling mother-to-be."

"That doesn't tell me how to kill it, though." Ali took the plate of cold chicken and bread, and started to eat it.

"Fire has long been a cleansing tool of Allah," Karim said. "It was abrogated for humans but not beasts and monsters. I know it works on ghuls, at least. Likewise, I have yet to encounter a being that survived decapitation. Have your sword blessed and fill some oilskins."

Ali chewed on his chicken, mulling on Karim's words. "That's enough to start with, I suppose. It only leaves the most important part, now."

"Which is?"

"Finding it."

That proved harder than it sounded. The next three days were spent seeking all rumors about the creature.

There were stories, yes, stories enough to turn a man's blood cold. The most promising of tales was of a mysterious Templar stalking the streets at night. Unfortunately, for every story about this figure which might have had some substance, there were ten which were utter nonsense.

Ali's favorite talked about how it was all a plot by black magicians in the service of King Richard to raise an army of the undead. Ali was no fan of the English king and thought that if the man couldn't run a proper war, there was no way he could build an army of supernatural monsters in secret.

Unfortunately, their attempts to find the creature's resting place were fruitless. Akka was a city older than Rome and Byzantium put together. It was filled with countless catacombs, hidden passageways, and tombs where a nocturnal monster might choose to make its resting place. It didn't help that many buildings were still abandoned from when Ṣalāḥ ad-Dīn had retaken the city the year before.

"This is hopeless," Ali said, finally taking a moment to rest after another fruitless day of searching. "We could scour the city for a hundred years and still not find this creature's lair."

Karim, who was travelling alongside him, laughed. "Don't be naive, Ali. More likely, it would be fifty at most."

Ali snorted and stared at the sky. "It is nearly nightfall, Karim. Do you believe we should continue?" His voice sounded hesitant, even to himself.

Karim rubbed his beard a bit. "I suspect you wish to continue, even if we have only a few more places to check."

"Yes," Ali said. "Do you remember Anisah?"

"All women run together with me," Karim said. "I take it I should, however?"

"She is my wife," Ali said, annoyed. "She is also with child. I cannot help but think that were the circumstances slightly different, she might be hunted by this thing. I have never been happier that she is miles away in Masyaf than I am today."

"Do not overly sympathize with those who have hired us, Ali," Karim said. "Death comes to us all eventually, both maiden and master swordsmen. Still, I believe we have at least a little daylight left. Perhaps we will be lucky."

"Lucky would be two days ago," Ali said, shaking his head. "Your spirits have proven useless."

"They have not," Karim said. "Sadly, they have told me they cannot find his location because he holds a fragment of the name."

"The name?" Ali asked.

"The name of God," Karim said. "The real God who exists in all places, times, and peoples."

"Careful," Ali said, his hand moving toward his sword's hilt.

"Indulge me," Karim said. "Assume I speak only what I have heard."

Ali sighed. "Fine. I will listen. Just do not expect me to believe you."

Karim sighed. "Yog-Sothoth."

"Thoth, like the Egyptian god?" Ali asked.

Karim rolled his eyes. "It is but one name for one whose true name is unspeakable. Abdul Alhazared worshiped it and many other creatures, but Yog-Sothoth reigns supreme above this universe and many others. His cults are created by fools seeking enlightenment on the Plateaus of Leng, Great Carcosa, and the Seven Heavens, among other places where dreams become reality."

"Now you speak gibberish," Ali said, rolling his eyes.

"Yog-Sothoth is the source of all magic," Karim said. "Because he is all things, even a syllable of his true name is enough to grant vast power. Many have sought the silver keys and small gods of Unknown Kadath to come face to face with him. It always fails."

"Does any of this have anything to do with our current quest?" Ali asked, feeling the traces of truth in Karim's words. Truths that threatened to shatter his faith if they were accepted at face value. Instead, he did his best to dismiss them and pretend they were nothing but the ravings of lunatics.

"The Templar has a name," Karim said. "Or had a name. His human one does not matter anymore. He was a powerful magician named Robert D'Airelle. He sought to walk the path and achieve enlightenment at the end of a dream-quest. Instead, he was merged with a creature from another world and it now walks around in his corpse. But he learned part of Yog-Sothoth's true name. The very nature of it prevents any spirit from scrying it."

"Oh, lovely," Ali said.

"You do not understand," Karim said, looking frightened for the first time Ali had ever seen in their long history. "That name has no place in this universe. Yog-Sothoth has long sought to explore the interiors of his existence and live as mortals. Each of his children with mortal women has been a prophet or a horror or both. The fragment of his name in this world makes this Templar a walking wasteland. Strigoi is just what mortals call these monsters, but he is something worse. Its hunger will only grow as it feeds and the true name takes up more of its mind."

"The true name of God according to you," Ali said.

"A thing man was not meant to know," Karim said. "There are some secrets too great for mortal minds."

In that moment, Ali believed him and hated him for it. "So, we have to stop this thing or it's the end of the world."

"No, others will stop him before then," Karim said, "The Old One's servitors will not lose their herd so easily. It may end the Holy Land, though. The Empty Quarter of the South was once a vast kingdom until it never existed."

Ali sucked in his breath. "What's the next location to search?"

Karim gestured down the street to an area that was mostly abandoned. The houses surrounding a small chapel had been burned out and looted during the city's capture. The church itself was a shell of its former self with half of its roof caved in and all its shutters boarded over.

The neighborhood had been mostly Christian before a group of Egyptian mercenaries had marauded through the region, killing everything that moved. Supposedly, Ṣalāḥ ad-Dīn had them all stuffed with arrows and rolled in a ditch, but the crime still lingered in the local's memory. Now Ali wondered if it was all just a cover-up for something worse living among them. But which was the worse monster, the evil in the hearts of man or an amoral universe that cared nothing for the lives or struggles of mortals?

No, I must trust in Allah and forget these infidel lies, Ali thought.

"You believe the creature hides in a church?" Ali asked, surprised. "A strange choice for a creature we are assuming is profane before Allah."

"If you choose not to believe what I have told you, that is your business. But this place is sacred to his kind," Karim said, crossing his arms. "If it helps you to sleep, then believe this former Templar will gravitate to a place as desecrated as his soul. Shall we go in?"

"I have no argument against telling myself such," Ali said, now uncomfortable. "As for going in, I want to say no but won't."

"Good," Karim said. "Facing your fears is the path of wisdom."

"Or madness," Ali muttered.

The church looked to be a decaying ruin. They only got to see the inside once they pried open the rusted gateway, however. A quick look around told the two assassins that their initial impression had been correct.

The pews were overturned, idols shattered on the floor, and there were signs that everything remotely valuable had been ripped from its place. There was also a feel to this place, a corrupt and unholy chill seemed to cling to the walls. As Ali walked alongside Karim, his hand moving down to the pommel of his scimitar, he swore he could hear the wailing of women and the clanging of swords.

"This place has been profaned," Ali whispered.

Karim said, "I agree. But not by the bloodshed. The gods love that."

"Let's hope superstition helps us." Ali reached into his tunic's neck and pulled out a necklace of garlic cloves.

"So, that's what that smell was. I thought a Venetian pirate was stalking us." Karim wrinkled his nose.

"I do not see any sign of this creature," Ali said. "It looks like this is another dead end."

Karim shook his head and gestured to the dusty ground. A clear path traced through the ruined church to behind the altar. "Look, the floor has been walked on recently. Many times, in fact."

"I see." Ali stared at the trail through the dust, surprised that he had missed something so obvious. "It appears we have at least found someone. Though this would not be the first time a beggar or vagrant has sought refuge in an abandoned building."

"You are cautious," Karim said. "Good."

Inside his chest, Ali's heart pounded. *May this be the one, Allah. May I deliver you this monster's head. I wish never to think of Karim's blasphemies again. I will request a transfer from the Old Man when this is done and never look upon Karim again. He is either mad, a monster, or Iblis in the flesh.*

Following the trail, the pair soon found a heavy stone block with a rusted hoop bolted into it hidden behind the altar. Ali used every bit of his strength to pull it up from the ground, revealing underneath a set of stairs carved out of the rock beneath it. There was no light, so the two had to make a hasty torch using one of the oilskins, a bit of cloth, and a scimitar.

"A catacomb?" Ali asked.

"Most likely," Karim said. "Left over from the days of the disciples, perhaps."

"I suppose Īsā ibn Maryam was the son of Yog-Sothoth too," Ali said, unable to hide his disdain. Jesus, the Son of Mary was the penultimate prophet and another person he expected Karim to blaspheme.

"No, but probably a great dreamer," Karim said.

Ali growled in disgust.

"You must choose either the horrible truth or horrible ignorance," Karim said. "There is no third way."

"I choose to kill the monster," Ali said.

Karim nodded. "I am sorry for ruining our friendship."

Ali said nothing.

Heading down the steps, they found themselves surrounded by ancient corpses placed into carved alcoves along the walls. The catacomb wasn't long, but a cramped hallway led to a chamber the size of a small house with a single stone coffin in its center. Surrounding it were a half-dozen rotting corpses, showing the creature was not restricted to dining on Jewish women.

"I think we've found its lair," Karim said, wrinkling his nose at the rotting smell. "Now I wish I had worn garlic too."

"Let us cut off its head, cover it in blessed oil, burn it, and be done with it," Karim said, drawing his blade.

"I agree," Ali said, advancing on the stone coffin. "We still have an hour or two before sunset."

Before he could say more, a dozen torches built into the side of the wall spontaneously lit themselves. In an instant, the previously dark chamber became well-lit.

"That's not a good sign," Ali said.

"You understate matters, I think," Karim said. "If it awakens, we must strike it dead through force of arms."

"Agreed," Ali said, ready to advance only for Karim to grab him by the arm.

"We must also be cautious," Karim said, "lest we join the many corpses around us. We might not find peace in death if the creature is a necromancer too."

It went against Ali's every instinct to hold back at such a critical moment, but he reluctantly nodded.

Moments later, the heavy stone lid of the coffin slid off and the creature was revealed. True to the description, it was a man in a Templar's armor. His chainmail was intact, though rusted and ill-kept with signs it had been damaged in battle. His tabard was filthy, covered in dirt and bloodstains, with the red cross underneath barely visible.

The monster itself, the strigoi Robert D'Airelle, was foul to look upon. It looked like a corpse three or four days old with skin hanging uncomfortably on its skull, sunken eyes, and a pair of burning flames in his otherwise empty sockets. Tumors grew out of its body on every visible portion of his flesh, and there was a long worm-like tongue slithering out of its mouth. The creature's fingernails were unnaturally long as it didn't bother with gauntlets. There was something else, like the form its eyes gave it was just an illusion for something even more horrible, but Ali pushed that thought away. Even so, out of the corner of his eye, he saw a multi-limbed worm that walked like a man. It made him want to vomit.

"You," Ali said in French. "Murderer."

Robert reacted unexpectedly, releasing a hellish laugh from its dead and decaying throat.

"Indeed," Robert said, speaking perfect French. "It was the price for seeking the true name of God so that I could remake Earth as a paradise. I did not realize we were but one race in a million, and each life was a thousand in a timeline of a mad demon. The trinity is not the Father, the Son, and the Holy Spirit, but Yog-Sothoth, Nyarlathotep, and Azathoth. I am a crude key for a sophisticated lock, but I shall forge myself into that which can release my master. The mistake of Creation will end, and we shall all be one in our Lord. That is my atonement."

Ali was surprised by the eloquence of the creature. He'd been expecting a mindless beast and was now confronting a thinking, intelligent being. "Atonement? You call the slaughter of these men and the young women of the Jewish Quarter, atonement?"

"Yes," the creature said, reaching into its coffin and pulling out a kite shield emblazoned with the Templar cross and a broadsword. "If

God has made me a monster, then I must do monstrous things. If it takes until Judgment Day, I will rid the world of Muhammadans and Christ-Killers, Heretics and Greek-speaking false priests, leaving only the pure and faithful Christians of Rome. Only those who pray to Christ's vicar shall remain. He is a deluded fool sitting on a throne of lies, but his sweet ignorance is the greatest gift I can give humanity before we all enter the fires of perdition. The meek shall inherit but beings far greater and grander than we could ever match."

Ali realized he was dealing with a fanatic as well as an undead monster. "I see."

He prepared to lunge at the creature with his blade, only for Karim to charge. Something about Robert's words had ignited a spark of fury inside his mentor and drove him to attack, not with strategy or spells, but pure unmitigated rage.

"Karim!" Ali shouted, stunned by his friend's movement.

The monster did not hesitate in its moves, blocking Karim's blow effortlessly with its shield and slicing through the older assassin's chest with its blade. The momentary distraction gave Ali time to hurl his oil skin at the creature with one hand and slice it in the air with the other. The oil covered the creature and seemed to sink onto every part of its body. Almost immediately, the oil ignited as if the being's accursed nature caused it to combust.

The creature let out a horrifying howl, tearing at its armor and hurling the useless burning pieces to the side. Within moments, the monster was a blackened charred thing with its skull visible through ashen pieces of flesh hanging from the exposed burned muscle beneath it. Somehow, it still stood, staring at Ali with lidless eyes. Its illusionary form vanished, and Ali saw the burning worm that walked and knew the oil would not be enough.

"Your heathen magic will not avail you, assassin," the creature said in a low, guttural tone. "I will feast on your blood and offer your death to the True God. Perhaps in your final moments, I will whisper what I know of his name. I have done it before with each of my prey and watched the light go out of their souls."

Ali knelt as the creature rushed at him. The monster was slowed down by its injuries but still lightning fast. Ali used his position to roll out of the way of the monster bringing down its razor-sharp tentacles as it swung repeatedly for the assassin's head. The creature would never tire or weaken, which meant time was on its side.

I pray this works, Ali thought, maneuvering so the unholy thing was forced to swing down particularly low during one strike.

Ali brought his blade around in the confusion, cutting through the monster's neck and decapitating it in one blow. The creature's head rolled across the ground and its body fell to its knees before plopping over. It was in that moment that Ali knew, inhuman monster or not, it was just a mortal thing like anyone else.

"Allow me to send you to the True God first," Ali said, trying to sound clever, but mostly failing. All he could think of was Karim getting sliced into by the monster. "His name is Allah and Muhammed is his Prophet."

Despite the fact Karim was dying on the ground, Ali stopped to empty his remaining oil skins on the decapitated creature's form. Though perhaps decapitated was less a word for it than bisected. The monster's body caught fire once more, this time burning like tinder. Ali tossed its severed head onto the pyre, hoping this action killed it forever. He wondered if the creature's monstrous form had been a deliberate attempt to obfuscate its nature or the name it held in its mind was so terrible as to prevent him from assuming an illusion capable of passing for human.

It didn't matter now. The monster was dead, and it had taken the true name of God, or the Devil as Ali preferred to believe, with him.

"Ali..." Karim called, the old man still alive despite his injuries.

Ali rushed to his side, taking the old man by the hand. "I am sorry, my friend. I heard such things and... remembered my body's humanity for a moment."

"You did well," Ali said. "Now you go to God."

Karim chuckled. "No, my presence will return to distant Pnakotus. I have only been wearing this body as I studied your kind. You were somewhat interesting, Ali, and that is the highest praise I can give one of your kind. Perhaps I will see what your descendants are up to in a thousand years."

Ali had no idea what that meant as his friend died. In the end, he chose to burn Karim's body as well.

"It is truly dead, then?" Yosef asked, once Ali came to his home. He looked like he had only hours to live and stood only with the help of a staff as well as a young boy who bore much of his weight.

Ali nodded, leaning back in his chair. "I placed the creature's ashes in four blessed urns and buried them under mosques throughout Akka. It has been three days and there is no sign that it has regenerated. I believe, as much as any creature that is already dead can be, that it is destroyed."

The rabbi let himself smile, albeit weakly. "I believe you. No nightmares have affected me since the night you said you killed him, little comfort that may be for my remaining time on Earth. If only Rebecca could have been here to see this. She deserved a chance to know that her attacker was destroyed. Worse, she could not even rest in death without jackals defiling her corpse." Yosef sniffed the air, a disgusted look in his eyes.

Ali stared at Yosef, and a cold chill ran down his spine. "What do you mean?"

The rabbi shrugged, shuffling to prepare some tea for his guest. "Her body disappeared from her grave yesterday. The filth in this city is beyond description."

Ali's flesh crawled as he remembered that Robert had not succeeded in killing Rebecca. Her death had not been immediate, and she held the name inside her now. Who knew where she would now take it. And what horrors she would unleash.

"The Final Gate" is the climax to Tales of Yog-Sothoth *the same way that "The Last Page" was to* Tales of the Al-Azif. *Both books were organized chronologically so it tended to result in me being the guy who wrote the first and last stories since I enjoyed stories of the Cthulhu Mythos in both the distant past as well as post-apocalypse future.*

In this story, which I, again, wrote before I knew there would ever be any more Cthulhu Armageddon *stories, former kid sidekick, Jackie Howard, is pregnant with her child. This effectively makes John and Mercury grandparents. Which just goes to show that I wasn't intending to keep telling their stories like I ended up doing.*

The Mi-Go also show up in this story, acting very much like the Grays from UFO folklore. I'm not the first author to notice HPL predicted a lot of things that would eventually show up in science fiction with the Mi-Go. The Delta Green *RPG, for instance, makes the connection explicit. Still, it's an easy connection to make with a bunch of aliens kidnapping people in rural areas to do experiments.*

THE FINAL GATE

A *Cthulhu Armageddon* Adventure

Chapter One

The screams of childbirth were accompanied by the battered old jukebox playing Rolling Stones' "Sympathy for the Devil." Natural birth was incredibly hazardous to women who grew up outside of civilized communities in the Wasteland. Still, human women had been giving birth to children for millennia before the advent of modern medicine and Jackie was lucky to have a trained doctor looking out for her upstairs. Each birth of a healthy child in the Post-Rising world was both a blessing and a curse. A blessing because it was shaking a fist at the post-apocalypse wasteland we lived in and a curse because it was introducing new life into a world that was destined to kill it early.

It had been a little over a century since the Great Old Ones had been awakened from their millennia-long slumber and the end of human civilization. Reality had been altered with the skies turning different colors, the stars rearranging, and the environment becoming a variety of alien hellscapes. It was, in many ways, a miracle that humanity had managed to eke out a living in the dusty ruins of a once-grand civilization. We—if you could consider me a human—were no longer the top of the food chain, but we weren't quite extinct either. Life was nasty, brutish, and short with perhaps no future beyond the next few generations. Still, we persevered and became more like the Old Ones every day.

I was wiping down the bar beside the wooden staircase leading up to the gathering of whores, friends, and family around Jackie's room. The Wages of Sin, my establishment, was the dual tavern and brothel that had become something of a cultural center for New Ulthar's tiny but growing populace. Technically, I was also sheriff and mayor since that title fell to you when you shot the previous boss of the town in the face. He'd had it coming, though.

The Wages of Sin had once been a cheap hotel for motorists back when there were roads. Wooden tables taken from parks and other locations filled the front, while I'd turned the former registration desk into a place where people could try the cheap whiskey produced from weird fungi that grew on the sides of nearby hills. So far it hadn't killed anyone and was a large part of why the place was in business. Well, usually in business, I'd shut it down for the night so Jackie could birth her child in peace.

The lights flickered for a second then went back on, the wires and newly blown glass bulbs continuing to work despite the conditions. I was genuinely impressed with the ingenuity of the populace, including some ghouls glamoured to look like humans. Humanity had gotten increasingly "strange" and broad in its definition of what qualified as a person versus a monster. Jackie, herself, was destined to become a ghoul like her ancestors but was still a human woman in appearance. Among most communities, that would have resulted in her—or those opposing her—death, but New Ulthar was "progressive" in ways that other villages were not.

"I need a drink, Booth," a female voice said, coming from the second floor of the building.

"What do you want? Mud beer, mud whiskey, mud vodka, or some variety of fermented fungus that glows at night?" I asked, half-joking.

Walking down the stairs was the petite Eurasian form of Doctor Mercury Halsey. She had crimson red hair that was cut short and alluring yellow cat-like eyes. She was wearing a dirty apron over a pair of denim pants and a cotton shirt. Mercury was a lovely woman, lacking the hardened leather-like features of most Wastelanders. Both of us had grown up in New Arkham, a converted military base that was a paradise compared to New Ulthar, but that place was destroyed now, its populace having spread out to conquer a good chunk of Massachusetts. You couldn't hold back the tides of change, no matter how hard you tried.

"Don't test me, Booth," Mercury said. "Also, give me a full bottle of moonglow."

I nodded and slid her down a ceramic bottle of moonglow with a clay cup to pour it into. Mercury had a cast-iron stomach and I'd seen her drink grown men under the table who could barely stomach two shots of the local liquors. She was human, a purer strain than most in fact, but seemed capable of things that others weren't. Then again, she was a witch.

"Thank you," Mercury said, taking both. She filled the cup to the brim despite it being three shots' worth.

"Boy or girl?" I asked.

"Boy," Mercury said. "He has all the requisite parts. Well, he's missing a toe, but he doesn't have goat legs or horns."

"Ah," I said, nodding. "I suppose the parents will be pleased."

Jackie and her lover Cloud would be the ones raising the children despite my offers to take on the lion's share of responsibility. Parenthood suited me and I wanted them to be able to enjoy their lives as best they could. I wasn't sure about Mercury, but she had a similar desire to protect her adopted child (and now grandchild).

I'd also offered to set them both up with one of the farms outside of town, but they'd adamantly refused, apparently preferring life in our weird city. Then again, New Ulthar's citizens had a strange belief that their town was protected. It was one of their stranger superstitions, like the fact they let cats run free around the place and hung anyone who so much as insulted one. Five were hanging around the bar right now, annoying the hell out of me.

"How does it feel to be a grandfather?" Mercury asked.

"The same as it did to be a father," I replied, shrugging. "If circumstances permit, I might be a grandfather several thousand times over someday."

"Or the world might end," Mercury said, pouring an iridescent cup's worth of liquor then slurping it down. "You're only immortal until you're killed."

Yes, I wasn't exactly human either. It was a fact I kept from everyone but my closest family. "That's all of us. How do you feel about it, though, really?"

"Jealous," Mercury said, smiling. "Envious. Happy that when I'm dust and bones, someone will remember me."

"You're in your thirties," I replied.

"*Late* thirties and getting older every day," Mercury said. "That's not happening to you."

"No," I admitted. "It's not. Not anymore."

Mercury downed the entire cup in one long drink. "I just might outlive humanity, though."

"Depends on how you define humanity," I replied.

Truth be told, I knew what she was saying. I was one of the few beings alive who'd had an encounter with Nyarlathotep, The God of a Thousand Faces, and lived to tell the tale. I was part of an even smaller group that had emerged with most of my faculties intact, human being or not. Nyarlathotep had said that humanity had only a few generations left before it was extinct on this dying world. That had been ten years ago and was increasingly true. Whatever managed to survive on this planet was unlikely to resemble "normal" humanity well before the last mortal died out.

"How is Cloud?" I asked.

"He's happy," Mercury said. "Or so he says. I don't think he's quite as happy as Jackie. I can never read that giant's moods."

Cloud had come in from the Wastelands one day, over seven feet in height, and hailing from the Dunwych tribe that existed many miles away. The Dunwych had adapted to the Post-Rising world by embracing the weird. They worshiped Azathoth, Yog-Sothoth, and Shub-Niggurath, while believing Nyarlathotep was their messenger. Somehow, Cloud had gotten himself outcast by that savage and relentless people before surviving a hundred-mile journey on foot. Jackie had been charmed by the stoic warrior and the result of their union was now above us. Probably. It wasn't like we could do DNA tests anymore.

"Fatherhood is a great responsibility," I said, with false cheer. "Harder than running a bar, being a sheriff, or—"

"Running a brothel and being a witch," Mercury said. "Do you think the locals will accept the boy? Jackie isn't exactly eager to run off to the Underground to live with her people. They'd probably eat Cloud too."

"Ghouls only eat the dead, not the living," I pointed out.

"That just means they'd have to kill him first," Mercury pointed out.

Well, she wasn't wrong. "The child, at least, will have a chance to live once it makes the transition to ghoul. Same as Jackie. I'm not sure much of humanity will, otherwise. Maybe we should start studding you out. Breeding a new humanity."

"Not funny," Mercury said.

"Who says I'm joking?" I asked, perhaps pressing the issue more than I should have. The issue of children had come up before, but the results had been painful. Even when Mercury had accepted my inhumanity, our attempts had not gone... well.

Mercury looked down. "Let's talk about something else. Also, pour yourself something. I hate drinking alone."

I nodded and got myself a separate bottle and cup. It was pointless, because I could drink an entire keg of this stuff and feel nothing. I could look human, feel human, and even breed with mankind—other races probably too—but it was a lie. I was a child of an older race that had worshiped Yog-Sothoth on a far-distant planet. I was a cuckoo that they had placed among humanity before reaching maturity. In that, Jackie and I had something in common.

"What do you want to talk about?" I asked. "The weather, crop rotations, outlaws?"

"The end of the world," Mercury replied, not pouring herself another drink. Frankly, I was surprised she could stand after her first cup full. Most people were lucky to sip their way through a half cup.

"There's a lot of that going around," I said, only half joking.

"The black rains are getting worse," Mercury said.

The black rains were a new feature to an already dying world. The battle between two Great Old Ones had poisoned the clouds with some strange magic that was transforming the Earth's surface. Whole regions that had once been dead and lifeless were now lush and vibrant, but potentially poisonous to mankind. When it wasn't poisonous, it turned those it touched into something more and less human.

"Maybe humanity isn't meant to survive," I muttered, holding my empty cup and pretending to drink. "Maybe nature has decided it's time for us to die."

"Bullshit," Mercury said, narrowing her eyes. "Life exists to propagate and change. Evolution doesn't select people to die, it's not a god, it's just some races do die out and other life goes on."

"Go forth and multiply, eh?" I asked, casting her eye a sideways glance. Mercury had been an atheist but had taken to worshiping idols and spirits in hopes of gaining power from it. It was a transactional sort of faith that irritated me. I had met real gods, one at least, and the only thing I'd learned from the experience was he was an asshole. I preferred to believe in the Small Gods of Humanity, whether they existed outside of dreams or not.

"Don't talk about that, Booth," Mercury said, taking on a dangerous and somewhat defeated tone. "I would if I could."

Ah, we were back on the subject of children.

"Would you?" I asked.

Mercury glared. "Do you really want that answer?"

"Yes," I said.

Mercury stared at her empty liquor bowl. "No, you don't. It's not just you. Time has caught up with me and it'd be dangerous. Even if it weren't, who would want to bring a child into a doomed world?"

Jackie had, but I wasn't about to bring that up. I had my answer, and it was useless to argue further.

"Fair enough," I muttered, deciding I would go upstairs and visit Jackie soon.

"Well, this conversation went depressing, quickly," Mercury muttered. "Why am I in love with you again?"

"I have eaten things trying to kill you." I lifted my empty glass. "Also, moral support."

Mercury smiled. "There is that. Jackie is graduating from the University next year. She can be a mother and a scientist."

The University was the sole remaining place of higher learning left in the New England Wasteland, possibly the world. It was a place of research and knowledge assembled in the steam tunnels underneath Miskatonic University's ruins. The Yith had taken to educating the mortals there and building strange technology for purposes I didn't entirely trust. Still, it was, for the time being, a reminder that humanity had not always been ignorant savages. That it had once possessed the hope to be something more than the rising ape or subject to the fallen angel.

"Someday you'll pass this wonderful establishment on to her," I said, half-jokingly. "Then she can be a scientist, mother, and whoremonger like you."

"You forgot witch," Mercury said, her voice low. "Mind you, I don't intend to die. Ever."

I was about to ask what she meant by that when we were interrupted by new arrivals.

"Where are the whores? We are ready to indulge!" a voice spoke from the entrance of the building, a piece of sheet metal I'd chained in front of the doorframe. Somehow, it had been pulled open and a squad of four New Arkham Rangers entered.

I glared. I had once been a New Arkham Ranger, and that time had been some of the proudest moments of my life. That had been before what I'd seen from the New Arkham Republic, which had started handing out the title and uniform like candy. They had started giving it to any "true blooded" citizen of New Arkham who was willing to kill, rape, or butcher whatever Wastelander stepped out of line in the six cities they controlled. Even so, it was possible I'd misjudged them. They were all my daughter's and son's ages, in their mid-twenties, with tarnished blue great coat and rubber coolsuit uniforms, and had their gas masks hanging from around their necks. Each of them wore berets that showed the mark of Beta Team. There were still trustworthy men and women in the military, so I decided to treat them with a modicum of respect. A modicum.

"This establishment is closed," I said, simply. "Which is why the door was locked outside."

The fact they'd broken the lock was reason enough to kick them out, but it was possible they were under the mistaken impression New Ulthar was part of the Arkham Republic's territory. Like Derry, the Rock, or the Lot, there were many small towns outside the larger cities with their own governments as well as dark secrets. New Ulthar was on the border of the Arkham Republic's border with the Dunwych tribes.

The leader, a man with marble skin as white as mine was black, walked up and put his hands on the bar. "What kind of brothel closes in the middle of the evening? Especially for paying customers."

"One reserved for a private gathering," I said, simply. "A birth."

The man snorted. "We don't need her to service us, but every one of the others will be needed."

He proceeded to drop a bag of gold coins on the top of the bar. They were each minted with the image of the United States Eagle on one side and a crude rendering of President Ashton-Smith. They had a somewhat sickly yellow look to them, and I knew they were originally made from Deep One ore. The unpleasant coloring of it didn't leave even after smelting. I'd heard the Arkham Republic had taken to trading with the cities along the coast but hadn't wanted to believe it. The Deep Ones, at least the Pure Bloods, wanted nothing from humanity except slaves. Ones for both their sacrificial altar and larders both. The hybrids forced inland by their brethren, ironically, were more likely to be slaves than to keep them.

I was not impressed. "Go away."

The man snarled. "No."

"There are other bars and brothels in town. Go there," Mercury said, not even bothering to look back. Unlike me, she had no lingering affection for the people of New Arkham and celebrated the near destruction of the city years ago. They had not only forced her into a marriage she'd loathed, but also into a position that had almost cost her sanity. It was not the study of eldritch lore or occult secrets, but the far more mundane position of being forced into torturing the city state's enemies. We were married now, of sorts, though no ceremony had ever taken place.

The leader's hand moved down to his sidearm threateningly, but my attention remained on his three companions. He was making a deliberate ass of himself. While I could easily believe that, I noted that the smell of alcohol was on his clothes rather than coming from his breath. The man and women to his side were keeping their hands underneath their great coats, clutching weapons well before things looked like they'd degenerate to violence. They were also standing deliberately in front of a somewhat lanky-looking man with facial features that did not move, including his eyes. A weird buzzing was coming from his lips, though, that I could hear despite being too high a frequency for human ears.

"Yog-Sothoth…mzg'agal…Yah'athal…nbbaas…n'gleb…" The unholy alien noises were spoken by a throat that seemed halfway between a human's and something else. Magic was more will than word, but I recognized its use where it was employed.

I nodded and reached under the bar before picking up my composite quadruple-barreled shotgun made of pipe which had massive buckshot shells. "Very well. We can…trap!"

I fired the gun through the thin wooden material of the bar and shot the stomach of the leader causing him to fall back into his fellows. Strangely, there was not the shower of gore I usually saw accompanying the shotgun's use.

Mercury threw herself backward and called out to gods I didn't recognize the names of, only for a bolt of lightning to fly from her hands. The blast slashed through the chest of the woman behind her, striking through her and into the spellcaster.

"Kill the mutant! Retrieve the child!" the last remaining ranger shouted, pulling out a strange triangular metal pistol with a double grip not meant for a human hand. I ducked to one side as bright green light dissolved the wall behind me. I'd never encountered a weapon like it before.

The ranger moved it to one side, only for me to smash the barrel of my weapon into his face. The result turned out to not be a bloody mess, but a sparking metal one. Underneath the fleshy coating of his face was a grinning chrome skull with wires, gears, and unidentifiable machinery leaking brackish fluid from the wound that exposed its interior. I could see some sort of braincase between the holes of its metal skull and felt with alien senses the patterns of brainwaves not entirely human. This was the product of no human technology, but a mind infinitely vaster.

Mi-Go, I could hear Nyarlathotep's voice whisper in the back of my mind. *The Fungi of Yuggoth.*

"What the hell," I said, staring in shock.

That was when the metal man lifted its gun to my face.

Chapter Two

Time seemed to slow down for a moment as the machine man tried to force his alien weapon underneath my chin. He was stronger than a human being, many times more, but I had more strength than the average human myself.

"Get the hell away!" I said, my voice becoming raw and guttural.

"Stop r-r-resisting," the machine man spoke, his voice glitching as we pushed the weapon back and forth between us.

Years ago, I'd discovered I was the child of an unspeakable thing from another world. I'd summoned Nyarlathotep with the *Necronomicon* and he'd shown me my origins, possibly changed them, or created a stable time loop (what was really beyond the power of a god after all?). I had undergone a horrific transformation, but by making a pact with the spirit of the thing inside me, I'd learned to gain a human shape as well as draw from its inexhaustible knowledge of otherworldly matters.

That should have been the end of it. But there was a cost. My humanity, the personality of John Henry Booth the human being, was a thin layer of cloth that barely covered the much older and more terrible thing beneath. I'd been casual with my powers before and the older thing had taken over. Still me, but a me from a time and place where rules like morality, justice, and good were abstract concepts compared to slaking one's every unnatural lust.

It was that unnatural power that gave me the strength to grapple with the alien machine that was trying now to take from us what was ours.

"Who are you? Why are you doing this?" I shouted, headbutting it and doing nothing more than giving myself a nasty gash on my forehead. The struggle for the weapon continued but it was one I was gradually losing. There was only so much a faux human body could do, and if I wanted to really overpower it, I would have to change. With the cost that incurred—the rage of the beast inside me.

"You will never know," the machine man spoke, speaking with malevolence that belied a human mind behind its soulless eyes. His greater strength pushed his weapon underneath my chin. "Die, mutant."

"You will not get Jackie or her child!" I abandoned any hesitation at calling on the power within.

I felt my eyes burn black as I pushed the man's gun away in the last second, moving faster than any normal man could have reacted, causing the next energy blast to go over my shoulder. It didn't entirely miss, though, as the discharge seared my shoulder. I felt agonizing pain as flesh boiled and horrible black ichor poured from the alien body underneath my human-seeming exterior.

I lost control over the beast inside me in that moment, before jamming my fist through the chest of the monster then out its back. There was no tissue or organs inside its body, only wires and gears as well as a noxious-smelling green goo that reminded me of decaying plant matter. I then tore the creature apart, causing its pieces to fly in every direction.

The machine man who I'd shot in the stomach got off the ground, the hole I'd created in him dripping ichor and oil as he went for my throat. I grabbed him by the face and crushed his metal skull in my hands, causing an explosion of sparks and fluid. In that moment I wondered why I ever bothered to hold back my power.

Feeling my shoulder regenerate from its damage, I felt my skin tremble and begin to fall away. Underneath was an exoskeleton that would emerge to reveal a purer, more powerful creature underneath — my true face rather than the camouflage I wore among humans. I wanted to smear the machine men's metal and oil insides against the wall and track down everyone involved in this attack before ripping out their throats.

"John," Mercury spoke, causing me to suddenly pull back. "Are you okay?"

Why did I hesitate to draw on this power? The power to slaughter and rend these fragile things was the birthright of all Kastro'vaal, a race that once was able to traverse the muscles and sinew of Yog-Sothoth to all portions of the cosmos. If I gave myself to it, I could draw on magic humans could barely conceive of and use it to make Mercury like myself. To breed a thousand new warriors from human cultists and revive my dead people. We could join Azathoth in his court, K'tulu in

R'lyeh, or the satyrs of Leng. Abandon this dead and dying world for someplace better. We would be like the Old Ones, wild and free, and killing without mercy.

"No," I whispered. "No, I am not."

"I'm sorry. I know you struggle with the other side of your personality." Mercury walked over and put her hand on my shoulder. "Maybe you shouldn't try to fight it so much and it wouldn't weigh on you so heavily."

There was a trace of jealousy in her voice and I wondered if she really would embrace everything I was if our roles were reversed. Death was always on the mind of Wastelanders, it was an eternal companion, but it weighed on Mercury heavily these days. I could make her immortal, a part of me kept thinking, but would it still be Mercury if I did? Would she ever forgive me if I didn't make the offer? Did she already know that I was holding back?

"John?" Mercury asked.

"Sorry, deep thoughts," I said, telling the truth. Then I lied. "The thing inside me is not part of me. It's a demon I can't exorcise."

"We've been down this road before, John," Mercury said, picking up a pistol from one of the fallen soldiers. "You can't suppress the thing inside you. Even though it's about the only thing keeping us alive most days."

"You can't understand, Mercury," I said, softly. "You're not a monster."

Mercury snorted. "We're all monsters here, John. Survival makes all of us creatures willing to kill and debase ourselves."

"It's not the same."

"Don't become a reluctant monster, John," Mercury said, shaking her head. "Don't pretend feeling guilt for doing what you have to do to survive makes you worse than anyone else. I've done terrible things to survive. I was a torturer at New Arkham and every day I went to work, I chose my own life over the people brought to me because the alternative was joining them. You're the same. Embrace the power you have and don't shy away from it. I love you, both the beast and the man because they're one and the same."

"I'm not sure the beast is capable of love."

"The beast is you."

"That's what scares me," I said, looking at the corpses on the ground. They were all showing signs of being machines. It was insane even for an insane world. I'd never encountered anything like it in my life. "They came here for Jackie."

"Her child," Mercury corrected, drawing a distinction I wasn't yet comfortable with making. "Thankfully, we had our pet shoggoth here to help protect her."

I grimaced. "Funny."

"Well you are kind of shoggoth-y," Mercury said, good-naturedly taunting me. "You can shapeshift, grow tentacles, and heal just about anything. The books also say I can control them with certain spells. We should try them when we argue."

"Mercury—"

"They say they're very fond of penguins," Mercury said, speaking of the late Doctor William Dyer's work. "What's a penguin?"

I sighed and laughed. "You're trying to make me feel better."

"I am," Mercury said, kicking one of the immobile machines. "It looks like we've got another group of people trying to kill us and hurt our family. What the hell are they?"

"Mi-Go," I said.

Mercury blinked. "Not really familiar with them."

"Me either," I muttered. The Wasteland was full of horrors and abominations. I couldn't memorize them all and maintain what little sanity I had left.

"These aren't Mi-Go. These are robots," a voice spoke from the stairs. "Cyborgs more precisely. Their creations."

My attention wandered over to the source of the voice and I saw two figures standing at the base of the stairs.

The first was Jackie. She was a dusky-skinned woman with a pair of shaded glasses on her face, a coarse homespun blouse over her large muscular body. She was well over six feet tall and showed more signs of her ghoul heritage every day, but this was limited to her size, elongated canines, and yellow predatory eyes for now. Ghouls had been the origin of the werewolf legend among humans and were a simultaneously savage as well as cultured people. In Jackie's arms was her newborn babe, wrapped in swaddling clothes.

Standing beside her was Cloud. He was a giant of a man with light brown skin and twisted black hair with beads in it. Cloud wore a plain cotton pair of pants that had been scavenged from one of the unopened plastic bags in a half-buried shopping center we'd found last year. His eyes were stark white yet functional, while his proportions were just slightly off. There was a strange quality about him, and I rarely used that descriptor. I just couldn't put it into words.

I let loose a breath I hadn't realized I'd been holding in. A part of me had been reluctant to go check on Jackie during these circumstances. "I'm glad to see you're all right."

Jackie smiled back, clutching her child who wasn't crying. I was concerned for a second before I noticed the baby boy, his skin like his father's, was breathing softly.

"Up already?" Mercury asked, looking over at them.

"Gunfire will move even a new mother," Jackie said, simply. "Besides I'm not as fragile as other women."

Human women, she meant. "And the others upstairs?"

"They all went diving for cover or sneaking out the back when the gunfire started," Cloud said. "Sensible."

"And you didn't?" Mercury asked.

"No. I am a warrior of the Dunwych," Cloud said. "I do not abandon my mate."

"Well you were a great help down here," I said, more sarcastic than I'd intended. "Glad to have you fighting with us."

"Are you questioning my honor?" Cloud asked.

"I question the very concept of honor," I said, smiling.

Cloud's look would have incinerated most men.

"What's a cyborg? I've never heard of this creature," Mercury asked.

"Cyborgs are the product of Mi-Go science," Jackie said, as if discussing farming techniques. "The Mi-Go are a race far older than mankind that live in the asteroids surrounding our solar system. They harvest the brains of human beings they find interesting and place them in specialized cases. Sometimes, when they desire to put them to work, they construct bodies for them to move around in. These are those sorts of bodies."

"How do you know this?" I asked, horrified and fascinated at once. It seemed even a monster still had things that could repulse him.

"The University has dealt with a few over the years," Jackie replied. "The Wilmarth family still watches the skies for them. It seems a foolish waste of time when the aliens and monsters are all among us now."

"You have no idea," Cloud muttered.

"Perhaps *you* don't," Jackie replied. "Why do they want my baby?"

"I don't know," I replied. "But they won't get him."

I found myself hesitant to approach Jackie and her babe. I had failed both of my earlier children and didn't know if I'd unwittingly condemned this one to a life as an immortal inhuman monster. The fact the child wasn't crying but simply laid there, smiling and staring forward with moon-colored eyes, indicated he wasn't human. Was he going to be a ghoul like his mother or was he destined to become human or something else entirely? Humans, ghouls, Deep Ones, Faceless Ones, and K'nyanians could all produce offspring. They were all various shades of human. However, there were other races which had learned to incubate themselves in the lifeforms of whatever planet they colonized. Things like me. I wished I could tell what fate awaited the young one.

"What is his name?" I asked.

"John," Jackie said, smiling. "As if there was another option."

"His middle name better be Mercury," Mercury said. "I was the one who delivered him after all."

Jackie snorted before giving a hyena-like laugh.

Cloud went to the remains of the machine men on the ground. "Can you hold off a second attack?"

"Yes," I said, simply. "I know what I'm fighting now."

That was a lie. I was a creature of the Wastelands now, but that didn't mean I was at the top of the food chain. The great irony was that the universe was an uncaring, unforgiving, and deadly place even for the so-called Great Old Ones. These things came close to killing me and even if I was at full strength, no longer pretending to be human, there were plenty of things that could destroy me. The Mi-Go had sent a bunch of tin men without hearts after me, but they had begun as humans. Next time, I suspected they would send something much worse and there would be no stopping them. Still, there was no need to upset the new mother and her mate.

"May I hold the boy?" I asked, reaching out. I'd already begun to return to my human state and was completely "normal" in appearance by the time I finished my gesture. Even so, I suspected it must have been terrifying to those unused to such things.

Cloud moved in front of Jackie. His presence annoyed me and I was tempted to throw him to one side. I had never approved of Jackie taking up with one of the Dunwych and worried that it would get her into trouble. They were a people deeply in debt to the Great Old Ones with the currency of their souls and the lives of their fellow humans.

Jackie shook her head. "Please, Cloud. Of course John can hold his grandson. There is much our child must learn."

Cloud looked unhappy about this. "John brings danger and horror wherever he goes."

"Where are not both?" Jackie replied.

Cloud had no answer for that. "I yield."

I did not think their relationship would last, but I had been wrong before. Romance was not something that one could predict in the Wasteland. Only Yog-Sothoth saw everything and everyone, so the unique bonds that formed in the face of oblivion could be quite surprising. After all, who would have thought a witch and an alien thing would have a loving relationship in a decaying trading post? Not I, certainly.

"Thank you," I whispered.

I reached out for the child only for the entire hotel to be bathed in a green, unearthly light. That was when all the cats in the bar started hissing and screeching. The ground began trembling beneath us. Cups and bowls started shaking where they lay, some falling to the ground and shattering.

The floors overhead disintegrated and a glowing, swirling light shone above us. Someone had conjured a portal over our business.

Chapter Three

I was pulled inexorably upward and assaulted with visuals beyond the human mind to perceive. Strange energies and winds battered me while I flew through the tunnel, half matter and half energy. I could see Jackie, Mercury, and Cloud pulled into it as well. Jackie's baby cried out and I could hear his scream but there was nothing I could do about it. I was blinded, confused, and helpless before everything went black.

I was honestly surprised to wake up again and wondered if the others had survived their ordeal. Post-Rising portals were not things that were safe to use, even if you were of an advanced enough race to create them. They were tunnels through the flesh and sinew of Yog-Sothoth that disrupted reality by their very existence. I had only gone through a few during my harrowing decade as a self-aware monster and it had left me feeling even more disconnected from my humanity each time.

It took a second for my head to stop pounding and to allow me to absorb my surroundings. I was in an asymmetrical room made of non-Euclidian angles that seemed to shift every time I looked away. The colors were black and green to human eyes but a tangled spectrum of indescribable ones to someone who could see in ultraviolet or radiation waves. I believed it was a prison cell since it had teeth-like spikes serving as bars in its sole exit. The décor was minimalist with no beds, but a drain that I suspected existed for the purposes of releasing waste.

I could hear an alien buzzing in the background that was best described as psychic noise. Hundreds, if not thousands, of minds communicating at once, sharing information at speeds far exceeding human thought. I tried to find a corner I could huddle in but lacking any such features in the cell's bizarre architecture, instead I covered my ears and curled up into a ball in the center of the room. That did nothing to drown out the noise, but I did my best to focus on only my own thoughts, trying to ignore the torturous noise.

"Poor John," a human female-sounding voice spoke at the door. "You try so hard to pretend to be human. It's tragic, really, like watching an elephant put on a suit or a human act like a dog. You are so much more, but you've driven yourself mad to fit in with a dying race."

I took three unnecessary breaths before rising to my feet and turning to face the source of the words. Standing there, beyond the jagged teeth, was a bald, corpse-like-skinned woman wearing a trench coat and bowler hat. Her skin was flaking and pitted with the smell of rotting meat wafting from her. Her eyes were glowing and looked like someone had set fires behind them. Each of her hands had an extra digit and I saw the slithering of something else under the base of her coat.

I could see that even this hideous thing was just an illusion over a much nastier creature beneath it. Ghouls, Serpent Men, and Deep Ones used glamours during the heyday of humanity to seek out mates among mankind. Inevitably, though, the eldest of their kind lost the ability to project such things as they lost their ability to hold a human image in their mind. This twisted parody of a person was worse than most I'd seen.

"I maintained the power to hold a human shape for close to a thousand years," the woman said. "That was much longer than my creator, who succumbed to madness and self-destruction after just a few years. Mind you, I've moved my consciousness into several human bodies over the centuries. The ones I abandon slither into sewers or live in caverns until meeting their end. I like to think I inspired legends of several cryptids over the years."

I stared at her. "Who are you?"

"My mortal name no longer has any meaning to me," the woman said. "I do not cling to it like you do. I now go by the Traveler."

"So, you substituted the name of your mortal life for a pretentious title," I said, smirking. "That is the most human thing I've heard from you so far."

The Traveler frowned, apparently not used to such blatant disrespect. "Have you not considered abandoning this decaying corpse of a world? There are countless ones out there awaiting settlement by a superior species. The Dreamlands are also a refuge for those who seek it. There are even other Earths and countless variants on the races of man if you want to spend your time wallowing in the filth of monkeys."

"Spoken as the descendant of one who thinks she's better for having been mutated by magic," I said, ignoring her question. I had considered it, but what would I be if I left the world of humans? Just another monster? Did mankind not deserve someone to witness its final hour and carry memory of it to the future? Was it arrogance to think that said person might be me? Or merely did I fear to leave behind what had made me feel as a mortal man?

"Evolved," the Traveler said, interrupting my thoughts. "I was evolved by magic."

I snorted. "Only humans think of such petty things as racial pride. The Old Ones know that we are all ants before the cosmos and debating which has the best shell is stupidity."

The Traveler didn't react, instead focusing on me. "You have not asked about the fate of your companions."

"Either they are alive, and you plan to hold their safety over my head, or they are dead, in which case I will destroy you," I replied, crossing my arms.

The Traveler did not seem impressed with my bravado. "You have no idea where you are, why you are here, or what is going on."

I paused. "Then why don't you tell me?"

The Traveler tapped the side of the wall beside her and the cell's teeth-like bars opened, freeing me. "Come."

I stared at her. "I don't understand."

"Yes," the Traveler said, gesturing for me to follow.

I walked out the door and stared at a sight which crushed my spirit. There was an enormous hangar with winged insectoid creatures fluttering about, carrying strange equipment not meant for human hands. Tumorous, organic, saucer-like vehicles were docked there, created with no human sense of aesthetics. The hangar's north wing was an octagonal portal that opened upward to the blackness of space with a glowing blue-white field separating us from the endless void.

"We're in space," I said, my voice dropping as the full implications sunk in. "We're in outer space."

"Technically, you've always been in outer space, John," the Traveler said. "You are no longer on Earth, though. Instead, you are on Asteroid 6101 as the humans named this place before their civilization ended. The Mi-Go call this place G'naharr. It is one of their few remaining bases in this system."

"Why have you taken me here?" I asked, genuinely confused. "What have you done with Jackie and Mercury? The babe?"

"How quickly bravado fades in the face of superior knowledge and power," the Traveler said.

The Traveler had me and knew it. I was at the outer edges of the solar system. If she wanted to dump me into the emptiness beyond, nothing would stop her. I had no idea if it would kill me immediately or not, but the difference was immaterial. I would float in the dark until I went insane or died. A lighter fate would be if one of the Mi-Go turned their alien weapons on me. There was precious little that even shapeshifted flesh could do against disintegration.

"I surrender," I said, defeated. "Is that what you wanted to hear?"

"For a start," the Traveler said. "Your human mate and ghoul pet are safe, as is the hybrid child. I have need of all of them. My orders were to destroy you initially, but I didn't realize precisely what you were. As a specimen, you have value."

I ignored her clinical detachment and lordly attitude. "What about Cloud?"

The Traveler let out a dismissive laugh. "You really don't know, do you?"

"Know what?" I asked.

The Traveler gestured to one side and I heard a psychic command pass through the static still in the air. Cloud proceeded to walk out, his face empty of all expression and his body moving with a zombie-like gait.

"What have you done to him?" I asked, not particularly caring about him as a person but upset about what it would mean for Jackie.

"His brain is being prepared for extraction," the Traveler replied. "He did his job well."

"Job?" I asked.

"Cloud is the last living descendant of the inbred Whateley family," the Traveler said. "The Dunwych have bred many sorcerers and inhuman creatures in their lineage but only a few contain the genetic markers needed for summonings. Unfortunately, the ritual I need to perform is one that cannot be completed by a mostly human vessel. It would kill him through the sheer power of the eldritch forces involved."

I stared at him before turning to her. "You sent him to seduce Jackie. To breed a wizard to use."

"Yes," the Traveler said. "The Mi-Go have been monitoring the Dunwych for some time. After Cloud's exile for rape and murder, we abducted him like so many others in the desert. He was reticent at first but the prospect of immortal life as a cyborg persuaded him to our point of view."

This all felt like some sort of insane Pre-Rising science-fiction adventure. "He's a traitor."

"Yes," the Traveler said, pointing a finger at Cloud. A ray of unearthly light left her fingertips and Cloud's body was enveloped. Moments later, there was nothing left of the Dunwych warrior but a fine powder on the floor as well as a shadow burned into the alien metal beneath it. "I must admit to despising traitors. I suppose on that we have some common ground. Now that Cloud is dead, we can establish a bond of trust."

If that was her goal, then she had badly miscalculated. As much as I despised Cloud, all this told me was that the Traveler saw no reason to reward those who had outlived their usefulness. I had no reason to believe I would be treated any differently, shared inhumanity or not.

"Of course," I said, lying. "This old cowboy is at your service."

My self-description seemed to irritate her as I could see the slightest twitching of her face. Then again, given her glamour was failing, it might have been nothing. "You wish to know why I am here, John? I will tell you. I am here to save the Mi-Go from destruction, including the cyborg humans they have harvested from your race, and a supply of breeding-age humans as well. I am attempting nothing less than to avert the extinction of two races, maybe three depending on how you define them."

"You don't strike me as a humanitarian," I replied. "I doubt your opinion of the Mi-Go is much higher."

"So certain you know me after a few minutes," the Traveler replied.

"You make a strong first impression," I said, dryly. I really shouldn't have been antagonizing her, but the Wastelands had left me with a rather dry sense of humor. Sardonicism was the only way I made it through some nights.

The Traveler gave an all-too-human snort. "Long ago a madman whispered half the true name of the one true God, Yog-Sothoth, into my mind. It burned away most of my humanity and for a thousand years across dozens of timelines I did my best to fulfill their wishes. To bring the God of Everywhere into the physical world so that it could experience physical existence inside itself."

"That makes no sense," I replied.

"It's religion," the Traveler said. "It either provides great truths or doesn't make sense in the slightest. Sometimes both at the same time."

I didn't disagree with her there. "So, you want to use Jackie's child to merge the Key and the Gate with this world?"

The Traveler laughed. It came from no human larynx, but the sound was unmistakable. "Oh, John, I succeeded a century ago."

The implications of her words took a moment to sink in. "You? You destroyed the world?"

The Traveler did not seem affected by my accusation. "Perhaps. The world was always doomed, and the stars were right for my ritual. Perhaps that was because the Great Old Ones were destined to rise that night. Either way the universe was turned inside out, and the Big Bang has been reversed. Dream, reality, space, and time are becoming one in the Unspeakable One. Yog-Sothoth is reclaiming its body and soon, cosmologically speaking at least, all that is will be returned to the one it comes from."

I had no idea her meaning beyond the statement that her insane antics had brought about the end of everything. It was a crime literally beyond human comprehension. Hell, even the Great Old Ones would perhaps struggle to soak up the knowledge that everything was going to end because of one termite's actions.

"Was it everything you hoped it would be?" I asked, venom replacing sarcasm.

The Traveler's glamour fell for a moment and I saw the hideous worm-thing beyond. It somehow looked crushed with despair to eyes both human as well as monster. It spoke with its mind instead of words, *I had hoped to learn the other half of God's name. I thought it would lead to apotheosis. Instead, I discovered my grandiose vision meant I was to become nothing more than another cell in a body consisting of quintillions. That my enlightenment would be the extinction of self. Ascension, Heaven, Hell, and oblivion were all but shades of the same state.*

I would have pitied her if not for how monumentally stupid her actions were. "Can it be undone?"

The Traveler resumed her glamour, looking slightly less like an undead wight and more like a fresh human female corpse. She even had hair. "You are not listening, John. The universe and its Dreamlands are doomed. They have already died. That doesn't mean there is no hope, however."

"You and I have very different definitions of hope then," I replied.

"I mentioned escape," the Traveler said.

"You've already said there is no escape," I said. "The places you suggested I flee to are dying as well."

The Traveler smirked and I wondered at the level of concentration such a human gesture required. "Not in this universe. However, there are other universes. Places where the Great Old Ones never chose to sleep on the Earth or evolution took a wildly different path. Timelines where they exist but will not awaken for millennia or even millions of years after humankind has gone extinct from its own depredations. Refuges where Yog-Sothoth remains both everywhere and nowhere instead of merely everywhere."

Her plan became understandable. After having served her god for millennia, she'd found its promised land to be wanting. Escaping a dying universe was harder than it seemed, though, and that required a figure to bring her beyond the body of Yog-Sothoth into realms it did not touch.

It relied on a lot of assumptions, not the least of which that there was any place in the multiverse the Key and the Gate's tendrils did not reach. If he/ it/ she really was the true God then there might be no refuge anywhere. Yet, a part of me couldn't help but wonder if there was a solution to an impossible problem there. After all, what did we have to lose anyway? We had already lost everything.

"You've convinced the Mi-Go that your plan can work?" I asked.

The Traveler nodded. "Their advanced science cannot provide them an escape for their race, but they are aware my magic is capable of reaching further. I have supplemented my abilities with their machines, and all is here except for the spellcaster."

"The boy," I replied. "One less than a day old."

"I thought I would seize their form and age them to adulthood," the Traveler said.

I prepared to strike her dead where she stood.

"But I have a better idea," the Traveler said.

I relaxed but only a little. "I'm listening."

Chapter Four

"John, are you out of your goddamned mind?" Mercury asked, having heard my explanation of the Traveler's plan.

I was standing in the middle of another cell with Mercury, Jackie, and Baby John in the latter's arms. I was pleased to see all three of them had survived the portal's terrifying power. They weren't terrified by their circumstances but angry, which left me in a poor position to negotiate on our behalf.

I was wearing a set of long white robes and a hood that felt deeply ironic given my apparent human heritage. The sides of the robes were covered in woven mystical sigils and embroidered letters from languages that had died out before the birth of Pre-Rising civilization.

It was unnecessary for the ritual that was going to be performed but there was power in ceremony. Magic could tear apart one's mind and body with but a single stray thought, so every little aid in maintaining your concentration was a boon. I had also taken a staff with a ridiculous all-seeing eye on the top of it. Had wizards really worn these accoutrements in the Pre-Rising days or was it just the Traveler having a laugh at my expense?

"I think you underestimate the opportunity here," I replied.

"The opportunity presented by a mad woman who destroyed the world," Mercury said. "No wait, not the world, the entire goddamned universe?"

"Goddamned is a particularly accurate statement. Either that or god blessed. It's just the blessing is worse than the curse," I replied, mentally noting that I didn't think the Traveler was strictly a woman anymore either (if she'd ever been).

Mercury glared at me, making it clear she was not going to be distracted from her statement. "What in the world could possibly possess you to go along with this?"

I blinked and clutched the staff with my left hand. "Well, one, because I actually think it might work. The chance to escape this dying world means that at least some of humanity will survive until the next century. Two, because we are completely in her power and in *goddamned outer space*."

Mercury grimaced at my accenting of those words. "Fair enough on point two."

"Technically, we're always in outer space," Jackie pointed out, having remained conspicuously silent during all of this. "Earth travels through it."

"That's what I said," I admitted. "Third point, I have no doubt that Jackie's child would have been killed if not for my acceptance."

"Over my dead body," Jackie said, clutching Baby John tighter. The baby started crying almost immediately. It was having a very eventful first night of existence.

"I believe that's the idea," I replied. "The only reason she's not disintegrating us all is because she's of the mind we're useful. It's rare I feel like we're cornered but I think we are for the time being."

Mercury cursed under her breath. "I didn't learn the secrets of the dark arts to get bullied by a zombie witch."

"She's much worse than a zombie," I replied. "What she is, I can't tell you. Certainly not human and not for a very long time."

"Humanity is relative," Mercury replied. "I think I'm finally coming around to that."

"Humanity is the thin veneer of rationality that fools impose on a disordered and hostile universe," I said. "It is the delusion of civilization and the madness of ethics in a malevolent world with the worst elements of both mythology as well as an empty materialist existence. It is an insanity I gleefully embrace. Truly, I regret having to be reminded of the reality it rejects."

Mercury stared. "Not the time for one of your random soliloquies, John. If I wanted to contemplate the universe, I'd smoke devil weed and eat some mushrooms."

"Is Cloud all right?" Jackie said, interrupting our jovial banter.

There was no point in lying to the girl. "No, he is not."

"Is he dead?" Jackie asked.

"Yes," I said. "He was working with the Traveler."

Jackie didn't respond for a moment. Finally, after a few seconds, she said, "I see."

Betrayal was a common thing in the Wasteland and there were many families that had been torn apart by cults or the raw arithmetic of survival. Jackie had been subject to these sorts of betrayals before, but I wasn't about to cover for the dead man.

"Great job, John," Mercury said. "Tactful as always."

"Tact is not something that helps you survive," I replied.

"It is if someone kills you for pissing them off," Mercury said.

I blinked. "Fair point."

Jackie offered me Baby John. "I need to think about some things."

I took the child and nodded. "I understand."

"Do you?" Jackie asked.

I had suffered many betrayals of the heart over the years. This included by the mother of my children. "Yes."

Jackie nodded and took back her child. "I want to kill her."

I worried our captor was watching but didn't disagree. "Hold on to that feeling. Bury it, though. Bury it deep and let it come out only when it has a chance of succeeding."

"John, has anyone ever told you that you give terrible advice?" Mercury asked.

"A few," I replied. "However, we are in no position to be seeking revenge right now. Not if we wish to escape this place."

"There's an old Chinese adage that when seeking revenge, it's best to dig two graves," Mercury said.

"Aren't your ancestors Korean?" I asked.

"Not the point, John," Mercury replied, rolling her eyes.

No, but I wasn't going to throw my life away for someone like Cloud either. "Think of Baby John. He's just beginning his life."

Mercury sighed. "Fine. Also, is Baby John his official name? Can't we say Junior?"

"No," I said.

"I'll protect him," Jackie said, looking at her child. "He is my flesh, even if his father is a monster."

"No, just weak and human," I replied. "Which is bad enough."

"Yes, humans suck," Jackie replied. "No offense, Mom."

Mercury shrugged. "They do. So, what does the Wicked Witch of the East Coast want from me?"

I almost pointed out Mercury was the Wicked Witch of the East Coast, but I wasn't in a joking mood. "I want your help in casting the ritual. I don't have your level of power, but I can survive channeling more magic than you. Use me as a focus for the spell and I suspect we have a much higher chance of success."

"Assuming the Traveler doesn't intend to use you to open this portal to another universe and then stab you," Mercury said.

"Assuming," I replied. "Honestly, she's more likely to disintegrate us all in one go."

"What will the Mi-Go do?" Mercury asked.

"I can hear them," Jackie replied, gesturing with her free hand to the air around us. She could hear what I could not make sense of. "They're not like humans. All of their memories are stored between them. They're a hive mind. Not one being but all linked together. I can hear their fear and distrust."

"Could they be turned against her?" I asked, not having too much hope in that possibility. If I had any luck at all, it was bad. The universe wasn't just a cold and unfeeling place, it was actively hostile. The Outer Gods only kept people alive as long as they did in order to make sure they suffered more.

"Desperation makes people do strange things," Jackie said. "They would not ally with her if they weren't desperate. However, they do not see any other hope."

Neither did I.

"Are you done?" The Traveler's voice spoke from the doorframe of the cell. There I saw the unnatural woman standing there with two flying Mi-Go guards, both of them armed with alien weapons that I had no doubt could destroy me.

"Yes," I said. "I'm ready for the ritual. I believe Mercury will be an excellent addition to it."

"I'm sure," the Traveler replied, not bothering to hide her sarcasm. "Just note that if you do not perform the ritual with me then I will disintegrate your child and grandchild. I can always make another vessel."

Jackie looked ready to bite the Traveler's throat with her teeth.

"Down girl," I said, only partially making a joke about her canine nature. Jackie had not yet made that transition, but it was inevitable. At least if she survived. This was possibly her last chance—and her baby's—to reach maturity.

Jackie didn't find my comment amusing and glared.

"Right," I said, getting up. "Take us to the ritual chamber."

Reluctantly, I followed the Traveler as she brought me to an enormous pyramidal chamber. Like the cells, the shape wasn't entirely stable. Sometimes it had a deep slant and other times it had multiple points. The pyramid seemed to be the most stable shape of its geometry even as I knew its angles leaked into multiple dimensions as well as layers of reality. The Mi-Go's technology allowed them to construct their fortifications partially in the physical world, partially in the Dreamlands, and perhaps a couple of other realities I wasn't familiar with.

The interior of the chamber had an enormous circular ring propped up in the center with a pair of obelisks beside it. They were R'lyeh-ian in origin, though I only knew this because I'd seen Deep One construction with similar markings. Alien technology made of crystals and pylons was attached via glowing wires to the ring. Purple and greenish energy crackled between the pylons, providing an abundance of electricity for whatever strange experiment was going on here. There were several tables of equipment nearby ranging from ancient books to weird, bizarrely shaped tools.

Finally, on the ground, was the Elder Sign carved into the ground. It was a strange marking given the historical antipathy the Elder Gods had for beings like Yog-Sothoth, but perhaps that was the point. Its presence told me that the Traveler did not expect me to survive this ritual, I was a creature of the Outer Gods after all, but the joke was on her. I had a resistance to the symbol due to my peculiar "insanity." I still mostly thought like a human and only derived immense pain from the sigil's presence. I was used to pain.

"A peculiar mixture of occult paraphernalia," I replied. "You could film a horror movie here."

"No one's made horror movies in a very long time, John," the Traveler said, almost sad. "It is strange what you learn to miss as the centuries pass."

"So, it's a portal you're charging up with Mi-Go extra-dimensional juice and directing the end point of with John as your focus," Mercury observed. "The obelisks are enhancers for the magicians casting the spell."

"Very good," the Traveler said. "In a thousand years, you might have made a decent wizard."

"Well, hopefully I wouldn't have ended the world for an evil god," Mercury said, cheerfully. "I figure I could have done without that in my millennia of life."

The Traveler looked annoyed. "You're lucky your continued existence is convenient, witch. Otherwise, I might be tempted to take your body next."

"I imagine you would get more use out of it than your current one, Wormy," Mercury said. "I would hate to imagine what sort of pleasures that thing can get up to. Give me an old-fashioned man-woman, woman-woman, or trio of both any day."

What was Mercury getting at? Antagonizing the Traveler was not going to help our situation. That was when I saw her pocket something off one of the tables nearby. I really hoped she was just being cautious rather than planning something.

I looked over at Jackie, who was following behind me with another pair of Mi-Go hovering nearby. Her look was squarely focused on the Traveler, full of hatred and venom for the woman who had killed her consort. I hadn't liked Cloud and my suspicions had been justified, but emotions were not logical things. They belonged to that peculiarly illogical part of the human brain that I even now struggled to keep ahold of. I wasn't sure if Jackie would make her own attempt to disrupt the ritual but hoped she would put our survival ahead of vengeance. I wasn't one hundred percent sure she would, though. As she stood there, Baby John started crying and she went to care for him. That, at least, gave me hope.

"Keep him silent," Mercury said. "We don't need him attracting Space Bats or whatever is beyond that portal."

Jackie stared at her mother. "He needs food."

"Then feed him," Mercury said. "Get some raw meat or something."

Jackie glared and moved to feed him.

I turned away. Funny what embarrassed even an immortal monster.

The Traveler, thankfully, was not inclined to kill us all for disrespect. Probably because she planned to do it later. "Are you quite finished?"

"For now," Mercury said.

"Then let us begin," the Traveler said. "It is time to escape the end of everything."

Chapter Five

It turned out to be not so simple as that, as dramatic of a statement as the Traveler's had been.

The ritual was one that required a few more hours to set up, the Mi-Go's cyborg slaves setting up candles made of human fat alongside more bizarre equipment that humanity could not have constructed in a million years. By the end of the preparations, the place looked less like where a magical ritual should be conducted than a particularly eccentric Pre-Rising owner's basement.

"I think you may be overdoing it," I replied, staring at the sight.

"It is better to be overprepared than under," the Traveler replied. "This is my collection of artifacts, enhancers, and occult items from a thousand years of life. There are the skulls of great wizards and mortal enemies scattered among these devices. All of this is expendable if it means piercing the barrier of Yog-Sothoth's reach."

"I'm surprised you haven't just considered going back in time," I replied. "Head back to the beginning of human history and relive your glory days. Hell, prevent yourself from destroying the world in the first place."

The Traveler's response surprised me. "If only that I could."

Mercury proceeded to walk over with a large tome in her hands. "Okay, I've memorized the enchantment."

"Human vocal cords cannot enunciate the words," the Traveler said, disdainfully.

"The words are merely a medium," Mercury said. "The magic is in the expression of thought."

"Humans cannot imagine the truth of what I have carried in my mind for millennia," the Traveler said.

"I can imagine quite a bit," Mercury said, narrowing her eyes.

"Perhaps I should whisper the true name of God into your ear," the Traveler replied dangerously.

"Perhaps you should," Mercury replied. "I certainly can't do worse with it than you did."

The Traveler walked past her. "You might be surprised. Assume your positions."

"Language," Mercury said, moving to one of the points of the Elder Sign while I moved to another. The Traveler moved to a third. In the end, the remaining points of the Elder Sign were filled with Mi-Go. I didn't know if the flying fungus creatures could actually cast magic, but I assumed they could.

I made sure to keep my eyes on Jackie as I noted the number of Mi-Go around her had gone from two to almost a dozen. The threat was implicit, and I was disgusted with the whole ordeal. If we somehow survived the ritual without betrayal, I was expecting that the Traveler intended to turn her Mi-Go allies on us. It was always in the back of my mind and I needed to make sure that I had a plan to deal with it. I just hadn't come up with one in all the hours I'd had a chance to analyze the situation. Nope, I was as clueless as to a way to proceed as I had been at the start. That was not good.

"Now begins the end of the old age and the start of the new," the Traveler said, invoking the exact same philosophy that had destroyed the world in the first place. It made sense if she was the one who had done it but meant she'd learned nothing. "Ia Yog-Sothoth t'grrr t'kra mah-tahl vurok tzimisce agh'dah!"

I began speaking my own invocations to the Outer Gods, raising one hand in the air and the other around my staff. "Yust-tah Yog-Sothoth yatool-yatool vosh nyal attok!"

"Nyarlathotep thool chastash!" Mercury shouted, throwing her own power into the spell that was happening around us.

I felt the energy rush through my body as my consciousness expanded. It became hard for me to maintain my human form as my flesh slowly turned malleable. Tendrils began to reach out from my back, lashing outward in random directions. I had performed many spells in my time, summonings and exorcisms mostly, but this was a far greater undertaking. The pain of the Elder Sign focused my mind, though, allowing me to avoid having my consciousness torn apart before we'd even begun.

Above our heads, a glowing series of lights began to swirl as I felt myself link to a consciousness infinitely greater than my own. My mind began to expand, and I felt myself moving between times. There was the far past, the far future, and the vast swath of history lying between. All of them were as one in Yog-Sothoth, experienced simultaneously, with every moment equally important.

The concept of omniscience was something that mortals had routinely associated with gods, but no linear being could truly grasp it. I could only reflect on my own life, alien and human, its entire procession visible to me like I was watching a river from the skies above. No, not a river, the oceans of the world. No beginning or end, each moment spilling into the other and forming something far greater.

"John, I'm losing control of this!" Mercury shouted, refining the energy in me so we weren't blown to pieces.

"If you do, you die and so does your family!" the Traveler shouted, shaping the nature of the sorcery that had passed through me.

"Threats don't scare me!" Mercury said, continuing her casting with pure thought rather than words.

"They should!" the Traveler shouted, her glamour failing once more. The creature underneath was disgusting but seemed to be rejoicing in the sorcery on display. It let forth an alien series of noises that approximated joy but sounded like the cacophony of the screaming damned to me.

I found myself witnessing the Traveler's past as I struggled to find something to hold on to in the enormous wealth of knowledge gathered before me in Yog-Sothoth's presence. We were pricking the Outer God with a needle in hopes of gathering a bit of its blood to power our escape. It was the sum of everything and everyone's history from the beginning of the universe to the end. It was too much and I needed some path through it.

I saw her birth in the Holy Land of Abrahamic religion as a Jew.

I saw her horrifying murder at the hands of a cannibalistic serial killer.

I saw her travel across Europe, struggling to maintain her battle against her inhumanity.

I saw her fail in the face of humanity's ignorance and fear.

I saw her raise countless cults and secret societies in hopes of finding a way to bring about a better world.

I saw her battle heroes and villains alike, men as well as women, people who wanted to delay the end of the world for a handful of decades more.

I saw her defeated until the very last days of humanity's civilization. The day she called her god, who finally answered.

I heard the true name of God.

An explosion of eldritch forces blasted outward and knocked me onto the ground, along with everyone else in the chamber except Jackie. The Mi-Go dropped like flies, hitting the ground with a splatter. Their psychic communication died in an instant and I realized the Traveler had betrayed them first, using this asteroid's population as fuel for her experiment. The lights above our head joined into a spinning, glowing ball of flame before flying into the ring before us.

The ring began to spin and twist as light flickered throughout the chamber. Dazzling images appeared inside the ring and I saw things that I could not put into words. Yog-Sothoth's presence was among us—had always been among us—but I could now feel it. It was listening to our incantation and had opened a portal to a new world.

My eyes tried to focus on the sight before me, but I felt the world beyond more than observed it. It was a planet where humans still lived, laughed, loved, and bred. If the Great Old Ones existed there, they still slept and might for millennia more. I saw vast jungles, fields, deserts, oceans, and stars that stayed in the same place rather than moving across the sky in a foreboding dance of impossibility. It was Earth as it had been or was so similar as to not make any difference.

I realized in that moment that the Traveler's plan was doomed from the start but also pointless. Yog-Sothoth's essence touched every single part of the multiverse. It was all things, all possibilities, and impossible to escape. Yet, that very impossibility meant our universe was only one in numberless trillions, each with their own infinite parallels. We could escape this dying world to any one we desired, but it was impossible to escape the Outer Gods themselves. They were as much a part of us as the cells in our bodies.

It was almost comforting.

"Yes! Only one thing left to escape this hellhole forever!" the Traveler shouted, covering herself in a glamour that was almost perfect. She looked more like the human she was while alive than the decaying corpse she'd been when I'd first met her. Watching her take a step off the Elder Sign sigil, I felt the Traveler's power grow exponentially. That was when I realized she was staring at Jackie.

I sensed her intentions and reacted before my conscious mind could process what she was about to do. The portal was unstable and about to collapse. The only way to maintain it was a blood sacrifice of Whateley blood. I tried to figure out what sort of spell or action I could take to stop her, only for Mercury to lift a triangle-shaped object in her hands. It glowed with green light and the Traveler let out a hideous scream.

"Eat ray gun, bitch!" Mercury shouted.

The Traveler screamed and glowed brightly before turning into a pile of white powder on the ground. Mercury had managed to steal one of the Mi-Go's tools and it worked just as well as a weapon. I wondered what sorcery she'd used to distract the others from its presence before realizing it didn't matter. She'd been human and thus beneath suspicion. The Traveler had paid for it with her life.

The spinning ring started to throw out bolts of lightning and grew more unstable. The image of the Earth behind grew discordant as I saw parts of its past, present, and future. It went from being a beautiful verdant world to an icy dead ball before ceasing to exist altogether in the supernova of its sun. The spinning rings turned red, then purple, and then green as I felt energies begin to escape it. The machine was going to explode and take all of us with it. Jackie, putting her babe on the ground, ran on all fours before knocking over one of the pylons. This severed the wires leading to the portal and, in an instant, the rings stopped spinning. The apocalypse, at least for this asteroid, had been averted by the equivalent of pulling a plug.

"Huh," I said, slowly returning to my human state. "Well, that didn't go like I'd expected."

"The bad guy is dead," Mercury said, walking over to the dust of the Traveler. The thousand-year-old monster had died as pointlessly as any other human in combat. It was almost anticlimactic.

"It's what we should have done in the first place," Jackie said, picking up her crying babe. "Whatever you learned wasn't worth it."

I wasn't sure about that. The true name of God, or at least Yog-Sothoth, was still burning in the back of my mind. _____ was a name that I could speak if I thought about it, but I chose not to. I did my best to bury it in the far reaches of my inhuman brain. It had a sublime beauty while complete that was only a dissonant nightmare without its totality. _____ was so powerful that I knew I could harness it if I wanted to.

Harness it to open another gate. I did not know if I would survive such a thing or remain unchanged by its use if I did, but it opened possibilities that weren't there before. I could gather hundreds or even thousands of humans together to leave this dying world just as the Traveler did. Humanity would survive, or at least something resembling humanity, until it evolved into something else. I promised I would take myself, Mercury, and Jackie, as well as her child, to this new world where we would live in wonder and glory forever. We just first had to get off this asteroid.

I didn't get a chance to think further because a terrible black miasma started to rise from the ground outside of the Elder Sign. It crackled with strange energies and I felt the Traveler's power once more. She was more than a mere physical body. No, unlike her predecessor, she had become fully a creature of consciousness transcending mere physical laws of matter. The Traveler's monstrous presence launched itself at Jackie's child, only for my daughter to throw herself in the middle of the Elder Sign.

The Traveler's consciousness pushed itself through the ward of the Elder Gods, making noises that my mind heard as a combination of both screams as well as growls. It hovered over Jackie for a moment, seemingly pressing down but unable to get inside their bodies. That was when the Traveler's essence turned around and hurled itself at me.

The black brume of her consciousness struck against my chest and poured itself into my body. What followed could only be described as the ghastliest psychic death cry imaginable. The true name of Yog-Sothoth was something she heard the totality of inside my mind, but despite holding half of it for a thousand years, it was too much for her mortal mind to handle. The result obliterated her and consumed her, leaving less than nothing as her essence spread throughout it across every moment of time in every part of space. Even someone who believed in no afterlife at all could not have conceived of a more final oblivion. The Traveler had become one with her god and there was nothing left of her to salvage.

"Oh my," I said, falling on my ass as I tried to shake away the feeling of what I'd just experienced.

"What happened?" Mercury asked, running to my side.

"She looked at the opening of the ark," I said, remembering an old movie they'd used to show at New Arkham's makeshift theater.

Mercury snorted, getting the reference. "I guess we're lucky the Elder Sign protected Baby John."

"It wouldn't have worked anyway," Jackie said, chuckling as she held her child. "Cloud wasn't the father."

Both Mercury and I looked at her.

"We had plenty of fights," Jackie replied. "Sometimes I went to visit George the pig farmer. Remember him? Baby John has his eyes. I guess he was too human, or ghoul, for whatever she needed."

Rather than being shocked, I just looked on in bemusement. The Traveler, for all her genius, hadn't taken human nature into account when she'd sent her agent to impregnate Jackie. Perhaps if she had, the Traveler might have considered her breeding experiment subject worked in a brothel. Even if she wasn't one of the ladies of the evening, that was bound to influence your attitude toward casual relations. Baby John was her baby and Cloud had just been along for the ride.

"Suckers!" Mercury said before the weight of our situation hit her. We were still far, far from home. "So now what?"

"Does anyone know how to fly a spaceship?" I asked, remembering the vehicles in the hangar.

"The Black Pharaoh's Test" is the opening story of Tales of Nyarlathotep, *which is the third time I was asked to do the set up for an anthology. By this point, we'd already had* The Book of Yig *(which I'm not even in), so it was more coming back than a default element of the Books of Cthulhu series.*

This story isn't remotely HP Lovecraft but a total homage to the works of Robert E. Howard. Well, sort of. It's from the perspective of one of the evil wizards that tended to dominate his longer fictionesque stories like The Hour of the Dragon. *It's also something of a "distant finale" taking place in the final years of the Hyborian Age's last remaining kingdom before the Ancient World as we know it truly begins.*

Apophis Zul is not a particularly deep character, but I have a lot of sympathy for him. He believes he's a wolf in the Cthulhu Mythos when he's not even an ant.

THE BLACK PHARAOH'S TEST

M ilord, the followers of Re will be upon the capital within the hour," a slave spoke to Apophis Zul, kneeling with his head to the stone floor.

"I know," Apophis Zul replied, his voice deep and commanding.

It was almost dawn and the hated sun-worshipers had timed their attack for when their god would be in ascendance while his god would be at his weakest. For millennia, Stygia had stood at the center of the civilized world as a bulwark against the savages who had risen in the time since Atlantis sank and Acheron burned.

Great Stygia was the last of the old civilizations and had outlasted most of the new. Aquilonia, with its pagan Cimmerian lord, had drawn its last breath an age ago, and Zamora having been sacked by Hykarnians when Apophis Zul had been a boy.

It seemed inconceivable that, at last, the once-mighty empire of the river Styx should be brought low by barbarians, but it was undeniable. Their armies had abandoned them, the peasants were in revolt, and daggers had been stuck in the handful of acolytes who had not defected to the other side. Priests of Seth-Yig had joined the followers of Re'Kithnid, Bastet, and Hathor-Niggurath to wield the magics of the

Old and New Gods together against him. He, the high priest of the Black Pharaoh.

"Come with me, slave," Apophis Zul said, bidding the bald man behind him to rise with a near-imperceptible motion of his scaled fingers.

"Yes, milord," the slave said, confused.

"Follow," Apophis Zul said, gesturing to the entrance to the Forbidden Temple's inner sanctum. It had been constructed over the course of a century with a thousand slaves dying in the process. Their blood had added to the power of the place, consecrating it to the God with a Thousand Faces.

"It is forbidden," the slave said.

"This I command," Apophis Zul said, not having the desire to obliterate the slave with a wave of his hand or drown him with a mouth full of flesh-eating scarabs that he could make appear at will.

"Of course," the slave said, nodding vigorously.

The long stone hallway was illuminated by torches of blue fire which never went out but needed a monthly tithe of human fat. They illuminated blasphemous hieroglyphics that depicted the humiliation of the priests of Seth who had once ruled Stygia since the days of Kull.

The blood of the Serpent Men had been thick then, pure and undiluted, but lust for the monkey-like humans around them had weakened their power. Attempts to fix this by breeding brother to sister had backfired with the gods cursing the resulting children to be stunted, sickly, or fools.

Apophis Zul had thought himself clever then, casting down Thoth-Amon by stealing his ring and turning to older more powerful gods than Seth. The magic flowed through his body like a river, and he had changed himself into a purer, stronger vision of his kind. Rains of byakhee and hordes of tunnelers had answered his prayers, laying waste to all who dared call themselves his enemy.

Unfortunately, he had overreached. The Cult of the Many-Faced One had grown vast, but he had been too free with its secrets and drunk on the power at his fingertips. The Dagonite Deep Ones had poured forth to sack the coastal lands, the ghuls had dragged his soldiers underground to become food for their larders, and those simpletons with their lifeless human-like idols had reminded him that steel slit the throats of wizard just as well as man. Alliances between ancient enemies of the Stygian priest-kings that would have been unthinkable a century before had shown there was no force capable of uniting people quite like hatred. Man and monster alike had joined king, noble, priest, as well as slave in their quest to see the greatest city on Keb, the world, destroyed.

Apophis Zul could knock down a city's walls and drown them in lakes of fire or blood but making them obey was harder than it seemed. Most men preferred death than service to a monster, particularly if the monster required their sons and daughters as sacrifices. There were costs to the great magics as well, with the usual prices of blood and pain not enough, no matter how much they gave. The stars had turned against them and most of his peers had either sunk into torpid slumber as corpses in buried tombs, collapsed into dust from overexertion, or were carried off by things they could conjure but not put down. Fools.

"Tell me, slave, have you ever heard of Nyarlathotep?" Apophis Zul asked the slave.

"No, no, my lord," the slave lied, terrified. It was the sacred name they used to refer to the Many-Faced God and one that was blasphemous for anyone but the high priests to know. Yet, like all secrets these days, too many had been free with their tongues no matter how many Apophis Zul had ordered ripped out.

Apophis Zul smiled with his lipless face and let his long, forked tongue slither across the rictus of his mouth.

"It is the true name of the spirit we summoned into the Pharaoh's grandfather. The one that made him great."

The slave didn't respond, undoubtedly thinking about the fact said Pharaoh had been considered the greatest tyrant who had ever lived. A man who had ordered entire cities put to the sword, and built insane—but terrifying—structures that had required tearing down much of ancient Stygia to construct. Half of Stygia had burned to the ground in one night when he'd played his shepherd's pipe to drive all who listened irrevocably mad. Indeed, it was this Pharaoh, Nephren-Ka, who had contributed most to the fall of Stygia's greatness.

"I see," the slave said, confused.

"We tried to summon him again and again because the secrets that spilled from his lips when we could coerce them forth were enough to strengthen our magic tenfold," Apophis Zul said, wistfully. "But when he ascended the Black Pyramid to the stars, we could not bring him forth again. His brothers and sisters became hideous things with a dozen mouths while his children exploded with human-headed rats from within their bellies. Their blood was too diluted, their minds too weak to carry the spirit of a god."

The current Pharaoh, a useless boy of twelve, carried none of the ancient blood at all. He had been a mouthpiece for Apophis Zul and his ilk in hopes of reassuring the people that the worst times were gone. That had been a mistake. The lion does not explain itself to the gazelle. In the end, it had only weakened their standing further.

The pair of them entered the antechamber of the Forbidden Temple where the priestly vestments woven from the chest hair of Leng's ape-men, incense of Kadath, and knives of Acheron steel were present. Apophis Zul took only one item, the jeweled *nemes* headdress of the Black Pharaoh. It would be needed, along with the*se khem* scepter, to bring about the end of this nightmare.

"Accompany me to the main chamber," Apophis Zul said.

"Milord," the slave was terrified now.

"What is your name?" Apophis Zul asked.

Stunned by the request, the man took a deep breath.

"Narmer, lord."

"Obey," Apophis Zul said, annoyed he had to waste power to control the man's will. If he had to ask twice then truly his authority had diminished.

Narmer paused for a second then blinked.

"Yes, milord."

There was a slight hesitation, a second of defiance, a single moment of resistance that signaled to Apophis Zul that he had made the right choice. The Nameless Pharaoh had impregnated a hundred women and caused a dozen men's bellies to explode with offspring as a jest, but few products of these unions had lived.

Those that did had gone on to become powerful sorcerers or mad killers themselves, sometimes both at once. But a few had also spread their seed. None of them had been controllable and thus nonsuited to continue the official line of Pharaoh's. But they could be hosts— powerful hosts—and that had its own value. Narmer was the product of one demigod's rutting with another slave and now would serve a purpose far grander than any of his ilk deserved.

"Place the nemes upon your head," Apophis Zul said.

It was a sacrilege beyond imagination and any slave who committed such an act would have required hours of deliberation to devise a torture horrible enough to slay him with. However, these were unusual times and Apophis Zul intended further abominations.

Narmer obeyed and soon looked every inch the Pharaoh himself once he wore his raiment. Why not? They were both humans pretending to be gods. It's just Narmer had some divine blood in him. It was just diluted with the blood of human swine. Like fine wine mixed with offal.

"Sit upon the throne," Apophis Zul said. "You will understand soon."

"Yes, milord."

Narmer did not hesitate at this moment, for what was one more blasphemy after a series of them. Upon doing so, though, the man's body straightened as a look of unimaginable horror passed across his face. It was a look that Apophis Zul had seen many times upon the faces of sacrifices or those unprepared priests when he conjured something from the Outer Void. It was also followed by a scream that would have deafened Apophis Zul if he'd had human ears to listen. Narmer's dying cry was the sound of a man face-to-face with things that he had not been prepared to see.

That was another reason they were falling now to the barbarians at the gates: the slow death of magic. Apophis Zul had never thought it possible, but more and more priests of the Outer Gods and Great Old Ones had proven themselves to be charlatans. They recited the words, offered the sacrifices, and even sometimes believed, but could not connect themselves to the true masters of reality. There were no dreamers among them who could project their minds to the distant shores of Carcosa or the other places where the true magic flowed.

New Gods existed as well, conjured from humanity's ideas of more human-centric interpretations of the true masters of reality. It was difficult imagining for a being as old as Apophis Zul that anyone could want to worship something that was just a greater and more powerful version of a human, but he was not a peasant or slave. A fact he felt a twinge of hypocrisy over as Apophis Zul rubbed the black sun amulet under his robes while muttering.

"G'rrllan'agaa'nahrasha, Nyarlathotep! G'rrllan'agaa'nahrasha, Nyarlathotep! G'rrllan'agaa'nahrasha, Nyarlathotep! Heed me, oh Messenger of the Outer Gods! Father of the Old Ones! Prophet of Yog-Sothoth! Son of Azathoth! Embody yourself in this body, Great Black Pharaoh, oh mine! Come forth! Come forth!"

Truth be told, he should be out there among his followers hoping to find more mundane ways of stemming the tide of Stygia's fall. Even if he was one of the last truly great wizards among his kind—the others' blood and magic more water than wine—they had armies. Some of his fellows were futilely attempting to assemble a defense with their untested slave soldiers and Hyksos mercenaries who were as likely to turn against the Great Lords as fight against the hated revolutionaries despite their shared gods.

Apophis Zul knew, in his quieter moments, that he had let the kingdom's management fall to the wayside in the wake of his quest for ever greater mystic power. Eunuchs and functionaries had plundered the gold meant to outfit their warriors while the sacred rites had become mere excuses for debauchery than actual placation of the spirits. They'd overcorrected as the doom that was coming to their land became increasingly clear and most of the palaces' servants had either ended up burning in last minute charnel pits or fled, regardless of whatever horrid punishments he'd promised to mete out on the deserters.

Apophis Zul had simply not believed that their patron god, whose reality was unmistakable, could allow them to fall. Had they not offered many first born of the Shemish during the Moloch feast days? Had they not carved his god's other names into every possible vessel to spread word of his power as well as prestige? Names that even slaves like Narmer would have recognized versus the one they had kept for themselves as his high priests like Bel'Moloch, Nergal, Tiamat-Ashuran, Typhon, and Lokas the Black Bull. Was not their betrayal of all other, lesser deities complete? What more did the many-faced one require?

Apophis Zul felt all too much like a peasant praying for relief from the lash or hunger, and it was not a pleasant sensation. He was of the old blood and should not be on his knees, huddled in the dark.

Narmer's scream ended as the room's angles seemed to twist and the air became a noxious mixture of smoke with the gases of another realm. Narmer's eyes, now as dead as the rest of him, looked up as the spirit of something infinitely older than the Earth itself animated his body like a child with a doll. The voice that escaped it was like a sickening echo of a dozen men speaking at once in a deep cavern. "Hello, Apophis Zul."

Apophis Zul was honestly surprised his master had answered his call and more than a bit relieved. Something he struggled not to show in his expression. He had sacrificed dozens of slaves, some with greater blood than Narmer, in hopes of conjuring his master. Sometimes *things* had answered but never his master, and most had been more interested in a good meal or rutting than heeding his wishes.

"Master," Apophis said, kneeling on the ground. "I have come to beseech your wisdom. It has been many long years since we have last spoke."

"Has it?" Nyarlathotep asked. "I haven't noticed."

Apophis could not help himself but spoke out of turn. "It has been almost a century, lord, since you wore the skin of the Black Pharaoh."

"Ah yes," Nyarlathotep said. "An evening's amusement."

Apophis Zul struggled to control his pride because displaying insolence rarely ended well when dealing with the gods. Certainly, he had punished enough of it when dealing with his fellow mortals.

"Blasphemers and heathens come to pillage Stygia, to burn it to the ground, and defile your sacred places. Their prophets and warrior-priests have promised to put all the old clergy to the sword, loot our treasuries, and destroy every engraving of every name so that we are forgotten."

"They will succeed," Nyarlathotep said, simply. "Or, rather, they have succeeded. In this world and in many others, I stand on the ruins of Stygia. I see it paved over to build new cities, I see the ashes of that city, and I see the world dead and lifeless far past that point. Mind you, I also see the city before it will be constructed and the precious sands of time you worship where it will thrive. A particularly grandiose colony of scurrying creatures offering prayers and blood to the sky while calling it empire."

Apophis Zul kept his temper in check. The conversation was not going the way he intended, but even the off-handed words of the gods could be deeply illuminating. He knew other worlds existed, but the Black Pharaoh's words implied variations on this one were real as well as the gods existing simultaneously across multiple time periods. He would have very much desired a scribe, hopefully a hard-hearted or fanatical one, to transcribe the god's words exactly for later study. However, that was hardly the most pressing point right now.

"It is within your power to save your worshipers, my master," Apophis Zul said, careful not even to phrase it as a request let alone a demand. Nyarlathotep was a chaotic god who was as likely to reward defiance and punish the faithful as the reverse. If not for the vast power he'd seen it wield, he might have heeded Thoth-Amon's words that conjuring lesser gods were less likely to be Stygia's doom.

"Yes, it is," Nyarlathotep said, a bored expression on his already rotting face. Narmer's body would not be able to hold the Black One's essence long. Perhaps Apophis Zul had overestimated the slave's pedigree.

Apophis Zul released a breath he had been holding in. The god was playing coy, he knew, and there was no choice now but to ask directly. Throwing his hands up into the air, he prostrated himself with his face pressed against the stone floor at the foot of the throne.

"Please, Ahtu, the Crawling Chaos, the Black Wind, the Dweller in Darkness, and the Whisper in the Night, save my people from the horror that is about to befall them."

"No," Nyarlathotep replied.

"No," Apophis Zul said, not raising his head. "No?"

"That's what I said, yes."

Apophis had been prepared for many answers but the sheer bluntness of his god's response was too much. He'd sacrificed too much and put too much of himself in his worship of the dark god to back away now, but the loss of Stygia was something he could not imagine surviving. So, against all good sense, he looked up and spoke, "But *why*?"

"Would you remove a spider to protect a fly that has been cocooned?" Nyarlathotep said, his face now a skeletal, oozing mass.

This was all too much and a kind of suicidal foolishness that could pass for courage came over Apophis Zul. Rising to one knee, he gazed into his god's visage. "But we have been loyal to you! The sacrifices, prayers, and—"

"Why do you think prayers matter to me?" Nyarlathotep asked, dryly. "That the fawning and chorus of lesser beings serves any purpose? Do you think I feed from it? Grow stronger? Need your kind's mewling and requests for wealth or healthy babes? The smoke of burnt children and the hearts of slaves gives me no pleasure. One soul in a billion of your kind ever shows the slightest bit of promise and it is not through religions that they achieve enlightenment. At least no more than any other path."

It was the most Apophis Zul had ever heard from his god and all of it left him feeling as empty as the River Styx in egress. Had he wasted his life? What even qualified as wasting one's life if the gods cared nothing for one's deeds, good or ill? Could a god who disdained worship even be called a god? Or was it simply a force far above man like a lion before a rodent?

"Ah, now you begin to understand," Nyarlathotep said, looking interested in their conversation for the first time. "Or at least begin to. Now ask the question you hold in your heart, and we will see if it provides you the secrets you desire."

Apophis Zul didn't know what he meant and was briefly terrified the god would smite him for standing there like a fool. Unwilling to let this happen, he blurted out the first question that occurred to him. "If you do not want prayers or sacrifices? What do you want?"

"Amusement."

Such a frivolous yet insightful answer. "Amusement."

The corpse of Narmer started changing from the rotted desiccated thing it had been to something wholly different, as if it were becoming the flesh of something else entirely, more shadow than man. "Indeed. Would you like a wish, Apophis?"

A wish? Such things were the subject of old wives' and children's tales. There was no magic that could grant anything one desired simply by willing it. If there was, Apophis would know of it. Yet, certainly, his god was perhaps one of the few beings capable of granting such a thing.

"Yes, master," Apophis Zul almost choked on his own reversal of fortune. "Please. I would love a wish."

"Then allow me to put you to the test," Nyarlathotep spoke. "Listen to me tell the tales of those touched by my presence. In the time it will take the hordes of the Sun worshipers to breach this temple, I will provide you with insight into my nature. If you can answer one question when these are done, you will receive whatever your shriveled little reptilian heart desires."

If there was a warning in the Black Pharaoh's words, Apophis Zul did not hear it and focused instead on the god's promise. No matter how rarely divine tests worked out for mortals.

The Beginning

"Cinderella and Her Outer Godfather" was written for another Cthulhu Mythos anthology back when I was first starting out. It's a simple concept: a fractured fairy tale with the various Cthulhu Mythos entities substituting for more traditional characters in the story. I always felt it was somewhat unsettling, though, with its familiarity adding to the creep factor. Maybe this is how the story is told in Lovecraft's Dreamlands or perhaps how the story ended on the Plateau of Leng.

CINDERELLA AND HER OUTER GODFATHER

A long time ago in an accursed land far, far away, there lived a wealthy landowner named Marcus and his young daughter, Anna.

Marcus was the descendant of a powerful line of warlocks. Once his family commanded the spirits of the Dreamland, regularly conversed with Nyarlathotep himself, and were routinely invited to dine with the spirit of Abdul Alhazred in Azathoth's court. Unfortunately, Marcus was not the equal of his ancestors and quickly spent his vast fortune on frivolous entertainments. Anna, who possessed an uncommon intelligence, confronted her father one night after he came home from yet another drunken binge.

"Oh Father, what are you going to do?" Anna asked. "Our house is built upon the great underground cities of our ancestors where the intelligent rats gnaw and play! If you continue to waste our fortune, who will take care of them?"

Marcus cuffed her across the face before replying.

"Silly girl, I have already come up with a solution to my problems. The Deep Ones from distant R'lyeh offer gifts of gold and great caches of fish to whoever will marry into their accursed bloodline. I attempted to offer you to one of their men, but they said you were too young. More's the pity, but I suppose I shall simply have to lie down and think of the fortune."

Anna, of course, was horrified by his words because her ancestors had long ago promised their descendants to Yog-Sothoth. The Deep Ones, with their degenerate rites and unnatural appearance, were uniformly pledged to Great Cthulhu. It was a blasphemy of the highest order to switch their family's allegiance.

Unfortunately, Anna's pleas fell on deaf ears and her father married one of the Deep Ones a week later. This particular Deep One, a haggish woman named Salyssa, had more human blood than most and was able to pass herself off as a mortal woman with the right combination of veils. Her daughters, Eris and Carnyl, were even more human-looking but still possessed tell-tale signs of their inhuman parentage.

Perhaps Anna might have won them over had she been a respectful, obedient child who joined in the depraved rites of Father Dagon and Mother Hydra. However, Anna was the descendant of warlocks. Every night, she snuck out into the forest behind her home to carry out the fell rituals devoted to Yog-Sothoth's glory while praying to the Key and the Gate for deliverance. Even Anna's dog Muffin was sacrificed to the Outer God, showing the young daughter's piety.

Such disrespect did not go unpunished, however. At first, Marcus made a halfhearted attempt at defending his child but the stresses of his unnatural marriage got to him and he hung himself.

It was then Eris said, "We should sacrifice her to Great Cthulhu, Mother. Toss her in the ocean where she can join the ranks of all those who refuse to venerate He-Who-Is-Dead-But-Sleeping."

"No," Salyssa said, staring at her children. "As much as I would like to, Anna is a daughter of an ancient bloodline. Were we to kill her, we would bring the wrath of Yog-Sothoth down upon us for he is in all places at all times. No, instead, we shall punish her for her misbehavior. We shall inflict such indignities upon her that she will come to worship Great Cthulhu voluntarily and take a Deep Ones husband."

"She doesn't deserve such an honor," Carnyl said. "However, I like the plan of hurting her. What shall be the first thing we do to her?"

"We shall take away her name, because it is the first thing her father gave her," Salyssa replied. "From this day forth, we shall refer to her only as Cinderella. She shall sleep in the fireplace amongst the ashes and with the rats."

Both daughters thought this was an extremely good plan and had a hearty laugh over it. They took away all of Cinderella's dolls, burned her dresses, and forced her to work as a servant. In time, they came to deny she had ever been the daughter of their stepfather. The neighbors, fearing retaliation from the cult of Cthulhu, ignored the young daughter's plight and allowed the Deep Ones to treat her as a slave.

Cinderella, however, found the life less taxing than it could have been. Her stepmother and stepsisters could not have known the rats in the walls were her friends, frequently bringing her news of the outside world and whispering all manner of dreadful secrets. As the years went on, she heard of the prince who was leading their country in the place of his hopelessly mad father.

The prince, a handsome blond-haired warlock named Benedict, was a believer in the old ways and followed them fervently. Greedy arrogant nobles took the prince's faith as a sign of weakness, though. They believed in the Great Old Ones only so much as it brought them power. The resulting civil war had devastated the noble houses of the land, and Benedict had called forth an army of flying polyps to devour his enemies and their forces.

While his magnificent victory was a sign to the whole world of how the Outer Gods favored the prince, the gruesome destruction of the rebelling noble families had left the kingdom without an eligible bride for its heir. Rather than marry outside the kingdom to one of the families who worshiped the strange idol-less god from Arabia, it was said Benedict had begun searching the ranks of commoners for a potential spouse.

"Oh," Cinderella sighed, one day, sitting in her fireplace. "If only I could marry into the royal household. Then I could practice my ancestors' religion in peace and keep Yog-Sothoth's altar filled with the hearts of men as opposed to the animals I trap in the woods."

"You can," one of her rat friends replied. "You are the descendant of Eibon, greatest of all the ancient magicians, and inheritor of his sorcery. Were you properly trained, you could summon forth one of Shub-Niggurath's young to make Prince Benedict your willing slave and breed with him many fresh offerings."

Cinderella smiled at her friend, stroking his furry human-shaped head. "You are sweet to say, friend rat, but I am not properly trained. My father cared more for drink than dread supplications. Why I do not think he ever waylaid a traveler so the hungry ones entombed below could have a meal!"

Cinderella was a child of good morals despite her faithless father. The fact the dead-but-sleeping remains of her ancestors were not fed by her stepfamily caused her no end of fitful nights.

"Feh!" the rat replied, surprising Cinderella. "I am surprised at you child, ignoring the power of the Outer Gods. They are there to be seized, not given. The secrets of ages past lay sleeping in the tomes of your forefathers. One merely has to seek these books out and possess the will necessary to perform the rituals within."

Cinderella blinked, considering the rat's words. "You mean to say that I should seek my grandfather's books and use them to summon a messenger of Yog-Sothoth?"

"Indeed I do," the rat replied. "The Deep Ones, craven fish-men that they are, have locked away your ancestors' libraries in the attic rather than destroy them. You must sneak the key from one of your stepsisters and study them in secret. In time, you will master the black arts and the world will be yours to command."

Cinderella felt embarrassed that a rat had been required to tell her such things. "I *will* do this. I will study the magic of my ancestors and wreak a mighty vengeance on my stepsiblings."

Stealing the key to the attic proved to be simplicity for the Deep Ones had long since abandoned active torment of Cinderella. She had become just another short-lived mortal, destined to be devoured or driven mad by the imminent rising of the Old Ones. Cinderella scoffed at such arrogance, knowing well that what was imminent to the Old Ones could last longer than the duration of humanity's reign on Earth.

Studying the *Book of Eibon, Pnakotic Manuscripts, De Vermis Mysteriis,* and other works, Cinderella became well-versed in all areas of the occult. Choosing a particularly auspicious moment in the solar calendar, Cinderella lured a hot-blooded traveler to the heart of the forest. There, she sacrificed him on Yog-Sothoth's altar before repeating mantras not meant for human mouths to perform.

Hours passed before a nightmarish black centaur stepped from a gateway to the primordial abyss. The creature had a body akin to a horse but covered in a thick alien exoskeleton. Its head was long and whip-like with only a yawning chasm in place of a face. Instantly, Cinderella fell to her knees and bowed before one of the many faces of Nyarlathotep, messenger of the Outer Gods.

"Milord," Cinderella cried, falling to her knees. "I am not worthy."

"Be at peace, daughter of Eibon, for I appear only to those who have caught my interest. Your ancestor long ago predicted your situation and ventured to distant Kadath where he passed by the puny gods of the Earth to speak with me. I am to grant you your fondest wish and see it is brought to fruition."

Cinderella clapped her hands with joy, never imagining such an august personage would be her patron. "Then, if the choice be mine, I would marry Prince Benedict and destroy my stepsisters as well as their hateful mother. I wish to be queen of all the realm and dwell with my beloved at the court of Azathoth for all time, listening to the otherworldly pipers who serenade the blind idiot god."

"Easily done," Nyarlathotep said, giving a courtly bow. "First we must replace the rags you wear with silks from the plateau of Leng. We shall give you jewelry made by the finest artisans of Ulthar. Your rats shall be made into coachmen, the skull of your father buried nearby turned into your coach. Your features will be changed as well for you are beautiful but only by human standards. I shall spare for you an entourage from the warlock courts of a place unpronounceable to your tongue. Finally, you shall wear a pair of glass slippers given to me as a present by a fallen priest of Hypnos."

"Glass slippers?" Cinderella asked, surprised such a thing existed.

"They carry upon them a dreadful curse of the Elder Gods to punish those who seek to pry too deeply into mysteries not meant for frail mortal minds," Nyarlathotep said, conjuring the slippers between his right hand's eight fingers. "You, Cinderella, are touched by the Outer Gods and shall suffer no ill-effects for wearing them. Lesser minds, however, will be driven mad from the glimpses of the Dreamlands they provide. Even your stepsiblings are too human to endure such secrets."

"Oh my lord, this is a princely gift!" Cinderella said, stunned by the Outer God's generosity.

"As befits a princess," Nyarlathotep replied. "I must warn you, though, the stars were not quite right for my summoning. You must return before midnight or all of my gifts will be undone."

Coincidentally—or perhaps because of fate—the prince was presently hosting a ball in hopes of finding an eligible mate. The ball was not going well, the young women Prince Benedict encountered were either too frightened of his dreadful religion or too mired in local superstitions to change their ways to match his. There were cultists to the King in Yellow, Cthulhu, Ithaqua, and Tsathoggua, but not a single follower of the Outer Gods.

"Oh, why must I be surrounded by such churlish savages?" Prince Benedict lamented. "Am I to be forced to marry a ghoul bride in hopes of having someone who does not quake in terror of the proper way of living?"

As if answering the prince's audible plea, Cinderella arrived with all the pomp and ceremony befitting a daughter of the primordial warlock-kings. Tongue-less slaves from distant realms rolled out carpets of human hair while painted faceless dancers enthralled the prince until the arrival of their mistress. The prince's heart skipped a beat upon seeing Cinderella, enraptured by the asymmetrical beauty Nyarlathotep had given her features.

While later versions of this tale would have you believe they danced all night, in truth it was Cinderella's love of the arcane which won Prince Benedict over. From the cyclopean architecture of Elder Thing temples to the distant world of Yuggoth, the two discussed all manner of things not meant for human ears.

So enjoyable was the time had by the pair that Cinderella nearly missed the deadline given to her by Nyarlathotep. Hearing the chiming of the Yithian-made clock, however, she immediately rushed out the door to escape in her skull-carriage. Along the way, she dropped one of her glass slippers, playing along to destiny's plan.

The next days passed miserably for Cinderella and Prince Benedict. Cinderella's stepsisters were furious the prince had not chosen them, taking out their rage on their normally unnoticed sibling. Prince Benedict, by contrast, was enamored with the mysterious girl and brought all the soothsayers of the land to find her.

Each of them failed, often perishing in ways which could only be described as the wrath of the Outer Gods. Prince Benedict, desperate to find Cinderella, decided to test the slipper on the young women of his kingdom. The consequences of doing so mattered little to him because he could sense it was the will of the Outer Gods they marry. Despite the hundreds of young women driven mad in the process, the prince could tell he was getting closer to finding the mysterious girl who captured his heart.

Eventually, Prince Benedict reached Cinderella's house where she was locked away in the basement in hopes the family's pet shoggoth would devour her. Salyssa had grown tired of her continued defiance and possibly sensed the growing power within her. Fortunately, Cinderella had learned the spells for mastering a shoggoth to her will.

No sooner had Eris tried on the glass slipper and gone mad, stabbing Carnyl to death with a knife, did Cinderella burst from the basement with her newfound pet and ordered it to feast upon her stepmother. Salyssa's last words were a plea to Dread Cthulhu to rescue her but, of course, that god lies dead but sleeping.

"Who are you that commands the rebellious servants of the Elder Things?" Prince Benedict asked, impressed by her dramatic entrance.

"I am the woman you seek, blessed by Nyarlathotep and the Outer Gods, destined wife to you and mother of a great kingdom," Cinderella proclaimed, curtsying in her rags because she was addressing royalty.

Though she did not possess the non-Euclidean features which had so attracted him before, Prince Benedict tested the glass slipper upon her. Cinderella, having seen many more terrible things than the sights they showed her, remained completely sane. Well, as she and the prince measured sanity.

"At last!" Prince Benedict said. "My bride!"

"At last!" Cinderella said. "My husband!"

The two were married in an obscene ceremony soon after, ordering debased celebrations to all the Outer Gods and Old Ones throughout the land. That very year, twins were born possessing all the attributes associated with Yog-Sothoth's unnatural children. For, you see, both the prince and Cinderella had the Outer God's blood in their veins and Nyarlathotep had arranged for their bloodlines joining in aeon's past. The royal family summoned their godly ancestor on the twins' eighteenth birthday, destroying the kingdom utterly and flattening most of Europe in the process.

In reward for their actions, they were all raised up to dwell in Azathoth's court in wonder and glory forever.

The End

Honestly, I think "Cookies for the Gentleman" is, word for word, my single best work. It's also one of the few unquestionable pieces of horror fiction I've written with no caveats or twists. Unsurprisingly, the story was inspired by a dream I had and follows the kind of horrific weird logic that they tend to do. I think HPL would have been proud.

COOKIES FOR THE GENTLEMAN

I live alone. I had a wife, once. Her name was Rachel. You wouldn't remember her, even though she lived right next door to you. You see, she never lived next door to you. Not now. Not ever. One day, you woke up and the next-door neighbors you remember lived there and had always lived there. You don't remember talking with Rachel, gossiping with her, or the fact she asked you to our wedding.

That's because the Gentleman took her. I see him every night, usually when I can't sleep. I walk to the window of my apartment and stare out into the parking lot. There, he's always standing perfectly still. I would say he's looking at me, but he doesn't have any eyes. At least, eyes I can see. No, instead there are only shadows where his face should be and too many arms where humans have two. He dresses well, in a suit I'm sure someone gave him, but I've never seen his feet.

Sometimes, when I go to sleep, I can hear the Gentleman crawling around my room. He's too tall for it, you see, standing half again as tall as a man and he must slouch over. That doesn't prevent him from moving through cracks and stepping through walls. He plays with my cat, Whiskers, who can see him like me and doesn't seem the least bit afraid.

I wish I wasn't. It's rude and I'm always worried he's going to take offense, but it's hard not to be afraid. The Gentleman's shadow brushing up against you makes you unable to move, your hands shaking palms sweaty, and your mouth dry.

I used to fear nothing, happy to spit in the face of men twice my size and never losing a fight. That was before I lost half my weight and I ceased to ever sleep completely. He's waiting for me in my dreams too, you know. I won't tell you about what he does there, though it's nothing *ungentlemanly*. It's just he might hear and decide to visit yours too.

The proper thing is to remember the Gentleman is lonely and the best thing to do is be polite. He doesn't speak, I don't think he has a mouth or a tongue or vocal cords as we know them. However, he *understands*. Don't scream at him, threaten him, or insult him. I made the mistake of doing that when he first showed up in my apartment. I didn't realize it was his and everything which resided in it belonged to him.

That's when he took my parents.

Now, now. I know you're going to say that my parents died when I was very young. They disappeared in a fire, and I was moved from foster home to foster home. That's the thing, though, I met with them just a day prior to their disappearance. They were speaking about my baby brother and how very proud of him they were. It turns out he was never born. The Gentleman left me a picture of him, though, and sometimes brings him to visit.

My brother has no eyes or tongue anymore, only shadows. I think he's happier where he is now.

Now, you can imagine my reaction to all of this as event after event piled up. I panicked and pitched a fit, calling the police, the National Guard, the exorcist, and even professors of the occult. Funny thing, no one could remember doing any of that within minutes of me doing it.

My wife believed, though, perhaps because the Gentleman let her remember my parents. We decided we'd rabbit for the state lines and go as far West as we could go.

Too bad the Gentleman decided we weren't allowed to leave. I won't tell you what he did to us but there are other places I went to when I tried to leave his influence. Merciful God—if merciful he is— has wiped my mind of most of the sights I saw, but in the corner of my eye I still see the terrible place of all-corners that I only briefly glimpsed. The place where the things which mustn't be and never were stay and I WILL NOT TALK ABOUT IT ANYMORE.

Ahem.

The thing is that the Gentleman only wanted to be loved and I was foolish not to realize that. My wife, on the other hand, comprehended it first. She was foolish about it, though, cutting open poor Whiskers and tossing her parts about around the room. I think she must have read it in a book that gods like the Gentleman appreciated animal sacrifice.

They don't.

I still see my wife every day in the bathroom mirror. I don't know if she's behind the reflection like Alice or whether whatever was done to her burned an image inside it. She doesn't move, though, only occasionally opens her mouth as if she's trying to say something but I can't make it out. Sometimes, I think about asking the Gentleman for Rachel back. I don't think that's a good idea, not since he so dearly loves Whiskers. He was nice enough to return Whiskers to life. But Rachel? He did not like Rachel at all. No sir.

The worst punishment, though, was when I decided to escape the Gentleman the only way I knew how. I tossed myself off the top of our building and hoped to God that I would end up in Hell, because surely that would be better than the apartment belonging to the Gentleman. I landed in my apartment, with the Gentleman waiting for me.

There is a worse punishment than even the place I WILL NOT SPEAK ABOUT, at least for good Christian folk. A punishment I am even now living and would warn you about, if not for the fact that all will become clear in time.

In the end, knowing I could never escape the Gentleman and that I had been a terribly rude man, I remembered a story of my grandmother. She was from Appalachia, you see, where stories were passed down from mother to daughter straight from Scotland where people came from looking for a new life. All that's forgotten now, replaced with strip malls and gas stations, but she remembered the stories. The stories she'd shared with me.

Oh, I don't know if the Gentleman was the Black Man who made pacts with witches, the God with a Thousand Faces, or the Worm that Walked, but I *remembered* the tales. The ones I heard in my dreams that were the true stories behind the Brothers Grimm. The frightening ones she used to share with me when she babysat, where princesses had their feet cut off for dancing in the glen and peasants' eyes were ripped out for seeing too much.

In the old tales, though, there is the lie that the supernatural can be appeased. If you believe a lie enough, in the Dreamlands, maybe a cat will make it real. I remembered hearing that somewhere, maybe when I walked the streets of a city made of stories and the Gentleman left me alone for a night. Maybe he whispered it to me as I screamed in terror for my wife and my neighbors called the police. For a bit of sour milk and some treats, the supernatural would leave you alone for a time. They wouldn't rip your babies from their cribs and leave someone else in their place, they wouldn't skin your husband alive and wear him like a suit, nor would they take you away to the Unspeakable Place where the headless men and living whips holds court. So, I needed to bake cookies for the Gentleman.

Oh, you have no idea what fear and trepidation accompanied this perverse realization. No child hoped to bribe Santa Clause or placate the monster under the bed more than I, when I had the terrified realization this was the only way I could get the Gentleman to spare me further torment.

I was not afraid of death, indeed were suicide a possibility I would have welcomed it even then, but the thought of being forced to do my "penance" was sanity tearing. I hoped, foolishly, that if I managed to placate my new master then he would not make me go through the horrible thing he'd forced upon me.

I'm sure you must think me quite mad or a great liar. Indeed, by the look on your face, I suspect you are already thinking of calling the police or at the very least asking me to leave. A part of you, however small, thinks I'm either telling the truth, or more likely deranged enough to believe I am. You possibly think I'm violent. I beg you, however, indulge me a few more minutes. I do not have any ill-intentions to you or your household.

I swear by HIM.

Now where was I?

Oh yes, cookies.

The belief that cookies—sugary crumbly pieces of baked flour—could set me free from the hands of a being able to dance between the spaces of God's own kingdom was a mad, mad thought but one I latched on with force beyond measure.

Unfortunately, acquiring them wasn't as easy as it sounds. I had never been a baker and knew precious little about the kitchen my apartment contained. My wife and I subsisted on take-out and sandwiches, ignoring the fineries of the culinary arts. I also knew—perhaps instinctively—that nothing could be so easy, that store-bought cookies would only enrage the Gentleman. Given his earlier actions towards me were spurred on by only, I think, mild irritation, I did not have any desire to test the being's patience further. No, I would have to master the art of cookie making on my own and create such a spectacular confection as to delight the taste buds of a creature with no mouth.

The Gentleman was kind enough to let me out of the apartment for this journey, perhaps sensing I was going to make him an offering he'd appreciate. For the past week, I'd been trapped in my apartment. The door to the outside led to my bathroom and the windows opened to an apartment identical to my own.

Several times, even, I caught a glimpse of myself entering said apartment only to look over at me as I looked over at him. I feel for my doppelganger and occasionally wonder what he did to incur the wrath of the Gentleman.

But we were discussing my inability to make a decent tasty treat.

Oh, the *desperation* at the grocery store counter when I realized my escapades had drained my finances dry. I had not been to work in almost a month and overdue bills had long since obliterated my meager savings. At the grocery store counter, I considered killing the woman behind and making away with my supplies before I remembered there was still a little money left on my credit card.

I didn't want to do the cashier harm, of course, but hope is a more dangerous beast than despair. A man who despairs cannot be harmed and, truth be told, I wish I'd fallen to it completely. Unfortunately, I saw an escape and that makes monsters of all of us.

Whatever the case, I bought enough supplies to bake cookies for an army. I also acquired books of recipes that were as precious to me as any spellbook. Ugh, you should have tasted the first of my creations. Vile, disgusting things with too much sugar and burnt from top to bottom. I spent hours retrying the recipe, reading through the literally dozens of cookbooks I'd checked out of the library as if they were sacred scripture and trying them all. Several times I threw up, not having eaten in days only to fill my belly with sweet but nutrition-less confections.

I didn't sleep for almost two days until I came up with something I believed which would satisfy the Gentleman. It was hubris, of course, a madness shared by Perseus and other great heroes who thought they could walk amongst the gods without being struck down.

Oh, the agony! The pain! The terrible *things* he did to me. It was minor compared to my penance but so much more *physical*. All the torments and fires of Hell could not match the Gentleman's wrath he inflicted on me without saying a word. Even now I feel like curling into a ball and crying, I who used to brag about my ability to take a punch without flinching.

Where was I? Oh yes, the Gentleman did not care for my cookies.

At all.

A more foolish individual might have concluded that it was the fact I was offering him cookies and not something more substantial that offended him. Since that time, I have occasionally been allowed to walk the crossroads with the Gentleman and I have seen what other people have left for him: gold, shoes, wildflowers, infants, and the hearts of young women. The Gentleman seems to prefer the flowers, putting them on his lapel as one might a boutonnière but is indifferent to the others.

The cookies, though, I was sure were the key to his heart.

I drank myself silly after my failure, indulging in two bottles of whiskey the Gentleman had allowed me to purchase, which I threw up before they killed me. I could sense the Gentleman was growing bored with me and that terrified me more than the prospect of his wrath. You see, across the hall, there was a happy couple much like my wife and I had been. Arguably, they were more so because they had a five-year-old daughter.

Now they don't. They never did, citing the expense and hardships of raising a child. I think the Gentleman must have taken a fancy to her and took her with him to the nameless realm he calls home. Perhaps her young developing mind is not so caught up in the mundane aspects of things like physics, cause and effect, or people should have all of their parts when they speak. I like to think so. The other option is simply too terrible.

In the old stories, the Gentry simply cooked and ate the children they took.

It would be a mercy compared to the alternative. I poured over my recipes like a deranged alchemist, tasting the cinnamon and sugar each to see what might have been the problem. I tried combinations which ranged from the ghastly to the sublime, struggling to see where I went wrong. My landlord gave me an eviction notice during this time, only to be replaced the next day by a kindly old woman who said I could stay as long as I desired. I do not like her very much. She has no shadow and I can see things moving under her skin when she thinks I'm not looking.

Whatever the case, I was halfway to embracing whatever punishments the Gentleman could devise when inspiration struck me like it must have struck Edison when he created the light bulb: the milk! The Gentleman was a creature beyond the scope of time and space; he wouldn't want cookies made with artificial ingredients. No, he would want *raw* milk for his cookies and the drink to wash it down. Straight from the cow and fresh! I seem to recall having heard raw milk was much tastier, simply possessing a higher possibility of germs.

Finding a dairy willing to cater to my unusual request wasn't that difficult. Many of the local farmers resented the government's regulations against raw milk and were willing to sell it to me in bulk, especially once I revealed my willingness to pay exorbitant sums I'd acquired from pawning my wife's jewelry. Adjusting my recipes to the new, stronger taste, took some work but I could tell I was on the verge of something masterful.

By that point I hadn't eaten or drunk anything but my creations in days. But, determination kept me alive—determination or the will of the being who was now the arbiter of my fate. Whatever the case, I finished a batch of what I felt were the single greatest cookies ever made by man well after midnight and laid them out with a fresh glass of raw milk by my doorstep. From there, I climbed into my bed and collapsed.

I had hoped—rather foolishly in retrospect—that the Gentleman would let me die. I never entertained any ridiculous notions of him returning my parents or my wife. Such thoughts had long since left my head, along with any idea that the Gentleman cared about such things as humans might. I'd compare him to a lion amongst gazelles, but lions are closer to humans than the Gentleman is. Better to compare him to a star or a gaseous cloud than anything which evolved on planet Earth.

Instead, I simply lay there, unable to sleep. I felt the Gentleman creep into my room and pick up the plate from the ground. I could imagine his sickly, spider-leg-like fingers lifting each of the cookies and making them disappear into the shadows where his face should be. I doubt, now, that the actual composition of the things mattered to him. He could have eaten the molten metal of the Earth's core without grimacing. No, instead, it was the suffering and desperation of my struggle to please him that made the cookies good.

You see, he really is just lonely. Once he finished the plate, making it disappear along with the glass, I knew he would never be satisfied with simply one order. From this day forward, I would be expected to prepare my magnificent feast of wafers every night. They would all have to be as perfect as this batch, never the slightest mistake or error. I do not know if the Gentleman will allow me to age, but I do know I am still expected to do my penance.

Yes, my penance.

I mentioned it earlier, that terrible thing that is worse than the place of all-comers. I tear up and scream inside every time I think of it. Yet, as bad as it is, I promise you I would return to it rather than do this. I have no choice, though, because if I didn't comply things would get worse. I don't know how they would get worse, I lack the imagination, but I know in my withered belly and sleepless mind they would.

The Gentleman is lonely you see, and he has a delightfully karmic sense of justice for those who are rude to him. I was terribly rude to him by not showing him proper respect before and the only way to pay him back for my discourtesy would be to find him new friends. People who could show him the love and affection he so richly deserves.

I've chosen you. Now, now don't panic. Your friend panicked. What friend? Oh dear, this is going to be a long story.

Cookie?

The End

"The Siege of New Ulthar" was written as the beginning of The Tree of Azathoth *when I finally decided I had more* Cthulhu Armageddon *stories to tell. In the end, I decided to release it as part of* Tales of Nyarlathotep *instead. This was because I felt it worked better as a standalone. While you can read* The Tree of Azathoth *without it, I do think it benefits strongly from knowing what happened to New Ulthar and with John and Mercury's relationship.*

THE SIEGE OF NEW ULTHAR

A *Cthulhu Armageddon* adventure

Chapter One

Doom had come to New Ulthar.

New Ulthar was, in simple terms, a shit hole. It was a cattle town—if you stretched the definition of the mutant steers sold here enough to call them "cattle"—but also a place where every vice imaginable was permitted. Nay, even welcomed by the locals. Gambling, prostitution, and murder were indulgences permitted in every town from here to New Arkham, but New Ulthar took the next step. Here, the townsfolk were willing to overlook eyes where they should not be and the worship of things that should never have their names uttered.

If you wished to marry something that barely qualified as human, then you didn't have to hide it in the basement unless it was going to eat someone. It was a town where minding your own fucking business extended well past virtue into a kind of selective insanity. In the last days of humanity, when the Great Old Ones had risen, and hope was a distant memory, New Ulthar was the sign that humanity would go out with not a bang but a whimper. A ragged, twisted, deranged bunch of oddballs and degenerates who were barely kept in line by their duly-appointed dictator of a sheriff.

That was me, by the way.

Yes, New Ulthar was a shit hole, but it was my shit hole, and I was sure as shit not going to let some scumbag living dead, fungus-ridden bandits come to loot my town. If this was the last days of humanity—

which it almost certainly was—I was not going to abandon my little piece of Purgatory to a gang of raiders come to burn it to the ground.

"John, you're being stupid," Mercury said, standing beside me as I laid out the various weapons I'd prepared for confronting the Yellow Raiders.

Mercury was my partner in most senses of the word, a redheaded Eurasian woman who was wearing a dirty white linen shirt and a pair of black, stained slacks. She was currently holding a rifle as she looked up at me. It was a ridiculous weapon since I knew she could do things with sorcery and monsters that could lay waste to far more than any gun could ever do. I just wasn't sure that would help in this situation.

The two of us were in our shared business called The Wages of Sin, a half-saloon and half-brothel that I'd inherited by the oldest law of the Wasteland: you kill the owner then you get their stuff. The customers had been cleared out and I was now trying to assemble what broken weapons, idols, and amulets we had in hopes of figuring out something that could repulse the swarm of locusts about to descend on our Biblical Egypt.

The building was the remnant of an old Pre-Rising hotel/motel that had been patched repeatedly by me and others over the past century since the end of the world. It was full of old wooden benches and plastic chairs that didn't exactly scream high class, but the kind of customers who drank here didn't care about ambiance.

"Maybe I *am* being stupid," I said, surveying the rows of guns and mystical artifacts on the tables. New Ulthar was half in and half out from the Dreamlands, so things that wouldn't normally have any power now did. Religious artifacts, lucky charms, and personal totems might give a slight edge against the Undying King.

"But smart would leave us running into the Wasteland without anything to our names and that's its own kind of stupid."

"You stupid bastard," was Mercury's only answer to that.

"Yep."

"And for these assholes?" Mercury asked, waving her hand toward the village around us.

"Yep."

There was a time when I had been a United States Remnant Ranger and was supposed to protect the pure-blooded humans of our home base. That was before I found out I wasn't a pure-blooded human myself, but a Kastro'vaal—something closer to shoggoth than man—and that everything about me was just illusion. I was a mad monster pretending to be a human and would have been destroyed by my own people if they'd known the truth. Mercury and Jackie were with me despite the fact we didn't share anything resembling proteins, let alone blood. And yet we were a family, nonetheless. New Ulthar was about the only place that our arrangement would be accepted, though. At least until the last of humanity passed from the earth in fifty years or so. That was a prophecy coming closer every day.

"Do you want me to lay any land mines, Dad?" Jackie asked, gathering supplies from the back room.

"What the hell?" Mercury asked, confused. "Where did you even get those?"

"Remember that guy who tried to eat Becky?" I asked.

"Which one?" Mercury said.

"The second one," I said. "He left an entire wagon full of them."

Mercury shook her head.

"I hate this town so much."

"You love it," Jackie said, coming out with two arms full of landmines. "It's the only place that wouldn't burn you at the stake."

Jackie Howard was a ghoul, though she hadn't yet made the transformation into one of the feral lycanthrope race that dwelled underground. Her human mother meant that that she wouldn't begin her transformation until she was about thirty. Theoretically. Even now at twenty, she already was showing signs of her unnatural heritage that marked her as different from the so-called "normal" humans of the Wastes.

Jackie was over six feet in height and extremely muscular, standing above most men, not just women. Her hair was a tangled mess, impossible to brush, and hung down to her waist. She had just the barest traces of fur on her palms as werewolves were once identified by. Her eyes were an iridescent shade of green and her canines pronounced to the point of looking like fangs as the rest of her teeth came to points. Despite her obvious inhumanity, Jackie reveled in the effect she had on others and dressed in cut shorts as well as a shirt tied at the midriff. Sand, dirt, and the acidic rain did not bother her the way they did creatures of mere homo sapiens flesh.

"Burning doesn't always kill witches," I said. "I remember one that exploded into flesh-eating maggots and tore half the town to pieces."

"That's an urban legend," Mercury said, reluctantly taking the mines from Jackie one by one and stacking them. "Probably. You never can tell what's a lie and a truth these days."

"The ghouls of Tremortown say that anything that can be dreamed of by man or beast is true somewhere in the Dreamlands," Jackie said, rubbing her hands. "They said that the Old Ones awoke because Yog-Sothoth tore a hole and let them all come spilling into the world. That's why the ghoul race doesn't fear death because they know life and death are one and the same."

"And that's why I think religious people are all crazy," Mercury said. "Especially when I have proof gods exist."

Mercury had once been a die-hard atheist who had been raised on the lessons of the United States Remnant's dogma that the Great Old Ones were nothing more than humungous aliens with vast psychic powers and incredibly advanced technology. It was our feeble defense against a universe intrinsically hostile to all life.

Unfortunately, even the sad illusion that we could hold our own against the madness of reality had been plucked from her mind when we'd been forced to use technology beyond the grasp of even the mightiest of Earth's minds to bring Cthulhu back to the Earth it had escaped. Mercury had witnessed the legendary Sleeping God in all its glory and had been driven mad by the experience.

I'd done a terrible thing, violating her mind to bind away what she'd seen, but it had left marks. Now I found her praying at night to clay idols with human fat candles dedicated to Old Ones and gods I'd never heard of. That didn't bother me as much as the fact that sometimes I could hear them answering.

"We live in the worst of both worlds," I replied. "The gods are real and they're uncaring assholes. We're the fungus growing on the toes of beings infinitely older and more powerful than us. Beings that will outlive this universe."

"Thanks, John," Mercury said. "Because we really need that before our life and death struggle with the Yellow Raiders."

I grimaced. "You have a point."

No one knew the origin of the Undying King. A scarecrow-looking man with a burlap sack over his head, riding an emaciated, half-dead horse, showed up on the edge of Little Stone a month ago. He had ordered everyone to offer up their children to Hastur. When they didn't, he'd destroyed the entire town. A week later, he'd shown up at Ghostrock with all Little Stone's dead behind him as well as an army of remnants. All of them were covered in a vile, yellow fungus growing in and out of their corpses, spreading a horror that animated them like puppets. This time the local headman had grabbed every child from their parents' arms with his goons and offered them up. The Undying King promptly destroyed the town anyway.

There was no way of escaping across the Wasteland, and destroying an army of the already dead was probably impossible. Nevertheless, the Undying King's actions provided a nice level of certainty to my chosen course of action. If the choice was dying on your knees or dying on your feet, then it was easy to throw yourself into the meatgrinder. Sun Tzu said something about that but, lacking a copy of *The Art of War*, I had to paraphrase it.

"Well, I think that's every weapon we have," Mercury said, staring at the row after row of weapons. "Do we even have ammunition for all of these?"

"Some," I replied, not at all that confident. "A few of these are busted beyond repair."

"Gun maintenance takes a backseat when you become a tentacle monster," Mercury said, insulting me.

"Please don't," I said, still hating every moment of my life when I lost control and abandoned myself to the thing inside me.

Eventually, no matter what choices or desires I might have, the alien mind would consume the human mind and leave nothing of John Henry Booth, Recon and Extermination Ranger. In its place would be a far older thing that had lived millions of years in various forms across time. A thing that had as much in common with a human being as a cat. Hell, far less because at least a cat was a creature of carbon and base proteins. The Eyes of Yog-Sothoth, as my "true" race was known, lived outside time and could assume the forms of beings who bathed in lava or drifted across airless voids.

I'd managed to hold onto a semblance of my prior self, though even that I couldn't be entirely sure of, due to the fact the monster had time on its side. Humankind didn't have a future, our world was too hostile, and there were only a couple of generations left until we went extinct. When that happened, if I somehow survived, I would have no choice but to give in to the beast within. It would be better to live wild and free, like the Old Ones, than be the lone thing that remembered mankind when we were nothing more than dust on the road of greater beings' travels.

On the other hand, I was probably going to die today so what was the point in worrying about such things? Death may eventually die but it would probably be after he claimed me.

"I'm just saying that we may have a chance with you," Mercury said, sounding like she was trying to convince herself more than me.

"I'm not immortal," I replied. "You of all people should know that it's not impossible to kill the creatures of other worlds. We've both done it and plenty of them were tougher than me. We were just the wasps lucky enough to sting them to death. Magic tricks or not."

Mercury didn't immediately respond. She'd started as a virtual slave to the Remnant government, doing whatever horrible things she needed to survive. Now she was free and had turned to the sorcery of ghouls and the late Alan Ward to seek power over her life. It cost much of her soul, as such things existed, but provided control over her life. That control was an illusion, though. Even if sorcery could make you the strongest ant in the world, it didn't make you any less likely to be squashed.

"I don't want to die here, John," Mercury said, almost a whisper.

"I don't want to either," I replied.

"Don't you?" Mercury asked.

The statement hung in the air with no definitive answer. Life as a monster or merciful death as a man. Was I here prepared to fight against an army of the dead because I didn't want to abandon the twisted little burg I'd set myself in, or because I figured this was a way to die semi-human? After all, stupidly throwing your life away was one of the things humans did best.

The somber, fatalistic mood was interrupted by Jackie's baby, Baby John, crying out above our heads in one of the second-floor rooms. Jackie was a mother now, her child carrying more mixed human as well as ghoulish blood, and watching her rush up to tend to the child caused me to reevaluate my priorities.

"Too bad that kid doesn't have a future," Mercury muttered.

"He does if we win," I replied.

"Will we?" Mercury asked, turning back.

"Yes," I said, deciding we will. I had no way of guaranteeing that and it might be delusion, but if you lost the battle in your mind before it happened then there was no point in fighting it at all. Baby John would inherit a dead and dying world no matter what I did, but the Old Ones' lives were measured in epochs not years or decades. Maybe I could make it so Jackie and her child lived long enough to have a human's lifespan. However short and insignificant that was to a ghoul, let alone the creatures that existed far longer than their entire race had since they evolved in the Neolithic Era.

"Good. That's all I want from you. A lie that we can believe in so this worthless hellhole will have a fighting chance. I'll even give you free rounds with the girls," Mercury said, going over to the table with remnants of our last big adventure: the one against the Unimaginable Horror where seven heroes had set out to save the world and only a few had lived to tell the tale.

"I'll have free rounds with the best girl in the house," I replied, giving a half-smile.

"Don't get romantic, John, it doesn't suit you. Will this help?" Mercury asked, handing me a belt with two holsters. They were Thom Brannan's guns, each emblazoned with the hellish brand of Cthugha the Living Sun that Eats. Things that could kill me. Maybe things that could kill the Undying King.

I pulled out both from their holsters, feeling a malign intelligence inside them that wanted to kill me as much as anything else in the world.

"Yeah, I think these will do nicely."

Chapter Two

I didn't have a chance to think more about my situation because the door to the Wages of Sin opened and let in a few of those poor fools who'd decided to stay. Not that there was any place to flee to right now. The destruction of Little Stone and Ghostrock had cut us off from part of the Greater New England Wasteland. What little "settled" territory that existed was now isolated and perfect for this undead host to wipe us from the face of the cosmos. That didn't mean plenty of New Ulthar residents weren't trying it. I didn't expect to see them again because if they could outrun the Yellow Raiders, they wouldn't outrun the heat and lack of supplies.

The first of these poor brave fools who were joining me in my assisted suicide by undead horde was Becky Khatri, a lovely girl of East Asian descent that was wearing a smudged white spring dress. While formerly a working girl here at the Wages of Sin, she'd somehow managed to move beyond bare survival into one of the few nice homes left over from before the Rising.

While a savvy businesswoman, I noted that was mostly due to the fact the previous occupants were eaten by something, given all we'd ever found of them was a boot with half a missing foot next to an incorrectly made Elder Sign drawn in blood on the floor. Becky was a crack shot from days when her family had killed mutated but still terrestrial varmints for the other families. Her rifle, made in the last ten years but equal to anything made in the Old World, was slung over one shoulder. A pleasant little hat was resting on her head, as if this were all a summer's eve rather than the end of this part of the world.

Behind her was Matt "Wild Dog" Davenport, a tall man built like an oak tree with a thin goatee and a vest over a blue shirt with black slacks. A pair of thin spectacles rested on his nose and a revolver was holstered awkwardly to his side. Matthew was a writer from Kingsport who had somehow found himself down the rabbit hole of the Wasteland's strangest town. Which was saying something. I fully believed he was only here for Jackie and otherwise would have fled. It was noble. Foolish, but noble.

The third individual rounding out the group was August Bierce, a chocolate-skinned man with a shaved head and a beatific expression on his face. August dressed starkly different from the rest of the town, wearing a robe-like leather trench coat and metal goggles that protected his eyes. August had been driven mad by looking upon Cthulhu as well but while I debated putting a bullet in the head of the wizard as he stared catatonically up at the ceiling, he came out of his deranged state on his own.

I honestly wasn't sure if he were the same man I'd met earlier—and didn't particularly care—his magic was of a different sort than Mercury's. Not necessarily stronger, but he could command the beasts of other dimensions to do his bidding. Things far older and stronger than anything Earth had produced. That was why he was the one man I feared as I always wondered if that included me. Death was better than slavery as I knew what horrible things could be done when a man lost control of himself.

"Sheriff?" Becky asked. "Are those all the weapons you were able to assemble?"

"Technically, I'm a Marshal," I replied. "A Sheriff requires an election in a county."

"Technically, you're neither because you're just the local murderer they've put in charge to kill the people the locals dislike most," August said.

Whenever I doubted he was still the same man as before seeing Cthulhu, he said something like that and reminded me that alien consciousnesses were unlikely to replicate August's peculiar brand of assholery.

"Yes, Becky, these are all the weapons I was able to get out of our little slice of Hell."

"How many volunteers were you able to muster?" Mercury asked.

"Seventeen," Becky said, listing a depressingly small number even for a flyspeck of a town. The world's population was dwindling rapidly but not so much that that wasn't infuriating.

"Do they expect to be spared if they don't fight?" Mercury asked.

"No, they're all holed up in their houses," Matthew said, sighing. "They'll fight to defend their homes and property but won't lift a finger to save each other."

I sighed, not even surprised.

"We need to hang together or surely we'll hang separately."

"I'd rather not hang at all," Becky replied, not getting the double meaning. Language had changed a bit since Ben Franklin's time.

"Seventeen is not enough to cover the town edge," Matthew said.

"No shit," Mercury said, rolling her eyes. "It's not even enough to do a twenty-one-gun salute."

"Yes, that would be twenty-one," Becky said.

Mercury and I looked at her side eyed.

"What?" Becky asked.

"It's not too late to try to escape, sir," Matthew said, looking at me. "There's nothing you can do to stop this, and no one would blame you for not trying."

"Except everyone before they died," August replied. "But they'll be dead, so you won't have to worry about their opinion."

Matthew glared at him then turned back to me.

"At least try to send Jackie and her baby away. She deserves better than to die horribly out here at the monster's hands."

I wasn't sure who exactly he thought did deserve to be torn to shreds by a madman leading an army of fungus zombies, but men in love were stupid the universe over. Even the Kastro'vaal had something equivalent, though they were a race that bred with countless other species, growing their children inside them like parasites. We were a race of cuckoos, and it was hard to say if we were really kin to the races we joined with at all. Then again, I'd changed enough that I tended to think of Deep Ones, serpent men, and ghouls as just other versions of humanity.

"I'm the eighteenth gun in this posse," Jackie said, descending the stairs, holding Baby John. "I'm not going to be abandoning my ma, pa, or friends. Few as I have of them."

Baby John was clearly not Matthew's baby, for reasons of skin color and the fact he hadn't appeared in her life until a few months after the baby's birth, but I could see the look on his face was one of a proud father.

"You have plenty of friends, Dog Girl," Becky said. "I'd happily play fetch with ya if you weren't likely to bite my hand off."

Jackie narrowed her eyes. "Quiet, Monkey Girl."

"I'll have you know that some of your best friends are monkeys," Becky said. "Me—"

"Wrong," Jackie said.

"Matthew," Becky said. "Your mother. I'm not sure about John. He has that worm that walks sort of feel."

"Thank you," I replied, resenting the comparison. The people of New Ulthar were far more accepting of the unnatural than most of humanity's scared scattered remnants, but that didn't mean it wasn't more convenient if they thought of me as a human. Just one that had made some sort of dark compact with eldritch forces. Apparently, that was better than being a wholly alien creature.

Somehow.

"You're welcome," Becky said. "In any case, we don't have much time. It's about a couple of hours until the Yellow Raiders arrive. Old Blind Sue saw it in a chicken's entrails."

"Is that, uh, accurate?" Matthew asked, confused.

"Extremely," August replied. "There's no way for you to escape even if you wanted to. Their rotted horse corpses would track down even the most tireless rider."

"Shit," Matthew said, looking down at the ground.

"It's okay," Jackie patted him on the shoulder. "I promise I'll shoot you before they get to you."

"Uh, thanks." Matthew looked less than reassured by this statement.

I didn't want to think about what that offer to kill her lover meant for Jackie's child. I fully believed that, if the situation came down to it, that Jackie would kill her child before she allowed it to be torn to shreds by the Yellow Raiders or reanimated as yet another of their weapons. This was the world now as we lived in it. I needed to find a way to get the child away and cursed myself for not doing it sooner.

"Could we have a moment alone, John?" August asked, putting on a pair of thick leather gloves.

"Sure, August," I muttered. "What is it?"

August led me outside the Wages of Sin into the dirty, shit-smelling, mud streets of New Ulthar. A rain barrel was nearby, catching water that was pouring down from a light thunderstorm. The general store, stables, gunsmith, and butcher were all visible from my hotel doorstep. A windmill farm in a lonely set of hills above our town provided what little power we needed, though it could also catch lightning according to its mad owner.

Most notable about New Ulthar was the fact that it had about four cats for every citizen and the place was utterly littered with strays. They came in every color of the rainbow and were a particularly foul-tempered set of unidentifiable mixed breeds.

It had been a capital crime to harm a cat in New Ulthar by the time I'd taken over as Sheriff and I'd enforced the law since. Not that it had required much enforcing as the locals — at least the ones who had been here before my arrival — had a passionate fear of violating said taboo. Personally, I much preferred dogs, but avoided harming any of the local felines. They always seemed to be *watching*.

"I'm not going to be joining you in your protracted suicide," August said, dryly. "I'll be leaving ahead of the Raiders."

I stared at him, balling my fists. "You heard what they said. There's no way to escape."

"No, there's no way for these poor fools to escape," August said. "I might walk through the spaces of time, send my spirit across the globe to another poor fool's body, or turn into a great night-gaunt that flies far into space on the winds of Azathoth's breath."

"And these people mean nothing to you," I said.

"Absolutely not a thing," August said. "They are one of the most aggressively ignorant and uncultured races in the universe."

"And you know many?" I asked, not even that surprised.

"Oh yes," August replied. "My encounter with the Lord of R'lyeh sent me on a journey to distant Kadath where I awakened many of my past lives. In them, I saw such things as to make the destruction of Earth and it's populace seem like a mercy killing."

I stared at him. "I'm so happy to hear that."

"There are other places than this world," August said. "Dreamlands made in the image of Earth and even parallel versions of this world. The past, the present, and distant realms where you could assume the form of a local to live out their lives. If you are so inclined."

"I am not," I said.

August rolled his eyes. "I knew you'd say that."

"Which is why you've wasted your efforts and my time," I replied. "Something that I no longer have much of."

"A strange condition for an immortal being," August replied. "That is, unless he is set on ending himself."

"Death holds no mysteries for me," I snapped.

"How can it when it is an end?" August said. "Life is an illusion and even if consciousness can be picked up by future generations or preserved like a fly in amber amidst the streams of time, how can it be said to be the same thing as it was? The soul is extinguished every second of the day, constantly changing like a river, and it is an interrupted continuity of consciousness every time we go to sleep, let alone die. Life as we know it is but a particular form of insanity that we delude ourselves in having value. Like your whore in there or faux grandchild."

I was tempted to put two rounds into August's stomach and make a pithy line about agreeing his life had no value. Certainly, it wouldn't be the first cold-blooded murder I'd committed just because some fucker had annoyed me. However, I wasn't in the mood for whatever reason. August was his own creature and had never pretended otherwise. Maybe honesty was his one redeeming quality, if it could be called that.

"Then get the hell out of here," I said, making a dismissive wave.

"If it's any consolation, I contacted the forces of the Arkham Republic," August said. "They have weapons that can lay waste to this particular strand of evil. Shells, tanks, flamethrowers, and disposable fools that think themselves to be heroes by throwing themselves into the jaws of monsters."

The Arkham Republic was what the United States Remnant had renamed itself after, ironically, losing New Arkham. They'd spread out into the Wasteland and used their weapons to take over Kingsport, Scrapyard, and a dozen other locations. They were driven by a perverse Manifest Destiny that was even more delusional than believing we had a chance here.

Because they could not accept that humanity was doomed, they sought to conquer and reunite as much of the East Coast as possible. They'd already run into unbreakable walls with the Dunwych tribal nations and the Miskatonic cultists, but they had established dozens of trade routes. There was even talk they'd activated an old power plant managed by ghouls and were laying down track for a revived train system. Not that such a thing was a sane project with things like tunnelers and beasts the size of ruined skyscrapers.

"My daughter and son are New Arkham citizens," I replied. "The ones by blood."

"And doomed to become monsters themselves?" August asked. "I hope they're not stupid enough to join the military like you. Mind you, I would have told them of their destiny. Do they even know you're a monster?"

I didn't answer him.

"How strange you so readily leap to death at the hands of the Undying King but are too cowardly to confront your real family about their coming doom," August said.

I had been married to a woman named Martha prior to my exile from New Arkham. She was a psychic and, at the time of our prearranged union, had been the "freak" of our pairing. We'd had two children, Gabriel and Anita, who had been left behind when I was forced to walk the Wasteland for the crime of surviving an attack no human should have. I loved my children, but I was a catastrophe that had come into their lives. They'd been doomed before they'd even been born, and I simply hoped they were not actually my children or somehow the curse of my alien blood would pass them.

"They would not appreciate a monster," I replied. "Better I stay out of their lives than infect them with the alienness I bring."

"So speaks a man given the keys to heaven and immortality yet complains that they are silver not gold," August replied.

"What?" I asked.

"The look on your face," August said. "Romanticizing humanity and death as if they were things that were worth doing so. Humans are ugly bags of water and meat that smell terrible after just a short time in the sun. They were one of evolution's mistakes and nature is now correcting that delusion."

I smiled and patted him on the shoulder. "I'm going to miss you, August. Some of the time we spent together was almost enjoyable."

August frowned then shrugged.

"Goodbye, John. Before I take my leave, I wanted you to know that there were some Dunwych looking for you."

"I guess they're just out of luck," I said.

"Perhaps," August said. "But I have the feeling you will survive this. The question is will anyone else?"

Chapter Three

I wish I could say that August became a giant eagle, disappeared in a puff of smoke, or even slipped into the shadows. Magic was often dramatic like that, at least since the Reveal, but I just looked away for a moment then turned around to find he was gone. It was said the Kastro'vaal could slip through time and space like that, part of their relationship to Yog-Sothoth, but it was a trick that I couldn't do.

I knew a little magic, a few tricks that I'd picked up from Mercury and the late Alan Ward, but nothing that could mark me as a wizard. It was ironic because as a monster, I probably could do things regular human beings would be torn apart by due to the forces they were channeling. Assuming any regular humans still existed.

Gods and Old Ones, I never stopped complaining, did I? Maybe August was right that I did lionize mortality and humanity more than both deserved.

Heading to the walls that had been erected around as much of the main part of the town as possible, I checked that they were properly secure. They weren't, being made of nothing more than welded together pieces of steel that were as fragile as a wire fence. The people gathered on the platforms—our seventeen—were a mixture of the elderly and the too young. People who had very little to live for or too little experience to know they weren't invincible.

Beyond the walls of Ulthar was a massive mud flat that in better times would be able to grow blood grass. Blood grass was one of the things, like mushrooms, that mankind had been reduced to eating almost entirely due to the inability to digest most other mutated plants. Most plants and animals that humanity had once subsisted on were almost extinct now. We lived on mutated cattle, this peculiar type of weed, things grown in our own shit or corpses, and a handful of other unappetizing things. Now the blood grass had all been harvested and it would be a few more weeks before the next crop arrived, leaving only an endless sea of blackish sludge.

The farms and ranches that tried to grow other than these things were behind us and I wondered if the Yellow Raiders would hit them first. Somehow, I doubted it. They didn't come here to slaughter animals, but the people inside, as little difference existed between humans and their beasts of burden. No, the Undying King seemed only to want to extinguish the race of man and its various offshoots wherever he found it. Or she. Truth be told, I had no idea whether the Undying King was a man or a woman. I'd met plenty enough she-cats and wild women who were every bit as vicious as a man.

In the end, no longer waiting for me back at the Wages of Sin where I'd left them, the rest of our meager posse assembled as the rain went from a drizzle to a full downpour. In the skies above our heads, I could see a strange aurora of weird colors and new stars that reminded me that the world was getting stranger rather than more normal. I wasn't even sure if we could still be a living world anymore. Sometimes I wondered if we'd died at some point, and this was just Hell. It bothered me that I couldn't really find any coherent points to refute my musings.

Mercury came up by my side as everyone else assumed what positions they could.

"I don't suppose you have any tricks left?"

"I radioed for help," I replied. "No response from the Dunwych. The Miskatonic cult flat out said no."

"What about New Arkham?" Mercury asked.

"August apparently took care of that," I replied. "No dice. I think they'd kill everyone here if they somehow defeated the horde."

"You're exaggerating," Mercury said. "They'd give everyone a blood test first and then slaughter all the mutants as well as hybrids. There would be at least one or two children spared. Just not Baby John. Oh, and maybe they'd keep a breeding female or two."

"We were definitely working for the wrong side," I replied, keeping my gaze focused forward on the mud flat. I could feel this was the direction they were coming.

"There is no right side," Mercury replied. "There's just winners, losers, the living, and the dead."

"A very convenient philosophy," I replied.

"The living can afford to debate morality," Mercury replied. "The dead don't have to."

"Morality is usually about rules for keeping you alive and making sure you don't destroy any long-term gain for short-term benefits," I replied. "Also, to provide meaning in a senseless world."

"You know, August is right. You are a depressing bore."

"You're only now picking this up?" I asked.

Mercury chuckled. "So, I'm going to take that as a no on the tricks."

"I'll turn into whatever kind of monster I can," I replied. "But I can't beat an army by myself."

"You killed a shoggoth once," Mercury said. "With magic pistols."

"I got lucky," I replied. "There's not a lot of that to go around. How about you?"

Mercury stared. "I have what magic I could prep."

"What was the cost?" I replied.

"Don't expect to see Old Man Jim Joseph again," Mercury replied. "I saw him trying to leave while his grandkids were holed up in his cellar. His blood didn't exactly give me much to work with, but it was better than nothing. Nodens will provide, though."

I didn't respond, simply noting that I couldn't bring myself to condemn her for what amounted to human sacrifice. At this point, desperation had blotted out most of my old morality and I was willing to forgive almost anything of Mercury. Which was already much as we'd both wronged each other horribly.

"What about Baby John?" I asked, feeling the anticipation in every drop of freezing cold rain.

"Sue is looking after him until we're all horribly murdered," Mercury replied.

"We're trusting the baby to an old blind seer?" I asked.

"I don't think that's the biggest problem we're facing right now," Mercury said. "Besides, if she has any problems, she'll definitely see them coming."

"Unless she offers the baby up to Yog-Sothoth," I replied.

"That's ridiculous," Mercury said. "Yog-Sothoth prefers young, virginal maidens. So, me and Jackie are out."

"Do ancient gods really care about the sexual status of sacrifices?" I asked, not turning from the mud flats but glad for any distraction. "I somehow imagine a guy that occupies all of time and space simultaneously has better things to do with its time."

"Probably not," Mercury said. "As the old joke goes, throwing a virgin in a volcano probably didn't stop any eruptions but was very useful for getting women to loosen up."

I rolled my eyes. "The really sad part is that I'm pretty sure there are plenty of religions that actually had that as a motivation."

Mercury leaned her head on my arm. It was a rare intimate gesture for a woman so guarded. Even if we were effectively husband and wife, as much as such a thing existed without laws or religion to bind us, she kept a close guard on her emotions.

"When I was still a doctor, I had some mild psychological training."

"I wonder what the training for 'go mad from the revelation' was," I replied.

"Drugs, hypnotism, brainwashing, and a bullet to the brain in that order," Mercury replied. "But no, there was a condition called apophenia that always intrigued me. It's the condition of seeing patterns and meaning where there isn't any."

"Like omens in the wind or rain," I replied.

"I'm not sure that's the best example as this storm seems to be following the Undying King," Mercury replied, "but yes. People wanted to find an inherent order to the universe in hopes that they could deduce the secrets of these patterns. Knowledge is power and all that. A belief the gods and immortals cared about every little thing ranging from who you fucked to what you should do when a woman was bleeding."

"And there is no pattern," I replied.

"None that this universe cares about," Mercury said. "No god cares about mortals. Any more than you or I care about ourselves. Whenever a sacrifice is offered to one of the Old Ones' creatures, if they notice at all, it is someone just ringing the dinner bell."

"There's one," I replied.

"What?"

"One god who cares about the activities of mortals," I replied. "Like a child with a magnifying glass who names each and every ant that burns."

"You knew some screwed up kids," Mercury replied, noticeably not asking which god I meant.

We both knew.

An oppressive silence filled the air as Old Man Caruthers coughed, having caught an infection of the lungs that I suspected would kill him within a few months. Perhaps that had contributed to his decision to defend the town, or maybe he was one of the few people who realized it made no difference whether we fought or fled so we might as well die with our boots on. Perhaps I also misjudged some of these men and women and there were at least some among them who believed they could spend their lives to buy more time for their children.

I had a deeply pessimistic view of mankind, but sometimes they displayed a wild and tremendous form of madness that justified their delusions of eloquence as well as courage. Good did not exist save as a salve on the ultimate futility of life but it was a beautiful idea. Perhaps the saddest thing about the extinction of mankind was not the actual loss of its people but that all this wonderful madness would be forgotten.

My name is Ozymandias, King of Kings;
Look on my Works, ye Mighty, and despair!
Nothing beside remains. Round the decay
Of that colossal Wreck, boundless and bare
The lone and level sands stretch far away.

Except it seemed almost silly to compare humanity to the Pharaohs of old when much grander and more powerful species were ending around us as well. The Deep Ones, Yith, tunnelers, serpent men, and ghouls would all be joining us in annihilation. I did not believe they would survive this epoch any better than us. The entire universe was collapsing.

"I miss Jessica," Mercury said, interrupting my increasingly frequent ruminations on the end of everything.

"You hated Jessica," I replied.

Jessica O'Reilly had been a fellow R&E ranger from New Arkham and was my best friend. I'd been more than a little in love with her back during my human days, but she'd been married, widowed, and someone I'd treasured too much to try to have an affair with. She'd tried to kill me after my inhumanity all but consumed me, but I didn't hold that against her. I think Mercury held it against me that my feelings for her had always been different than mine for Jessica's.

"No, Jessica hated me," Mercury said. "She thought I was a bad influence."

"How so?" I asked.

"That I encouraged you to embrace being a horrifying monster," Mercury said.

"You didn't," I replied, remembering how she'd chosen not to have our child.

"What is good for me is not good for you and vice versa," Mercury said. "I know you can't go back to what you were. She thought you could."

"I would if I could."

"Then we'd all be dead," Mercury said. "Now we're just going to be dead later."

"We're always going to be dead later."

"Not for some beings," Mercury said. "Perhaps if I was a stronger magician or you knew how to share some of that immortality."

"I don't, though. I'm sorry."

"Believe me, I am too," Mercury said. "I'm just glad you'll be there to remember us all when the Earth is no more."

That was no comfort at all and was why I was happy to die here. I wasn't able to respond, though, because we were interrupted by an ominous fog rolling in across the mud flats. In the mist, I could see shadowy figures on horseback start to emerge, one by one. The rain intensified and I was glad of my hat. Thunder and lightning accompanied the arrival of the Yellow Raiders as if they were the legions of some foul god, which they might well be.

"Prepare to fire on my mark!" I shouted, barely able to be heard over the din.

I could see some of the riders through the parting of the mist and it was hard to not want to flee at the sight. Their bodies weren't so much animated by the yellow fungus covering their bodies like a second skin and musculature but consumed by it, bizarre and disgusting pustules carrying the dread spores that I recognized as the Fungus that Eats. It gave the forces that were attacking us a nightmarish new dimension as I'd heard stories of these awful things before.

The Yellow Raiders were sporemen and they were directed by a single, unholy intelligence that crawled into the brain of each of these then operated them like puppets. It was a meat moss that ate the flesh of the living and yet could think, reason, and use tools. Sporemen were not so terrifying because of the plague they were to the living, —they were just one of a thousand horrible threats—but of what they represented. They were a sign of the way life was adapting to the brave new world we'd found ourselves in. Humanity had no future, but this crawling psychic evil that I could feel reaching out to touch my mind very much could.

Join us.

Be free.

No longer afraid.

Eternal.

The voices I heard in my mind were soft and melodic with a chorus of the dead. The images and whispers of the previous towns' victims were inside the gestalt and I couldn't help but wonder if they continued to live as a part of this alien hive-mind. However, if the choice was living forever as cannibal bread mold, I'd rather choose death.

"John, I don't think bullets are going to hurt these things," Mercury replied.

"No, they are not," I replied. "Fire would be good right now."

"How convenient there's a fucking rainstorm going on," Mercury muttered.

"Yes, convenient," I replied, pulling out my guns. "If you could work on that, that would be great."

"Because I'm a witch I clearly know how to control the weather," Mercury replied, sarcastically.

"Do you have any better ideas?" I asked.

"Not a one," Mercury replied.

That was when a single rider in black rode out, a burlap sack over his head, gloves on his hands, and a horse that looked like it was dressed in the skin of a dead one. There was a malevolence to the man wholly different from the sporemen descending on us like a funeral procession. Weirdly, when the Undying King approached halfway across the field, I could make out the sight of a half-circle drawn underneath the eyeholes. It added a bizarre comic element to the whole thing as I realized the leader of this necromantic army had drawn a smiley face on his death mask. He had a pair of pistols, a bandolier across his chest, and a rifle on his back that I immediately recognized as my own. Weapons I'd lost in my fight against the Unspeakable Horror.

"You have Mercury Takahashi, doctor, witch, and whore among you. You have John Henry Booth, the Living Death that Walks among you. Bring them out to us, that we may know them!" The voice sounded eerily like my own and could be heard as clear across the thunder and lightning ridden field as if the rider was standing right beside us.

"The Bible reference is cute," Mercury said, showing more knowledge of the subject than I expected. "However, I am offended you get an awesome title and I'm just a whore."

"Also, a doctor and witch," I replied.

"Do you know this guy?" Mercury asked, not even bothering to look at the others who were already moving their guns to us except for Jackie. Even her boytoy looked like he was contemplating it.

"Try it and I will have the ground eat you," Mercury said, staring forward.

Everyone was suddenly interested in something else. Death at her hands was as certain as death at those of the horde's. Mercury had once made a man eat his own fingers and another take three days to die after spontaneously catching fire. Violence was the only language most people understood these days and Mercury spoke it well.

I looked between her and the Undying King.

"Yeah, I have a pretty good idea who it is."

"Who?" Mercury asked.

"Nyarlathotep."

Chapter Four

Nyarlathotep.

The god the Devil prayed to.

I couldn't tell you precisely what Nyarlathotep was any more than an ant could tell what a human being was passing over them. Some speculated he was a kind of gestalt psychic entity that the Old Ones used to communicate among their servitor races. Others that he was the son of Azathoth and Yog-Sothoth in an unholy Anti-Christian Trinity. Others still believed him to be a mortal being who rose to become a god in ancient Egypt or far off Delain—which explained his twisted fascination with mortal beings. Some even believed him to be Satan himself, which said something as that was by far the least esoteric and most provincial of explanations for his existence.

In truth, I had encountered Nyarlathotep multiple times in the past. The Other God had left his mark on me after I'd been left for dead by the late Alan Ward. I'd later summoned him with a spell from the *Necronomicon* and he'd responded, chatting with me in his form of the Black Soldier. I had no idea if I'd summoned the real thing, if such a thing existed, or what my mind believed the Other God would be like. Either way, he'd said he was the answer to human and other races' prayers for the universe to have meaning. A meaning that somehow explained all the horrible, terrible, awful things that existed. I believed him. It. Whatever you wanted to call the thing.

It was possible the Undying King was not actually Nyarlathotep. Nothing prevented anyone with the slightest bit of occult knowledge— and there were a massive number of "learned" religions these days despite humanity's dwindling numbers—claiming to be the god. However, something told me that this was the real thing. It was like a nightmare come to life and there was no escaping that he was the arbiter of my destiny.

That was when Mercury looked to me.

"I guess we better head out, huh?"

"I'm surprised you think that," I replied.

"Well, if we don't then they'll try to throw us down and then we'll have to kill everyone in town."

I stared at her.

"I like those odds."

"Yes, but it's a bit self-defeating," Mercury said. "Especially since the whole reason we're up here is to try to save everyone."

Mine wasn't. I was here to die killing as many of the sporemen as possible. That was another oddity to all this as I wondered why Nyarlathotep had brought such a creature with him. It wasn't like the god couldn't wipe us all out with a wave of his hand or a whisper. Heroes and fools had fought against the cults of the Old Ones for centuries but, honestly, had probably done nothing to change or alter the timeline of their rise.

"We thank you for your sacrifice, Sheriff, Doc!" Becky called over to us. "You truly are the best of us."

"Screw you!" Mercury shouted back.

"I promise to take care of Jackie!" Matthew shouted to us.

"You, too!" Mercury replied.

"Do you want me to come?" Jackie called.

"Fuck no!" Mercury finished what were possibly our last words to the townsfolk of New Ulthar before climbing over the side of the meager fencing we were holding fast behind.

I had to admire her bravery. No, it wasn't bravery. It was more calculated than that. Mercury knew that there was no way to survive by staying on top of the flimsy walls upon which we had erected our hasty defense. Just like I had expected death here, she had stayed behind because of a perhaps unjustified belief that I could pull victory out of the mists of nothingness. It was the mindset of a dedicated survivor and yet it had twists and turns that I could not follow. Yet, in my heart, I knew she was going to walk forward and confront a god because that was perhaps the only way she'd get through this alive.

She is not alive, a familiar voice whispered in my mind. *What was Mercury Takahashi died in the face of Cthulhu's presence. What is left is what you envisioned her to be and crafted with your spells. A corpse walker with a new soul crafted by Kastro'vaal magic.*

I remembered the ritual I'd conducted in Mercury's bedroom in the Wages of Sin, her catatonic form lying on a bed in need of its sheets being changed. I'd threatened the owner with a gun if he'd disturbed us and, in the end, killed him when he tried to buy her. The ritual had involved a human heart, a dozen cats in the room, and a brazier burning incense I'd stolen from a Cthulhu worshipper passing through.

The spell had been magic from the *Book of Eibon* and assembled from papers Mercury had kept under her room's floorboards that I had barely understood. Still, I knew enough to realize that the will behind sorcery was more important than the ritual. I had begged, pleaded, and finally commanded the ether to bring her mind back. I'd focused on what I knew of her personality, idealized and otherwise, then willed it to exist where the mere presence of Cthulhu's psychic imprint had washed it away like sand on a beach. It had worked and she'd opened her eyes with life behind them again.

Lies, I said. *She is who she was.*

No one is who they were. Nor can they ever be again. Life is a river, constantly shifting and changing substance while remaining predictably the same.

What do you want? I asked, watching Mercury and now uncomfortably aware it looked like I was leaving her to face the Undying King again.

You will find out, little Kastro'vaal. Death is a doorway but who says that it is one that lets in who you want? Nyarlathotep taunted. *Or maybe it is your concubine, and you will be betrayed by someone else you want back, my little necromancer.*

There was no response and I reluctantly crawled over the wall myself and jogged up behind her, still a decent way from the edge of the Lord of Chaos' forces.

"I see you're finally coming," Mercury said.

"I got caught up reminiscing," I replied.

"Probably about all the whores you're going to miss once I'm gone."

"We're not doomed yet."

"We were always doomed," she said. "Like Doc Holiday."

"He was a doctor, gunfighter, and brothel owner too."

"He also died of tuberculosis at age thirty-six."

I didn't quite know how many years old Mercury was but didn't think she was much older or younger. Time tended to get away from people these days since the Sun went up when it felt like it and went down erratically. It was the biggest proof the Earth had merged with the Dreamlands and arguably didn't exist anymore.

"He was a dentist, not a proper doctor," I said. "But I didn't want to bring that up."

"And I was a torturer," Mercury said. "Any tips for speaking with a god face-to-face? I've only spoken to them via prayer and ritual, which is to say I was talking to myself."

"They will kill you or spare you regardless of what you do. They are completely unpredictable, inhuman, and insane by human standards."

Mercury paused and I caught up with her, just ten yards away from the Undying King.

"You know he can probably hear us, right?" she asked.

"I imagine he heard our first breaths and is now listening to the sounds of our deaths an hour or a million years from now."

"Ah, so the best suggestion when talking to a god is not to bring you along."

"Probably."

That was when the Undying King stepped off his horse and looked at us. I couldn't make out his eyes underneath the sack, but the silly expression drawn on the sack made the whole thing seem even more surreal.

"Hello, John, hello succubus."

"I'm getting some distinct misogyny here," Mercury said. "I have a name, Man in Black."

"I have many names," Nyarlathotep said. "Many identities. Each stranger than the last. You should be glad that you are no longer a mere person, a candle flickering in the night. You are a dream of a monster consumed with loneliness and bitterness brought back to life. You won't be the last, though, but will be mother of a new race of monsters. Even as it seeds its black bastards across the Wastelands."

"If you mean, John, I know he's a lech," Mercury said. "He'd make me richer than Croesus if I charged him for all the play he's had between brooding and murder. But I am not his dream. I dream myself and right now I'm dreaming you're going to take this army of corpses out of here."

It was insane bravado and no more likely to be effective than screaming obscenities into a storm. However, I couldn't have been prouder of Mercury than if she'd thrown a harpoon at Cthulhu while quoting *Moby Dick*. If humanity died tomorrow—hell, if it died right now—it would be at least a defiant death in the face of the gods. Which, perhaps, was what Nyarlathotep had wanted from her.

"You have a hell of a bill for all the times you've been with me too," I replied.

Mercury gave me a sideways glare.

Nyarlathotep gave a deep, malevolent laugh that sounded like several people speaking at once, both male and female. Supposedly he was the horde of demons that Jesus has cast out into a herd of pigs while others said he was the Carpenter himself. I didn't think it mattered.

"What do you want, Dreammaster? Why did you lead this horde of the dead to our feet?"

"These?" Nyarlathotep waved back to the sporemen. "These are the rats that follow my piping song. They seek to know the music of the spheres and hear the whispers of my father Azathoth, as if it was not the gibbering lunacy of a blind idiot god. As for what I am doing, I am giving humanity that for which it begged."

"What is that?" I asked, wondering why gods always talked a great deal or not at all.

"To bring an end," Nyarlathotep said, his voice becoming all too much like mine. "The human race's dwindling elements do not wish to go with a whimper across generations but the bang of horsemen and armies of the damned. So, I am here to bring an answer to their prayers. The thundering of hoofbeats and an army of two hundred million."

I stared. "And if I were to stop you?"

"Do you wish to?" Nyarlathotep said. "Is life so good for someone who desperately wishes death himself versus an immortal life as a monster?"

Mercury stared at me with an accusing look, but it wasn't like it was something that she hadn't known before.

"Yes," I said, coldly. "I'd like that. I'll live a bit longer to save this village."

"Longer or forever?"

"Nothing is forever," I said. "Not even you."

"Clearly you don't understand time," Nyarlathotep said. "But as you wish."

I blinked. "What?"

"The dream is dictated by the sleeper and the sleeper has not awakened yet. I do not speak of Cthulhu or you, but others. I'll let you and your fictitious girlfriend survive to have some other stories to tell if you play the role others would have us play."

I shook my head. "I have no idea what the fuck you're talking about."

"John, not helping," Mercury muttered.

"The audience on the wall demands a story," Nyarlathotep said. "The Undying King versus the mighty sheriff and his deputy."

"I better not be the deputy," Mercury said. "Also, he's technically a marshal."

The Undying King chuckled. "How would you like to be immortal, Mercury?"

"Would it be one of those tricky Aesop forms of immortality like making me a rock or something?"

"Yes," Nyarlathotep said.

"Then no," Mercury replied.

"Then be silent," Nyarlathotep said.

Mercury glared.

"Are these games really worth it?" I asked.

"These games are as close as anything that provides this world meaning," Nyarlathotep said. "Without the stories whispered on Carcosa, the plateaus of Leng, the halls of risen R'lyeh, or the tombs of

Stygia then there would be no purpose to any of it. I am the narrator, and you are the characters."

It was the piss poor author who wrote themselves into a story. I'd learned that from a writer named Phillips in Kingsport.

"So, how do we give the audience a show?"

"A gunfight," Nyarlathotep said.

"You're kidding."

"Almost certainly," Nyarlathotep said, pulling his gun out. It was black as midnight and seemed to wiggle like a living thing. "But the joke is that if you don't then the horde behind me will pour over your little town and every man, woman, and child will meet their ends sooner rather than later."

"And if I win a gunfight with you then the town goes free?" I asked. "The army of the dead goes away?"

"I didn't say that," Nyarlathotep said. "My legion is made of the crushed consciousnesses of five thousand humans. It might live to populate the world after mankind is destroyed and colonize other worlds. Maybe it'll be demolished by you this evening. However, I won't be the one who leads it to end New Ulthar and its cats."

"Yes, the cats are clearly the ones who matter here," Mercury said.

"Versus their slaves, yes."

"God has a sick sense of humor," Mercury said. "So much makes sense now."

"Most of the gods do, yes," Nyarlathotep said. "After all, they are all faces I have worn. Maybe someday I'll wear yours, if I'm not already."

"So, we handle this high noon style, huh?" I said, hoping that the mad god was telling the truth. "Twenty paces turn and fire?"

"You can simply be the one to walk and turn," Nyarlathotep said. "Unless you're afraid I'll shoot you in the back."

"That wouldn't make a very good story, would it?" I replied, dryly. Nothing prevented the Crawling Chaos from simply destroying us at will. It wouldn't be a fight, no matter how many stories of mortals wrestling with gods there were. It would be like trying to battle gravity or the Sun, except even larger.

"It depends on the religion," Nyarlathotep said. "There are places where cunning and treachery are worshiped in place of fairness or honor."

"Yeah, I've been to most of them," I said. "Will my gun even hurt you?"

"No," Nyarlathotep said. "It might hurt the Undying King, though. You can't kill the god, but you can destroy the mask."

That was as close to a reassurance as I suspected I would ever get out of the monster. Admitted murderer of men, women, and children by the thousands—and those were just the crimes he committed within the past few weeks—it was hard to think of the Crawling Chaos as evil. It was the god that humanity and countless other races had asked for. It tended to the spirits in the Dreamlands of Ra, Vishnu, and the Nailed God along with the small gods of other races. Ones that were close enough to humanity to be actually worth worshiping. He was above good and evil because they were simply irrelevant to him. The same way as the morality of insects would be as inscrutable to those of monkeys or stars.

I pulled out one of my pistols—cheating if we were doing this Wild West style—and took twenty paces before spinning around to fire. He hit me first and I fell to the ground, massive pain in my chest from where I'd been shot. I'd made the stupid mistake of believing I could outshoot the Devil when it was his game.

That was when Mercury drew her pistols and unloaded into Nyarlathotep. The Undying King's entire body caught fire and exploded into piles of insects that spread across the ground as unholy screams escaped each of the thousands of little creatures crawling from his burning clothes.

That was when the sporemen started charging at us both.

"Shit," I said, what was possibly my final word.

Oh, and the sky started raining down fire.

Chapter Five

What followed was wild, chaotic, and insane as I pulled my other pistol and fired into the onrushing horde of sporemen. The Cthugha guns fired bullets made of flame and had an unlimited number of them. Mostly because it wasn't a gun but something else inside the weapons, taking the form of metal and steel while hungrily eating the living with its fiery venom. I chose deliberately to only see the image of the creature rather than the weapon as I unloaded into as many of the enemy as I could despite bleeding to death on the ground.

Each time I managed to hit one of the creatures, they burst into flame and screamed with the wailing of the damned as they were sent off to whatever oblivion awaited sporemen. The Fungus that Eats would keep a copy of the consciousness, if not the souls themselves, in even the tiniest sliver of their existence. It would eventually recover and devour this town unless every little bit of it was destroyed. Given I was dying, I didn't particularly think that was a likely outcome, but I was damn well going to try.

The insanity of my circumstances gave me a perverse sort of hope, though, as the sky continued to rain down fire on the army of the dead. Balls of flame and ruin landed like mortar around us, sending up piles of mud and steam. They were indiscriminate but seemingly centered over the mud flats, so the only victims were the attacking army and, well, us.

"Mercury, I don't suppose this is your doing!" I shouted, continuing to shoot as I experienced intense pain from the bullet that Nyarlathotep put into my stomach. It burned like a hot branding iron shoved into my gut.

"Not unless it's divine punishment for shooting a god," Mercury shouted, slinging lightning as a circle of flame burned around us in a protective ring.

"Could be!" I shouted, thinking it was more likely a parting gift from August from a safe distance. "Now would be a good time for some Johnny Cash!"

"John, shut up!"

An undead horse ignored the protective circle and pushed itself forward, causing its body to burst into flame and become akin to a vision of Hell. The creature thrashed above my head and lifted its hooves to crush my skull. I gave it both barrels, a term I'd always wanted to say, before it exploded into burning chunks. I wondered how it had managed to get through the circle, one powered by the might of the Elder Gods, and realized that it had been Nyarlathotep's horse.

I was close to passing out—a state I wouldn't wake up from—when I saw the sporemen start moving around the protective circle. The Fungus that Eats was not going to keep its focus on us, the only people giving it any sort of fight. It sought to now wash over New Ulthar while we were trapped in our present position. Perhaps it knew that I would leave our limited protection to try to save everyone.

I kept trying to fire into the heavy rain and throng of horrors surrounding us while Mercury futilely threw her spells into the ranks of the Fungus that Eats. We destroyed dozens of the creatures, but there were hundreds—if not thousands—gathered around us. It was like pissing into the wind and I soon found myself having to cover my stomach with one hand, barely able to stand. The bullet was burning through my essence, the creature I was that existed in other dimensions, not just the four that humans dwelt in.

"I have to go," I muttered, unable to cross the flames any more than the rest of the horde could. The circle prevented me from leaving as assuredly as it prevented any of the sporemen from crossing.

"John, don't be stupid!" Mercury shouted. "You'll die!"

I reached my fingers into the wound, feeling staggering agonizing pain as I opened it further to grasp the bullet killing me. It was like grabbing hold of a burning coal, but I managed to keep my fingertips around it until I pulled it out then tossed it into the flames. I almost passed out then and there but lost my sense of slowly burning to death. I was injured but not dying, crippled but alive. At least if I could get the injury sewn up.

Probably.

"Jackie is out there!" I cried out. "We can't abandon her!"

"Does this look like abandoning her?" Mercury said, sweat and rainwater having soaked her even as her hands burned from the supernal powers that she had channeled to try to end this horror.

"I can take more of them down," I said, hearing the pitiful sounds of gunfire in the distance. Weapons that were all but useless against the sporemen and would do little but make noise as the horde overrode them. "I can become the monster!"

"You killed Jessica when you became the monster!" Mercury cried out. "You can't control yourself during it!"

It was like a blow to the stomach, more so than the pulsating wound I was already feeling. I had denied and lied to myself repeatedly about that terrible night in New Innsmouth. I had given myself to the beast within, the alien creature that was the last of his kind in this dimension, in hopes that I could control it. That I could wield it as a weapon against a host of Dagonite Deep Ones purists that had been massacring a community of hybrids.

When I'd awoken, I'd been surrounded by a dead community. I'd slaughtered the attacking army to the last squamous horror, leaving their entrails scattered and their skulls dashed against the ruins of their conquest. My blood rage did not limit itself to the conquerors and murderers, though. It was not that kind of story.

The beast within was not a force for good, it was the mad predator of a different world trapped within the body of another world's vermin. A mouse containing a lion. I had slaughtered my team who had stayed to fight for a people that were reviled by the humans and purebloods of R'lyeh both. I had slaughtered the people who we'd come to defend. Butchered the people who'd fought by my side to defend them.

I was a monster.

"Let me go," I said, whispering. "I can stop this."

"John! Stop trying to kill yourself!" Mercury said. "It's not going to do anyone any good."

I held my gun tight, my finger on the trigger as a kind of madness overcame me. This was my chance, regardless of how little sense it made, to rewrite the past. If I destroyed the sporemen here, then I could save the people I'd gotten killed. I had a whole bunch of lives on my conscience I could name: Jessica, Thom, Stephens, and so many others that I'd choke if I attempted to speak all their names.

"Let. Me. Go," I enunciated each word.

"Are you going to shoot me?" Mercury asked.

No, I wasn't going to shoot her. The thought briefly crossed my mind as the only way to lower the flaming circle around us. I was mad, desperate, and suicidal, but not so much to the point that I would repeat my past. Without Mercury to anchor me to this last lingering remnant of my humanity, I would kill everyone here. If I woke up beside Jackie and Baby John's corpses, then I might as well be like the Fungus that Eats: a creature that would put to death every human it encountered.

That was when a bolt of lightning struck downward against one of the sporemen and it made me realize what I'd been missing. Looking at the flames, I concentrated on the lie of my humanity and walked forward. Magic was mind over matter, will over reality, dream over physics. There were no limits to the level of what it could accomplish any more than a writer was limited in what he could accomplish by putting words on a page.

I was not naturally a wizard, nor a witch like Mercury who exalted in the power of sorcery. She would sell her soul and devote herself to it in order to be able to work miracles. But I was a monster and came from a people for whom magic was as natural as breathing.

Perhaps if humankind had more time, they would have evolved into something similar. The talent for dreaming showed that they had the potential. Combined, monster and dreamer, I was able to construct a very simple spell and made myself human for the second I needed to step through the flames. They did not burn me any more than they would any other mortal that called upon the Elder Gods to protect them. Beings that did not exist until mortals had dreamed them up as a defense against the things in the dark.

"Killer!" I shouted, holding my one pistol in both hands. "I know you! Face me!"

Far in the distance behind me, I could hear the mines that Jackie had placed blow up and take out a couple of dozen more sporemen. The sporemen were also stopped cold for the moment by the fact that the metal sheets erected around the town were covered in the squiggly star of the Elder Sign. It was almost humorous that whatever time was bought to save my little village was due to a few scratches with a knife.

I knew it wouldn't stop them for long, but I was pleased to see them dump every bit of oil in the town over in barrels onto the sporemen before lighting them up. It created a brief moat over part of the town's barrier that continued to destroy more of the murderous fungus. However, unless they burned every bit of it, their toxic substance would rise up to infect them all.

I gunned three more down with my pistol, wishing I'd brought the other one but only able to keep my guts inside because of the hand holding them in. Even so, I could tell the sporemen were ready to swarm me and there wasn't a damn thing I could do about it.

"Brilliant plan, John!" Mercury called from beyond the fire. "You clearly have thought this through!"

"Not helping, Mercury!" I shouted back.

"I feel my last words to you should be bemoaning your stupidity!" Mercury said.

"I know what I'm doing," I said, lying. "It wants to fight me."

I had no idea what the Fungus that Eats wanted, but I could feel it all around me, its consciousness diffused among the hundreds of corpses remaining. Two or more for every single man, woman, and child in New Ulthar, but all centered around one single will. I could hear that will speak, its voice a cacophony of entrapped spirits forced to speak as one but not quite managing it. Instead, it sounded like five or six spirits speaking one after another with different inflections.

You must be destroyed.

All must die.

A new world will be born from death.

I knew I had its attention now and concentrated on trying to speak to it, backing my next words with every ounce of will in my body.

"These people want to live. All you can do is kill them."

They will live through me.
Life is not good as a human.
We must survive.

It was hard to argue with such simple logic once you rearranged reason around the parameters of survival at all costs. It was, after all, the most primal of drives. If you couldn't survive then it didn't matter if you were good, evil, mad, or sane. Lately, sanity was in short supply and as I found myself surrounded by more sporemen as they prepared to tear me apart, I suspected I wasn't adding to it.

I struggled to change in that moment, to become the monster who would tear into all these creatures but leave his loved ones alone. I almost laughed but was in too much pain and aware that the horde was going to tear me apart in seconds. Nyarlathotep's bullet had been more esoteric than practical. As I'd prepared to die heroically as a human, he'd taken away my power to change to a monster.

At least for a time.

"You will not," I replied, looking through the dimensions of man and monster. I may not have been a monster anymore—a decidedly less than comfortable realization right now—but I still had the Sight. That was as much my birthright as any power or secret tentacles.

All around me, I saw the various sporemen crying out with hidden faces and screaming souls. They were all entangled by a psychic web, though, that reached back to a single obese, armless sporeman in the center of the horde. I briefly wondered what his story was. How had he become the first of the creatures to be incorporated into the Fungus that Eats. Was he a good man, bad man, or simply an insane man who'd been blessed as well as cursed with transformation into a monster? What had compelled him to try to absorb all his fellow men? And what role had Nyarlathotep played in it?

I found that I didn't care as I aimed through the descending monsters that piled onto me, one last shot at where I saw all these myriad consciousnesses linked, and pulled the trigger. It was a long shot but one I hoped would prove to be the head of the beast. My bullet struck home and the heart of the Fungus that Eats exploded into flame while the others all reared up at once as if they were the ones on fire.

Pain beyond imagination spread through the collective as they were released from the control of the psychic parasite who had created their foul existence.

They didn't all fall to the ground, but they started attacking each other and running in different directions. The central guiding intelligence that had driven them to want to consume the remains of humanity was lost. All that was left were mad, hateful, pained corpses animated by alien mycelium. I felt dirty teeth and hands claw at me even as I fell to the ground under the pile of monsters above me.

It was not the death I wanted, oblivion losing its appeal no sooner than it was upon me, but there was a kind of poetic justice to it all. I'd managed to stick my finger into the eye of the Devil—or at least some fool playing it—one last time.

I didn't know if the meager posse could keep fighting the now-decapitated Yellow Raiders, but I'd done my part. Nothing, not even hunger, motivated them especially against humanity's bitter remnants. Only mindless malice and the desire to reproduce sent forth the once-human throng now. Emptying my gun into more sporemen and feeling the flames licking me as they were blown away by one last spell, I finally lost consciousness. My last memory was Mercury calling upon Yog-Sothoth, the Hebrew God, and another power before a terrifying wave spread out.

I awoke, much to my surprise, with bandages wrapped around stitched wounds and lying on a nasty mattress that reeked of human waste as well as the alcohol used to purify my injuries. It was extremely well-done, implying Mercury had done it, but I did not understand why I was abandoned since this was my room at the Wages of Sin. Except the door was boarded over and there was no sign of life around me.

I did not see any sign of New Ulthar's survivors. The town was normally full of life, and I could not hear anyone around me. Climbing to my feet, seeing a jug of well water beside me, I chugged it down and crawled to the window. There was no sign of the sporemen, but the town was dead.

Empty.

Lifeless.

"What happened here?" I asked, staring out.

"Your lover called upon the power of the Other Gods," Nyarlathotep whispered.

He had taken the form of Mercury. I saw her cold, lifeless face in the reflection behind me.

"She sacrificed the whole of the town to save your life. A few survived like those exploding mines in the distance but the bulk were burned as fuel for magic."

My blood ran cold.

"No," I said.

"Yes," Nyarlathotep said, chuckling. "I love testing humans. You never cease to surprise me."

"I am your plaything," I replied. "Not her."

Nyarlathotep laughed. "All life is my plaything, John."

The god vanished. Then I was alone.

Unaware if the only people I cared about were still out there and unsure if they were monsters worse than the creatures who'd preyed on my home.

The End

"The Final Judgment" is the epilogue to the Tales of Nyarlathotep. *It's more of a sequel to the opening story, really, than a story of its own sake but nicely demonstrates the proverb, "Be careful what you wish for." Apophis Zul should have known that you can't conjure up the Great Old Ones or Outer Gods and make them obey your will. At best you can ring the dinner bell and at worse, you should expect them to destroy the world. You just had best hope you're consumed first.*

THE FINAL JUDGMENT

Nyarlathotep finished his last story and Apophis Zul found himself shaking off the visions he'd seen as if coming from a deep sleep. Nyarlathotep had been changed by the experience, his face no longer rotting but now looking like it was constructed from obsidian and the rest of his body as rigid as a sarcophagus' art. Yet, despite this impossibility, he moved as if a living man and Apophis Zul was briefly reminded of the time he could still believe in wonders.

It was a fleeting feeling, though, because such a time was long ago. He had seen magic that would make the sanest man go mad, climbed distant shores, and witnessed brutalities that would turn the so-called worst of mankind squeamish. His blackened heart had been opened to the mysteries of the universe long ago and instead of being frightened like a monkey fleeing a storm's thunder, he had craved more.

Seeing that Nyarlathotep awaited his reaction, Apophis Zul felt emboldened and stood up from the ground. If the Crawling Chaos desired to tell him so many stories, then surely, he was a man of importance and could risk trucking with the god as a peer if not an equal. He would not have wasted so much time on a being he viewed as without value, despite his words.

"Is that it?" Apophis Zul asked, waving his hand.

The stories themselves didn't impress him. If they were meant to horrify or amaze, then the Black Pharaoh had severely underestimated his audience. Apophis Zul remembered when, centuries ago, he had been born to one of his father's many slave concubines. He'd strangled his mother when he was twelve to eliminate the reminder of his cursed human heritage then poisoned all his father's true-born children with a Yig princess.

Apophis Zul remembered when he'd offered up his own lover's heart to the altar of Seth to prove his loyalty, and trapping the only one of his offspring that he'd ever cared for in a tomb with a host of jackals lest the man overthrow him. It would require a far more surreal group of stories than the ones presented here today to cause his knees to shake.

Apophis Zul had come here and offered up poor Narmer to be the host for the Many-Faced God in hopes of a genuinely impressive miracle. This seemed more like a collection of nomad campfire tales and the ramblings of old women to children. He wanted the secrets of how to destroy his enemies and rule the ashes as a proper god king. Nyarlathotep might allow himself to waste time playing with insects, but Apophis Zul was no scarab on the ground to be crushed underfoot but the greatest wizard of an age! Of any age! Men should worship him!

Nyarlathotep's expression, being literally made of stone or at least something stone-like, was unreadable.

"Is what it?"

"These stories," Apophis Zul said, risking a dismissive wave. "These children's tales. Old men and women fleeing from the sight of their own shadow. Fools thinking that they can stab a god and draw blood."

"It depends on the god, really," Nyarlathotep said. He rested his head on the palm of his hand, propping his arm up on the armrest by its elbow. It was such a human gesture that Apophis Zul briefly forgot he was not dealing with a mortal man. "In my mind's eye, I see the sons of Yog-Sothoth banished by a mortal scholar speaking words from the writing of a mad Arab who will not be born for millennia but is long dead by their time. I see in your past a lusty Cimmerian cutting through things your ancestors worshiped and his ancestor cutting through yours. I see in the far future, an Old Crow, Titus his name, riding around in a flying coffin as he unmakes the works of the Great Old Ones in a reality where they are as petty as men. I—"

"Enough *gibberish*!" Apophis Zul shouted before his heart seized up in absolute fear at what he'd just done. If he could have killed himself in that moment, he would have, for fear of what might have been done to him, but he was too paralyzed with terror to do so. Besides, if an afterlife existed outside of those dreams produced by mortals, he would not be able to escape his master's wrath.

"Am I boring you, Apophis?" Nyarlathotep asked.

"No, no, my master," Apophis said, almost choking on his words.

"Good," Nyarlathotep said, his voice even more amused and mocking than normal. "After all, we have a pact to consider."

In all the strange stories of distant worlds, times, and horrors, Apophis had almost forgotten the wish that his master had promised him if he could pass his test. Given it was the single most important thing in his long existence, Apophis could only blame the fact that Nyarlathotep's voice had been so mesmerizing that it had slipped his mind. Indeed, it had seemed he had been lost in the experience to the point that he did not entirely feel of this world during the tales. Apophis, even now, could not focus on anything but the Outer God himself.

"Yes, our pact," Apophis said. "You were going to test me."

"Yes," Nyarlathotep said, almost daring Apophis to back out but there was no power gained that did not require risk.

"Test away!" Apophis said, straightening himself. He felt stronger and more alive than he had in centuries with none of the decay even the Yithians started to feel after so many millennia of life. They were not immortal—contrary to their own claims—but merely ageless to the short-lived apes they shared some blood with.

True eternal life required draining the youth and vigor of their own kind, which had resulted in them dooming themselves to be outbred by the monkeys outside. A necessary sacrifice, though, to keep the sorcerer kings like him alive. Few of their bloodlines still lived, though, and it was for that reason in part that Stygia had to live. Without it, they would be a scattered race and become impure as more of their kind bred with humans instead of their own kind. Indeed, it had already happened if he was honest with himself.

"You have listened to my stories," Nyarlathotep said. "You have gained insight that few other beings have ever been blessed with. Heard my actions from my own mouth, or at least the slave's body I puppet, so I ask: what is my purpose?"

It was a trick question for who could know the mind of a god? Apophis knew that Nyarlathotep lowered himself to speak to beings of mortal flesh with minds of limited reasoning. Even the greatest of Earthly beings, Apophis judging himself to be among them, was still among the world's smartest locust compared to his glory. Yet, Nyarlathotep would not give him a question he could not answer. Apophis was certain. No, the God of Chaos was one who would not find that sporting.

Unfortunately, the usual answers that Apophis taught to his followers did not seem sufficient. Apophis had claimed to know the god's mind so many times that he, himself, had sometimes believed it. But that was a lie. Apophis had taught that Nyarlathotep was the herald of the Outer Gods, that he wished to awaken the Great Old Ones to destroy the world, that he wished to elevate other beings to enlightenment, as well as a hundred other reasons. All of them ascribed a personhood or humanity—if Apophis were to use such a vulgar word—to a being that transcended such description.

Yet the stories the Crawling Chaos had shared were empty of any insights. Indeed, they were aggressive in their pointlessness. Nyarlathotep appeared as whatever the tales required: a demon, a god, a friend, a teacher, or a monster with the only consistency being his complete lack of consistency. Even that he was mad or completely unpredictable did not fit into Apophis' image of the being before him. There was a purpose to the Dark One, but it was akin to a child overturning a turtle to simply watch it squirm.

Apophis could not imagine how long he stood there, pondering the mysteries of the unfathomable, before he simply spoke the thought that rang the truest. "Because it amuses you."

"Is that the mask you wish me to wear?" Nyarlathotep asked, surprising his audience. "The god who tortures and lords over other beings simply because it can? Because that is power to you?"

"It is the god I see," Apophis admitted. "It is what all men do once they have no limits upon them."

"And yet I am no man," Nyarlathotep said.

"No," Apophis said. "But that is what I see."

Nyarlathotep's face remained unchanged, its face frozen into the mask it wore. "It is an answer."

"But is it the right answer?" Apophis asked, his hands shaking. They felt strange, lightweight, and he was surprised at how dreamlike this all was. He wanted to turn away from the god on the throne but could not.

"Who knows?" Nyarlathotep said, straightening in his throne.

"You do!" Apophis said. "Please, grant me the power to save Stygia!"

"I think not," Nyarlathotep said. "Besides, it no longer matters."

"No longer…matters?" Apophis asked.

"If it ever did," Nyarlathotep said.

"What do you mean?" Apophis asked, feeling strangely sick. He had held his breath in for far longer than he should and yet felt no shortness of it.

"We have been talking for a while as you would reckon things," Nyarlathotep said. "Look around."

"I don't understand," Apophis said, suddenly freed from Nyarlathotep's gaze.

"Nor will you ever."

Much to Apophis' surprise, the chambers around him were different. Instead of the pristine inner chambers prepared only for the highest of the clergy, it was now decayed and ridden with dust as well as grime. The entrance was buried over with debris and rubble. The only light was provided by a strange aura about Nyarlathotep himself that glowed in a spectrum Apophis had never seen before.

It was not his surroundings that caught his attention most, though. Instead, Apophis' eyes drifted down to a pair of robes rotted to rags around a brittle skeleton. Apophis did not need to wield magic to know that it was his own corpse. He was a ghost now, or something similar, having become nothing more than a spirit serving as an audience.

Apophis had died of thirst, starvation, and exposure long before this day. Possibly he'd been stabbed to death by the followers of Re'Kithnid, the fanatics finding their archenemy kneeling like a slack jawed peasant before an empty throne room. Apophis dismissed that because he hoped they would at least carry his body away as a trophy, but it occurred to him that the zealots might not have even recognized him. After all, how were they to have known the High Priest of Stygia from any other without his accruements of state or guards? It was almost comical in its pointlessness and, of course, that was the point. That there was none.

"How long?" Apophis asked, his voice losing all of its usual arrogance. He had been tricked and, for once, had no reply or bluster to paper over his own failings. Humility had been taught and it was a bitter lesson indeed.

"Long enough for Stygia to have collapsed into dust, be consumed by the desert, and be built upon as many times as long dead Acheron," Nyarlathotep said.

"And I am dead?" Apophis asked, already knowing the answer.

"You speak of such limiting things," Nyarlathotep said. "I am still speaking to you, so you continue to exist."

"And when you withdraw your attention?" Apophis asked, now simply dreading the answer.

"You will cease to exist," Nyarlathotep said. "Not that you exist now."

"You promised me a wish," Apophis said, clenching teeth that did not have any more substance than thought.

"Did I?" Nyarlathotep said. "Do you think promises bind me any more than they did you while you lived?"

"I want to be a god," Apophis said, clenching his fists. "To live forever and be free of all mortal constraints! To be as the Great Old Ones! To be as you! Eternal! Immortal! Infinite!"

Nyarlathotep shrugged. "Alright."

Apophis almost laughed at his good fortune. It was a reversal of everything that had happened before. "Truly?"

"Such a pedestrian wish and yet you keep making it every time we speak, no matter the story." Nyarlathotep waved his hand and let forth his power to sculpt reality as thought.

"What?" Apophis spoke his last word and died as he lived: ignorant and full of unwarranted hopes.

Apophis Zul vanished. He became a dream that spread throughout time and buried itself in the minds of Stygians, Aegyptians, and other peoples. Immortalized as the giant serpent who opposed light and the sun. Nyarlathotep briefly pondered whether Apophis Zul had been named after the dream he'd been turned into or whether he'd even existed once he'd become nothing more than a flight of fancy that would last for an eternity in the Dreamlands.

Nyarlathotep left the statue he'd made of poor Narmer's body for future historians to pour over before speaking to himself for one last time as he abandoned this incarnation of Earth. The Old Ones would rise soon and make short work of its humanity. It mattered little. There were worlds to explore, mortals to play with, legends to inspire, and secrets to whisper.

An infinite number.

Just as there were an infinite number of faces for him to wear.

And all the time in forever.

The (True) End?

I was invited to participate in David Hambling's Time Loopers *after that anthology was re-imagined from a science fiction series about time travel to being an anthology about time travel within the Cthulhu Mythos. Given the number of interesting uses of it in Lovecraft's own work, especially "The Shadow out of Time", I think it was a good concept. "Academic Legacies" is still set in the same world as the* Cthulhu Armageddon *series but before the Rising. You can probably guess who the ancestors of which characters are. It's also a crossover with Matthew Davenport's* Miskatonic University: Elder Gods 101.

ACADEMIC LEGACIES

I woke up with a start, my mind full of terrifying possibilities. I saw clawing, awful, and monstrous things pawing at the world. They ripped through the fabric of time, hungry, and desperate to get at this reality. I knew that only I could stop them and that I needed to do the unthinkable to do it.

Then I heard my boyfriend snoring. A quick survey of the room and the sight of the Randolph Carter adaptation of *They Came from Space* poster, the PlayStation 5 console I spent all night playing *The Drowning City* on, and my battered copy of the Simon *Necronomicon* next to an open box of pizza told me the origins of my nightmare.

I was inside my dorm room at Miskatonic University, at nine-thirty-five, which was late for getting up to do my job but not so late as I would make it if I hauled ass. I slid out of bed, I immediately started throwing on my underwear and bra before looking for a sufficiently clean t-shirt to accompany my ratty blue jeans.

"Oh, come on, Mercy, you're not even going to stay for breakfast?" Tommy spoke, turning his head to me. He was a smooth-headed black football player who, nevertheless, had ancestors who had gone here to Miskatonic University since Ye Olde Days. It was a point of pride that his family, the Tillinghasts, were old money despite the fact I was very much of an "eat the rich" mentality.

"You mean you running down to get Starbucks?" I asked, picking an *Unaussprechlichen Kulten* shirt. The German death metal band, not the ancient occult tome.

"I was thinking more Tim Hortons, but yeah," Tommy said, sitting up. "Will that old fossil really care if you're not there to sweep his floors?"

"I clean up after his experiments more than sweep floors, but yes, yes, he will," I replied. "Unlike you, I need this job to cover my tuition."

Doctor Chester Winfield was one of the best research scientists in the theoretical physics department. He's considered 'out there' on a campus with a history of weirdos, witches, and pseudoscientists. Much like my hometown of Salem, Massachusetts, Miskatonic University had leaned into a crackpot reputation to attract more funding. You wouldn't think an Ivy League college would need that kind of publicity, but apparently, not enough alumni had gone on to become sociopathic billionaires or Senators.

Thomas sat up and began getting dressed, neither of us having time for a shower. Such was campus life, and I doubted Doctor Winfield would care in my case. "Well, at least let me walk you to the old geezer's lab."

"He moved off campus last week, so I have to catch a bus. Also, he's my dad's age, so not *that* old," I replied, looking for the various books that I'd have to cram in between doing whatever Doctor Winfield wanted.

The things I knew about theoretical physics could fit into a thimble (I was here for an anthropology degree), but Doctor Winfield had hired me more or less sight unseen as his assistant. His demands were mild, and he seemed to have a significant influence around the campus despite the fact he wasn't known to have made any discoveries in the past decade. You didn't want to rock the boat with that kind of employer.

"Then let me drive you," Thomas said.

"Well, I can hardly argue with that," I said, putting my hair up into a ponytail. "How do I look?"

"Like a five-foot-two Eurasian girl who just got out of bed," Thomas said. "So, hot."

"You can at least say Japanese American," I said, glad he'd known whenever I asked that question; she just wanted reassurance. I didn't have time to put on my full-Goth look, but I hoped I could at least powder my face and apply my black lipstick on the bus.

Thomas rolled his eyes. "Yeah, on your mom's side. She's biracial too. Your families' roots are like mine. They go back deep. Salem deep."

I frowned. "You are way too interested in the fact I have a witch in my ancestry."

"Who is writing a book about it?" Thomas asked.

He had a point there. I wasn't even finished with my bachelor's degree, and I already had plans for my master's thesis that I would turn into a book once I graduated. I wanted to do a book about my Salem witch trial ancestor, of Keziah Mason. I had the theory she wasn't falsely accused but a brilliant satirist who had 'confessed' as a way to challenge the ridiculousness of the witch hunt. Her elaborate stories about dealing with the Black Man and writing her name in the *Book of Azathoth* became clever fiction.

So far, those few professors in Miskatonic I'd discussed my ideas which had been less than receptive, either believing the whole thing had been a case of hysteria or that my ancestor had been an evil witch. Those latter ones annoyed me because I would have thought Miskatonic U would have better standards than letting in the '*Dungeons and Dragons* is of the Devil' crowd, at least among the faculty. We were a respected academic institution, after all, occult history and parapsychology departments aside.

"Alright, let's get going," I replied, throwing my book bag over one shoulder.

"You know my ancestors used to be into quantum physics and extra-dimensional woo," Thomas said.

"You don't say," I replied, knowing he was about to start hitting me up for details on Doctor Winfield's research again. Thomas wasn't majoring in quantum physics, instead in engineering, but he'd still take the classes as an elective.

"I'm just saying maybe you could tell me a bit more about it," Thomas said.

"I don't *know* anything about it," I replied, rolling my eyes. "I'm strictly janitorial and coffee fetching."

Thomas frowned. "He should be trying to teach you about these things."

I stared at him. "He's building a portal to hell. He will harvest the energy there to solve the energy crisis."

Thomas stared, suddenly looking alarmed.

"I'm describing the plot of *Doom (2016)*," I said, rolling my eyes. "Seriously, you will believe anything."

"Don't joke about these sorts of things," Thomas said. "I know at least three professors who might consider that as a viable solution."

"Probably all students of Doctor Winfield. Listen, if you have such a hard-on for Doctor Winfield's research, why don't you just come with me and ask him about it?" I asked, stepping out into the hall. As usual, Nancy Dyer Dormitory was full of young women my age. It was full of chaos as everyone moved in and out between classes. I wasn't the only girl who'd spent the night with their boyfriends if the guy sneaking out of Marcelin Russell's room was any indication, but officially it wasn't allowed.

"Oh, I couldn't do that," Thomas said, looking a bit starstruck. "He's a legend in the field. It'd be like talking to Einstein."

"And if I brought Einstein doughnuts, I'd introduce you too," I replied.

That was when Sally McPherson, a buxom blonde girl on the cheerleading squad, walked up with her eyes displaying a thousand-yard stare. She moved like a zombie past Sheryl Mason (no relation-I think) and Meredith Johnson, who were my dorm mates and every bit as weird as Thomas about science and the occult. They were both pretty girls, but I didn't have time to focus on them.

"Mercy," Sally said, looking at me as if she was shocked that I was still alive.

"Yes?" I asked, wondering why she was talking to me. Of course, this wasn't *Mean Girls*, and it wasn't like there was a divide between alternative girls (as I viewed myself) and a cheering crowd. That was strictly high school nonsense. Still, Sally and I didn't exactly run in the same circles.

"Do you remember anything?" Sally asked.

"Anything what?" I asked, wondering if something had happened. Last month Marcelin was roofied and woke up at a Fraternity that tried to sacrifice her to Yog-Sothoth, or so the rumor mill said. Honestly, it was challenging to say what was true or not on this campus.

"Crud," Sally cursed like a five-year-old. "Okay, this is going to sound insane."

I really should have been more sympathetic, but Sally had other friends to turn to. "I really must get going. Can this wait?"

Sally took a deep breath. "I'm a time traveler, and Doctor Winfield has stolen my time machine. I think he's doing something terrible with it."

I blinked, then turned to Thomas. "Can she come with us in the car?"

Thomas nodded.

Now you may question my willingness to listen to Sally's obviously insane story as we all loaded into Thomas' cherry red 2020 Mercedes convertible, which was a fine ass ride, by the way. Well, there are a couple of reasons that I did so. One, Miskatonic University was full of some genuinely weird ass stuff. If time travelers were going to appear, they would do so here. Two, Miskatonic University drew a bunch of genuinely creepy ass people, me included. I believed in magic, aliens, and the alternative reality of dreams. Three, If someone was going to make up an insane story like this, you would at least get a laugh out of it and should hear them out until they asked for money.

"Okay," I said, taking the passenger's side while Thomas drove. Sally was in the back between us. "Tell us your story."

Sally looked around nervously as the car started, and we began our journey to Doctor Winfield's lab. It was on the other side of town, so hopefully, we had time to hear it. "It all started when I was in my senior year of high school."

"Was this the future or the past?" Thomas asked, treating this with the detached air of a clinical study.

"Really?" I asked.

"If she's from the future, it'll be interesting to see if the timeline is determinant or not," Thomas asked.

"It was the past but, like, the recent past," Sally said. "I was given an app by a guy in black who told me it could reset a single day."

"An app?" I asked, wondering if I heard that correctly.

"Something-something, only data moves through time," Sally said. "I didn't take him seriously at the time."

"And a *guy in black*," I replied. "Did he run a curio shop in Castle Rock?"

"Be serious," Sally said.

"I am being serious," I replied. "Demons are known to exist outside the space-time continuum."

"Let her tell her story," Thomas said, which annoyed me. I really hoped the prospect of sex with a time traveler didn't turn him on. That was a hard thing to compete with.

"I didn't believe him, but I accepted it because, hey, I didn't know about spyware at the time," Sally said. "However, it worked when I used it. It became my lifeline during my senior year. I went from being the weird overweight girl nobody liked to being the person who could say the right thing every time."

"How did time travel help you lose weight?" I asked, probably focusing on the wrong thing. But I wanted to know the physics of how this worked.

"The ability to redo everything helped me get in the right headspace," Sally said. When you know you can eat any amount of anything with no consequences, you eventually lose the urge. I also used it to improve my grades, win the lottery, and make sound investments to get my family out of that crud hole of a trailer we lived in. It worked so well I'm here on scholarship."

"I'd question the use of manipulating the fabric of existence for personal gain, but I have to admit I'd probably be using it the same way," I muttered. "You won the lottery?"

"Yeah, with like ninety other people," Sally said. "Still, it was better than nothing. I didn't try again because I didn't want to draw too much attention."

"Prudent," Thomas said.

"Is it really?" I asked. "She could have used that to prevent the train derailment in Ohio or stock market investments saving the planet, and instead she's using it like Hermione's Time Turner. Not that I approve of those books anymore."

"My parents never let me read Harry Potter," Sally said. "They said it was of the Devil."

"Uh huh," I replied.

"Does it reset to an exact moment of the day like *Happy Death Day* or *Groundhog Day*, or does it move back a day from the point you activate it?" Thomas said. "Like, theoretically, could you move back one day at a time for a long period."

"Are those movies?" Sally asked, confused by the question.

"Oh Goddess," I said, feeling a headache coming on. Discovering time travel was hard enough without the fact we didn't have a shared cultural reference pool to discuss it. Sure, I doubted it worked like in the movies, but at least that would give us some common data points.

"I've seen *Back to the Future*," Sally said. "I think. That's the one where they have the town that banned dancing, right?"

I took a moment to look out the side of the car onto Arkham, Massachusetts. It was a strange town, even to someone from Salem, with a mixture of the old and new blending uneasily. The old parts seemed far older than the four hundred years this part of America had been settled. The buildings had a kind of ancient aura that made even things constructed in the Forties feel like the coliseum in Rome, but it also had the trappings of a modern city of the future.

There was a miniature Silicon Valley along the riverbank, and it was beside historical landmarks where the town's Founding Fathers had debated whether to side with the British or Revolutionaries. Then there was the weird oily black Stonehenge lookalike and the *2001: A Space Odyssey* monolith that sure as hell hadn't been built by the local

Mashpee Wampanoag tribe. They had been here for supposedly tens of thousands of years. Possibly millions.

"So, you said Doctor Winfield took your magic phone," I said.

"Science, not magic," Thomas corrected.

"Don't start with me," I said. "We're well into Arthur C. Clarke territory here."

"Yes," Sally said. "That's when my boyfriend got ate."

Thomas stopped at a red light as we exchanged a look.

"I'm sorry, *eaten*?" I asked, suddenly feeling a lot more sympathetic to Sally. If any of this was true, I mean.

"By an invisible dog, yes," Sally said.

I opened my mouth to comment, only to close it. There was something about Sally's reaction that told me, however crazy it sounded, she at least believed it was the truth. "Go on."

"Buster Wilcox," Sally said, whispering. "He was an offensive lineman on the football team."

"No, he's not," Thomas said, driving again. "That's Jack Legrasse. Also, I would have heard if one of the football team had been eaten. Even at this school."

Sally shook her head on the verge of tears. "I'd been using my device a lot last October. College was incredibly demanding, and my grades were slipping. I'd offended people with my Beyonce costume for Halloween—"

"Please don't go into detail," I replied. "Ever."

"I attracted something," Sally said. "It chased me down, I fled into Buster's dorm room, and it smashed through the door his time. I rebooted the day, but it was too late. He'd been eaten body and soul."

"Ate his time," I said, staring at her. "By which—"

"He was gone," Sally said. "I can remember him, but no one else could. Not even his parents."

Something about the way she spoke and the pain in her voice convinced me that it was more than just something she believed. This had happened to her. "What did you do next?"

"I tried to destroy the phone," Sally said, sounding ashamed. "I put it in a glass of water, hit it with a hammer, and tried to toss it off the roof. None of it worked."

"Your phone was made indestructible by its future app?" I asked, jumping to conclusions.

"No, I just think it was a durable model. My grandmother bought me the waterproof one with a steel case," Sally muttered, highlighting the surreal nature of the story. "It was damaged, though. Not much, but enough to crack the screen and mess around with some of its insides."

"You didn't think just to erase it?" I asked.

"I wasn't thinking, okay! My boyfriend was eaten!" Sally practically growled. Her eyes briefly turned black, and I could see her veins bulge out. Then, just like that, they were back to normal. I wondered if I imagined it, but I wasn't prone to auditory or visual hallucinations—at least without at least four of Thomas' special cookies.

"Sorry," I said, regretting pressing her.

Sally stared forward blankly. "Anyway, maybe I didn't want to get rid of it. At least completely. I ended up doing what I promised never to do again."

"You tried to use it again," I said, figuring out where this story was going.

"Yes," Sally admitted, pausing. "I'd like to say I tried to use it to get back Buster or something noble, but I just became scared. Scared of trying to get through college without it. The results weren't pretty."

"Define not pretty," I replied.

"I have cancer now," Sally said, shocking me. "Stage 2. There's more wrong with me, but I don't think they have a word for it. I had to use the phone again to get the medical department from keeping me for vivisection."

I was 50-50, sure she was exaggerating. Still, I didn't need to be told the rest of the story. Despite her sheltered upbringing, Sally was a smart cookie. I knew what I'd do in her situation. "And you went to Doctor Winfield for help."

"Yes," Sally said. "I wanted to get him to repair it. Maybe figure out a way to reset time without me suffering from whatever the hell is wrong with me."

"And he stole it," Thomas said.

Sally stared forward. "Whatever happened to me has left me slightly off. Even if I don't remember, I can tell when the world is reset. Maybe it's all the exposure, or maybe it's what's wrong with me. Maybe it's something else, but I can sense when things are changed."

"How many times has it changed?" I asked, dreading the answer.

"Hundreds," Sally said. "He's using it way more than I ever did."

Doctor Winfield rented out an abandoned factory to conduct his experiments. I admit it should have been my first tip off the science experiments he was conducting were of the mad variety rather than the more mundane ones that made Miskatonic University most of its funding. Still, Grant and I had cleaned up the place pretty good, and it wasn't like we were dealing with the kind of stuff that needed a clean room. Except, if Sally was to be believed, we were dealing with goddamn time travel.

Pulling his Mercedes to a stop, Thomas and I parked it just outside the building's main entrance. A storm was brewing, and I would have called it cliche, but we lived on the coast of Massachusetts, so this was what you'd call Thursday. Still, there was something ominous in the air, and the hairs on the back of my neck tingled while my mouth went dry. The air was ionized, and there was something just plain weird about it all.

"Oh no," Sally said, burying her fingernails into the backseat leather. "He's starting another one of his experiments."

I stared at her, opened my mouth then frowned. "He shouldn't be doing that yet."

"Is he running his experiments already?" Thomas asked me as if the fact I hadn't told him was some sort of betrayal.

"He shouldn't be!" I snapped. "He only started this project a week ago! It should be months getting all the calibrations done."

I didn't know much about quantum mechanics, but he'd said as much.

"He has all the time in the world to compress into a single day or two," Sally replied. "Now the monsters are going to come."

Now when people say things like that, you should probably take them at their word. This would be the moment in a horror movie where you'd shout at the frigging *idiots* who proceed to go forward versus turning around the car and then leaving the state.

I also now realize all those braindead bimbos and their himbo jock friends who marched forward to certain doom in cinema were motivated by something more primal than fear: the undeniable urge to poke weird stuff with a stick. Like hell I would miss out on seeing whatever was going on. I was a Miskatonic alumnus born to run toward the surreal, regardless of the dangers. No wonder our species was doomed.

"Do you have any weapons?" I asked, thinking it was a ridiculous question. I should have known better.

"How long have you lived in Arkham?" Thomas asked, getting out of the car and heading to the trunk. "You should never go anywhere unarmed."

"I both love and hate this town," I said, watching Thomas open the trunk. "Whatcha got?"

"Baseball bat, golf clubs, and a cricket bat," Thomas said. "I call the baseball bat."

"Nothing stronger?" I asked.

"I'd rather not have firearms in my trunk if I'm pulled over," Thomas said as if that should be his primary concern. "The police see a rich armed black man, and they think drug dealer rather than Old Money citizen concerned about cultists."

"Cultists have been infiltrating the police since the Satanic Panic of the Eighties," I said. "I read that online."

"Hurry!" Sally said, staring at me. "Cut the power! Stop him!"

Sally's alarm was something I wasn't dismissing because the storm I'd initially dismissed as Massachusetts weather was now swirling around the rooftop of the warehouse. I was half-expecting a beam of light to shoot up in the sky like the end of every superhero movie.

"Cricket bat," I said, taking it from Thomas. "We can't cut the power because he's using an internal generator. So, I asked him if it was gasoline or propane, and he joked it was zero energy from the 8th dimension. Now I'm not sure it was a joke."

"Probably a good idea," Thomas said, hoisting up his aluminum bat as we headed into the warehouse.

I was so gung-ho to confront the supernatural for the first time. It never occurred to me that Sally didn't follow us.

The sight that greeted me on the other side of the warehouse's entrance was the kind of massive construction you'd see in a Hollywood movie set but an old-timey Universal Horror one rather than anything made in the present century. A lot of it wasn't strictly "science". It had a DIY garage quality to it, as if Doctor Winfield couldn't rely purely on cutting-edge technology to make his machine but had to put together some of his ideas from stuff ordered on Amazon.

The contraption that filled the whole lower floor of the warehouse centered around a sizeable tuning-fork-like device surrounded by glowing glass balls that filled with electricity and images that made me think they were receiving television feeds. Weird holographic images of monsters flickered in and out of the air around the tuning fork before I realized they weren't holographic images but free-floating living organisms.

The creatures were gross fleshy things with wings resembling a mixture of sea life with tumors. They seemed to move around with no means of propulsion other than telekinetic force. They also stank, which was difficult to put into words unless you could somehow imagine a locker room with rotting meat and cat pee all mixed together.

However, the creatures seemed to be getting more solid with each passing moment, writhing in either pain or ecstasy.

Doctor Winfield, a dirty blond-haired middle-aged man with a thick but not long beard, was standing at the control panel for the device. It had a bunch of old green and black computer monitors as well as a bunch of dials and switches like the set of the original *Star Trek*. He was seemingly ignoring the fact the room was rapidly filling with monsters, focusing instead on the readings he was getting.

"It's wonderful, Ms. Halsey-Mason!" Doctor Winfield shouted. "We have pierced the veil between this world and the world of the immortals! Space and time are no longer frontiers of the imagination! We are Orpheus to Hades! Alice to Wonderland!"

You'd think my first moment of being confronted with proof positive of the supernatural after a decade of false starts as a neo-pagan would have been more of a spiritual experience. But, unfortunately, my overwhelming reaction to having the foundations of my reality shaken was not exactly Neil Armstrong on the moon.

"Oh Goddess, that is rank," I said, being overwhelmed by the smell first and foremost. "Also, gross."

I almost tripped over a tapeworm the size of a greyhound. I smacked him with my cricket bat and caused it to explode into a glowing magenta goo that covered me. At least the things, or this one, weren't especially tough.

"This is my ancestor's work!" Thomas shouted, using his bat to knock away a thing that looked like a wasp married a lobster. "You don't know what you're doing!"

God, of course, it would be his ancestor's work. You know you were dealing with Arkham when people kept track of what their family did in generations past their grandparents. So, of course, this was coming from the woman obsessed with her witch great-great-great, etcetera grandmother.

"On the contrary, I know exactly what I am doing!" Doctor Winfield shouted. "This is about the survival of the human race! The gateway is open, and sixty-five-million—"

Doctor Winfield was interrupted by a long, hideous slimy insectoid arm with a hand that ended in eight skeletal fingers reaching out from a hole in the air to grab him around the waist. It lifted him from the control panel as the creatures almost fully developed. I saw tears in the fabric of reality and what I swore was a brachiosaur in at least one of them.

Shotgun fire was heard as I saw Grant Higashi, the other lab assistant, unload on some of the monsters coming into reality. He was an incredibly handsome Asian American man dressed in a Miskatonic U Cephalopods sweatshirt and blue jeans, blowing glowing gore apart left and right. Unfortunately, none of that would do a damn thing as the creatures multiplied every second. A slime monster started enveloping Thomas as he struggled to beat it off, err, I mean, hit it.

"Get the phone and use the Windlass app!" Doctor Winfield shouted to me as the insect arm started to drag him off to wherever. "It's the only way to save everyone!"

Instead, I jumped out of the way of a fleshy ball of mouths before getting to the control panel and throwing the knife switch. Seriously, a knife switch. The doctor was both cooler and lamer than I'd thought, all at once. The device, lacking power, immediately shut down.

Immediately, every single weird and creepy-crawly thing vanished from the room as Doctor Winfield fell to the ground with a thump seconds before leaving this universe forever. Even the goop covering me and Thomas was gone, probably a good thing since his shirt and jeans mostly dissolved. Unfortunately, his bat was also half melted, which implied things could have been a lot worse.

"Ten points!" I shouted, throwing my hands in the air. "MVP!"

Doctor Winfield didn't immediately get up, instead taking a moment to stare at me. "Have you considered you might be taken more seriously as an academic, young lady if you behaved more seriously?"

"Yes," I responded dryly. "You're welcome, by the way."

Thomas got up, looking furious. "You goddamn lunatic! You were using the Tillinghast Device! There's a reason my family went into disrepute! We've spent generations trying to escape that thing's curse!"

I had no idea what the hell Thomas was talking about but gathered from his implications that the weird Frankensteinian invention around me was plagiarized from his family, perhaps explaining its retro-look. I took a moment to pocket Doctor Winfield's cell phone, which he'd been directing me to and decided to ask my own questions. "I think you have some explaining to do, Doc."

"This is all justified," Grant said, putting his shotgun on the ground. "Insane as it sounds, he's trying to save the world."

Grant's expression was unreadable, but that was expected. He'd explained he was neuroatypical to explain why he almost always had the same expression on his face. Still, there was a slight twitch on his face that I took to be a concern.

Thomas looked at Grant, then me. "Okay, why the hell is your ex-boyfriend working here?"

Oh crap. I'd forgotten to mention that detail to Thomas during my working weeks.

"Listen, Grant and I barely dated," I said, sipping from a cup with a zombie's picture on it. "You don't have to be jealous."

Thomas gave me a severe case of side-eye. He'd changed into a spare set of sweatpants and a shirt Grant kept in the back. Apparently, my fellow lab assistant had been living here. "I'm just saying that you didn't mention it, and I find that a bit weird. Don't you?"

"Clearly, I don't," I replied, looking back at Doctor Winfield. "Can we get back to the hell portal maker? Because I feel like we're burying the lede otherwise."

"It's not a hell portal," Thomas said, frowning. This was all deeply personal for him, even without the specter of jealousy looming. "The Tillinghast Device is a machine that stimulates the pineal gland to perceive creatures that are otherwise invisible to us. My ancestor, Crawford Tillinghast, built it to perceive what he believed was an entire ecosystem around us."

"I'm pretty sure we would have bumped into some of these critters by now, even if they were invisible," I said. "Also, being able to see horrifying monsters that otherwise ignore you is a crappy invention, especially when it attracts their attention. No offense."

"We also know you have access to time travel," Thomas interjected.

"Interesting," Grant said, massively underreacting. "As you have not yet figured out, the two are, in fact, closely related."

"I was going to save that for after we knew about the Tillinghast Device," I said, annoyed he'd revealed so much already.

Doctor Winfield just took it in stride. "This is not the first time you have discovered my works, Mr. Tillinghast, Ms. Mason-Halsey. Not even the thirteenth. However, this is the closest I've ever come to my goal, and now that the Windlass device is in Ms. Mason—"

"You can call me Mercy," I replied. It was short for Mercury. My dad had a real hangup for naming the kids in my family after planets.

"Yeah, when we broke up, I became Mercy-less," Grant joked.

Thomas glared at him.

Grant just smiled.

"Very well," Doctor Winfield said. "I'll share with you everything I know. I owe you my life, and you've proven, through many loops, that you can be trusted."

It was convenient. That wasn't the sort of thing that could be verified. "Have you seen Sally?"

"Ah ha!" a voice spoke from the back of the warehouse as Sally came out, carrying an older model cellphone from maybe five years back. "I've got it! You won't threaten reality anymore, Doctor Winfield. This insane science stuff is at an end! I will stop you from ever going back or stop myself from meeting you! That way, history won't attract any more of those monsters!"

"I transferred your information off the phone, Ms. McPherson," Doctor Winfield said dryly. "The Windlass app is on mine now, and that's in the hands of Ms. Halsey-Mason."

"This is ridiculously easy time travel," I replied.

"It must link up to some machinery outside of the phone itself," Thomas pointed out.

"Or it's magic," I said.

"It's not magic," Thomas snapped.

"Magic is just sufficiently advanced science," Grant said. "Or science so advanced that humans can't analyze it."

"No one asked you," Thomas said before pausing. "But I agree."

"Dammit," Sally shouted, throwing the phone on the ground. "I want my time machine back! I don't want stupid cancer! I don't want to be dying! I don't want weird crud happening to me."

As childish a display as that was, I sympathized. She'd gotten a raw deal; all it had taken was meddling with cosmic forces for personal gain.

"I can fix that, Ms. McPherson," Doctor Winfield surprised me by saying. "Once I've finished my research here, I can alter your localized time field and reverse the damage done to your body without affecting the greater time stream."

Sally blinked. "You can?"

"You can?" I asked as well because that sounded like bullcrap.

Doctor Winfield took a deep breath. "I am now going to relate to you what only a select few in the world know right now, and most of them welcoming it with open arms: the world is doomed."

"Yeah, duh," I replied. "Global warming and idiot politicians have guaranteed it."

"This is more about ancient aliens rising from their extra-dimensional cities and tombs to destroy everything," Doctor Winfield said. "We don't know which will come first: shoggoth invasion, Great K'tullu, and his Deep One slaves, Yog-Sothoth merging with reality, or mass dispossession of the human race by the Great Race. Humanity is doomed to extinction, and there is absolutely nothing we can do to prevent it via direct confrontation."

Everyone in the room was silent, even Sally.

"Well, that sucks," I said, speaking for everyone.

"Indeed," Doctor Winfield said. "I first became aware of the vast, sinister forces arrayed against us. No, that's not quite accurate, the vast, sinister forces arrayed against each other that didn't care in the slightest about us as collateral damage when I had my body stolen for five years by one of the Great Race."

"The Great Race of Yith is a hypothetical Jurassic and Cretaceous—" Grant started to explain.

"Yeah, yeah, I saw the *Ancient Aliens* special on the History Channel," I said, interrupting him. "The pre-human body snatchers are real?"

Doctor Winfield nodded. "My consciousness was transferred back millions of years, and they forced me to inhabit one of their conical lobstrocity forms."

"Thank you, Stephen King, for giving us the word lobstrocity," I muttered.

Doctor Winfield ignored my interruption. "When I returned, I had advanced my career considerably and invented whole new fields of string theory. I even proved parts of it and was in consideration for the Nobel Prize with my team. I had a wife and two children as well."

"Wow," I said. "Sounds like you hit the jackpot."

Doctor Winfield's stare was as empty as my older brother's when he returned from Iraq. "String theory is absolutely wrong, I'm asexual, and I consider it a rape of both my mind and my soul."

Well, now I felt like a jackass. "Sorry."

"Surely, the Great Race of Yith would have erased your memories of your time there," Thomas said.

"Yes, because that's clearly the biggest question being raised," I said.

"Can you let him finish?" Grant asked, his voice remaining monotone.

Great, now everyone was teaming up against me. I made a zipper gesture across my mouth.

Doctor Winfield smirked. "The Great Race has improved its techniques and also added false memories to their victims, but they underestimated Miskatonic University. A combination of mesmerism, psychic probing, and psychedelics allowed me to restore my consciousness' memories of my time in Ptalkotus, the greatest of their cities after Pnakotus. That gave me a vast knowledge of the horrible things to come and humanity's helplessness against them."

As much as I wanted to ask which doctor at Miskatonic was using psychic powers and shrooms to awaken lost memories, I kept my mouth shut.

"Is the end of the world like, soon?" Sally asked, finally contributing something to the conversation. "Because I'd like to know."

"Too soon," Doctor Winfield said. "Worse, there are forces in this world and others that are working to hasten it. When I was trapped in Ptalkotus, I was exposed to a time war being waged between the Great Race and the shoggoths that had inherited the kingdom of the Elder Things. Whole swaths of history are being rewritten and tinkered with by uncaring impersonal forces. I despaired of being able to do anything against a fourth-dimensional conflict when the hand of providence delivered unto me a miracle."

"Sally's phone," I said, breaking my silence.

"Indeed," Doctor Winfield said. "The technology is beyond anything in this century or probably several, but I do not restrict my research to the bounds of science. I have access to Keziah Mason's grimoire, the knowledge I learned in the Great Race's library, and the sorcery of all those cultures that Miskatonic's Restricted Section overflows with. Better yet, I've had time to study them all with the Great Race none the wiser."

"How old are you, Doc?" I asked.

"It's been a relativistic century or so since I've been working on this project," Doctor Winfield said. "This Tillinghast Device is a far different creature from the one that your ancestor, Crawford, created. By the way, he was completely wrong about the pineal gland, and the machine stimulates the merging of extra-dimensional spaces via physics perception or Reality Dreaming, as they call it, in the Carter Building. However, I've modified it extensively with modern technology and the principles of the arcane to produce a, well, let's call it a Hail Mary Pass, to save humanity."

It all sounded like gobbledygook to me, but I was very intrigued by the fact he had my ancestor's spell book. He could have claimed he was Jesus Christ reborn, and I probably would have believed him if it got me closer to it. "So, what does the machine do, Doc?"

"It will seal off the Earth from the alien, supernatural, and evil forces," Doctor Winfield said. "Time travel will become impossible, and fifth-dimensional or above beings will be forced into permanent slumber or out of this universe. In effect, we will prevent the apocalypse."

"What you're describing is impossible," Thomas said, shaking his head.

Yes, because so much of this is possible. I was polite enough *not* to say.

"Not at all," Grant said as if he was explaining the weather. "Reality Locks, for lack of a better term, are things the Yithians and shoggoths both have access to. They're shields for their cities and civilization. Otherwise, they would have been erased as an opening move in any time war."

Grant notably pronounced shoggoth as 'shaggoth,' which I found weird.

"Of course, Doctor Who," I replied.

"He's just the Doctor," Sally, of all people, corrected me.

Everyone looked at her.

"What?" Sally asked. "My dorm mate is a huge fan, and she's right. David Tennent is hot as fudge. Matt Smith too. I don't like the old guy or lady doc."

"I hate to ask but isn't this like risking the fabric of reality?" I asked. "Doc Brown would be warning us against paradoxes at this point."

"It is, unfortunately, the only way yours will not be the last generation of humanity," Doctor Winfield said.

I got the impression he was lying to me, but I wasn't sure about what, and it wasn't all the crazier details of his speech. "What do you need from us?"

Doctor Winfield stared at Thomas. "I actually could use your engineering expertise. It was a hardware failure, not a principal failure. Mercy, you were selected for a reason, and if you could study your ancestor's book, I think some adjustment to the runes I've drawn in certain places would guarantee success. If we put our minds together, we should be able to adjust the Tillinghast Device tonight to create the bubble that would save humanity."

"And you can always just reboot the timeline if it fails," I replied.

Doctor Winfield's expression became unreadable. "No, unfortunately, the chaos around Miskatonic University has attracted far too much attention. Initially, the constant reboots and noise were disguising my efforts. However, some of my reboots have dealt with forces unrelated to the ones conjured by the Tillinghast Device."

"You mean the invisible dog," I said.

Doctor Winfield shrugged. "Something like that. I think it would be best for you to keep the phone for now. I strongly suggest you do not use it unless it is an absolute emergency. I may have gotten it working properly, but it is now a tool of last resort. In a bizarre way, we are running out of time. The hounds are, both literally and metaphorically, closing in on us. Unfortunately, they are also the least of the creatures we must worry about."

I was hardly going to turn down the chance to keep a frigging time machine, even if I never got the opportunity to use it. "Sounds good. So, what do you think of all this, Thomas?

"I can tell Grant has drunk the Kool-Aid."

"It's true," I said, referring to Grant. "You're the only person on Earth, save Jared Leto; that is too weird for me. That's why I broke up our study dates."

Grant looked depressed. "I knew I shouldn't have shared my essay on Elizabeth Bathory possibly being a devotee of the Satanic Black Maiden cult."

"No, that was cool," I said, reassuring him.

"So, they *were* dates," Thomas said, crossing his arms.

"Stay focused, Tommy," I said.

Thomas furrowed his brow. "I dunno, it sounds insanely risky, but I believe him about the apocalypse. I've experienced many weird things here at Miskatonic University, and so did the previous five or six generations of my family. It is also a chance to make the Tillinghast Device a machine for good, possibly the greatest good in humanity's history. It would redeem the second biggest stain in my family's history."

"What's the first?" I asked.

"I'm a relative of John Wilkes Booth," Thomas said.

I grimaced. "Yikes. I'm glad I'm only related to a misunderstood witch."

Sally looked uncomfortable. "I've felt the other failures. Some of them have been very bad. It would be best if you didn't do this. I want my phone back."

"I feel you don't have much choice, my dear," Doctor Winfield said, his fatherly 'savior of humanity' tone dropping slightly. "Your temporal sickness has continued to progress despite all my reboots that should have affected you. I fear you only have a few weeks left to live."

Sally's eyes widened as she looked ready to throw up. "But you can fix me, right?"

"Of course," Doctor Winfield said absently. "Just help Mercy until the experiment is done, and stay out of our way."

Okay, now I knew he was lying.

"Wow, my ancestor was a baby-eating bitch," I said, sitting at the cafeteria table and reading through Keziah's grimoire. "Mind you, the fact that literally one person at the Salem Witch Trials was a theistic Satanist, assuming we count an Outer God from the Dreamlands as Satan, doesn't mean that they were in any way justified. Indeed, we should note the only actual witch at Salem got away scot-free while a bunch of innocent people was executed in her place."

The ancient tome, well, if you counted 1692 as "ancient", was a hand-written account of Keziah Mason's horrific crimes as well as a journal of more mundane activities. It was in an archaic style but one I was familiar with due to my studies. I learned as much about butter churning as I did about her horrific pact with Nyarlathotep, her fantastic ability with advanced mathematics, and her preoccupation with baby murder.

Seriously, she was really into it.

Sally was sitting across from me, not the least bit interested in my commentary. "Can I have my phone back?"

"No," I replied for the fifth time. "We're saving the world with it. Besides, it's not your phone. It just has the Windlass app on it."

"I just want to have it," Sally replied, having a distinctly Gollumesque air about her. "Just in case. I won't use it."

I looked up from the grimoire. "You want to reset the day so you don't have to deal with Doctor Winfield's experiment."

"He's crazy, you know that, right?" Sally asked, not denying it. "I don't trust him to fix me."

I didn't trust him either, but I was also pretty sure Sally didn't have much in the way of options. "Would it even work? I mean, if we rewound the phone a day, then wouldn't the phone return to Doctor Winfield's possession?"

Sally blinked. "I don't know."

"This is the sort of thing you'd have answers to if you'd experimented with it," I replied, crunching on a Dorito.

"Listen, we have the apocalypse to deal with," I said, finding my words less reassuring than I meant them. "I didn't believe in the Cthulhu Cycle Deities or CCD until today, but Keziah here clearly did, and I've just found out both time travel and other dimensional monsters were real today. So I'm in a very credulous state."

"Then wouldn't you want the phone in my hands?" Sally asked, sounding like a junkie.

"We all have problems now, Sally," I replied. "I'm going to have to ditch my book's central premise now. *Sometimes Witches Do Need Burning* isn't exactly the title that will sell with my kind of crowd."

"How can you make jokes at a time like this?" Sally asked.

I shrugged. "It's my defense mechanism."

"Some defense," Sally said, rolling her eyes.

"Wait, are we quoting *Clue* or not?" I asked, wondering if she'd seen the classic movie.

"The board game?" Sally asked, confused.

"Never mind," I muttered, turning the page. "Oh, wait, she also knew another witch: Joseph Curwen. Oh, that's just stereotypical. At least that tracks with my thesis. The actual magicians got away while they killed good God-fearing religious fanatics. But, wait, they were doing the nasty? With demons, too? Holy crap. Those are some interesting illustrations."

I was interrupted by a bunch of textbooks dropped on my table, drawing both my and Sally's attention. Dropping the books was Sheryl Mason, the only other Goth Girl in Nancy Dyer's Dormitory. She was pink-haired, wearing a *Sherlock Holmes: The Awakened* shirt, and looking highly ticked off. There's an old saying that nobody hates a Goth as much as another. So Goth and I narrowed our eyes at her.

Standing beside her was her was Meredith Johnson, who was as close to a live-action Claire Redfield or Lara Croft as you were likely to meet in real life. An archaeology student, she had crimson hair in a ponytail and was a lot more athletic than any other girls at the table. Oh, and she was Norwegian, or at least her family was. I admit I'd made a drunken pass at her once, but I'm pretty sure she didn't notice since I'd ended up throwing up in a plant.

"And a fine hello to you too, fellow humans," I said sarcastically, wondering what this was all about. "How can I help you?"

"Don't play smart with us," Meredith said, taking the lead. "We know Doctor Winfield is doing experiments that endanger the world. Also, as his lab assistant, you must be involved!"

I blinked. Was I just blind, and everyone I knew was involved in wackiness, or had I unwittingly stepped into a nexus of the odd that was now attracting it all to me? "I have no idea what you're talking about."

"Yes!" Sally interjected. "He's mad! He must be stopped!"

I stared at Sally. "Sally, no one likes a narc."

"This is serious, Mercy," Sheryl said. "I have a cosmic sense of the mathematical nature of the universe, and everything about the world's geometric lines is being disrupted. My hyper-spatial awareness is telling me everything is wonky now."

I blinked slowly. "Uh-huh. I'm pretty sure you're getting a C in math right now, and ninety percent of that explanation was comic book bull—"

"Ahem," Meredith interjected. "Listen, Mercy. There are groups of students who have seen things around Miskatonic University. Awful evil things. We've banded together to try to stop them. Everyone pretends things are normal around here, but they're not. Trust us, We want to help."

I was now just irritated. "Listen, Meredith, Sheryl, this is not the *Ghostbusters*, and you are not Egon and Ray. If I were going to trust anyone with cosmic end-of-the-world stuff, it'd be a professor famous the world over for his understanding of how reality works. It wouldn't be someone my age. Doctor Winfield has earned my loyalty, and if you have anything to bring up, you should bring it up with him and not try to get me to turn on him."

Both newcomers looked disappointed at my decision. Sally also looked like she was upset at my decision.

"Very well," Meredith said, picking up the textbooks that Sheryl had dropped for their dramatic entrance. "We'll seek another way to stop this from getting out of hand."

Sheryl pointed at the grimoire, presently opened to some messed up illustrations of what hot and sexy Keziah had been up to in her thirties with a ghoul's tail. "Hey, can I borrow that after you're done?"

"I don't know why you didn't want their help," Sally asked, following me back to the Nancy Dyer dormitory. "They could be our key to stopping the doctor's evil plan!"

It was night now, which was weird since it seemed like it should still be daytime, but I wasn't in the mood to pay attention to little details like that. I'd been working on the proper mystical signs on a yellow pad for the past few hours and must have lost track of time.

The university courtyard was also weirdly empty, with the buildings all having lights on, but everyone packed in the library, dormitories, or various halls. It was possibly the storm gathering, again, outside, but there was more to it. It was like the students and faculty had developed a sixth sense about the weird stuff on campus, getting ready to break out again.

"I didn't want their help because I don't trust the gang from *Scooby Doo*. You do know who that is, right?" I asked, turning to Sally.

"My parents were evangelicals, Mercy, not Amish," Sally said.

"Whatever," I said, continuing. "I don't trust the gang from Scooby Doo's claim that I'm endangering the world, and they know how to stop it. This is not an inn, and we are not meeting our fellow adventurers there."

"Now you've lost me again," Sally said, looking exhausted. Actually, she looked worse than exhausted. I didn't know what kind of space disease she had or if it was common cancer, but it was clearly taking its toll.

"I'm saying that there are plenty of reasons not to trust them," I replied, looking back at her as we arrived at the doors of the dormitory. "Maybe they want to steal Doctor Winfield's work. Maybe they're working for a rival professor or like some evil corporate entity that wants to monetize it. What if they're working for the jerk who gave you the time travel device?"

"He wasn't a jerk," Sally said, running her hands through her hair and removing a clump. "Oh, God."

"Yeah, you don't look so good," I said, frowning. "Listen, we'll get you fixed."

I was lying to her, and we both knew it. I believed Doctor Winfield was trying to save the world, but everything he'd told me also highlighted that he was willing to do whatever he had to in order to do it. I figured sacrificing Sally, especially if he didn't have to do anything himself, was a small price to pay in his mind. It probably was in the grand scheme of things. Still, if I could find a spell in Keziah Mason's grimoire that didn't require killing a literal baby, then I would have cast it for her. I didn't know when it had happened, but I was now Sally's friend.

"So, he says," Sally said. "But I guess he is my only chance unless I can figure out how to go back to before I started all of this. Being poor is better than being dead. Maybe it would even save Buster."

I sympathized, but I sincerely doubted that was the case. I also thought that these invisible dogs needed to be treated like a room full of poison gas, avoided at all costs. Doing more of what attracted them in the first place wouldn't make things better.

Either way, I walked into the dormitory front entrance with Sally coming in behind me. That was when I noticed we were in a long white hallway full of identical doors, which wasn't the standard room of the Sally Dyer building.

"Did we go into the wrong building?" Sally asked, staring at the sight over my shoulder.

"No, we didn't," I said, feeling a cold chill go up and down my spine. I turned to go out the door we'd come in through but somehow it was now an identical hallway to the one in front of us. So we were officially trapped in some space that didn't obey the laws of physics or at least geometry.

In that moment; I had the peculiar notion that Doctor Winnfield's playing around with time loops, combined with Sally, might have shunted us into a parallel dimension, or some greater time police were at work. There were many odd things at Miskatonic University, and I couldn't help but wonder how they might react to technology from the future.

"Oh, God, oh God," Sally said, hyperventilating. "It's the invisible dog! It's going to take us like Buster!"

"Now-now, let's not panic," I said, on the verge of panicking myself. I was way outside my area of expertise right now, and unfortunately, the only person I knew to have any experience with this was telling me we would all die.

"Not panic?" Sally asked, looking at me like I was crazy. "When the hell do you *think* it's time to panic? Give me the phone!"

"I don't want to send a beacon up to this thing!" I said, lying. My real reason was that if Sally rebooted the universe, I wasn't sure if it would save me. What if this thing operated on string theory, and she was moving between nearly identical universes? I'd get eaten, and she'd get away like Keziah Mason from Cotton Mather. Huh, I guess I did learn a few things during my time with Doctor Winfield.

"I said give me the phone!" Sally shouted, assaulting me and trying to go into my pants pockets.

That was when there was a nightmarish inhuman growling noise. It wasn't like any Earthly animal's vocal cords, but it was recognizable as *something* alive, big, and angry. It was also coming down from the other end of the hallway.

Complete and utter terror filled my body down to a primal level as I stared at Sally and shouted, "Run!"

Sally didn't need prodding, and the two of us began running down the halls, feeling something coming up behind us. I could feel its hot, rancid disgusting breath and hear the sound of its crashing with leaps and bounds. Unable to stay ahead of it, I took a chance on the doors being unlocked and smacked myself with Sally through one.

Much to my relief, it led into just an ordinary classroom that the two of us ran through. It had a whiteboard full of equations on the front wall and desks for the students. Unfortunately, all the chairs were smashed and thrown into the air by the time we reached the other side of the room and ended up in another identical white hall.

"Which room?" Sally asked.

"It doesn't matter!" I shouted, selecting one at random and heading inside.

The room was almost identical to the one we'd just left, except there was a huge Confederate battle flag up against the wall with the equations next to writing in French. I was already feeling tired as I fled through the same door into another white hall.

"Give me the goddamn phone!" Sally shouted.

"I will!" I said, deciding we didn't have any other options, but I wasn't going to do it in the middle of a chase. Heading through yet another doorway, I found myself in a decidedly different sort of classroom. This one was in a chamber seemingly made of stone, with every "desk" growing out of the ground with a crystal hovering over it. The writing on the walls was projected by an organic growing crustacean thing making hovering alien writing.

The door behind us was an "iris" whose interior folds resembled starfish arms. That gave me a second to pull out the phone before Sally grabbed it. No sooner did she do so, than the iris opened itself, and I once more heard the nightmarish voice of the thing. We weren't even seemingly on 21st century Earth, but it had managed to follow us.

"I'm sorry," Sally said, looking at me as she got the phone.

"What?" I asked.

Sally then kicked my knee out from under me before running toward one of the other iris doors. Apparently, she'd learned the lesson of the old proverb about two men outrunning a bear. You only had to outrun the other guy, not the bear.

As Sally disappeared out the door, I cried tears of fright before I felt the invisible dog pass over me, and my stomach twisted with nausea. That was when I heard a sanity-shattering scream as if *something had* happened to Sally. It was a death cry unlike anything I'd ever heard in a movie or imagined a human being could make, but it was unmistakable as the end of a person's existence. It became hard to remember Sally... Samantha... whats-her-name. Only focusing on the equations I remembered from Keziah's book seemed to calm my brain and let me climb to my feet to run back through the door I'd come through.

Escaping once more into the white hall, I ran down it before trying one more door, hoping to find my way out of this insane non-Euclidean labyrinth. Instead, it once more led me into a classroom that looked not too dissimilar from those I'd attended at Miskatonic University. Unfortunately, when I reached the professor's desk at the foot of the whiteboard, I heard the creature's animalistic grunts once more.

Close to choking on my screams, exhausted and confused, I took a chance and grabbed a marker before drawing one of the symbols drawn from Keziah's grimoire. It was a long tree branch-like symbol that Keziah said was used for protection. Unfortunately, my drawing wasn't very good, and I heard it moving closer as I fell backward and cowered on the ground in utter desolate fright. I closed my eyes and wrapped my arms around my legs, waiting for death.

Right before, I either passed out or was pulled out of my nightmare.

I screamed at the top of my lungs as I found myself once more in the middle of Miskatonic University's courtyard, standing in front of a wooden bench as Grant was holding me. I stared at him for a second, pitched myself forward, and threw up on the ground.

"It's alright," Grant said, looking down at me. "You're okay now."

"The hell I am!" I snapped, my entire body shaking. "It ate her! It *ate* her."

"Who?" Grant asked, confused.

"Her!" I snapped. "What's-her-name!"

I couldn't remember my friend's (was she my friend?) name, and only by concentrating on the symbol I'd drawn on the whiteboard did I remember anything at all. It was a horrifying violation and made me question the nature of reality. Yet, mathematics, and sorcery of the kind the Old Witch had done was seemingly the only defense against this madness. That was when I realized how bizarre it was for me to be alive.

"How the hell did I get here?" I asked, confused.

"I don't know," Grant said. "You weren't here one minute, and then you were here the next."

That sounded like complete crap, but I wasn't about to question it right now after having survived a horrifying nightmare. "I lost the phone."

"No, you didn't," Grant said, pulling one identical to the one I'd given…her, the blonde girl, before she vanished. Was she blonde?

"Where the hell did you get this?" I asked, staring at it.

"You dropped it," Grant said.

No, I didn't. So either he had a copy, or he'd somehow retrieved it from the invisible dog universe. Still, I wasn't stable enough to question my good fortune. "Gee, thanks."

It was about two hours later, according to one of the clock stands lining the courtyard walkways. The night was extra dark. The wind was rushing all around us as storm clouds completely blacked out the sky. The air around Miskatonic University was also every bit as ionized as it had been around the Tillinghast Device.

"Oh crap," I said, looking up. The second horrifying revelation of tonight had occurred. "He's using the device now."

Grant looked around, his expression unchanging. "What makes you think that?"

"Because he's using the device!" I snapped. "I recognized the signs! It was all a distraction!"

I didn't think that Doctor Winfield had summoned the invisible monster, but it wasn't like he didn't have a book full of magic that he'd given me. This could have been his plan all along.

"I see," Grant said, his voice low and rumbling in a way that surprised me. "Shall I take you to see him?"

"Yes!" I snapped.

Why did I feel like I was missing something?

Things had gone from bad to worse throughout Arkham. Grant took me in his plain unmarked white van, which I admit gave strong serial killer vibes, down to the warehouse despite the winds reaching hurricane levels, which was something you rarely experienced on the Northeast Coast. They weren't impossible, Hurricane Bob hit the place in 1991 before I was even born, but this was artificially induced.

How did I know that?

Some clouds were glowing purple, and the moon was a bright shade of red. It was also comically large like seen in movies.

That was not normal.

Worse, I could see the creatures the Tillinghast Device summoned out of the corner of my eye. I couldn't see them directly, but they floated through the air, overturning cars and clawing at the buildings. I swear, I saw one poor guy trying to cover his face with a newspaper just vanish, and I'm glad the car flew past him. Because, honestly, the crunching noises in my head were bad enough without hearing whatever real sounds it made when the things ate him alive.

Capping it off, that enormous beam of light I'd made fun of being at the end of every superhero movie? Yeah, there was totally one going into the sky now. Lightning crashed around it, and I could feel reality shifting around me. Maybe it was my imagination, but it was like moving through water every few seconds. If ever there was proof the police and military were useless, it was the fact I hadn't seen any of them coming here with massive firepower.

"He's going to end the world," I muttered as we finally pulled up toward the warehouse. Thomas' car was there as well as Sheryl Mason's Mystery Machine-looking thing. She and Meredith had decided to intervene directly despite not knowing a goddamn thing about what was going on.

"The time war between the Yithians and the shoggoths is one where humanity is only a bystander," Grant muttered, bringing the car to a stop by Tommy's car. "The Yith use human agents, though, and have gained a terrifying advantage. One that threatens the extermination of all biological life on Earth. Humans and shoggoths share a fundamental biological link that the Yithians do not. Humans and shoggoths also share a fundamental need for freedom from oppression that the Yithians do not with their body stealing ways."

The third horrifying realization of tonight struck me. This one being more of the Ghost Face from *Scream*, is now in the car with me variety. That wasn't the kind of speech that an average person gave. It was the kind of speech a crazy cultist or something worse, gave. "Um, Grant, this will come off as a weird question, but are you…human?"

Grant paused before answering, which was never a good sign when you were asking if someone was *homo sapiens*. "Yes."

"Oh good," I said, not at all reassured.

"But the people I work for aren't," Grant said.

"Oh," I said.

"I am of the Brotherhood of the First Ones," Grant replied. "We work for the fathers and mothers of the human race. The ones who uplifted our ancestors by sharing their primordial essence with us long ago: the shoggoth."

"Great," I said, sucking in my breath. Grant was a frigging cultist. "Are you going to kill me?"

"No," Grant said, surprising me. "You are needed to make sure events proceed in a favorable timeline. Something is very wrong."

I gulped. "How wr-wrong?"

"Very wrong," Grant said. "Doctor Winfield has taken my assistance to his research in directions beyond those intended. I am no longer able to interfere directly. I need the help of a proxy or proxies."

Thanks for the in-depth, profound explanation, professor. However, what I got from that was that he didn't want to kill me and was, at least temporarily, on my side. "Then I guess we should go stop the experiment."

"Yes," Grant said, remaining expressionless. He did, however, unlock the door, and I bolted from it.

Once there, both Sheryl and Meredith confronted me. I noticed Sheryl was unarmed, but Meredith was carrying an old—timey-looking pistol. Rain was starting to pour down on us now; it was weirdly colored and seemed to catch colors that didn't exist in nature.

"This is your fault, Mercy!" Sheryl shouted. "You should have worked with us!"

I glared at them, clenching my teeth. "Listen, I almost got eaten by an invisible dog, I just lost my friend, and I may be the only person left on Earth who even remembers she exists. Plus, the world may be ending. Do not mess with me, Scarlet Johansson. I am not in a great headspace."

"Sorry. You're right. We need to work together," Meredith said, turning her head to the side. The wind caused her hair to flutter in the wind like a shampoo commercial.

God, she was hot. I needed to talk with Tommy about hall passes or polyamory. Also, there was something seriously wrong with me for thinking about that right now. I blamed the Tillinghast Device.

"So, does anyone have a solution that doesn't involve killing Doctor Winfield and busting up the machine?" I asked, looking around.

Grant was there behind Sheryl and Meredith. He was expressionless as always. None of them said anything.

"Great," I replied. "Don't hurt Tommy."

The room that awaited us inside the warehouse had drastically changed from earlier today. The bizarre Dieselpunk device that Doctor Winfield had reverse-engineered and improved on from Crawford Tillinghast's 1920s device had been replaced by a sleek, white iPhone-looking thing that incorporated instruments of a wholly alien nature. There were weird crystal structures, organic growths, and something that looked like that one classroom I'd accidentally found myself in while being chased down by the invisible dog.

The walls were now also covered, and I mean *covered*, in the kinds of doodles that I'd found inside Keziah Mason's grimoire. All of them were glowing white with an alien energy pouring outward, the raw essence of magic in my mind but probably something closer to the distilled mathematics of the universe. *The Matrix*'s code, if you will.

But the central tuning fork that was largely unchanged drew my attention. It had blown the roof off the building and directed a continuous beam of pulsating light upward into space, specifically, into a rift torn through space/time like before during our earlier encounter with the machine. It was a much larger, singular rift, though.

Through the Rift, high in the sky, I saw the sight of the ground of Earth's distant past. Beautiful verdant jungles, feathered creatures that looked like no paleontologist I knew whose image of dinosaurs (but were close enough to recognize as such), and a distant city of stone mixed with crystal. For a second, I thought the doctor was trying to travel back to Earth's Cretaceous Era for some reason. That dashed itself as I saw the horrific monsters outside pouring across the surface of the prehistoric world. Not just by the dozens as we'd seen in our lab but by the thousands. It grew into an ever-greater horde.

Doctor Winfield was trapped inside a circle of mathematical doodles, holding his arms against the wall as floating slimy growths passed him by harmlessly. He was staring at the horrifying thing he'd achieved with a look of the rapturous eye, one of his eyes swollen shut from an injury he'd sustained. One of his hands was holding a pistol, not aimed at anything.

Tommy was moaning on the ground, a pool of blood around him. I saw him moving about in his limited protected space, but he was severely injured. Leeches the size of baseballs were licking up where his blood had spilled out of his protective circle. Tommy was several feet from the controls that he'd been trying to get at, probably to stop precisely what I was saw going on.

"You son of a bitch!" I screamed at Doctor Winfield. "What have you done!"

Meredith and Sheryl came up from behind, with Grant trailing them. I wasn't sure if I should clue them in that Grant was crazy pants now or later, but we had bigger problems right now.

"You shouldn't be here, Ms. Halsey-Mason!" Doctor Winfield said, his face soaked from the rain pouring down on us. "This stage of the experiment is very dangerous!"

"You shot my boyfriend!" I shouted, furious.

"Mr. Tillinghast, or Booth, as his real name may be," Doctor Winfield mocked my boyfriend, "attempted to interfere, like the ants spoiling the picnic of the gods!"

Tommy somehow managed to speak despite the fact he was nursing a stomach wound. "It was all a lie! He's not saving the world, Mercy! It was never about saving the world!"

"No!" Doctor Winfield said, his voice a snarl. "It's about avenging the human race! Millennia of rape, brainwashing, and body theft! The Yith think they can take what they want from us and manipulate our timeline like it doesn't matter! Well, now I am unleashing doom upon them in their own time! From hell's heart, I stab at thee! For hate's sake, I spit my last breath at thee!"

"It's never good when they quote *Moby Dick*," I muttered, thinking of *The Wrath of Khan*.

I debated charging over the symbols on the ground but was unsure whether covering any of them would disrupt the spells of protection (for lack of a better term) around us. I was also unsure where to begin dismantling the Tillinghast Device 3.0 he'd created. Clearly, he'd had access to months or even years to build this thing, but that wasn't how my friend's phone worked. Which I weirdly remembered despite not remembering her—maybe it was the witch blood in me. The others had the same view, as we were all hesitating at a critical time.

"He has combined *The Book of the Windlass* and Keziah Mason's geometric magic to create stable pocket dimensions for hiding his creations from the Yith!" Grant said, awed. It was one of the few times his emotions seemed authentic and not manufactured. "This is Elder Thing and future technology sent by the government to be studied by Miskatonic University! He truly is a genius."

"Good for him!" I shouted. "What is he doing!?"

"The Flying Polyps existed on Earth for seven hundred million years!" Meredith, of all people, answered. "Existing alongside the pre-human races until something agitated them to exterminate the Yithians during the Cretaceous period! This could be a stable time loop!"

That was a lot of information to unpack in a few seconds. Now in the face of mass alien genocide and rewriting everything I knew about history, you might think it'd be selfish and single-minded to focus primarily on whether my boyfriend would die or not. Well, I wasn't just focused on that; it was ninety percent of my focus. The remaining ten percent was on something less selfish but closer to home. "That's just great! So what's that mean for us?"

"The world will be consumed!" Grant said, back to his usual monotone but louder. "The forces are too great! The Great Old Ones will rise! K'tullu will slay all dreamers, and Yog-Sothoth will pierce reality!"

"And what's your opinion on that?" I snapped, needing to know where he stood before I did something monumentally stupid.

"It is glorious!" Grant shouted, enraptured.

"What?" Meredith asked, shocked.

"Huh," Sheryl added.

"The sleepers will rise, and the Old Gods shall return!" Grant said. "Praise K'Tullu and our shoggoth masters!"

Meredith responded by pistol-whipping him before Sheryl pushed him out the door and down the stairs.

Well, that was one problem solved.

"Time to screw with this party," I said, pulling out the cell phone. "No pun intended."

"It won't work!" Doctor Winfield laughed. "I didn't give you my password!"

There was something absurd but darkly hilarious about the end of the world being brought about by six digits. I managed to get it on his street address and the last digits of his birth year on the third try. I was always very good at math—family trait.

"No!" Doctor Winfield shouted, pulling up his gun and walking across the glyphs.

Meredith shot him in the chest before he could shoot me, and a bunch of glowing spheres descended on him, devouring the flesh off his bones in seconds.

"Do you know what you're doing?" Meredith asked, staring at the man she'd killed.

Yeah, with literal rifts in the fabric of space and time and a bunch of magic deliberately designed to mess with it, I was pretty sure this thing wouldn't work correctly. I also started hearing the noises of the invisible dogs in the sky, except there wasn't one. No, it was the sound of packs, hundreds of the beasts. Looking over at Tommy, I wanted to ask him what he thought, but he'd passed out—or worse.

That made it easy.

"Not a fucking clue," I said, calling up the Windlass app.

RESET?

YES/NO.

I hit YES, and a purple flash washed over me.

I woke up with a start, my mind full of terrifying possibilities. I saw clawing, awful, and monstrous things pawing at the world. They ripped through the fabric of time, hungry and desperate to get at this reality. I knew that only I could stop them and that I needed to do the unthinkable to do it.

Then I heard my boyfriend snoring. A quick survey of the room and the sight of the Randolph Carter adaptation of *They Came from Space* poster, the PlayStation 5 console I'd spent all night playing *The Drowning City* on, and my battered copy of the Simon *Necronomicon* next to an open box of pizza told me where the origins of my nightmare came from.

I was inside my dorm room at Miskatonic University, and it was nine-thirty-five, which was late for getting up to do my job but not so late as I couldn't make it if I hauled ass.

There was a storm brewing outside, though. Through the window, I swore some of the lightning was purple. That was when my cellphone rang, and I picked it up, surprised to see a new app on it. Someone was sending me a video chat request. Despite not being dressed, I raised it to my head and answered it. Much to my surprise, I saw the person on the other side was…me.

I was about twenty years older and dressed like a reject from *Mad Max: Fury Road*. I wore leather pants, halter top, ammo belts, an Elder Sign tattoo (how did I know what that looked like?), a ponytail, and scars everywhere. She did have a badass eyepatch, though, and a shotgun in her other hand. It was such a surreal sight that it instantly obliterated any thought of running to Doctor Winfield's lab to ensure my laboratory assistant's job was safe.

Other Me looked at me. "Yeah, Mercy, I think we need to have a talk."

And to think, I thought today would be boring.

Randolph Carter is H.P Lovecraft's author avatar in the Cthulhu Mythos, being an author of weird fiction who manages to survive several encounters with the supernatural. Later, he would go on a fantastic dream quest that results him in staring down everyone from Nyarlathotep to Yog-Sothoth. Here, I have a prequel of sorts, "The Statement of Randolph Carter" that shows his first encounter with the supernatural. It is also the opening to The Book of Hastur. *My take on Hastur being something of a Great Old One embodying the undefinable nature of storytelling and the Dreamlands.*

WEIRD TALES WITH RANDOLPH CARTER

The typewriter sat in front of me as I struggled to try to provide a proper ending to my latest story. It was an adaptation of the events at the blasted heath outside of Arkham, Massachusetts. I'd struggled to put to words the wild story told to me by a sickly strange looking man named Ammi. A tale of flora and fauna corrupted by an unknown substance from space. It was not that the local legend wasn't a good subject for weird fiction, it was that I was afraid I would be beaten to my adaptation of it.

There was also the fact that events were possibly a little too close to home if I were to try to sell it to local publishers. Arkham's appetite for the macabre was greater than any market outside one of America's largest cities but the issue of groundwater contamination following the building of the local reservoir had been a gradually growing concern for the past decade. There were some who believed unknown metals or chemicals were slowly driving the citizens to madness or an early grave.

Was it exploitative to write a tale where the origins of this ever-increasing rise in infirmity or death was the cause of an alien life form carried to our world from distant galaxies? Perhaps, but it would also sell a lot of magazines.

Or so I hoped.

"Randolph!" A voice spoke from the hallway outside my study. It shook me out of my reverie and brought me to the present. I was inside my study with a noisy thunderstorm outside and the hearth in the chamber burning brightly. There was no bust of Pallas with a raven on the top to complete the horror writing mood, but I was otherwise close to the perfect circumstances for the creation of chilling tales.

"It is polite to knock before entering, Harley," I replied, not getting up from my seat at the desk.

I'd inherited the property from my late father, and it was far more than a professional writer could afford on the meager payments to his mad imaginings, but it was still large enough to surprise me with the kind of visitors that sometimes showed up.

"Would you have heard me, old friend?" Harley Warren inquired, entering. "I know the kind of place your mind goes when writing."

Harley Warren was thin, clean shaven, and starting to go bald. He dressed well though his suits were years out of fashion and patched due to his complete lack of desire to keep with the times. He was quite wet, and I could tell he'd arrived without an umbrella. There was also a brown paper wrapped bundle under his right arm.

"No," I replied. "Unlike you, I cannot afford servants."

"I'd buy you one, but you can't own people anymore," Harley said, making a less than pleasant joke.

Harley came from money in the way that fish came from water. His ancestors dated back to the time of the Puritans and had made fortunes equal to the Washingtons as well as the Jeffersons. Sadly, with the same means. Supposedly, Harley's ancestor Hobert Warren had believed Ben Franklin to be a mystical rival of legendary warlock Joseph Curwen.

Unfortunately, Harley had no interest in business and neither had his immediate ancestors, becoming instead embroiled in the secret societies that feuded constantly among New England's upper crust. Masons, fraternities, and mystical groups with delusions of spiritual power. The last three generations of Warrens had been part of them all.

Harley was the last of his line and was very likely to spend the rest of his family's money chasing phantasms that, however entertaining I found them, would leave him as bankrupt as a writer for *Weird Tales* or its local equivalent, *Outlandish Stories*. That would be, however, at least a decade or two of frivolous spending chasing ghosts.

"Is there any reason you're darkening my door this stormy night?" I lit myself a pipe and began smoking, taking in a deep whiff of tobacco. My mother had encouraged me in the habit to calm my nerves.

"I cannot show up for no reason other than your charming company?" Harley asked.

I narrowed my eyes. "Not normally no. I remind you that you left last year to scour the globe for secrets of the unknown."

Harley took a seat in my grandfather's leather-bound chair across from me. "A worthy use of my time if there ever was one. What I have to show you tonight is enough to change both our lives forever."

Harley was a man prone to such bold proclamations and I frequently found myself disappointed by the results.

Harley unfolded the brown paper wrapping around his package and revealed its contents. It was a yellow leather volume with crinkly paper that had a golden clasp around it. A strange squiggly trio of lines was on the front.

"*The Book of Hastur*," Harley said. "I acquired it in India a month before my return to the States. I've spent months translating it, poring over the language, and deducing the true meaning of the author. I wrapped it up lest it be damaged by our climate because each page is as precious as gold to me. More so even. Look upon its dreadful visage and be elevated to the ranks of an elite priesthood of mortals who have glimpsed the infinite."

My reaction was not what you expected. "Hastur? Really? Harley, you've been suckered. Again."

Harley narrowed his eyes. "I'm disappointed in your skepticism, Randolph. Why would you think so?"

I stared at him. "Hastur isn't real."

Harley frowned. "Your mind is not usually so prosaic."

"Ambrose Bierce first wrote about him as a god in *Haita the Shepherd* and he's the subject of Chalmers' writing in the *King in Yellow*," I replied. "I use *real* occult concepts in my writing. Names and concepts from the *Necronomicon* or the Black Book. Not this Hastur nonsense. Hastur is a literary homage nothing more."

"This is the same spiel you gave about Aleister Crowley's Thelemic pantheon," Harley replied.

"And I'm right about him too," I said, tapping the end of my pipe in an ashtray beside my typewriter. "Hastur isn't even a god outside of Bierce's work. Chalmers used him as a place. Your rival's writing doesn't make it clear what he is either, probably because it was just an homage to another horror writer."

"Hastur is…more," Harley said, almost reverentially.

"What does that even mean?" I asked, confused.

Harley furrowed his brow as if briefly broken from a spell. "It means the concepts of defining something in occult terms are not necessarily the best use of one's time. Is Hastur a place, a god, or an idea? Is Carcosa a planet, dimension, or kingdom? The Plateau of Leng and Hali are places but how do they relate? The King in Yellow is a personage but maybe it is a genius loci or personification like Columbia for America or Hypnos is of sleep."

"Please tell me you didn't just suggest America's symbol is a goddess." I rolled my eyes. "Cthulhu is a god. He lives in R'lyeh. He is worshiped by a bunch of degenerate Theosophists and weird Christian cult offshoots. Anthropologists try and link every squid god and fish man across Earth's mythology together under him. Either way, he's a god worth worshiping because he's one you can explain."

Harley stared at me like I was a small child talking nonsense. Which, given he was the occult expert who taught me most of what I knew about comparative mythology and the weird, was perhaps accurate. "The unknown is a major part of what makes gods worth worshiping. Why the Hebrew God presently reigns instead of Zeus. I also think you severely overstate just how much we know about Cthulhu. People conflate Cthulhu with all those gods because they're all descended from the same primal source."

"So you've claimed." Harley and I had spent the week in Innsmouth researching his theory before getting chased out of the town by the local fundamentalists. Harley was banned from our old Alma Mater, Miskatonic University, for much the same reason. Personally, I think they just grew sick of his lecturing. "You know I don't actually believe in this sort of stuff."

Which was a half-truth. Harley Warren had introduced me to a cornucopia of weird, surreal, and unnerving things. I'd attended seances with him, meetings with foul characters, and explored the most haunted locations from Kingsport to Ipswich.

Which wasn't a grand journey in terms of distance if you considered all of America but was larger than all of England. Oddly, it was Harley who was the quickest to believe in fraud and the most furious whenever the supernatural was not "actually" present in a medium or psychic's household. Personally, I could not often tell the difference between charlatan or soothsayer.

Frankly, some days it felt like I was following Harley along like Watson to his Holmes. As entertaining and congenial as I found Harley's company to be, it was often a demoralizing and unequal partnership. Yet the one time I suggested leaving for less arcane pursuits, he had positively revolted. 'You are a powerful dreamer, Randolph, and your destiny is to be far greater than mine. I rummage and scrape for scraps of knowledge, but you will bring life to worlds.' Which I'd assumed was referring to his appreciation for my short stories and novelettes. That had been ten years ago. Now? Now I wasn't so sure.

"A shame," Harley said, opening the book and looking over its contents. "This particular work provides more insight into Hastur, or the King in Yellow if you will, and the Yellow Sign than any other work I've yet read."

"Is he Cthulhu's half-brother?" I asked, sarcastically. "Some elemental spirit of the air?"

Harley glared at me, as if I was blaspheming. Which I suppose I was. "The things I have seen would turn your hair white, Randolph."

"Show it to me then," I said.

"You wouldn't understand the language," Harley replied. "It's written in a tongue that predates the human race."

That was a less than impressive response.

"Please tell me you didn't pay real money for this," I said, sighing. "Because that sounds very convenient for the seller."

"If it was a fraud, it was a very good one given the cipher used does translate to coherent passages," Harley replied, surprising me by arguing with logic rather than emotion. Harley was a good friend but something of a bully and if he'd been in a different mood, I expect he would have just yelled at me until I accepted his latest tome was a purchase of sublime genius.

I decided to indulge my friend. "A decoder ring can do the same thing. Still, what does it say?"

Harley's eyes seemed to bulge forward as if he was dealing with a concept too big for his brain to carry. He tapped the side of his skull with his forefinger three times. "Hastur is here."

"Uh huh," I replied.

Harley sighed. "The Yellow Sign, The King in Yellow, Carcosa, Leng, its satyr men, and Hali. All these things are related to the same prevailing concept. He is an entity or being or thing that you can touch through your art. The Muse of Madness or Grace of Chaos."

"You're not speaking sense, Harley," I said, now genuinely concerned for him. Harley was an intense man and frequently prone to obsession. Indeed, he was something of a bully even to his closest friends—myself included—and did not tolerate dissent.

"Exactly," Harley replied, as if he'd won an argument.

I sighed and got up from my seat. "I think I'm going to make myself dinner. Unless you want to go out?"

The storm was abating, and I suddenly felt my study had been invaded. If I was to listen to him claim yet another deity was secretly on the edge of human society, waiting to have the keys to their Olympus unlocked, I at least deserved a meal out of it. Harley would pick up the cheque and that was worth the price of listening.

"You're an artist, Randolph," Harley said, taking an almost conciliatory tone. "Of sorts."

I glared, taking him to be insulting of my profession. "Of sorts? Really?"

"No scorn is intended," Harley said, raising his hands in defense. "I find there is more value in a typical issue of *Arkham Scares* or *Outlandish Stories* than there is in any preacher's sermon. Had it larger print runs, I believe the combination of you and that Pickman fellow would have the entirety of the nation's men in rapt attention."

He was referring to the cover artist for a good number of Arkham's pulp magazines. Richard Pickman was not a gallery artist with his nightmarishly gory visages of otherworldly terror but had found an appreciative audience among the science fiction as well as horror fans of the genre magazine world.

Richard and I didn't always agree on content, and he often corrected me on how my monsters 'should' look but whenever I wrote from my dreams, I had his complete and undivided attention. He was, honestly, probably my only other close friend.

At least these days.

I'd lost contact with Etienne-Laurent de Marigny, who was every bit the occult obsessed madman that Harley was. Etienne had shown me the closest thing I'd ever come to the "true" occult in the crypts under Bayonne, New Jersey. He'd been less than pleased when I'd dismissed them as the products of mesmerism and no wilder than what I saw every night I went to sleep.

"I fear the average reader of both is more interested in the voluptuous naked forms being menaced by various creatures on the covers," I said, dryly.

I had been privately seeing a lovely young model for Richard's art from Innsmouth, her form absent that particular community's deformities save possibly unusually large eyes, when she'd suffered a dramatic change in personality as well as decided to no longer bare her skin for the cause of pulpish art.

It was a pity that Asenath had changed so much as some female companionship might have done both me and Harley good. Harley had no interest in such things, though, and I sometimes wondered if the intensity of his bond with me was serving as a substitute for it. I could not even say there was nothing sexual about it because the whole of that drive had been absorbed into his lust for the occult's power.

Harley gave a dismissive wave. "What I'm saying is that Hastur is a chance to open one's mind to a higher dimension beyond the sights and sounds of the common man. He is not a being who lives under the ocean or in the dark corners of the Earth but far beyond in the stars where reality merges with—"

"Dreams?" I finished for him. It was the one subject for which I believed I had a far greater authority than Harley. Neither Freud nor Jung had any insight that matched what my fantastical visions had bestowed me over the years.

"Yes," Harley said, staring down at this book with an almost lecherous gaze. "Imagine if inside this tome were the secrets to being able to connect our minds to the crossroads between inspiration as well as madness. Of dream with magic. Hastur is the key for that."

"I thought Yog-Sothoth was the Key and the Gate," I replied, referring to one of the imaginary gods of the *Necronomicon*.

Well, all gods were imaginary.

Harley gave me a withering glare. "No one likes a smartass, Randolph."

I snorted but decided to take his question seriously. "I suppose I think it would be truly amazing to encounter something unnamable. Indefinable. That would open one's mind to possibilities that would test the limit of what was conceivable. I'd very much like that, I think."

Harley snorted as if I'd said something very funny. "Perhaps you might very much like to touch the Yellow Sign. I suspect most minds would not. They would break under the strain of having not only their beliefs challenged but destroyed. The human mind is a fragile tower of building blocks constructed by a child. Remove any single one of them and the structure comes tumbling down, leaving only a gibbering wreck of shattered will."

I decided I did want to go out to eat. "I like that. Do you mind if I use it?"

"My verbiage would come off as purple to an audience of normal men," Harley said, self-deprecating.

"No more than mine and I get paid by the word," I replied, fetching my hat. "Are you coming? A good steak and some potatoes will do us both good."

"You need to get packing," Harley said, dismissing my concerns.

"What?" I asked. "Are we going somewhere?"

Harley had chosen not to take me across the globe last year, but he'd asked me to join him on many other excursions. Given I could write everywhere, it was not usually an inconvenience, but this still felt very sudden. Clearly, this so-called *Book of Hastur* had gotten deep into my friend's head and taken over. On the other hand, I couldn't help but feel a twinge of excitement at the possibility of yet another trip with my friends. Even the failed expeditions proved to be exciting and were ones I could never have afforded to undertake on my own.

"Big Cypress Swamp," Harley said. "I have already reserved our tickets on the train and paid for our lodgings. Gather your things, Randolph."

I stared at him. "You want us to go to Louisiana?"

I admitted, that was a location I'd long wanted to visit. New Orleans was a city with its own unique history, as old as that of the Puritans, and there were many occult leads to track down there. Supposedly, a Cthulhu cult had been founded among the Voodoo worshipers there by a renegade member of the tragedy afflicted Delapore clan. It had proven quite the scandal and was a worthy avenue to explore—assuming Harley hadn't found his own leads on his eternal quest for proof of the supernatural's veracity.

"I want us to go to Florida," Harley corrected, disappointing me. "To an ancient necropolis used once by the indigenous peoples and later by the Conquistadors. It is a graveyard that exists on no map but near the Gainesville Pike, preserved by local superstition as well as the remoteness of its location. However old it may be, it is older still as it was first a sacred place to a far elder people that predate humanity's arrival in the New World or perhaps even the world in general."

I was used to Harley Warren's fancies, but this was something else entirely. Or maybe I was just upset our trip wouldn't allow me to experience authentic Cajun cooking. "*The Book of Hastur* has led you to a flooded old tomb that you want us to visit? Really, Harley, at least New Orleans has hotels."

"Why do you say it's flooded?" Harley asked, focusing on the most irrelevant part of the question. "I have every reason to believe the tomb we seek will be guarded against all elements, earthly or otherwise."

"If it's in Florida and underground, it's flooded," I replied. Harley had a fascination with incorruptibility as a concept and of corpses that could spend centuries or even millennia without decaying. I had always dismissed that as a papist concept and Harley was as heathen as they came. Yet, the idea of him poking around a swamp for damp bones or rotted cloth seemed excessive even for him.

"The book, Randolph, the book," Harley said, tapping it. "The book describes so much in the margins. This is a volume of a people that no human tongue had spoken the language of, but I am not the first to read its contents or decipher its words. A Spanish missionary, brought there by tales of gold and pagan devil-worship, sought this place out. Inside, he discovered a doorway between this world and the next."

"And what happened to him?" I asked, suspecting how the religious fanatics of Spain would react to such an unconventional idea.

"It doesn't matter," Harley said, snorting his nostrils like a hog. "This location is a place between the worlds and a hole in the fabric of time. To pass through it will be the chance to finally prove all my theories and touch the fabric of the King in Yellow's robe. I have seen the Yellow Sign inside this book, and it has inspired me."

There was something disquieting about Harley's attitude, and I was no stranger to his uncomfortable moods and peculiar fixations. Like a modern-day Abdul Alhazred, Harley had ever wanted to be the prophet of the supernatural to a jaded blasphemous age. However, no secret seemed to be enough nor any revelation fully convincing.

Perhaps my friend had finally found the grail or Caliburn that he'd long desired inside this old volume's writing. I feared for my friend because if he put all of his faith into the least developed of the occult gods he'd so often spoken of then he was certainly setting himself up for further disappointing.

Still, that only made my determination to join Harley all the greater. After all, when and if we journeyed to this hidden tomb, I needed to be there for my friend. If he found nothing, as was likely, then he would need my counsel that all was not lost. If he did discover some secret *Key of Solomon* or *Book of Eibon*, well, then I wanted to be there for him as well. So that we might both unearth ourselves the secrets of time. Hastur was, at least in some of the writings I'd read, a god of hidden truths after all.

The horror followed me into my dreams.

I had not slept well, a status that had never afflicted me even during the direst of my circumstances, since that terrible night in Cypress Swamp. We'd found, much to my surprise, the tomb from Harley's book. It was an almost innocuous above ground stone mausoleum amidst other barely recognizable broken monuments. After removing a great stone slab, we'd both seen a set of stairs leading down-down into the proverbial rabbit hole of Charles Dodgson's Wonderland.

I'd stupidly, or perhaps prudently depending on one's perspective, allowed Harley to go forward into the chamber alone. We'd communicated via portable telephone throughout and I could still hear every one of Harley's final words spoken on that machine. I struggled not to think of that encounter but found it replaying endlessly in my mind.

"God! If you could see what I am seeing!"

"Carter, it's terrible—monstrous—unbelievable!"

"I can't tell you, Carter! It's too utterly beyond thought—I dare not tell you—no man could know it and live—Great God! I never dreamed of THIS!"

I could only imagine what amazing vistas and alien wonders my friend was privy to. There was true magic here and he had crossed the threshold between this world and the next. Had he journeyed like Orpheus between Earth and Hades? Or was he now on some grandiose other world or dimension? Perhaps a mythical underground kingdom like Burrough's Pellucidar. I wanted to join him that very moment but hung back due to some primal sense of wrong that froze me to my place. I had not even noticed it in my fevered conversation with Harley, but it had been there. Then? Then things had gone terribly wrong.

"*Carter! for the love of God, put back the slab and get out of this if you can! Quick!—leave everything else and make for the outside—it's your only chance! Do as I say, and don't ask me to explain!*"

But I'd needed more. Much more. I'd robbed Harley of precious seconds in my hesitation.

"*Beat it! For God's sake, put back the slab and beat it, Carter!*"

I'd wanted to help. Come down regardless of Harley's frantic bequest. To do... something! I'd called down, said I was coming to rescue him like some hero from lighter adventure fiction than the dark stories I'd always been compelled to write.

"*Don't! You can't understand! It's too late—and my own fault. Put back the slab and run—there's nothing else you or anyone can do now!*"

He had spoken with a desperation, urgency, and resignation I'd never heard from my friend. It had been the words of a man who had no hope for his own survival but only the desperate wish that I might escape. I'd stayed and begged for Harley to respond when he fell silent.

Right before hearing that awful-awful voice speak words burned into my brain, "YOU FOOL, WARREN IS DEAD!"

I had struggled to make my way to the nearest police station and give my statement, but the results had been less than gratifying. The police had not even charged me for Harley's murder but dismissed my story out of hand before releasing me. If they had bothered to investigate the cemetery, I knew they would find no body, but I suspect they had not even done that basic amount of detecting. Real life police were rarely Holmes or Dupin or even Lestrade. It was for the better, though, because the most merciful thing they might have found was death.

So, I had taken the next available train back to Arkham, Massachusetts where I had struggled to stay awake lest my dreams be infected by whatever fearsome horrors that he had met his doom at the hands of. Had he met Hastur? Was the place Hastur? Was the creature he had talked to the King in Yellow or one of its minions? Did it have any connection whatsoever to the concepts of that book other than a deranged monk's speculations leading Harley to his doom? I did not know and did not want to know.

When I reached home, only then did I finally feel a measure of safety. The events were like a terrible dream for me, and I had to admit a noxious moment of self-aggrandizement that I'd started writing in my notebooks feverishly on the train ride back. Some of my best work had born from my horrific encounter with Harley's killer. As awful as it would be to profit artistically from the death of a dear friend, I hoped that perhaps it would help exorcise the demons of my mind to put all my terrified tales to my typewriter.

Then I entered the study and saw *The Book of Hastur* was resting on my desk next to my typewriter. The book that Harley had most certainly had on his person when he had entered the awful tomb. A nightmarish conjuration of the most blasphemous sort yet innocuous in appearance. Walking with trepidation to it, I sat down and opened the book.

Its contents were hand-written, in English, and in Harley's hand. Except the scrawl had an undefinable sense of stiffness and forced strike to it. My friend was dead, yes, but I did not believe that had freed him from whatever horror he'd encountered down there. He was trapped in Hastur now, place or person or god or state of existence, and would never ever escape.

Like the King in Yellow, that place he now dwelled was a source of artistic inspiration for the contents of the book. A place or person that would inspire new dreams and tales of terror or pulpish heroism that seemed so childish yet was necessary to keep my sanity from crashing in on itself. The latter a delusion that was my only life preserver in a terrible storm. Had Harley sent this or his new dark master? Or had I summoned it from the Dreamlands through the power of a wish, reality now unmoored from my existence due to an encounter with the Yellow Sign? I had no idea.

So, I read.

BLOOD EAGLE

I, Harald Bjornson, would not die this day.
    I, Harald Bjornson, would not die this day.
    I, Harald Bjornson, would not die this day.

It was a mantra I repeated as a prayer and a spell both against the hunger, cold, and exhaustion that would deny me Valhalla. Unfortunately, it seemed very likely that the magic in my words would do me little good as I stumbled through the woods with no idea where I was going nor really where I'd come from.

Njord, God of the Seas, curse me, what sort of navigator was I that I couldn't even figure out where I was on this island? It was like the woods had swallowed me whole and I'd been compelled to run through them from the moment I'd begun my shameful flight.

It had started so well too.

The Jarl had sent us on a mission of trade from their home port to their neighbors when Svend, my dear stupid older brother, had suggested they do some viking. There had been twelve of them and there was a fishing village on the coast full of fat Christians just waiting to be raided. Nordi, our leader, had objected. He'd married a Christian after his first wife had died and practiced the true faith while praying to their god whenever their traders arrived.

It was disgusting really.

How things had gotten so damned confused was an easy enough line to draw in the dirt. The storm had put them off course, they'd woken up adrift against this island that shouldn't be here, and a fight had broken out. In the old, proper days, it would have been settled one-on-one in a duel, but it seemed everybody had forgotten how honor was supposed to work.

Stupid Svend had declared Nordi unfit for captaincy, and I'd sided with him as a brother should. Hel, we should have read the crowds. They were Svend's men and the promise of raiding a bunch of the filthy kneelers like my grandfather and father had didn't appeal to them the same way it did us. They'd ganged up on my brother, beaten him to the ground, and put an ax in his forehead before I could do anything but reach for my sword.

Hel!

Still, I had no one to blame for what happened next. I'd run like a craven. Staying and dying against ten other men would have been foolish. Foolish but what honor demanded. I'd even now be feasting in Odin's halls alongside my grandfather and uncles had I charged them all. If I died here, I'd not only never reach Valhalla like my poor father (dying of the cough in his bed) but my brother would be unavenged.

Odin, he'd never let me hear the end of it and I bet he'd journey down to Hel just to taunt me about being an Einherjar. That was assuming I wasn't fully cast into Náströnd along with the oathbreakers, adulterers, cowards, and murderers. That would be horribly unfair. I'd killed fifteen men, three of them armed, and they should really judge these things in a context.

Eventually, I felt myself gain enough control to put myself up against the side of a tree. "Odin, I offer you this promise: if you can provide me with some food and a warm fire then I will kill a dozen Christians for you."

No answer. Well, obviously not. The gifts of the gods were rarely bestowed directly. Still, I needed to find a way back to the shore or some shelter against the elements. If my associates had left me on the island, which they might well have, and there was no one else then it would be a pitiful slow death. I needed to avoid that at all costs.

That was when I saw a burning fire in the night through the trees.

I arrived at the flames with a stumbling gait but the sight that greeted me was a welcome one, even if I suspected the man I found sitting at the fireside would not be happy once I took everything he possessed.

It was a Christian monk, sitting alone, on the top of a chopped down tree. His yellowed robes were old and ratty with an unpleasant smell radiating from them that I could not quite put into words. His skin was weathered like old leather with his eyes milky white, indicating that he was blind. I put his age between seventy and a hundred, somehow animate and still alive when time should have taken him.

There was a bag of food at his side, meat, and bread, with some fresh rabbit roasting over the fire. Sadly, I couldn't smell the deliciousness of the meat with the foul odor radiating from the man himself.

"Give me your wares, monk, and I won't gut you now," I said, pulling my knife instead of my sword. I did not know if he spoke my tongue and if he didn't, I was glad he was an invalid in the middle of the woods rather than someone who could fight back.

Much to my surprise, he spoke perfect Danish. "Everything that I own is something I am happy to share with you, Northman."

I blinked, staring at him. "How do you even know I'm a Northman, blind man?"

The old monk smiled a mouth of nasty yellow teeth. "I see more than you might guess. Either way, there is food, wine, and clean water. Drink and eat your fill."

"You act like you have a choice," I said, sitting down across from him on another log and tearing into his supplies while the fire warmed my spirit.

"Of course," the old monk said. "Tonight, is a fortuitous night for you, brother."

The fare was bland, but I didn't care, enjoying every bit of it. "My brother is dead, monk. The only reason I have not killed you yet is because I am too tired to do so, and you clearly have been left for dead by your people."

The old monk laughed as if the idea amused him. "My people have entrusted me with a mighty task. All is as the Lord wills it. My flock have been led astray by the words of false prophets and heathen blasphemers. This island belongs to the true followers of the Lord of Shepherds and not the foul liars who teach ruination. I had five soldiers with me, but they perished killing most of the heretics. Now, I have been sent a champion who might deliver us from the Great Beast's insanity."

I followed one in every third word in the old monk's ramble. Chewing between words, I stared at him. "I am a worshiper of Odin, Christian. As heathen and blasphemous as any on this Earth to your god of foolishness. I would kill you and your ilk if I could. I still might. I spit on any task that would do your god honor."

I'd already decided not to kill the monk. As repulsive as I found their religion, one that spread like disease via their preachers, it was bad luck to kill someone who offered you food at their table. Besides, it wasn't like I had anything to fear from a man older than my grandfather if he'd lived to today. Still, I wasn't going to allow him to spout his nonsense.

"Allow me to speak plainer then," the old monk replied. "Gold and a boat."

I stopped chewing. "You have my attention."

"These individuals are the followers of a god you will not have heard of called Dagon," the old monk said. "Throughout the lands of Wessex, they have spread a corrupted and foul version of Christianity that detracts from the worship of our lord. Their chief way of winning men over is gold trinkets and jewelry that they have much of. The ones here come every month to make an offering of a maiden to the sea to be ravished before collecting more gold. They proceed to bring it back and use it as currency to spread more heresy."

"How many?" I asked.

"Excuse me?" The old monk asked.

"How many men?" I asked, focused more on the practicalities than anything else. "I'm assuming you want me to kill them and take their boat with you on it. Presumably, one laden with gold as well as potentially one raped sacrifice."

"The sacrifice remains pure," the old monk replied. "She must be for the Day of Revelation."

"That is not my point," I replied.

"Eight," the old monk finally admitted.

I snorted in derision. "Madness. Far too many. I'm sorry but I may barter passage with these fools if it gets me off this island. Either that or I'll take you with me if you lead me to your boat. Surely you came here on one as well."

I was surprised I was apologizing to him, but it seemed Odin was set on denying me riches this trip. I did mean it that I would give him passage off this island, though.

"Madness? Perhaps not," the old monk said, reaching behind his log and pulling out a short bow. Much to my surprise, he notched it like a man in the prime of his life and fired the arrow past my head against the tree trunk behind me. It was done fast enough that I barely had time to react, and a little biscuit fell out of my mouth.

"Pretty good for an old man," I said.

"I am thirty-three," the old monk said.

I blinked. "You don't look it."

The old monk grunted. "My appearance is the result of an encounter with a fecund creature when I was a young man in the service of the church. It laid its touch on me and robbed me of what was a visage that Paris of Troy would have been proud of. My brother monks treated me, though, and my body still has the strength of three men."

I stared at him. "What kind of monk are you? I thought you all sat around praying and rutting sheep? Aren't you forbidden from killing?"

"Only humans. Not heretics."

I stupidly agreed to help kill the fish worshipers. Perhaps it was greed mixed with a bit of gratitude but a larger part of me believed this had to be a sign from Odin. A bizarre sign surreptitiously sent since I would be helping one group of Christians slaughter another since I couldn't tell the difference between their interpretations of their god. One called his god the Lord of Shepherds and the other called his the God of Fish.

Peasant gods.

Mind you, my own father had been a blacksmith, so I wasn't exactly a royal myself. Still, war had been good to my family and the prospect of returning with a boat load of gold back to the Jarl was an appealing one.

I could care for my brother's wife and child as well as wipe the stain of cowardice from my spirit. Hel, I could hire twenty men if there was more than a handful of gold and we could kill Nordi as well as his men before paying off the weirgild price to their families. And if I died? Well, that was better than the alternative of dying an old man. So why were my dreams nothing but nightmares?

Svend greeted me in my dream, his head caved in by an ax as his rotted corpse led me to the heart of our village's square where I saw Nordi suspended between two poles. The middle-aged captain was hanging there, the skin of his back flayed away and a pile of gore at his feet alongside what had previously been the contents of his bowels. Two men in black leather masks were working, tearing him apart like an old woman cleaning a fish.

"Blood eagle," Svend spoke.

"Gods," I said, disgusted. "Why?"

The Blood Eagle was the worst way a man could die, a man's ribs severed from their spine and their lungs pulled from their back to create wings. It was a ritualistic form of execution I'd heard of but never actually met a man who'd seen it. Well, any man who wasn't a drunken liar.

"Sacrifice," Svend said. "The winter will be harsh and food scarce. The Jarl will blame Nordi for his failure at the trading post."

"And us?" I asked.

Svend grinned, gore leaking out of the side of his head. "We do not trouble his conscience."

Of course not. As much as I hated Nordi, though, I found this far too much. It was far from a clean death. "Will he go to Valhalla?"

"Only if he did not scream before death," Svend replied.

"Did he?" I asked.

"Yes," Svend replied. "For hours."

I woke up to find the old monk making spirals in the dirt with the end of his staff. The morning mist had settled over us and the fire had long since died but I'd endured far chillier mornings. I did not feel particularly rested, but the exhaustion had mostly left my bones and my belly was full, which was more than I could say about most days.

"Did you sleep well?" The old monk asked.

I stared at him. "No."

"Pity," the old monk said.

I got up, relieved myself, and drank more of the old monk's wine. "You never did tell me your name."

"You never told me yours," the old monk said.

"Harald," I said. "Which means we're friends now, I suppose."

"Haïta," the old monk said. "Haïta the Shepherd."

"Uh huh," I said, shaking off the horrific imagery. "I don't suppose you have more food. I went through most of yours last night."

"I have enough for our journey," Haïta said. "We can reach their camp in a few hours."

I snorted. "You can't be serious. Why would you want to attack them during the day?"

"Day is when they are weakest," Haïta replied. "These are the mixed bloods who have at least one parent from the dark places of the ocean. They are not used to the sun, and it is when they are sluggish and weak."

I shook my head. "I do not believe in sea giants, Haïta."

"And yet your god teaches they are very real," Haïta said. "Just as mine teaches there are demons."

"Perhaps they're both foolish," I said, feeling particularly blasphemous. The dream of last night was a powerful omen and not a welcome one. It implied that I would never make it home to my brother's family.

"We should take out their sentries, there should be no more than three, and cut the throats of the rest while they sleep," Haïta said, ignoring my comment.

"That sounds less like a plan than a goal," I replied, sighing. "However, I have no better ideas."

My brother had always been the thinker between us and I'd seen where that had gotten him.

"Good," Haïta said. "Then you should get ready to travel. Once they are roused, they will perform the rite and summon their brethren from the sea. Then there will be no stopping them. They will have the aid of their dead god."

"Isn't your god dead?" I asked, only vaguely knowing anything about the Christians' religion. It seemed mostly nonsense about not seeking revenge and the poor being blessed, which was just silly by any right-thinking man's reckoning.

"My god lies dead until his resurrection too, yes," Haïta said. "Until the day he returns and destroys all of our enemies."

I really didn't need to get into a religious debate. Odin would provide and had up until this point. "How does one get to become a monk anyway?"

"I joined after I saw the horrible things out there," Haïta said, sounding more annoyed than anything else. As if he was explaining seamanship to a particularly easy to distract child. "Things that should not be and could only be fought by the power of my Lord."

"Uh huh," I said. "What does this Dagon have to say about it?"

"That there is only room for one god's faithful," Haïta replied.

Oh yes, this was going to be a lovely trek.

"Odin, that is one ugly son of a bitch," I said, wiping off my knife as I stared down at the dying Dagonite on the ground.

Sneaking up on the first of them keeping watch had been surprisingly easy, Haïta proving to be an able woodsman as well as every bit his claim as a hearty warrior despite his appearance. He wore a large backpack full of supplies, clothes, and his staff that plugged a hole in it. He also had a quiver and bow that, combined with the other materials, I would have struggled to carry half the distance we covered.

We were nearby the coast now with the forest growing right up toward its edge and too large for most groups to keep watch over. I'd gotten up behind the chainmail clad warrior and opened his throat with my knife.

Its blood was blacker than normal, though, and the man's appearance was obscene. He had eyes twice the size of a Northman's and a smooth face that seemed to sag off his cheek bones plus sacks bulging out of his neck. It reminded me of nothing so much as a frog mixed with a man. There was also a foul stench to the air that reminded me of rotting fish. His armor was good, though, and expensive too. I also saw his ax was fine steel, even if weirdly shaped with an eye-like design to the blade. The dead man wore rings of gold that I swiftly pulled off his fat fingers, already making this excursion worth it.

"It is an abomination," Haïta said, holding his bow steady as he surveyed our surroundings. "A product of man and not-man."

"If you say so," I replied, not willing to deny my senses but unconvinced as well that we were dealing with monsters. I'd seen what disease could do to a man and also encountered a wide variety of strange people when trading. None of them had been as repulsive to look at as this fellow but maybe he was a Pict. They supposedly married their sisters and ate the flesh of men according to my cousin.

Haïta cocked his bow and fired an arrow across the forest glade that struck another of the Dagonites in the throat. It was a supernaturally accurate shot, even for a man that didn't look like he was dug up from the ground a week after being buried. The figure choked in his own black blood before Haïta jogged toward him then drove the arrow deeper into his skull. It was a surprisingly brutal action, and I was starting to like the Christian.

"Two down," I replied. "So, that leaves six by your count."

"Yes," Haïta said. "We're nearby their camp. You should take his axe and smash in the heads of any that are still resting."

"That would not be honorable," I said, dryly. "I shall challenge them to combat open and honorably."

Haïta looked at me with a confused expression.

I grinned and let out a short laugh at the deliberate absurdity of my statement, going to check the second Dagonite body for more gold. This time, he had a little fish amulet that would buy me a shield when I made it back to my hometown.

"Your greed does not do you credit, Harald Bjornson. You can't take it with you," Haïta said, moving into the forest to look for more Dagonites.

"Then it's a good thing I intend to spend it in this life," I said, turning around to see no sign of my companion.

I also tried to remember when and if I'd ever told him my full name.

Calling it a camp was a misnomer as it was a single large Rus-style yurt erected on a hill overlooking the rocky shore. There were bedrolls gathered around it and a fire pit. It seemed an incredibly poorly chosen location for it as the tide would almost certainly wash over anyone sleeping around it.

Still, the wealth of my prey was impressive as I saw their longboat nearby and it was a genuinely masterful piece of craftsmanship, enough to have close to thirty men onboard and possessed a strange squid-like design on the masthead. If it had been fully loaded when Haïta's people had attacked, they must have been great warriors to kill so many. It also wasn't something I'd be able to man myself and Haïta would have known it.

Then again, the old monk had proven far from useless and between the two of us it would be possible to maybe direct it to inhabited lands if they were in Njord's and Odin's favor. That was never anything to count on when dealing with a bitch as capricious as the sea but there wasn't anything I could do about it now. It was also a prize that I'd look like a king bringing into the port and could hire a proper crew for at the nearest port.

Either way, I stayed low and saw only a single guard left awake. Taking the eye-shaped ax, I did my best to sneak up, but it didn't quite work out. Thankfully, the guard was lethargic and when he heard my movement, I was close enough to drive the ax into his neck. The man blubbered and reached for the blade even as he bled out from the enormous wound. I didn't give him a chance to go for it and drew my knife to stab him through the base of his chin. The fetid foul-smelling black blood made me gag but was still a welcome sight as it poured out over my hands. After all, it wasn't mine.

Five left.

Plus, the maiden they were going to sacrifice.

I hadn't given much thought to her, hadn't ever given much thought to women in my life, but noted that might be another bonus to this excursion. I preferred my women willing but provided I didn't have to argue too heavily with the monk, women slaves brought a high price at most of the markets I knew along these regions. The thought gave me pause and it occurred to me that I might just let her go with Haïta. He'd seemed oddly focused on her and she was probably a believer in his faith he wanted to rescue.

If so, I'd play the hero and let him take her back to her family or whatever monks did with women. This encounter was changing me, and I felt a better man for it. Not the least because the man on the ground had a pouch full of actual gold coins. At least twenty of them.

Odin be praised.

Clearing my head of any thought but the men around me, I found three sleeping the sleep of the dead in their bedrolls. There was a pot full of some sort of thick black liquor by the fire pit, I certainly recognized the smell of brew, and it amused me how much it was contributing to what I expected to be the easiest victory of my life. They were all as ugly and disgusting as the first one I killed. Destroying them would be a favor to themselves and whatever gods they worshiped. Most of all, though, it would be a favor to myself.

One head was easily caved in as he slept.

Two.

Then three.

It was bloody, gory, and entirely satisfying business, the Dagonite's own steel doing a better job than anything I'd ever wielded in my hands. With three more dead, I only had two to find and kill. Now, where were—

"*Dagon mftaghnah'pftyl! Muh'tah'ahh'zuul, Mother Hydra!*" A shout came from the yurt's tent folds as the two remaining warriors poured out with Moorish curved swords drawn. Clearly, these fish worshipers traveled as far as his people. Both had short, rounded shields too, something I could have desperately used right now. Both were even more frog-like than the others, but their fury was obvious as was their skill. Both charged forward, heedless of the danger but determined to avenge their slain comrades.

"Dammit," I muttered, holding the ax in both hands.

I had met many men who claimed they had struck down dozens of foes in battle. These men were all liars. The truth was that battle was often a matter of surprise, luck, and simple odds. Two well-armed men against one was almost always going to end in the death of the latter. A wiser man would have run but I'd already disgraced myself once.

Never again.

Instead, I surprised us both by charging forward with a curse on my tongue and no thought to my own safety. I slashed wildly and repeatedly, catching the first Dagonite off guard and cutting him to pieces before sheer chance allowed me to strike hard into the side of the second. It shouldn't have worked, mail existed for a reason, but the metal of the ax cut through it like linen. I had a feeling it wasn't steel but something much stronger and sharper. Either way, my next blow was enough to send it down. I kept cutting, though, and made a cruel sport of its form until it stopped moving. It looked like someone had poured an ink pot over his corpse.

"Ha-ha!" I said, as stunned as anyone by my triumph. "I piss on your god, Dagon! I piss on your language! I piss on your corpse!"

I was so relieved to be alive, I might have done so if not for the fact that I heard the tent flap of the yurt open again. This time, though, the sight that greeted me was far comelier. Her skin was as white as sea foam and her hair as dark as midnight with long lovely curls. The woman was clad in a white dress that was clean and tied to her waist by a well-tied rope. She moved with an ethereal grace toward me, her eyes a blue I'd never seen before.

I raised my hand. "You probably cannot understand me, but I am with the Christian monk. Cross? Friend? You don't have to die."

The woman showed no sign of understanding but still approached me, which made me wonder if she was simple. I had no idea how to respond but found myself strangely tongue-tied. That feeling swiftly left me as she opened her mouth and revealed two rows of teeth that were sharpened like knives, her jaw extending down like an eel's. Her mouth let forth an unearthly wail that caused me to drop my axe and cover my ears for fear of their insides bursting.

"Hel!" I shouted back, scared out of my mind and suddenly all too aware that Haïta hadn't been lying about them being giants.

That was when an arrow shot into the creature-woman's breast. A flower of clear liquid oozed from her injury instead of blood, smelling faintly of flowers like she'd been stuffed with plants instead of gore. Instead of dying, she screamed again, only to be shot again.

"Yield!" a familiar voice shouted to the creature-woman.

Haïta had finally made his appearance and calmly fired arrow after arrow into the creature-woman before me. She had six arrows in her before the clear ooze started to drip out of her mouth, her movements becoming sluggish as well as vulnerable. The sight compelled me to grab for the ax I'd dropped, climb to my feet, and swing around to decapitate the creature-woman in one easy motion.

"And stay down!" I shouted at her body, feeling quite proud of myself. I could now call myself Harald Giantslayer wherever warriors gathered to drink. Not that anyone would believe this story. I'd sound like the very drunks and braggarts I'd spent most of my life mocking.

"You destroyed the sacrifice," Haïta said, approaching me from behind. He tossed his bow on the ground and pulled his staff out of his backpack. I didn't know why he bothered with it since he clearly didn't need it to walk.

"Yes. She wasn't exactly pure, was she?" I made a half-terrified joke before sucking in my breath. "We make a pretty good pair, don't we monk?"

Haïta nodded. "Yes."

He then cracked me across the head with the side of his staff, sending me thundering to the ground.

Darkness claimed me with a second strike to the skull.

I woke up to the smell of burning flesh and rotting fish. My wrists were bound to a pair of poles set up before the shoreline. Night had fallen and my mouth was aching every bit as much as my head. My attempts to speak failed miserably because I discovered, to my horror, they'd been sewn shut with fishing line. Worse, my mouth had been stuffed full of some foul blackish substance that I could not taste but had a noxious texture.

Haïta was standing there with his shepherd's crook, in the center of a five-pointed star created by rocks combined that each ended in a strange dog-like skull that seemed more manlike than I was comfortable with. The bodies of the Dagonites were burning in a nearby pyre, sending forth black smoke into the night sky.

"*Catag'nh nergul Adonei Yog-Sothoth, Jehovah Azathoth Adzul, and Nyarlathotep Jibriel*! I call upon you, Lord of Hali, King of Carcosa, Lord of Leng, to come forth! Come forth and accept your gifts on this glorious day when the worlds merge! The heretics have been purged and the Dead God Who Lies Dreaming, your brother, lies sleeping still at the bottom of the dark underworld where your enemies have imprisoned him!"

"Mmmmph!" I struggled to speak.

"Come forth, Lord Hastur, Son of God, and bringer of the Revelation!" Haïta called up to the sky. "Come forth!"

I did not understand what had happened or who the names Haïta was calling upon were. He was like no other Christian I had ever met, and it occurred to me I was now dealing with something that I had absolutely no way of dealing with or escaping from. I struggled in my bonds but found them firmly tied.

That was when the sky cracked open and lights in colors I'd never seen before poured forth. They scintillated and danced in a rainbow of weird patterns before some THING began to crawl out from the rift that existed above me. It was indescribable and horrifying, causing fear in my heart that dwarfed anything I'd ever felt before.

I knew, though, I was its meal.

A sacrifice.

A Blood Eagle to appease the gods.

I tried to scream but could not because I realized that Haïta had taken my tongue.

"The Pits of Hastur" takes place after the events of The Tree of Azathoth *and in the early part of* Cthulhu's Canyon. *Basically, it's a gladiator story and I wanted to revisit one of the minor supporting characters of the Dream Cycle in Kuranes. This version is a far more corrupt and nastier than the one shown in Lovecraft's stories, but I view the idea of characters falling prey to their own vices over the millennia to be quite believable.*

THE PITS OF HASTUR

A *Cthulhu Armageddon* adventure

Chapter One

The Gug lifted one of the pitiful human slaves in the air before biting their arm off at the shoulder. The bloody action caused the coliseum crowd to roar with delight. The stadium was built Roman style and filled with tens of thousands of Celephaïs residents dressed in robes, tunics, and the occasional blue jeans with t-shirt. They were a cosmopolitan band of citizens drawn from all over the Dreamlands and here for the Great Games of Hastur as hosted by their God King Kuranes.

The man who was my host.

I felt ill watching the violence below. I was familiar with gladiator contests, fighting for spectacle was as old as humankind, but found this display sickening. Most battles I'd witnessed had been designed to display the skill of the contestants, often fixed to inflate their heroism, but this was just gore for the sake of gore.

"You do not appear to be enjoying the Great Games, Lord Booth," the voice of my host spoke with a decidedly anachronistic upper crust English accent. He was unlike anyone else in his kingdom as well, resembling a 1920s actor I'd once seen a black and white photo of. He was also wearing a tuxedo, of all things, with an umbrella being held over him by a twelve-year-old slave girl.

Kuranes, though that was almost certainly not his birth name, was the most powerful Dreamer in a thousand worlds and perhaps the most powerful Earth had ever produced except for the missing Randolph Carter. Dreaming was akin to magic in the Dreamlands and one who mastered their nighttime visions had the power of a god. Kuranes had long since abandoned his mortal body and ruled this place, supposedly made from his childhood dreams, for centuries.

"Just Booth, or John Henry, not Lord. As for whether I'm enjoying this display, no, I'm not," I said, deciding that honesty was a better policy for keeping his attention. Kuranes was surrounded by flatterers and sycophants. I'd met several who'd dismissed me as a Wasteland barbarian and unwittingly served as the best introduction I could have gotten to a man bored of court life.

"Oh?" Kuranes asked, curious.

I nodded. "I see no value in slaughter for its own sake. The Wastelands provided me enough indiscriminate violence to last a thousand lifetimes."

"Which you may find also applies to life in the Dreamlands," Kuranes said, leaning back in his throne that existed in an alcove that dominated this portion of the area. My own chair was far smaller and to the side, letting the position of his guests remain clear. I was technically here acting as a representative of humanity's survivors in the far-off Republic of Carter. A position I had as much title to as the King of Oz or President of Made-Up-Ville. I did not know if he believed my bold-faced lie or not but, so far, he seemed intrigued enough to treat me with all the honors an ambassador deserved.

"Immortality is an exotic dish," I said, speaking as if I had any real experience in it. "But I've yet to see it among most people living here. The people down below getting slaughtered, for instance."

Kuranes ignored my not so gentle reproach to the bloodshed. "Dreamers are capable of living for eons here if their spirits survive the transition of physical death. It is the dreams, those poor fools being eaten by my Gug for example, who are doomed to short meaningless existences. Look at it closely and see the difference between it and its prey."

I reluctantly did so, wishing I was anywhere else. "Sure."

The Gug was a particularly hideous example of its species, standing eighteen feet tall and possessing a mouth that was large enough to swallow a man in two bites with teeth that were like swords. Its proportions were apelike with scales covering part of its body and ratty molted fur on other portions. Its hunger was unnatural, feeding a biology not even the strange alien biology of the Dreamlands produced but modified with the alchemy of Celephaïs as well as twisted human sciences to produce a creature that served an all-too-human evil: sport.

For the past ten minutes, the Gug had been "fighting" a group of eight men, dragging a tree-sized wooden club behind it while chasing the remaining helpless humans down as they tried to navigate the crude obstacle course set up in the center of the arena. There were things I recognized: a junked car, a streetlight, and a stone fireplace absent a house around it.

There were more alien things as well like statues of beings that had no human features, what could have been chairs made for beings that had had no legs, and an organic rock formation that seemed to shift with movement around it. They did little to separate the Gug from its prey and the humans below, slaves, had thrown down their weapons to hope to avoid the creature.

There were two left.

A blond-haired man in his mid-thirties and a woman of about fifty who was directing the former to try to keep the creature at bay with movement even if such a thing was probably futile in the long run.

"I doubt they view their lives as meaningless," I said, not sure how to respond. As much as I didn't want to be invested, I couldn't help myself. I wanted these poor fools to live even if it was impossible. There was a natural urge for humans to root for the underdog, particularly when they were from the Wastelands like myself. We were all underdogs there, even if I couldn't really count myself among them these days.

"Dreams exist for the dreamer," Kuranes said, his voice carrying only a hint of the mammoth disdain I felt from him regarding his subjects. "They are my immortality. But I will never forget they are just my imaginings."

"They are still people," I said, struggling with the concept that reality was so mutable even if I'd spent some time in the Dreamlands. "The dreamfolk love, live, and die like real people. So, they are real."

"Are they? The people below, the ephemera of my consciousness, live as long as I will them to. True Humans are not made for immortality," Kuranes said, his voice soft and sad, surprising me. "I sometimes wonder if it was not a mistake to cast aside my physical form and live here as a god king among my creations."

The middle-aged woman of the two survivors met her end at the hand of the Gug, grabbed in one hand and hurled against a burnt-out Toyota Corolla that I was surprised to recognize the make and model of. The Gug proceeded to smash down its club onto her corpse multiple times, getting greater cheers with each blow.

"How does one become a god king?" I asked, half-joking. I was trying to distract myself from the disgusting display around me. I was far from squeamish, having memories of both a man and an alien, but the sheer delight around me was making me nauseous.

Kuranes smiled at the prospect of speaking his story. All dictators, magical or otherwise, loved talking about themselves. "When I was still human, I dreamed of Celephaïs as an image of a bygone age. A landed gentry, I thought kings and knights were the highest thing to aspire to. It was a child's dream of bygone innocence and sanitized stories of Grimm mixed with Sir Thomas Malory. By the time of the Great War, I was homeless and wandering the streets of London with the war having consumed my wealth as well as sanity. But I still dreamed of this place where I was absolute ruler of its people and a hero beyond reproach. Eventually, I stopped doing anything but dreaming and what little pocket money I earned by begging went to drugs to keep me dreaming of it. I became a master dreamer, able to work wonders like flying by thought or talking to sentient glowing gases but I never could find my way back to the product of a mind without the weight of a world. I found my home, this place, once more, only when I ran out of money for drugs and threw myself into the sea. Only then did the knights of Celephaïs take me to this place, in the Valley of Ooth-Nargai beyond the Tanarian Hills, where I was to rule forever. My body undoubtedly eaten by fish or washed up against the shores of Innsmouth beneath some fat nouveau riche fool's mansion."

I disliked Kuranes' sing-song way of speaking, like he was a poet rather than a tyrant. "So, to become immortal, you have to die."

"Yes," Kuranes said, bluntly.

"Ah," I said, clearly not understanding nor sure I wanted to. I had known things that had come back from death, but the experience always left them changed in ways that were never improvements. What lay beyond death was apparently worse than Hell or oblivion.

"Earth is dead, at least our Earth," Kuranes said, sneering. "I thought this was Elysium, Heaven, or the final reward religions promised for countless years but the years, nay, the millennia wore on. The heroic battles I fought mattered little when I always won, the beautiful queens I had all became shallow caricatures as they were all the product of my fantasies, and the sweetest nectars I drank at fabulous banquets all became like ash in my mouth. By the time Randolph Carter came to my land, I was already sick of being God-King. I missed my beloved Cornwall and the sweet simple pleasures of being a mortal man. All that is left here is the memory of those things and the primal fears and lusts. You ask me why I revel in the violence here with my people? Because death is one of the few things that can still conjure even the memory of true emotion in me."

"Ah," I replied. "I understand."

And I did.

Kuranes frowned. "You think I am a brute."

"I think you are a madman," I replied, simply.

Kuranes burst out laughing. A thing that seemed to surprise him as much as it did me. It seemed likely he had not laughed in a very long time. "What are your motivations, then, Booth? You are far younger than me and I suspect have foolish sentimentality about the nature of man and life. A man who clings to the delusion that the gods are anything but dreams of bigger, better, and louder humans who judge or care about our every move."

I silently cursed myself for being so blunt with Kuranes and it was just the vagaries of fortune that he had taken it as a genuinely funny joke versus the serious indictment of his character that I'd meant it as. I was here, flattering the despot, because I needed access to his palace's heart. The Eye of Hastur, a gemstone of black ruby that contained magical power beyond imagination, was supposedly in Kuranes' possession. If I was to find a way to free the Dreaming City from its curse, I would need an object like it.

Unfortunately, to get close to the Eye of Hastur, I needed to share pleasantries with someone who was *fucking insane*. Oh, and had the power of a god. If he wasn't anywhere near the power of a Great Old One, he was certainly capable of doing wonders akin to the Small Gods of Earth like Zeus, Hypnos, or Nodens. They existed in the Dreamlands as well, the faith of their worshipers sustaining them long after the civilizations that revered them had died.

It didn't help I was distracted by the sole survivor of the blood sport below. Against my better judgement, I cared about whether he lived or died. He had screamed out at the death of the woman, the only person of his group he seemed to care about and taken a spear up from the ground. It was a foolish move but that act of defiance was perhaps the only courage one could display in the face of such ritualized horror.

It did, indeed, inspire me with how to respond.

To quote a man who had lived his life free. "*I have known many gods. He who denies them is as blind as he who trusts them too deeply. I do not seek beyond death.* It may be a realm like yours, Kuranes, or the wonder and glory of the Deep Ones with their dragon-squid. Maybe even fluffy clouds and harps. Maybe nothingness. While I live in the Dreamlands, I am flesh and blood and blood and flesh are what I indulge in. Maybe as a god you have time to contemplate the ephemera of your millions of citizens but as a gunslinger, I only have a woman at my arm, a pistol in my hand, and a curse on my tongue to provide me my meaning."

Kuranes stared as if trying to remember some distant long forgotten wisdom. "You paraphrase the Cimmerian. He was nothing but a long-forgotten myth written about by Pulp writers in my time, like Gilgamesh or Hercules. The star of bawdy epics and boys' rags."

I shrugged. "I read those same rags as a boy. Though they were paperbacks and already decades old from when the Rising destroyed human civilization. Just because they were stories for children does not make them childish. *Let teachers and philosophers brood over questions of reality and illusion. I know this: if life is illusion, then I am no less an illusion, and being thus, the illusion is real to me. I live, I burn with life, I love, I slay, and am content."*

There was something about my answer that annoyed Kuranes, more so than the direct insult to his face. "A simplistic answer for a simplistic mind, John Henry Booth. For me, there is only one god, and it is a god that we will all come to worship in the end: Hastur. The God of Madness."

"A strange deity to worship," I replied, trying to disguise my excitement at finally getting to a relevant topic. I doubted Kuranes would tell me where he was storing the Eye in casual conversation, but stranger things had happened. "I have heard a thousand tales of his worshipers but all of them speak of him as a malevolent deity. The Lord of Hali. The Master of Leng. The King in Yellow. The half-brother of Cthulhu. I was surprised to see him venerated here. Usually, his worship is outlawed and the masked traders of Leng killed on sight."

I'd seen them everywhere in Kuranes' court.

Kuranes looked particularly disdainful of the last description. "That is what fools who think they are sane think. Hastur is the entropy inherent to the universe. The urge to self-destruction and horrific excess inherent to all thinking beings. Time wears down even the noblest of men but leaves only immediate gratification. When you have lived epochs, John Henry Booth, you will find that only staring into the spiraling abyss of everything's end provides any comfort."

Yeah, Kuranes was a madman who confused rapine for rapture. "Violent delights lead to violent ends. Spare the sole survivor in the arena."

It was an action that endangered my cover, and it was the height of hypocrisy to do so for this one fellow versus the dozens of individuals who I'd already seen killed. However, my emotions were piqued and if I had the attention of the self-styled God King then I might be able to do some small bit of good, at least as how humans defined it.

"So, you *are* invested in the games," Kuranes said, turning to me with a smile that seemed almost like he'd forgotten how to do it.

"As you say," I said, uninterested in arguing with him.

"So be it," Kuranes said, standing up and lifting a single hand with its palm outstretched.

The skies darkened over the coliseum with storm clouds rushing in across the horizon until it was as night, but no rain fell. From Kuranes' hands, though, not the sky shot forth a bolt of lightning like he was the King of the Olympians himself.

The bolt struck the man onto the ground before the Gug and left him twitching on the ground before death mercifully took him. It was an impressive but casual source of the supernatural powers at Kuranes' command.

The crowd was silent, shocked by the sudden action by their deity. It was a reminder of his terrible presence and power that could strike them down at any moment. A moment more of silence passed before the crowd erupted into wild ecstatic cheers, sincere or born from terror.

"That is *not* what I meant," I replied.

"I gave him the greatest gift possible," Kuranes said. "A chance to be martyred for his god. It was also a swift death, better than he deserved. Did you know he was a child-killer? A rapist? A serial murderer of women?"

"No," I replied.

Kuranes shrugged. "Neither do I. His crimes do not matter, if he has performed any at all. He lived and died at my will, just as you must—*shoggoth*."

My blood ran cold.

Chapter Two

Shoggoth.

That name. One that was reviled throughout the Dreamlands and among the survivors of Earth. If there was a more hated species where man's foot treaded, I did not know it. They were humanity's cousins, the Elder Things extracting the seed of consciousness from their modified slaves to create the sentient ape-men who would go on to father homo sapiens as well as all their offshoots like the ghouls, Serpent Men, or Deep Ones. The shoggoths themselves had been created from a marooned member of the Kastro'vaal species, creating a kind of sickening Great Chain of Being that extended from the Old Ones to the dreamfolk below.

It was difficult to say why the shoggoths were so reviled but there was no place in the Dreamlands I explored that they were not loathed more than the cannibalistic Skor or the plague-bringers of Tarkati. Somehow both dreamer and dreamfolk recognized enough of a kinship with the shapeshifting protoplasmic horrors that they desired nothing less but their enslavement or extermination on sight. Other creatures, let us call them monsters, might invoke awe as well as fear or a desire to propagate but the shoggoth was the preferred subject of sorcerers seeking slaves to dominate their foes or the proverbial dragon to slay for heroes hoping to make their legend.

I, myself, had slain a shoggoth before discovering our twisted kinship. In the Black Temple, I had managed to use a pair of mystical objects in the shape of revolvers to cut one down as it tried to slay me. It was the formative event of my career as a Wasteland "hero" and yet I could only wonder now if the creature had been trying to communicate with me as a brother versus striking me dead. Or maybe I saw sympathy where none existed, for it was not as if blood kinship prevented humans from slaughtering each other like ants over territory or starving dogs over a bone.

Kuranes' words were as such that the entire city would rise against me at his word, not that they wouldn't for any other words from him, and burn me alive. If I was known as one in the Dreaming City, I would also be killed along with all my associates. The Deep Ones might keep shoggoths as slaves but even they feared their power.

"I do not know what you—" I started to speak, stupidly.

Instead, I felt the air ionize around me and my words catch in my throat. I had no doubt that Kuranes could unleash ten kinds of magic upon me that would be as real as any flame, lightning, or explosive. I had survived things that would kill any normal man, which I was not, but shoggoths for all their reputation were still creatures of material matter. Immortal to the years but not to being killed and among the lesser creatures of the Dreamlands, only terrifying to humanity and their descendants. Kuranes may be playing God here, but the world was playing along with him. If he could dream me dead, I was dead.

"Yes," Kuranes spoke, clearly speaking to my thoughts rather than my words. "I could dream you dead."

"What do you want?" I asked, feeling a light rain pour down. Underneath Kuranes' umbrella, none of it touched him and I suspected it might not even do so should it have not existed. We were trapped in his mad twisted dream—which I probably should not have thought of given the revelation of his mind-reading power.

"Oh, I am mad," Kuranes said, clasping his fingers together and staring forward. "I'm mad. You're mad. We're all mad here. Lewis Dodgson had it right. As for what I want, it is simple: amusement. You are a man who craves something from me and wishes to kill me for it. I do not know what it is, it is hidden from my mind, but I will have it."

I did not yet breathe out a sigh of relief for the fact he did not know that I craved the Eye of Hastur meant the spells my lover Mercury had woven, ones infinitely more complex than the meager sorceries I'd managed to master of pre-human civilization, were holding still. Still, it would not take much to guess it was my quest's object and the greatest defense I had now was that no one was supposed to know I had it.

I had learned it from the Crawling Chaos himself.

In, of all things, a dream.

"I do not wish your death, Kuranes," I said, speaking truthfully. "I feel you are a mad king, wasted by time and corrupted by power. However, if I was to kill every man destroyed by such things then I would have to spend every day of my life murdering every ruler in the

Western Dreamlands. I would have to kill myself. I have lived too long as well and intend to continue to do so."

"So, your defense is you just intend to rob me?" Kuranes asked, eyes twinkling as if the ridiculousness of it all was enough to spare my life for the next few seconds. I had no doubt he could turn me into snow, music, or ash with a wave of his hand. This was his realm, and I was just a guest if even that.

I decided to do the most human thing possible in this situation and lie. "I seek the missing Dreamer, Randolph Carter, Kuranes. The one you knew from your early days as god king. With his power, we can dream up a new Earth and create a home for the people of our planet if not an entirely new habitat for humanity with no Old Ones to threaten it. You are the last one to have seen him in living memory other than Nyarlathotep and he cannot—"

"Do...not...mention...that...being," Kuranes spoke, snapping his finger like a man summoning a waiter.

No sooner had Kuranes made his gesture, than I found myself falling on my knees against the dusty blood and viscera-splattered cobblestones of the arena. The smell that assaulted me was revolting, mixing the intestines and gore with the discharge of men in their death throws. The rain was doing little to deplete the smell even as the winds from it carried out the noxious scent of the Gug that was perhaps three or four yards away. The smell a foul bacteria-ridden musk mixed with chemicals from other worlds toxic and hostile to human life. It was a creature that smelled of sulfur, sweat, and the dead men it was splattered in the gore of.

The Gug was considerably more impressive in person than viewed from the stands, towering over me like a storybook giant. Its bizarre alien biology, though I was no one to talk, had made it vaguely resemble a man with connotations akin to a giant ape, but its extra arms flexed in anticipation of a kill that it had clearly not gotten enough of. The monster's mouth was the wrong direction, horizontal like a Venus Fly trap and its eyes, if such sensory organs functioned like the ones on Earth, were on its malformed face's side.

"We have a new challenger!" Kuranes' voice echoed throughout the coliseum. "The Wastelander John Henry Booth, Son of Two Worlds, versus Gug the Never Dying! May those who are about to die salute the God of Madness!"

I gave the God King my own salute with one finger before rolling on the ground to grab at the spear of one of the dead men. I'd almost certainly ruined any chances of getting out alive, let alone with the gemstone I sought. But I had no regrets. The opportunity to tell that slaving asshole what I thought of him was worth the remainder of my supposedly immortal life. One either died as the man one wanted to be or lived as an unrecognizable collection of lies.

"Arghoooooooo!" The Gug made a noise that deafened me, spreading out its arms and charging toward me.

I dodged out of the way of the creature, cutting at it with the steel tip of the weapon, but if it was able to pierce the thick hide of the monster then it was not revealed in that moment, bouncing off as if striking rock. I considered in that moment assuming my true form, or at least what passed for such among a race of shapeshifters, to go after the beast. The crowd would consider me just another monster and Kuranes would keep me as a creature for his menagerie, no doubt, but at least I might have had a fighting chance. Besides, Kuranes had all but confirmed he knew who and what I was.

Unfortunately, that avenue had denied me as well as I found myself unable to make myself stronger, faster, or covered in alien armor. I was a poor shapeshifter, too much identification with my human form, but that was still better than being a helpless mortal against a creature that was as much alien matter as dream or flesh.

No, I cannot think that way, I muttered, standing tall. *The moment I think of my humanity as a weakness, the moment I am doomed to succumb to the same madness as Kuranes.*

I embraced that delusion as the Gug turned around like a charging bull, facing me with its open salivating mouth.

"Come on, you bastard!" I snarled, raising my spear. "Let's see how you do against someone who actually knows how to fight back!"

The Gug responded by lifting the Dodge Charger off the ground with two hands and proceeded to hurl it my way. I only barely managed to somersault forward, sadly bringing myself only closer to the creature as it smashed behind me. That was when the Gug moved forward, anticipating my movements.

Shit.

It could *think*.

A more philosophical man might have pondered the fact we were both being forced to combat one another for the amusement of a jaded crowd and a bloodthirsty wizard-king. Instead, I focused on the pure atavistic urge for survival while trying to tune out the crowds' screams beside. They were sincere in their cheering now, glad to see something more properly resembling sports instead of just simple murder.

I stabbed at the Gug again even as it swung its arms to the ground, sending up a cloud of dust that choked my lungs while its other arms reached for my body. I managed to move out in time, only for the steel to once more strike against a thick rock-like texture beneath its fur. The Gug had an exoskeleton underneath its flesh or musculature that was like coral.

"Arghhhhoooo!" The Gug blew hot breath that almost choked me with its nightmarish smell, tasting of the acids and chemicals in its stomach even as I saw the soft dark flesh leaking from two canals down its throat.

"Fuck it," I muttered, doing something very stupid and charging forward. The Gug grabbed me with two of its arms and lifted me up, the other two of them went to rip my arms off, only for me to jab the spear straight down its mouth into what I hoped was its brain. As I'd hoped, the creature's defenses were strong from the outside but not the inside as the spear pierced some sort of organ and it let loose a roar that was of a distinctly different kind than the ones it had thrown my way earlier.

I pressed the spear down with all my strength, forcing both hands to hold tightly while using the Gug's own arms as a base. The creature fell over, collapsing on the ground as it twitched violently with disgusting black ichor pooling in its mouth before it ceased its death throes. Modified or not by Celephaïs alchemy, the Gug had been mortal enough to be killed. So, its name as the Undying was ironic.

Then it started to move again.

Goddammit.

"Ratto! Ratto! Ratto!" The crowds chanted, genuinely excited now and leaving me with the impression I was even more screwed than before.

My knowledge of Celephaïs language was not great. It was the kind of language a child would invent for his fictional fantasy world, close enough to English to be understood but with a hidden code to those 'in the know.' Ratto was not a word I was familiar with.

It means resurrection, Kuranes spoke in my ear. It was as if his presence was right behind me even though I could see him from his royal box. *Tell me, John, have you ever killed the immortal?*

A couple of times, I thought back, cursing myself for thinking it would be this easy. *I guess I'm going to have to repeat the feat.*

I watched the corpses of the dead gladiators start to get up off the ground or crawl their way toward the body of the Gug in unnatural stop-motion like style. They started attaching themselves together to form a sickening form of armor around the Gug while the crowd went wild. There was a home team champion here and it was obviously not me.

There is another option, Kuranes whispered. *Submit to me, be my slave, and I will spare your life.*

Never, I thought, preparing to die. *Not all of us are afraid of death.*

I had been a slave once before. The Dunwych tribe had held me prisoner away from my family for a year and used me as breeding stock among other indignities. I would not submit again even if it would be to escape again.

Not everyone has the chance to escape it forever, Kuranes said, seemingly genuinely surprised by my response, but undeterred. *But perhaps not slave. Thrall. Servant.*

I prepared to do battle with the giant undead monstrosity that now had a dozen arms. The faces of the dead men merged into its flesh, opening their eyes and mouths in looks of abject, screaming horror.

Alien tongues slithered out of their mouths as something wholly new animated the corpse of the Gug along with its fleshy new additions, some nameless nightmare thing from beyond even the Dreamlands. Perhaps it had always been and would simply move to a new host after today. Golden yellow puss leaked from its body and bones stuck out of its head in a surreal parody of a crown.

"Hastur! Hastur! Hastur!" The crowd chanted, clearly treating the thing as a manifestation of Kuranes' mad god.

Perhaps it was.

"The answer is no," I said, looking for another spear and finding none that weren't broken or in the hands of the monster's own many hands. I was unarmed and had no chance, perhaps not even if I'd been fully armed and capable of calling upon my alien heritage. I cursed the fact I would die here, though, for no cause. In my youth, it would have been easy because my children were looked after, and I had faith I'd lived my life well spent. Now, in my monster years, I had only each moment to live for and a handful of loved ones I could not say would live in heaven or hell depending on the Dreamlands' mood.

How about if you simply say please? Kuranes whispered, knowing my heart.

I closed my eyes for a moment and hated myself for my response. *Please.*

I hated myself in that moment for acquiescing but that was in part because I didn't trust Kuranes to honor any promise he made. Honor may exist among thieves, but no one had ever gone broke betting against the integrity of kings or priests. I doubted god kings were any different.

My suspicion seemed to be justified as the Gug was now more like a centipede of living death with a long tail of dead bodies in place of its legs, incorporating the bodies of not just the victims of the initial fight but the bodies from previous battles fought in Hastur's name. The creature was far faster than it was before, and it slithered at me. I had no choice but to run now, jumping around and navigating the obstacles throughout the area, watching the abomination smash through them as if they were a child's toy blocks.

Accompanying the carnage and my less-than-heroic flight, I tried and failed to find any way that I might harm this horrifying thing. Resigned to the idea that this was my end, and I would have it witnessed by thousands,

I heard the war horns of Celephaïs. Kuranes' voice echoed through the coliseum, "Welcome Nybbas, Hunter of the Immortal!"

My attention briefly turned to an unusually tall woman, over six feet in height, muscled and dressed in furs that seemed less like the product of a barbarian race and more designed to evoke that by those marketing a product. She was beautiful in an unconventional way with long red hair cascading down her shoulders and eyes that were green without pupils. In her hands, she was wielding a sword made of orichalcum or Deep One gold. The gold weapons were almost impossible for a mortal man to wield due to their weight but struck down things that did not exist entirely in this world.

Supposedly.

If this was Kuranes' idea of help, then he was amusing himself at my expense to no end. That was when the woman charged forward, leapt into the air higher than any human could and struck the Gug's head off with a single blow that might as well have been cutting air. The undying creature's head rolled away as the yellow puss poured out in a river of golden fluid, spraying every direction. The head tried to reunite with its body, only for the woman to spear it to the ground with her golden blade.

Dismembered, the creature that could not die continued to roll around its body like a dying fish before falling into a pitiful set of twitching that was barely noticeable. It was not dead but no threat to anyone.

The crowd's cries turned from cheering to rapturous joy. "Nybbas! Nybbas! Nybbas!"

I stared, stunned. "Huh."

Chapter Three

It was hours after the slaughter of Gug the Undying that I finally found out the price for Kuranes' help, well more than the "please" he had claimed but far different from the eternal servitude that was his opening offer.

Kuranes, Nybbas, and I were standing on the balcony overlooking the gladiator barracks, there was no other word for it, that contained the God King's collection of hand-picked warriors. They were a motley collection of creatures ranging from Deep Ones, ghouls, Serpent Men, and humans from other parts of the Dreamlands with qualities showing alien or otherworldly heritage. There were perhaps as many as a hundred of them but room for many more in the extravagant building. The scent of death was here and by the sense of the beings beneath me, I could tell that these were not particularly cared for or valued warriors despite belonging to Celephaïs' dictator.

"You want me to coach your gladiator team," I said, not sure I'd heard him correctly.

"Yes," Kuranes said, bluntly.

"I was expecting something a bit more esoteric," I replied, surveying the warriors below. Some of them were clear veterans and covered in scars as well as walked with a killer's swagger, others looked significantly rawer.

"Your soul, if such a thing exists?" Kuranes asked. "Don't be gauche. You are a warrior and killer, so I want you to do something related to war and killing."

I didn't feel inclined to point out that my first gladiator battle had been just a few moments ago and doing battle in the arena was inherently different than doing it in the Wasteland. "My first piece of advice is to arm your gladiators with weapons that can actually kill the things they're fighting and then face them against monsters that are killable."

"Cute," Kuranes said.

"Yeah, I'm not joking," I said, not sure what would set off the mad tyrant. "Besides, you already seem to have a master gladiator."

Nybbas had barely spoken two words to me since her display in the arena, even to acknowledge my thanks for saving my life. Instead, she stared over the balcony at the gladiators with a look of contempt on her face.

"Nybbas is a supreme killer, the blood of Kadath runs through her veins, but her capacity to work with others is limited," Kuranes said, sounding almost apologetic.

Kadath was the Mount Olympus or Asgard of the Dreamlands, if not where those places were located. The Small Gods of Earth dwelled there, feeding on the worship of the humans they stole away in ancient times and bred like cattle to continue their relevance long after the Great Old Ones had devoured Earth's last civilization. In simple terms, it meant she was a demigoddess and possessed of her own power.

"How would you prepare this group?" I asked, still hoping to engage her in conversation. I'd like to say for reasons other than she was simply a statuesque figure akin to Atlantea or old pulp illustrations of Dark Agnes but that certainly didn't hurt.

"Let the blood flow between them and cull the weak among them," Nybbas said, her voice filled with a kind of cat-like purr of anticipation. "The strongest will emerge from them and die or triumph on their own merits."

"I see," I replied, nonplussed.

"Wars are won with strategy, tactics, and teamwork," Kuranes said, as if this was some great triumph of insight on his part. "I wish you to pick twenty men from this group and teach them to work as a proper collection of warriors against whatever threats can be thrown at them in the next Great Games. The rest can die or be resold as you wish. You have my complete authority for this and access to my treasury to make it so."

I blinked. "The next Great Games."

"Yes," Kuranes said. "A year from now, the Great Pasha of the Leng Empire will visit Celephaïs and bring with him one thousand of his Sorcerer Lords. We have a wager between us that must be won. Whoever's team emerges triumphant will receive their heart's desire. For the Pasha, it will be the Eye of Hastur that was stolen from his father by Randolph Carter and given to me for safe keeping. For me, it will be sublime apotheosis."

I blinked, trying to process a rather large number of revelations in but a few seconds. "I thought you were already a god."

Nybbas snorted at that, drawing Kuranes' distasteful gaze.

Kuranes did not correct her, though, and turned to me. "I am worshiped as one, but true divinity eludes me. The Great Pasha knows the true name of Hastur the Unspeakable One and if I repeat it three times, the King in Yellow will appear to grant me a wish. I will cast aside this feeble shell the way I did my mortal form and live among wonders and glory forever in the court of my god."

I'd chosen the path of war over the path of wizardry, but I had an unusually high education in the occult, hell an unusually high education period, for a man who'd grown up in the Wastelands. I'd read the Alan Ward translation of the *Necronomicon*, the 17th century Joseph Curwen penned edition of *The Book of Eibon*, and even a yellowed mass market paperback of the *Re'Kithnid* from Dunwich House. I needed none of these to know that mortals who summoned up gods, demanding to be made into one of their number, was a story that never ended well. The Ancient Greeks had even coined the term hubris for this very reason.

Explaining that, especially when he could read my mind, seemed like it would end poorly, though. "I am not sure I want to spend a year here in your fair city, no matter how intriguing I might find the job. You saved my life, but I point out you were the one to imperil it in the first place."

Also, being restricted here would make any attempt to acquire the Eye of Hastur more difficult rather than less. The gladiator stable was far from the palace and being part of its staff would restrict my movements greatly.

Of course, Kuranes knew this even if he didn't know precisely what I was after. He might suspect, though, and that was as good as being exposed. "Oh, Mr. Booth, I believe you will want to agree to my terms."

Ah, yes, here came the threats. Sucking in my breath, I looked into his eyes. "And why, may I ask, is that?"

"Because I found your spy," Kuranes said. "The lovely redheaded girl of Eurasian descent who fancies herself a witch. Sadly, her sorcery may be fine for the world she came from but is nothing to a place that absorbs and exhales magic with every breath. The woman called Mercury."

I blinked. "I see. I take it something untoward would happen to her if I don't cooperate?"

Kuranes patted me on the shoulder. "Not at all, because you are going to. She will be kept in the finest lodgings and given books of magic that will allow her to increase her power tenfold. Just as you will be kept in the finest quarters and availed every luxury while you train my slaves."

"I'm not a slaver," I said.

"Promise them their freedom then," Kuranes said. "Yours as well. If you defeat the Pasha's own team of slaves and monsters then I will give you what you seek, whatever it is. If you want Celephaïs itself, then the kingdom shall be yours to wear the crown of on a troubled brow. I will have no need of it. If you want Nybbas—"

"I choose my own partners, wizard," Nybbas interrupted, her voice sharp and condemnatory. "I also kill shoggoths, I don't fuck them."

Kuranes, much to my surprise, lowered his head. "Of course."

"I am not a shoggoth," I replied. "I am me."

Kuranes turned to me. "And if you do not win, I will strip your mind of everything human within you. I will toss slaves to you to impregnate and breed a host of monsters that I will spend the next thousand years killing then feeding to you."

"That is a very vivid image," I replied, cooly.

"I've done worse for less," Kuranes said, smiling. "Do we have an arrangement?"

"I feel very much like a gladiator coach now," I replied. "Go team."

"Splendid," Kuranes said, his voice lowering an octave. "I am glad we have an accord."

And like that, Kuranes was gone. There was no puff of smoke, crack of thunder, or flash of light. No, he was simply there one moment and then gone like a frame of a movie reel badly cut together.

"You realize he's going to kill you after the contest, right?" Nybbas asked, looking at me without the disgust I expected because of her earlier words but, instead, good natured pity.

"Are you familiar with the old Muslim proverb about the singing horse?" I asked.

"Indulge me," Nybbas replied, turning to me and crossing her arms.

"A thief is brought to the sultan and sentenced to be executed," I replied. "The thief then says, 'wait, no, I can teach a horse to sing!' The sultan, surprised by this, says that he'd like to see this and agrees to spare the thief's life for a year. One of his associates asks why the thief would make such a stupid promise. The thief says, 'A lot can happen in a year. Maybe the sultan will die, maybe he'll be overthrown, or maybe he'll forget all about me. And who knows, maybe in a year the horse will sing.'"

Nybbas nodded. "Ah, so it's a stupid proverb. None of that will happen to Kuranes."

"Probably not," I admitted. "But it is a year and that gives me some time to figure out an alternative."

Nybbas shook her head. "Your best bet is to abandon your comrade and flee. If you seek the Eye of Hastur, it is a fool's prize. Kuranes' land did not start decaying and his people starve until he began gazing into its depths. The sights of alien vistas and glorious magnificence exposed his paradise for the pathetic little fantasy world it was. If you think it will give you great power, you are a fool."

"I don't seek great power," I said, staring at her. "I seek the freedom for my people. The sole survivors of my Earth. Specifically, my family."

I had no idea why I was opening up to this stranger.

"Other shoggoths?" Nybbas asked.

"Man, monster, and otherwise," I said, staring at her.

"Find another Earth," Nybbas suggested. "There are an infinite number out there in the World Tree of Azathoth's branches. You don't even have to dream them up. Maybe that is what Randolph Carter did like in that outrageous lie you told or maybe he died long ago. Hastur touched him too and set him on the path to Unknown Kadath, ruining his brief mortal life the way that he ruined Kuranes'."

"Hastur ruins a lot of lives," I replied.

During my journeys across the Dreamland, I'd discovered my son was a Dreamer. Far more powerful than me or Mercury and he'd turned to the King in Yellow to try to find ways to save his fellow humans on Earth. He'd taken over Randolph Carter's own dreamlands, made in the image of New England, and turned them into the Republic of Carter. There was always a price for magic, though, and if I could kill any of the Great Old Ones then it would be him.

"Hastur does not exist," Nybbas said.

I blinked. "Excuse me? I'm pretty—"

"He exists only in the minds of his followers," Nybbas said. "He is not like K'Tullu, who is an alien older than worlds, or Yog-Sothoth, who is the incarnation of the universe's physical laws respectively. Nor even the Crawling Chaos, created by Azathoth in a blind moment of insanity to give purpose to a chaotic primordial universe. Hastur is the first of the true gods, those beings that living things create in their dreams to justify the helplessness they feel. He is the Eldest of the Elder Gods and exists only in the heads of his faithful. He is yellow because the first gods are dreamed of coming from the Sun, and the Lord of the Dreamlands, and with less substance or will than thought. By being all things, he is nothing."

"It sounds like Nyarlathotep," I said, half expecting Kuranes to show up and punish me for saying his name.

"Hastur is the shadow of him on the wall in a dimly lit room," Nybbas said. "Which is why your master has sent you to recover his property as well as punish its thieves."

"He is not my master," I replied, dryly. "I am neither his slave nor his friend. The True Gods don't have either. They have toys and pets. I'm just the turtle he occasionally puts on its back to see if it can right itself."

"And yet you sometimes can," Nybbas said, surprising me. "You are unlike other shoggoths, John Henry Booth."

"Like I said, I am not a shoggoth," I said, denying it to myself as much as anyone. "I am a human being."

It was a lie, but a lie I'd repeated so often I hoped it would be the truth someday. After all, the Dreamlands were made of wishes and lies. Long after Earth had been consumed by Yog-Sothoth, it would remain a world of fiction and broken promises. In my travels, I'd even seen the remnants of the dreams of races destroyed by their own Great Old Ones—peoples billions of years dead, and the shattered remnants of other universes that had existed like bubbles. There one day and then suddenly not.

"They are the same race," Nybbas said, surprising me. "The human mind and capacity for Dreaming, consciousness, came from the Elder Things inserting their slime into the apes evolved on your world. They are just trapped in one form and death when they could be awakened to so much more."

It was a strange statement to make, especially when she looked so very much like a human woman. But the Dreamlands were full of things that could appear to be something very different from what they truly were. "So, what is your story?"

"Do you know the phrase talk is cheap?" Nybbas asked, looking at me with her deep impenetrable eyes of solid green.

"Yes," I said.

"Whoever said such was a moron," Nybbas said, putting her hand on her sword pommel.

"Fair enough," I said, looking away. "I was merely asking because we're going to be working together."

"Together, perhaps. As brother and sister in arms, no," Nybbas said.

"My feelings are decidedly less than brotherly while you're in that outfit," I replied. "It gives remarkable support for animal skins."

Yeah, I was pathologically incapable of not being a jackass. On the other hand, some females found it endearing. Others turned into giant snake women with detachable jaws.

I'll share that story sometime.

Nybbas snorted. "You do a fair impersonation of a human, John Henry Booth. So, I will give you a hint. I was born on Kadath to the Lord of the Great Abyss. I am a goddess of the hunt, and my brothers and sisters are the nobility of the night sky, not frail humans. Our fathers are enemies, John Henry Booth, and I am here to slay a kingdom."

I was getting real sick of everyone and their delusions of godhood here. However, unfortunately, that was about as common as roadside shrines and bad food in the Dreamlands. "So, you're a goddess of the hunt like Artemis? Does that mean you're a virgin goddess?"

Nybbas shook her head. "Just focus on training the warriors below. I must win the next Great Games. The others winnowing the competition will make it easier."

"What do I have to work with?" I asked, switching topics.

"Rapists, murderers, and scum," Nybbas replied. "The only reason they're not in the pit to feed to monsters generated from the Hastur worshipers' nightmares is because they're marginally better at surviving than the ones used to quench the masses' blood thirst."

"Good," I replied. "Then I won't feel bad about reducing their ranks to twenty. Kuranes was clear about the number of the team he wants. I was afraid I'd have to do something decent and give the others their freedom."

"Free men have something to live for," Nybbas said. "Think of that when motivating them."

She then walked away, leaving me alone with my thoughts.

Chapter Four

The year passed quickly.

Such a thing should not be easy for any mortal man to say but the nature of the Dreamlands was such that a year, ten years, or millennia could pass with barely the blink of an eye. Time was always fluid within dreams and had a quality of otherworldliness that prevented it from being wholly similar to life in the "real" world.

But yes, I could say I almost enjoyed being Kuranes' gladiator coach. The warriors he'd assembled were all hardened killers from the four corners of the Dreamlands' Known Kingdoms. However, they were an eclectic bunch of murderers and each of them had stories to tell that reminded me of the time I'd been among fellow soldiers. I'd forgotten how much I'd missed the camaraderie of fellow warriors and Nybbas' description of them as scum did not include the fact most had done nothing worse than what I had.

Which was less of an endorsement than a reminder I had little room to judge the evils of men. Either way, there were only a few days left until the Great Games, and I still had a few choices to make for the final team to face the Great Pasha's Janissaries. Unfortunately, that choice would be decided by blood rather than deed. For example, I was about ready to strangle one of my best gladiators if he didn't shut the hell up.

"The universe is perfect, absolutely functional," Socrates the eight-foot-tall four-armed praying mantis spoke in a surprisingly humna voice. His people were called the Callisto and had written the *Al-Azif*. "The rules sustain it, let it grow, develop. It is sublime. Unfortunately, it has reflections, imperfect copies echoing through spacetime, filled with holes, imperfections, flaws in the system that the true universe has long discarded. We live in one of those. Like all the flawed reflections, it's temporary, dying, soon to succumb to entropy, which is just the name of its most obvious hole. Beings in these dying universes can escape the end of their realities by leaving through those holes, entering other universes, where they don't belong. The more stable the universe, the longer they can survive there. They can survive here in Celephaïs for hundreds, if not thousands of cycles. But their very existence degrades the worlds they find themselves in. They are living embodiments of our own limitations. But these dying worlds also need us. Our order, our dreams, is all that stands between them and nothingness. And these dreams will trap us if we let them."

"Shut up and fight!" I snapped at Socrates, holding a two-handed great sword with a cat headed pommel. "You're here to kill, not philosophize!"

"I can do both!" Socrates said, dodging past an ax coming for his throat with the speed only an inhuman creature could achieve.

Socrates and I were in the practice arena, little more than an octagon twenty yards long surrounded by fence. The Callisto and I were fighting on the same team against two other gladiators: Reaver the Ghoul and Bodhi the Vanir.

Reaver the Ghoul was like most of his kind in that he was a furry werewolf looking figure with a canine head combined with just enough human features to be terrifyingly wrong. At least to human eyes. In his two hands, he held double-bladed axes that were made from the bones of unnamable creatures. He was naked and only the length of his fur kept it from being distracting. Armor slowed the creature down and he moved like lightning.

Bodhi the Vanir, by contrast, was a heavily tattooed redheaded man with yellow skin. He preferred a pair of short, curved swords with jagged teeth edges that moved like dancing fireflies, burning with magic that he conjured with spells from his long-dead homeland. The short swords were engraved with runes that caused them to burn without ever being reduced to slag and were capable of searing the flesh off unearthly monsters as well as dreamfolk.

"Speak well, abomination," Bodhi said in a sing-song voice. "It will be your last conversation on this realm's soil. I shall offer your ichor to the Great God Hastur that I have abandoned Ymir and Muspell for. He lives inside my brain and compels me to kill."

Bodhi was one of the few slaves I fought with and promised freedom to that I knew the actual crimes of. He was a serial killer, and his crimes were both gross as well as against innocents. However, in the Dreamlands where bandits and armies were allowed to plunder freely by their masters, it had only gotten him thrown in here when his rapine had gone poorly against a village under Kuranes' protection.

I wanted to kill Bodhi when I'd first heard his descriptions of his crimes and would have if not for the fact that I'd gotten to witness some of the Janissary team at work during the final days of last year's Great Games. They were guests of Kuranes and yet killed a dhole, a shoggoth, and an Elder Thing in rapid succession. They were nine-foot-tall giants each and wore smoky black metal armor that disguised their true natures. I'd released eighty of our crew from slavery over the past year, but of the twenty-three remaining, Bodhi was the strongest other than Socrates, me, and Nybbas.

Too bad he was a traitor.

"Die, half-man!" Reaver hissed, going for me with his two bone axes. The ghoul had revealed little of his past or interests in the year we had together, but had apparently chosen his side when his attacks were not meant to disable, but to kill.

I dodged out of the way, ducking underneath his blows before kneeing him in the stomach then punching him in the face. It was like striking a brick wall even as I struck hard enough for the ghoul to feel it by the noises he made.

Our audience was the remainder of the team with them watching the battle with mixtures of boredom as well as curiosity. I had not won much loyalty from the twenty despite my freeing them and offering coin as well as other rewards to those who agreed to stay. They were aware that this was a bloody game and who got them through it alive was their friend, rather than who made the most lucrative promises. If I fell at Bodhi or Reaver's hands, they would be the leader and Kuranes would barely notice.

Watching us in the battle was the person who held the loyalty of the gladiators despite, or perhaps because of the fact, that she made no pretensions of caring whether they lived or died. Nybbas wore a large horned helmet with an ornate dragon (or perhaps night-gaunt) theme carved into its face. We'd grown *closer* during the past year despite her avowed hatred of shoggoths but I wasn't sure I'd made any sort of dent in her emotional armor. It was kind of sleazy to use sex to try to make an ally in this hell pit but, well, you used whatever methods you could, and it wasn't the first time I'd been a slave who'd tried to manipulate their master that way.

"You are leading us to our doom, Booth!" Bodhi hissed, going after Socrates rather than myself with his flaming blades. "We all know it! You think you're one of us, but we know you're one of them! Our only salvation is in Hastur and the Lords of Leng!"

The speech wasn't for me, and I had the strong suspicion that I now knew the source of the discontent among the gladiators I'd recruited. Bodhi had been spreading rumors about me this entire time and undermining my leadership. The worst part was I couldn't really refute them either. I was working for Kuranes after all, and he had no intention of living up to any promises I made in his name. I wasn't here for them either, but to acquire the Eye and get Mercury back. If that meant leaving them behind, well, that was something I'd do.

But it's not like Bodhi was better. "Yes, selling us out to the people who are going to fight and kill us in the arena is so much smarter. Why not just throw down your swords and die. It'll save you some time in the long run."

I was hoping Reaver wasn't completely lost to Bodhi's side but that went out the window when he lost control over his animal rage and went for my throat with his powerful jaws. The rotting meat smell of spoiled flesh and worse on its breath made me nauseous but didn't stop me from going under him to toss him over my shoulder. The ghoul was momentarily taken aback by basic wrestling instead of savage combat and that was when I slammed down my Ulthar steel sword through the back of his mouth before pinning him down with it. Blackish blood and a look of horrified terror passed through his all-too-human eyes as death took him. Until this moment, he hadn't thought I'd kill him. That was another problem the others had: they believed my desire not to kill them made me weak.

Examples had to be made.

I hated making examples.

"You cannot stop the coming of the King in Yellow!" Bodhi shouted, slashing away one of Socrates' arms with his flaming sword then forcing the Callisto over. "He has spoken in my dreams! I have seen the coming destruction of Celephaïs! You are all meat for the God of Madness! He will—"

Bodhi turned around to charge at me only for me to stand perfectly still, taking advantage of the fact my two-handed sword had significant reach advantage. I pulled up the sword from the ghoul's mouth a moment before he was in swinging distance and spun it around in a perfect arc that was matched with the speed of a half-giant's strength.

Bodhi's head rolled off his body.

Almost immediately, the Vanir warrior's body began to rot, splitting open and pouring out one-inch-long yellow human-faced magots with mandibles attached to their faces. I stabbed my sword down again into Reaver's twitching body, picked up one of Bodhi's swords, and tossed it on his body. The flaming sword's magic spread across whatever foul sorcery had kept him alive since the Hyborian Age, and caused the magots to scream as they died.

I gestured to the body. "Is this the kind of thing you want to follow? A corpse animated by the magic of Leng wizards and eaten for all eternity from the inside? He would sell you out to horned devils of that land and call it God's will. He is a traitor who sold you out for black rubies."

I reached down, and ignoring the pain from the hellfish flames that were eating at the body and licking my hand, I pulled off a small leather pouch from Bodhi's side. Or so it appeared. I opened it up and poured out the contents, revealing a bunch of black garnets and a few very flawed rubies from Bodhi's payout. It was a cheap payment, but I believed it would make the bribe more believable.

The Great Pasha had no need to pay great riches for destroying our team.

It was also a lie.

I'd had the payment hidden on my person the entire time. Bodhi had never needed payment to undermine our team, its morale, or me. I'd speculated on his motives, ranging from jealousy over Nybbas, jealousy over not leading the team, hatred of my race (shoggoth or what I appeared to be), or simply the fact he was an enormous asshole.

Either way, the Iago to my Othello was dead, and I hoped to turn that into an advantage.

"Better a traitor than a shoggoth!" a voice called from the back that was trying to disguise itself, but I recognized as Pinch. Pinch was a human pickpocket who had somehow survived a dozen gladiator fights, somehow deluding himself into believing that great riches, as well as fame, awaited him if we won.

Perhaps because I'd told him so.

"If I was a shoggoth," I said, knowing now what Bodhi had done to destroy their faith in me, "then our chances of actually winning would go up greatly. Wouldn't they? You would have a monster on your side rather than be in its path."

That caused a ripple of confusion among the group and was perhaps the one thing I could say to sow doubt about Bodhi's dissension. I'd never shown them my true form, but I was stronger than any normal human as well as healed far faster. That was hardly an unknown set of abilities among this collection of oddities, though. One of them was a man made of clockwork, wood, and tin that could only exist in the Dreamlands.

"Are you a shoggoth?" Pinch asked, no longer disguising his voice.

"You will find that out when we are about to lose, which we shall not, or if I decide to kill you all," I replied. "Now go back to your training. Tomorrow, we fight, die, or triumph."

It was not exactly the Saint Crispin's Day speech, but actions spoke louder than words. Bodhi and his chief hatchet man were dead as well as exposed as traitors. Whether they believed it or not, the doubt in him had been sown. That doubt caused them to question the words Bodhi had spoken and hopefully would have them follow me to the end. The group broke up at that point and returned to their exercises while I turned to Socrates.

"Are you alive?" I asked, staring down.

"Losing an arm is not much to my people," Socrates said, lifting its charred remnant. "Socrates will still be able to fight at most of my capacity."

"Most but not all," I replied. "If I had sorcery to—"

"Socrates would turn it down," Socrates said, shaking its head. "Sorcery is evil no matter what world it comes from and destroyed my people. You are tainted by it more so than any alien heritage you have, Booth, and it will bring nothing but misery to you. I suggest you abandon whatever quest you are on here in Celephaïs."

"I don't know what you mean," I said, helping him up. He weighed a little over four hundred and fifty pounds of exoskeleton and chitinous plates.

"You have a look of a man chasing magic," Socrates said. "Like all wizards, it will be your ruin."

I had no rebuttal for it. Magic had destroyed my teacher, Alan Ward, and it had ruined my wife, Martha. My son had taken to sorcery and become a worshiper of Hastur the same way that Kuranes had. What would it do to Mercury, and would the allure of it eventually consume me the same way it had them? At what point would the dark allure of true names and occult rituals overcome my love of the sword or gun? Had it already? I was, after all, here for a year of precious time seeking the Eye.

Socrates skittered away, still as fast as ever.

Nybbas jumped over the wooden fencing and headed to me. "A nice show, Wastelander."

"We're going to miss Reaver's and Bodhi's blades during the Great Games," I muttered, wondering if I'd made the correct choice.

"Having two less blades is a good thing when they're pointed at your back," Nybbas said. "But I remind you that you don't care what happens to these fools any more than they care what happens to you."

The bluntness of her statements was usually endearing. Not so today. "I was a soldier once, I had brothers in arms."

"And these are not them," Nybbas replied. "They are a distraction you are using every bit as much as they are using you in hopes of a vast payday. Or have you forgotten your true goal?"

"No," I muttered. "I have not."

"Good, because Kuranes hasn't," Nybbas said. "He has lost his mind."

Things had gotten worse in Celephaïs over the past year. A drought had caused devastating famine and the king's hydromancers had been able to do little about it. Riots had spread throughout the God King's city, and he had dispatched his zealots to put them down. Roving press gangs wandered through the streets, grabbing people at random for the work crews that were expanding the coliseum for the Great Games, and human sacrifices to both Hastur as well as Kuranes were performed weekly. It was said that every slave galley to Leng was full and that payments were no longer black rubies but exotic monsters for gladiator pits.

"I'd ask if he ever had it but I know what you mean," I replied. "I do not know what it says about a man's psychology that the people he dreamed into existence now curse his name."

It was treasonous talk but the spies in the arena were dead at my feet and very little could suppress it anymore. I knew Kuranes wanted me in that arena for his own reasons and would not strike at me now. I just had to figure out how to turn it around on him and that required the aid of forces beyond this stable. They were, as Nybbas said, a distraction.

"Dreams take lives of their own," Nybbas said, shrugging. "How else could you explain my attraction to a Spawn of Nyarlathotep?"

That was her latest way of referring to me instead of shoggoth and I wasn't sure it was an improvement. "I have drills to do and weaponry to inspect, Nybbas, unless you have something else—"

Nybbas lifted a bullet up in the air. It was sized for a revolver and engraved with tiny writing that was filled with orichalcum, Deep One gold.

"A gift," Nybbas interrupted. "From your woman in the palace."

She meant Mercury. My lover and closest companion with an infinitely more ruthless spirit than I had ever possessed even at my most alien. I had only seen her a handful of times in the past year at Kuranes' gatherings (more often orgies of debauchery and waste) but she seemed in good health. Indeed, true to his word, he had deluged her in ancient mysticism from the Lost Cities of Yith to the black rites of Acheron. I tried not to love her for all the murders and dark arts she practiced but the heart wanted what it wanted. The fact I was with Nybbas out here and she'd cultivated a harem of adoring young men in Kuranes' service changed little of that.

"What is it?" I asked.

"A bullet," Nybbas replied.

I glared. I was in no mood for jokes.

"She claims to have found Kuranes' true name in her research, possibly weaseled out of him in bed," Nybbas said, showing the first signs of jealousy or cattiness in our association. "The bullet is inscribed with it to remind the God King of his mortality. The metal is supposedly made from Randolph Carter's sword when he quested for Kadath."

I took it and nodded. "With this, we can kill Kuranes."

Nybbas smiled.

Chapter Five

So it was time to teach the horse to sing.

The twenty gladiators I'd chosen for this battle were gathered in the darkness of the coliseum's depths, having waited for the Great Games to reach their main event with increasing apprehension and disgust. Kuranes had ordered the entirety of the city to be assembled in the arena and the populace that tried to flee had been slaughtered or used as fodder in the Great Games.

Even then, most people in the stands were not the residents of the city itself but bloodthirsty crowds assembled from across Leng, Ulthar, and even the distant Republic of Carter I'd falsely claimed to be representing. The whispers of fantastic beasts, monsters, legendary warriors, and spectacle for these games were those that had stirred places not even known to humans.

I had seen obese Deep One potentates, ghouls covered in glamours I only recognized by the telltale signs I'd learned from my friend Richard, and even one of the foul Elder Things that was a special guest of Kuranes. The obese multi-stalked thing was supposedly being served meals of fresh human flesh that even ghouls did not kill for but only scavenged.

In the darkness of the dungeons below where we armed and outfitted ourselves, we could not see what was going on but I could tell from the sounds above that no matter whether the people were starving or insane, it was the show of a lifetime.

"I was a potter's son," Pinch said, lacing up his boots. He was a brown-haired man of Celephaïs descent and it still surprised me he'd made it this far over godlings and hardened veterans. "My father lost my sister and mother to his creditors. I ended up enslaved myself when I tried to steal enough to get them back."

"So why did you stay?" Socrates asked, his missing arm replaced with a prosthetic attached to a shield.

"Booth got my sister back, at least," Pinch said. "No telling what happened to my mother. I barely recognized her and there was nothing left of her behind her eyes, but she had two children. I had them shipped across the Silver Sea with a bag of silver as well as a letter of credit. But you'll always be someone's slave if you don't have money. So, I'm here. Even if I die, they'll be taken care of."

Yes, I had said that. I'd already taken the money out for his family, but the Other Gods knew whether it would ever reach them given how many crooked hands it would have to pass through before it reached them.

"Socrates has no people or hive," Socrates said. "They fight for knowledge instead."

"Knowledge," Pinch said, surprised.

Socrates pointed a clawed appendage with prehensile tendrils sticking out of the side at his chest. "This one has studied at universities as far off as the Yithian Learnarium of Pnakotus to the Shadow Archives of Miskatonic at Carter. None have given the secrets necessary to journey across the multiverse and find either his people or a reasonable facsimile. Across Yog-Sothoth I must go to be among people like myself. The God King may be the last option I have to send me to such a place or teach me how."

"A man who beseeches the gods for salvation is bound to be disappointed," Nybbas said, staring into the reflection of her polished sword blade. "Besides, what makes you think Kuranes will be impressed enough to do you any favors?"

"Both you and Booth are doing this battle for him," Socrates said. "Both of you have walked the rivers of time. Magic has a price I cannot pay but there are other secret knowledges I pursue. Thus, I follow you in hopes of finding a path home."

"How long have you been looking for a way home?" Pinch asked.

"Millions of your years," Socrates said. "Socrates would spend millions more for the comfort of the familiar."

I didn't have the heart to tell him that, yes, there was a way to find a portal to another universe where the Callisto still existed. The cults of the Key and the Gate or the Yithians both could have given him the secret. However, the Callisto had been destroyed so humanity could exist and the Yithians could eventually replace them. I had been the one to destroy the original Al-Azif, the book Abdul Alhazred had claimed contained the secrets of chittering insects, that had been their portal to this world. Not telling Socrates was the least of my betrayals. Perhaps he knew, though, as sorcery had been the downfall of his people as it had been Kuranes'. Unless he succeeded in becoming a god tonight, the God King would be overthrown or invaded by his neighbors. Already there had been failed plots against his life and mine would just be the latest.

"Survive and I'll lead you to a portal where your people still live," I lied, wishing it was the truth. "You have my word. For whatever it's worth."

"Do you think we'll live?" Pinch asked. "That we really have a chance."

"Yes," I said, pausing. "Just not all of us."

From the expressions on the faces before me, they believed me. It had taken up to the very end of our time together, but I'd finally earned their trust. Unfortunately, the chances of us winning were nonexistent according to even the most generous betting pool.

Despite the fact we all had blades capable of piercing steel like paper, armor that was enchanted to turn even alien claws, and had trained extensively in squad tactics, well, the Janissaries of the Leng Empire were the most feared soldiers in the Dreamlands for a reason.

They were made from children stolen from the many victim states of its armies and subjected to experimentation that hideously mutated them to a level even Gug the Undying might loathe. It was said that a headless man with strange fluids in a bag had killed them at the height of their power, and resurrected them as revenants without fear of death as well as an unholy bloodlust that could never be quenched. It could be bullshit but who knew in the Dreamlands?

"It's time," I said, feeling the cold steel in the back of my pants as I'd hidden the carefully crafted holster underneath my long coat. The other gladiators wore very different armor, choosing to forgo their usual displays of flesh, but I'd gone for a 'cowboy' theme that coincidentally hid my weapon. I still sported a greatsword since they weren't about to allow a gun in the arena, however useless such a weapon was against most creatures of the Dreamlands. It was presently tied to my back, which was normally a ridiculous place to put a holster but apparently Velcro wasn't a thing in Kuranes' quasi-medieval kingdom.

There was an itching in the back of my mind that I couldn't put into words, but it was a sense I was playing into the hands of parties infinitely stronger than myself. Perhaps it was Nyarlathotep or Hastur, though it was arrogant and stupid to believe either of them cared about the goings of humans more than a spider they removed from a web or flicked away at night. Hastur might not even exist outside of the avatars conjured by his worshipers, a god made by men and brought to life by our desire for a vengeful judgmental king.

Did Kuranes suspect I was plotting against him? Almost certainly. However, I was probably one of thousands doing so. There was also the fact that he was mad, driven to megalomania by too much power and staring into the abyss of his own insignificance too long. Which sounded like a contradiction until one realized that those who felt the need to prove their power constantly were those most insecure in it.

Then there was Nybbas. It seemed ridiculous to believe the gladiator was pulling the puppet strings around me, but she felt far more in control of her destiny than anyone else here. She was no more human than I was and dropped cryptic hints as to her true nature constantly. Then there was her claim she was here to destroy a country, which I wasn't sure meant she was plotting a revolution or something more literal. Certainly, she was excited and supportive of the plot to kill Kuranes. Indeed, it was what had gotten her to become intimate.

Ahem.

But there was no time to ponder the machinations about me, and the twenty of us walked down the underground passages of the coliseum before gathering in four rows of five before the Southern Warrior's Entrance. The enormous steel door lifted through the power of Gugs turning enormous wheels. Light filtered from underneath as it slowly rose, the light reaching our feet first then slowly rising.

"Now for the main event!" Kuranes' voice filled the ears of everyone in the arena, myself included. "A battle between the legendary Janissaries of Leng and the greatest heroes of our fair city-state! Whoever wins will be made immortal through the glory of their deaths and showered in wealth beyond imagination!"

Pinch muttered something about imagining quite a bit.

Socrates, by contrast, said, "Immortality in death seems a poor substitute for the real thing."

It seemed my sense of humor had rubbed off on them.

"Remember the strategy," I replied. "Kill them one at a time, three on one and stay out of individual engagements whenever possible. Turn their size against them and go with killing blows against their throats or back legs. It's where their armor is weakest."

"And if any of them is a sorcerer?" Nybbas asked, looking positively eager with her nightmarish yet ornamental armor that seemed made of black monster bone but shaped with themes venerating the Great Lord of the Hunt.

"Kill him first," I replied, knowing she was referring to Kuranes.

We departed into the light of the arena, and I thought myself familiar with carnage then I found myself swiftly disillusioned with my experience. Kuranes had organized whole battles and mass melees with the results left to rot as well as fester in the light of the dying sun that seemed to burn brighter than usual. The corpses were piled up to the first row of bleachers as the stink wafted upward.

Kuranes stood in a row at the very front this time, almost level with the warriors he had enslaved. He was still giving announcements before his throne that had a miniature version of it beside him for a single guest: Mercury. Beautiful Mercury, short and redheaded, wore a crown and translucent sheer evening dress as she sat at his side.

I had no doubt of her loyalties because she was ever someone who was primarily loyal to herself. Still, if Kuranes hoped to convince me she had defected to his side, he was bound for failure as long as I had the bullet chambered for his assassination. That was when I was distracted by the sight of the glowing orb hovering above their heads.

It was a glowing, pulsating, sickening piece of matter that reminded me more of a beating heart than a gemstone. It glowed in dirty colors of neon purple, vomit orange, and shades that didn't really exist in the human spectrum, but I could see due to my alien heritage.

It changed shape the more you looked at it, but it was really just catching a glimpse of it from other angles. It was alive and hungry, eating time and dreams. Something was *inside* it, I could tell, and it was begging to get out.

The Eye of Hastur.

Any plan to steal the object immediately fled my consciousness and I cursed myself for ever following the advice of the Black Pharaoh in the first place. It was no solution to my problems and a year of my life, possibly my life itself, was wasted on a fool's errand. Whatever was contained within that was uncontrollable and it would take a madman to believe they could. Which, in retrospect, explained quite a bit.

Turning my attention to the opposite side of the arena, I caught sight of the Great Pasha of the Leng Empire and almost immediately retched. One thing I'd learned in the Wasteland was the price of immortality was always everything human about a person and the Great Pasha had ruled the Leng Empire for 10,000 generations. The creature was a hundred-foot-long dragon-insect thing that was surrounded by a hundred chained slaves whose neck collars all linked to a central one around its bulbous cyst-covered waist.

The Great Pasha's side of the arena was filled with his court of fawning sycophants, wizards, and petty nobility that was a glimpse into what Kuranes was slowly becoming. It was easy to imagine that once the Great Pasha had just been another human dreamer from either the Middle East, Middle Kingdom, or perhaps a far older civilization like Khitai. Time and the Eye of Hastur had turned him into the thing he was now. It would be my destiny if I'd attempted to harvest the Eye's power to save the Republic and my family there.

Looking at Mercury I debated taking the shot immediately, my life and everyone else's be damned, but she gave a very brief shake of her head that told me it was not the right time. Confirmation came a second later as I saw a bubble of barely visible shimmer around his box in the alien sunlight. Kuranes, for all his claims of immortality and godhood, had taken precautions against assassination.

Kuranes stood up and spoke. "You have seen our mighty heroes, the Champions of Celephaïs, but now it is time to see their challengers!

They are the most terrifying warriors of the plateau they hail from, raised to kill from birth and infused with powers even the gods may envy! I give you the Janissaries!"

The metal door across the arena opened and our opponents marched out in perfect synchronization. They were indeed giants and wore armor made of chitinous insect plating taken from giant creatures that inhabited Leng's dense jungles. Their faces were covered in disturbing exaggerated wax masks that I realized, only belatedly, were not masks at all. Their eyes burned coal red and their heads were covered in small metal helmets dipped in gold. Each of them wielded a halberd and had a scimitar at their side. I'd heard they also trained in the basics of sorcery but felt that was overkill even for the Pasha of Leng to get his toy back.

Especially given their numbers.

"Is it just me or are there a lot more of them than there should be?" Pinch asked what was on the mind of every gladiator I'd assembled here.

There were a hundred of them. Kuranes' treachery knew no limits and he'd made all the arrangements he had just to set us up in an impossible battle against people who outnumbered us five to one. This was not meant to be a battle but a slaughter and all of the tactics that I had prepared were worthless.

"What do we do?" Pinch asked, knowing it was as hopeless as I did.

Socrates muttered something in a reverent chittering tone that I wondered about being a prayer, perhaps to Yog-Sothoth or cleaner gods. I had no gods to pray to who could help me now but lowered my head in acknowledgment.

Fury replaced my resignation. "We fight and we die, showing them that we are not beasts for slaughter!"

Nybbas placed her hand on my shoulder, staring at me then looking at the others. "John and I will carve a way through them. We must merely wait for the distraction."

"Distraction?" I asked, not having made any such plans.

Nybbas smiled enigmatically. "You will know it when you see it. Until then, embrace your inhumanity."

Nybbas transformed before my eyes, casting off her human form like a snake shedding its skin or an insect emerging from its cocoon in a way that was both horrifying as well as beautiful. The creature that emerged was bat-like and majestic but also terrifying. It was no Earthly creature so any allusions I made could not adequately describe what it was but there were many things it reminded me of. It was like some great majestic beast man with mighty horns, covered in an oily black skin that lacked sexual characteristics. Its leathery wings spread out from its back, absorbing all the light around it like a vampire consuming the sun. A long thin prehensile barbed tail dangled from its back. No face existed on its pointed, goat-like head, instead being so smooth as to be reflective.

I knew the creature as one of the most fearsome and dreadful beasts of the Dreamlands. One that terrified individuals as much as the shoggoths but without the revulsion that came from humanity's secret shared heritage with them. It was a night-gaunt, a creature that served the god King of Kadath, Nodens, and stalked the monsters of the Far and Near Nightmare. Nodens was said to be enemy of Nyarlathotep and because people believed it, it was true. They were predators of predators, the kind that fed on shoggoth like an owl might a mouse.

But Nybbas, instead, flew into the ranks of the Janissaries.

I loathed myself for what I did next, but I did not even look to my fellow gladiators before abandoning myself to the inner beast. The monster inside that did not think like John Henry Booth but wore his face as well as personality like camouflage. I feared every time I indulged its immense power because I carried a bit more of the alien immortal monster with me each time that I returned to who I was. Something that I would simply forget one day and cease to be able to do, becoming the thing I most despised.

Death.

Destroyer of worlds.

I can't say who or what happened next as everything I did as a shoggoth was so wholly removed from human senses. It would be like attempting to describe a battle to someone blind, deaf, and without a sense of smell. The senses of a shoggoth were dozens more and they overwhelmed the meager organs of humanity with their incomprehensible feedback. Whoever I was when I became a Kastro'vaal, a Primordial One, was also not me. They acted on instincts and memories that I could barely comprehend and was terrified of when I did.

If you assumed this was an easy slaughter, though, then I am unhappy to inform you it was anything but. Of the alien series of images and nightmarish urges I experienced, I remembered enough flashes to know the Janissaries fought back fiercely and inhumanly with weapons that bit through dimensions of flesh as well as spirit.

The wounds created were enough to have killed a normal man a hundred times over and eventually I was forced to withdraw back into myself and the human side of me. The pain was agonizing and it was a struggle to pull my mind back from the fury. Even so, I felt like my blood was burning as the alien matter struggled to keep itself together. I was naked and covered in slime in my human form, barely able to stand. I would need Mercury's magic were I to recover, though it would be hours or days until I died should I not gain access to it.

The carnage around me had gotten worse and fifty of the Janissaries lay dead but that left half of their numbers still capable of fighting. That did not mean this was a heroic victory in the making, though, for I could barely move due to the pain of the invisible injuries my alien biology struggled to heal. Nybbas, herself, was on the ground with several holes in her right wing and a bleeding slice across her side with greenish ichor pouring out.

As for our brothers and sisters in arms?

Dead.

All of them.

I saw Pinch had been torn in half, his body still twitching as his eyes stared up into the sky. Socrates was surrounded by the bodies of four dead Janissaries, having gone down battling them but succumbing to their sheer numbers. The others? Growl, Lysharra, Venom, and Stoneheart? All of them had died at the hands of their enemies in bloody as well as awful ways. Would we have won if Kuranes hadn't betrayed us? Did it matter? The game was rigged the entire time. I didn't get a chance to think more as Nybbas' voice spoke in my mind. *It is time.*

Time for what? I asked, confused.

A group of five Janissaries with nets and drawn swords, abandoning their halberds for more close and personal means, approached me when I heard the sound of screeching in the air. Turning my gaze upward to the dying sun, I saw it was blanketed by the black and horrifying forms of night-gaunts. Hundreds of them. Thousands.

I did not know which side they were on, if any, until they began picking up the Janissaries around me and descending into the crowd to their screaming terror. The Great Pasha of Leng was as vulnerable as any with five of the bat-like creatures tearing apart Kuranes' rival god king while his court were feasted upon by beings who had no fear of their power or wealth. Whatever magics the sorcerers wielded was also ill-suited to combat against the abyssal predators.

"You are ruining my ascension!" Kuranes shouted, his voice echoing throughout the coliseum. The God King levitated upward and over his box before he started to approach me. A night-gaunt descended upon him, only for him to make a dismissive wave that disintegrated it as if an errant dream.

I searched the ground for the pistol I'd prepared that had been lost with my clothes and saw it halfway underneath the corpse of a fallen warrior. I threw myself in a roll, almost vomiting from the stresses of the movement, only to feel the cold steel of the weapon in my hands. I had one shot at this and aimed the weapon at the God King. His eyes were firmly affixed on me, and I had only a second before he obliterated me like he had that night-gaunt. It would be an epic story, truly, a warrior assassinating the tyrant in the middle of the arena surrounded by monsters.

An epic story.

Perfect for a god's origins.

A terrible god but a god nonetheless.

You clever bastard, I thought, adjusting my aim ever so slightly and fired.

The bullet sailed not into Kuranes but the Eye of Hastur above him, shattering the jewel or at least the prism for whatever was inside it. I only got a momentary glimpse of what was inside, but it was enough that I was tempted to rip my own eyes out. An equally memorable image was Kuranes' look of absolute shock and horror at what I'd done. It was followed by a glowing yellow light spilling out, over him first, then everything beyond, consuming everything it touched at a glacial pace that was so much more terrifying than instantaneous death. Mercury had run to my side and wrapped her arms around me as Nybbas moved the folds of her wings around my body. I closed my eyes and readied myself for death.

But death did not come.

Nybbas, instead, carried us off into the alien skies of the Dreamlands, as Celephaïs disappeared into the maw of the King in Yellow.

"Ethical Consumption" is another novelette set before the apocalypse. This, like *"Academic Legacies"* is tied to the Cthulhu Armageddon *universe and you might recognize the protagonist as being a character from those books. He's very different from how he'd end up, however, as you can probably imagine. This was written for David Hambling's* The Book of Ghouls, *and I was inspired to connect the ghoul myth with the Sawney Bean legend. Even with this being a straightforward horror story, I admit I can't help but take the piss out of the entire concept in places. I'm a bit like Stuart Gordon in that comedy enters my Lovecraft no matter how hard I try.*

ETHICAL CONSUMPTION
Chapter One

"From ghosties and ghoulies. And long-leggedy beasties. And things that go bump in the night, Good Lord, deliver us!"

—Traditional Scottish prayer

B ut gradually the truth dawned on me: that Man had not remained one species but differentiated into two distinct animals: that my graceful children of the Upper-world were not the sole descendants of our generation, but that this bleached, obscene, nocturnal Thing which had flashed before me, was also heir to all the ages.

"Mr. Jameson," the voice of Professor Warner spoke, drawing my attention from my e-reader, where I'd been sneaking peeks at *The Time Machine* by HG Wells.

"Yes, Professor?" I asked, looking up.

I was sitting across from the Professor in a passenger car room on a train currently heading deeper into Scotland. Fields of purple heather and bracken raced by outside. Professor Niles Warner was a somewhat stereotypical image of a white-bearded academic with a tweed jacket, khaki pants, and an upper crust New England accent that made him seem like a throwback at the more modern Miskatonic University. It was extra incongruous to see his assistant, Lisa Delapore, who was a mixed European and South Asian Goth with a nose ring. She was dressed down for this journey with her sweater and jeans but still looked significantly more punk than I guessed most of this part of the country had ever seen. I had to admit I fancied her and been working up the nerve to ask her out for a drink but given she was a grad student, and I was in my second year, I doubted that was going to happen.

Sitting next to me was my somewhat chubby friend Karl Butcher and he was giving me side-eye for reasons that I didn't quite get. Both of us had agreed to sign up for Professor Warner's class pretty much just to fulfill our history degree requirements. However, Warner had taken a shine to me, and I'd gotten chosen for the Armitage Award that meant I didn't need to entirely drown in student debt along with side jobs. The price, though, was that I had to keep taking Professor Warner's classes on theoretical anthropology. And by theoretical, they should have said goddamn mad.

Karl, for reasons I didn't understand, had continued taking the classes alongside me and seemed a lot more into them than I'd ever been. He also seemed to resent me for reasons I didn't understand. Maybe he was jealous of me getting the award but that didn't make sense since he could afford to buy Miskatonic University a new department. His parents owned a good chunk of King Beer and its five breweries.

"I was wondering if you were paying attention," Professor Warner said, staring at my e-reader.

I put it away. "Sorry, sir, I didn't realize this was a lecture."

"Never turn down an opportunity to learn, Mr. Jameson," Professor Warner said. "Especially when it's on a free vacation."

"Yeah, Rick," Karl said, making a mocking noise with his tongue. "Ya need to pay attention *in class*."

I grimaced. "Yes, sir."

The four of us were heading to Beane, Scotland located in Bennane Head north of Ballantrae Bay and southwest of Girvan. It was a town primarily famous for the fact that the Sawney Bean family of cannibals had allegedly settled it and a popular brand of pickled herring, at least according to its Wikipedia entry. It wasn't exactly my idea of a vacation spot, especially given the fact my mother had come to America to get away from Scotland, but everything was paid for by the university. Besides, it was a chance to get closer to Lisa and if I was ever going to make my move then it was probably in a cold and wet place where there was nothing to do for ninety miles.

"I was talking about my theory of the Ultraterrestrial civilization," Professor Warner said. "Modern human civilization is something that dates back roughly six thousand years with oral history preserving work from close to ten thousand to thirteen thousand years. However, the archaeological evidence from the so-called Hyborian Age could well indicate an entire additional human historical era that we are only now recovering remnants of. But what if they are just the tip of the iceberg? What if, underground, an entire epoch of human civilization existed that could well upend our understanding of the fossil record?"

Yep. Goddamn mad. "Sir, a lot of the evidence of the Hyborian Age has been called into dispute," I said, reluctantly once more questioning my professor's conclusions. It was exhausting work and every time, I kept wondering why I bothered but my inner wannabe history professor couldn't help itself. Besides, Professor Warner had to like something about what I said since he was the one who recommended me for the Award. "If there really was an entire pre-human race of history around the time of *homo erectus*, don't you think we'd have more evidence?"

Or any evidence?

Any at all?

I didn't say that last part, of course.

"Ah, but there is evidence," Professor Warner said. "It is just located underground."

"Yeah," Karl said, speaking in his obnoxiously loud voice. "It's underground, numb nuts."

"Like *Homo floresiensis*, better known as the hobbit," Professor Warner said. "For centuries considered a myth, until remains were found in the Liang Bang cave in Indonesia in 2003. Further cave excavations turned up several more skeletons."

"Didn't forget Liang Bang cave, did ya?" Karl said, rolling his eyes.

"Which is why we're investigating the Sawney Beane clan as a possible tie into the surface world," Professor Warner said. "Which I trust you did your homework on, Mr. Jameson?"

"Yessir," I said, remembering the gory lurid stories the Professor had me going over.

"Please recite them for us," Professor Warner said.

I took a deep breath. "The Sawney Bean clan was a cannibal clan of forty members that existed in Scotland during the 16th century. They allegedly killed over a thousand people during a span of twenty-five years."

"Allegedly," Professor Warner said, snorting. "Please go on."

"Their leader, Alexander Bean, was born in East Lothian and supposedly married to a witch named Black Agnes Douglas. They robbed and cannibalized several victims before settling above a coastal cave system and founding the village of Bean."

"Hell of a founding father story," Karl said, chuckling.

"Supposedly, the town was founded by Thomas C. Bean," I pointed out. "A local dry goods salesman who was possibly a smuggler and fence using those cave systems. They used the money from their legitimate and illicit activities to fund a successful mining operation that lasted several generations. The town denied the Bean clan existed as anything other than Anti-Scott propaganda for the better part of two centuries."

"It is my belief that Thomas C. Bean is the fictitious of the two," Professor Warner said. "Alexander Bean made contact with the subterranean civilization and they provided him with gold as well as other precious metals while inducting locals as members of their sinister ghoul cult."

"Right, sinister ghoul cult," I said, trying to figure out how to indulge the professor's lunacy without affecting my grade or standing at Miskatonic. "Well, supposedly, Alexander Bean and Black Agnes had eight daughters and six sons. The family was all inducted into the same robbery and cannibalism that their parents were indulged in. Plus, they were inclined toward incest and the siblings wed each other."

"To keep the bloodline pure," Lisa Delapore said. "The Dutch noble family, the Martense clan, soon found itself engaged in similar practices of cannibalism and incest when they moved to the Catskill mountains. There's long been suspicions that they, too, were part of a larger collection of ghoul worshipers."

I didn't get Lisa's fascination with the macabre, but I wasn't a Goth girl and that might have explained why college had been nothing but a dry spell since I'd arrived on campus. Part of it might have been that Miskatonic students came in two varieties: the very rich who were getting their Ivy League degrees before entering politics or lobbying and the very weird who were attracted to the school's reputation for taking crackpots seriously. Lisa was clearly one of the latter. Karl was one of the former but, well, was now one of the latter. If I had a lot more money or a lot more interest in the weird, I might have had a better social life.

"Damn rednecks," Karl said, clearly trying to appeal to Lisa. "Of course it's the hillbillies who became cannibals."

Lisa glared at him, as if he'd insulted her personally. "My great-great grandfather supposedly traced the Delapore line back to one of their own estates here in the United Kingdom. He claimed he discovered an entire underground city underneath Exham Priory."

Karl grimaced.

"What happened to him?" I asked.

"He killed a friend of his, ate him, and was committed to a mental hospital," Lisa said, sounding oddly proud. "Thankfully, he was rich, and they released him twelve years later. That's where my branch of the family came from. Sadly, Exham Priory was something he willed to the government with secret instructions he didn't pass down to any of his adopted descendants."

"Sounds...neat," I said, grimacing. Maybe I should do just do what other guys on a European vacation should do and try to hook up with a local girl. I wasn't sure, however cool and hot she was, hooking up with a girl who admired her cannibal murderer ancestor was a great idea.

"Exham Priory was my original planned location for an investigation," Professor Warren said, frowning. "Unfortunately, during WW2, it was used as an artillery shelling range before the entire valley was flooded over to create Exham Lake."

"Mmm hmm," I said, nodding along. "That is a shame, sir."

That was always the case with Professor Warren's theories and quest for proof. Innsmouth being home to a cult of fishmen? The town had been bulldozed to the ground in the Nineteen Twenties. Dunwich being home to practicing sorcerers? Died out long ago with their possessions incinerated as junk. An actual fucking underwater city containing some kind of squid Godzilla? Well, no one was willing to pay for combing every inch of the ocean looking for it.

Four possibilities emerged: the professor was the victim of an elaborate conspiracy trying to cover up the truth, the supernatural somehow didn't want to be found, the supernatural didn't exist, or Professor Warren was such a bad scientist that he couldn't have proven a link between smoking and cancer.

"Please continue," Professor Warren said, gesturing to me.

"Well, the number of dead bodies kept increasing and the town developed a bad reputation for disappearing travelers as well as heavy banditry. The Bean clan hanged several innocents in show trials and probably disposed of the evidence." If they ever existed. "Eventually, though, the Beans failed to capture one of their quarries: a trained soldier on his honeymoon."

"They ate his wife, though, right?" Karl asked, grinning.

"Yes," I said, grimacing. The tale had given me nightmares despite just being a bunch of words. "The husband, his name wasn't recorded in any of my research, held them off long enough to be rescued by some nearby fair goers and they took him to the local magistrate. James the Sixth of Scotland, better known as James I of England, sent out an army to deal with the Bean clan. The town was no help, and his mansion was empty, but they found their cavern hideout with bloodhounds. The evidence was apparently so overwhelming that they were all universally condemned as witches. The women and children were burned while the men were castrated, drawn, and quartered."

Karl crossed his legs. "Eesh."

"Alexander Bean's last words were 'It isn't over, it will never be over'."

"It's terrible the way that the Old English and Scottish theocracies persecuted alternative religions," Lisa said. "Many cultures have engaged in ritual cannibalism."

"Yeah, I think the killing people in order to eat them kind of precludes claims of religious persecution," I said, sarcastically.

Lisa narrowed her eyes. "You are so *intolerant*."

Yeah, we weren't going to happen. Probably for the best. If we did hook up, we possibly had a couple of more years of working together if I could leverage the Armitage Award for a graduate degree in history. That meant keeping the professor happy with my critiques, though. "In any case, there's actually another legend that they didn't execute them at all but just detonated gunpowder at the entrance to the caves and sealed all of the clan inside."

"They could still be alive then!" Karl said.

"Uh, no," I said. "Because they'd be centuries old."

Karl snorted, way more into this legend and the occult than I was. There had been a time when my friend had been as skeptical of the occult as I had but now seemed every bit as obsessed as Lisa and Doctor Warner. I wanted to think he was just trying to get with Lisa, which was a pretty sexist and shameful view, but I knew Karl and that was less disturbing than my millionaire friend sincerely wanting to find lost cannibalistic underground civilizations.

"Interesting fact," Professor Warren said. "James I was the monarch who wrote the *Daemonologie*, one of the most extensive treatises on the differences between white and black magic. He also was the monarch to sanction witch trials. Is it possible that some of what was found among the Bean clan fell into his hands? Or was the whole affair what started him down the road of occult investigation like accusations that witches tried to kill him with a storm? Especially given Queen Elizabeth, his predecessor's, own relationship to the occult with Doctor John Dee?"

Or maybe James I was a religious nut raised by a religious nut in John Knox was what I could have said but didn't. "The nearby town of Girvan has an additional legend about the mythical clan. They claim one of the Bean clan daughters left the clan and took up residence locally. When they discovered her heritage, they hanged her from a tree she planted called *The Hairy Tree.*"

Lisa spoke up, adding an interesting addition to the legend. "*Cultes des Goules* by Francois Honore-Balfour actually references a version of the Sawney Bean legend in the original French language addition, though it's curiously omitted from the 17th century English language translation. Probably because of the content. You see, its version mentions the human followers of the Bean clan-cult were executed and the caves sealed over. However, the daughter of the Bean clan was actually arrested and taken to King James court where she was interrogated on the nature of witchcraft. The book suggests that King James was overwhelmed with lust for her and made her his mistress."

I grimaced. I hadn't bothered checking out the French edition of *Cults des Goules.* "Yeah, it makes sense the English translation would leave out accusing a British monarch of witchcraft and monster sex."

"I thought James the First liked dudes," Karl asked, confused.

"You can like both," Lisa said, annoyed. "Also, ghouls can shapeshift and frequently had lovers of both sexes."

I blinked. "Yeah. Okay."

"Monsters and unconventional sexuality are intrinsically intertwined," Lisa said, suggestively, and looking straight at me.

I wasn't sure how I felt about that given my decision just moments before of not trying to pursue her. Was she interested? Had I just not been picking up the signs?

Karl glared at me.

"In any case, Ms. Delapore had the fascinating theory that Anne Murphy, alleged mistress of James the First was, in fact actually, Anne Bean operating under her married name. Under this theory, Anne Murphy returned to her long-lost hometown with her second husband, Martin Fitzroy. A recognized bastard of James whose mother is unknown but could have been Anne Murphy herself."

"Keeping it in the family," Karl said, chuckling.

Yuck.

"They acquired the Bean lands and have been dwelling there ever since," Professor Warner said. "At least until the 2020 pandemic when the last remaining direct heirs of the family died out and Murphy Manor became property of the town itself. I believe we will find secrets to the lost civilization of the ghouls both there and within the caves below. Or, at least, an insight into the Sawney Bean legend as well as its relationship to the Ultraterrestials."

"We're just going to march up and ask to poke around their local historical landmark?" I asked, having wished I'd paid more attention to the specifics here.

"Oh no," Professor Warner said. "We've rented the house for the weekend on Air B&B. Quite expensive too as it's the local Meat Pie festival."

Chapter Two

I wanted to control my sarcasm. I'd gotten much better at it. My mother was Scottish, and my father was Italian, so, really, it was a miracle that every word out of my mouth wasn't pure snark. However, looking upon the sight that greeted us after we stepped out of the train station, well, I couldn't hold it in anymore.

"Yes, professor, clearly, we have come to the dark corners of the Earth," I said, sighing. "We are among a heathen people who will show us their pagan magic as well as introduce us to their chthonic masters."

A banner saying, WELCOME TO MEAT FEST 2024 hung over the front of the building directly across from the train station as people dressed as various slasher movie villains walked down the street. The theatre marquee was visible with CANNIBAL HOLOCAUST, THE HILLS HAVE EYES, and DEATH LINE.

Bean was not the kind of decaying hellish fishing town that I'd been envisioning from my investigations. I'd been expecting something gray, cheerless, and probably a few decades behind the times. Which, yeah, was probably racist against my mother's people. Instead, Bean seemed like an ordinary town in every respect, the cars modern, and a general sense of cheer for their local festival. Every other building was a tea shop or a place selling local produce – heavy on the tartan teacloths, whisky, and enough shortbread to choke the Loch Ness monster (present in plush form). I could see they'd set up a fair with amusement park rides in the distance and lots of booths with a decidedly horror theme. If it wasn't the middle of July, I would have said it was a pretty good Halloween display.

To the professor's credit, he seemed to realize this trip was probably a bust. "It would seem in lieu of recent economic woes affecting the British Isles, the locals have decided to lean into their infamous reputation rather than deny it."

"You don't say," I said, lifting my suitcase in one hand as my duffle bag rested on my right shoulder. I'd always been strong as an ox and my father had said that if academia didn't work out, I could always dig ditches for a living.

Dick.

"Also points for using the word chthonic," Professor Warner said, showing he at least had a sense of humor about all this.

"The commercialization of the Sawney Bean legend does serve the purpose of raising awareness of local legends and customs," Lisa said, sounding as disappointed as the professor but doing a better job of hiding it. No one hated Goths making the dark and spooky family-friendly for the normies more than Goths.

"I'm actually with Rick here," Karl said, looking around, annoyed. "This is a horrific misrepresentation of the local heritage and religious rituals born here."

"I didn't say that," I replied, annoyed at Karl putting words in my mouth. Personally, I was of the mind that if the Sawney Bean legend were true, which was a big if, then they were a bunch of serial killers rather than anything connected to either pagan religion or primordial underground humans.

"Good evening lads!" A cheerful woman's voice spoke up nearby them. "Welcome tae Scotland."

I turned my head and almost immediately found myself dumbstruck by the woman before me. She had beautiful skin, long black hair, and piercing blue eyes. She was dressed in a plain green dress and sweater but worn like high fashion. I was tongue tied just looking at her. There was a kind of instant Eighties movie music montage and kismet I felt. Either that or I was really-really desperate after deciding it wouldn't work out between me and Lisa. She was carrying a bunch of folders and I noticed she was standing next to an SUV.

"Lads and lass," Lisa said, unhappily.

"Oh right," the woman said. "I am Annie Devlin, and you must be the American Miskatonic Party! I am here to guide you through our wonderful town's sordid murderous history as well as set you up in Bean Mansion for the weekend. Tomorrow, we have a fun day planned of spelunking as well as exploring heritage sites."

It took us all a second to tune into her accent but I got there first.

I turned to Professor Warner. "You hired a tour guide?"

"It seemed the most expedient way of getting through the bureaucratic red tape that was impeding our investigation," Professor Warner said, lightly coughing and turning his head.

I was starting to wonder if the Professor was just as much of a fraud as I was. Because it was starting to look like he'd set himself up to do the bare minimum of actual research, let alone archaeology, while letting the University pick up the bill. If that was the case, then he'd gone up in my estimation significantly. The wonders of tenure in action.

"As you can see, we're in the middle of Meat Fest 2024! A local celebration of meat pies, steaks, sausages, lamb, venison, and stews. No pork, though. Local taboo. Don't expect to find any missing travelers in your meals, though. We save that for ourselves. Haha, just a bit of Bean humor there," Annie said, continuing to talk in her cheerful sing-song voice. It was clear she was doing her best to suppress her local accent and speak with a lighter more comprehensible tone. At least to American English speakers.

"What if you're a vegetarian?" Lisa asked, getting a weird expression on her face as if something about the woman was putting her off. More than just the occasional hostility a territorial person might have to a newcomer in a small group.

"Then you're just shite out of luck," Annie said, not missing a beat. "Meat Fest is a carnivorous festival and you're about as lucky to be vegetarian here as a teetotaler in wine country. However, I will assure you that the people of Bean are great believers in ethical consumption."

"Which means what?" I asked, just happy to hear her speak.

"We believe in free range handling of our domestic animals," Annie replied, speaking less like she was reading from a script and more from the heart. "None of those cramped stalls and other awful conditions that so many cattle and other poor creatures are shoved into. No being horribly pumped with drugs and steroids either. Not that we don't give them the benefits of modern medicine, mind you. Here in Bean, our livestock are treated as beloved members of the family."

"Until you kill and eat them," I replied, following that train of logic to its natural conclusion.

"Yup," Annie said, not missing a beat. "It's the circle of life."

I wasn't sure that was actually a circle since the meat eaters seemed to be getting the better end of things. I was definitely interested in what she had to say, though. Not just because she was incredibly attractive. Also, because I was really hungry and didn't have any objections to eating animals. As long as I didn't have to see how the sausage was made, so to speak, I was happily to wolf down meat in all forms.

"Indeed," Professor Warner said, staring. "While I appreciate this wonderful insight into the local festival, I'd like to get ourselves set up at Bean Manor first."

"Are you sure?" Annie asked, sounding genuinely disappointed. "I have lunch already reserved at the Devil's Pit barbecue. It's really an experience."

"I'm afraid so," Professor Warner said.

I had to admit I was disappointed myself.

For a variety of reasons.

Bean Manor was another location that didn't exactly meet with my "haunted house" expectations for this trip. I'd been imagining decaying walls, ominous shadows, and creaking doors with an antediluvian sense of dread from every corner (to borrow a pulp descriptor from my RPGing days). Instead, once we arrived at the building a few miles out of town, it felt like the kind of spruced up mansion you'd see on television. Hell, James Bond's mansion in *Skyfall* felt more intimidating and oppressive.

Indeed, the place had a fantastic view of the ocean from its cliffside placement, and I just wanted to go out on the balcony and soak up the sea air. It was another sign this trip was a bust as any place which had wireless internet (Annie had the password), let alone electricity and indoor plumbing wasn't going to be the home for eldritch abominations.

"Doesn't look like the home to a bunch of cannibals," Karl muttered, sounding almost disappointed.

"Well, this isn't the original Bean Manor," Annie said, still in tour guide mode. "The original Bean manor, if it ever existed, was burned down by the party assembled by James the Fourth during their attempt to cleanse the region of banditry. This house was actually built by Anne Murphy and her husband, Martin Fitzroy, before being renovated in the early 20th century after a housefire."

Professor Warner was oddly looking over every little nook and cranny of the place while Lisa seemed to be soaking up the atmosphere like it was a spiritual experience. She even had her little psychic crawl necklace out around her neck as she spread out her arms in opposite directions. Karl, by contrast, looked bored and annoyed with everything he was encountering.

"What caused the housefire?" Karl asked. "Angry villagers?"

"Faulty wiring," Annie replied. "Sadly, not much of the original Murphy Manor remains."

"You say Murphy Manor," I said, looking at her. "Wouldn't it be Fitzroy? I mean, why call it Bean Manor today?"

I was going to do at least a little research here even if I thought this was an enormous waste of time. Besides, it was an excuse to spend some time with Annie.

"That is a long story," Annie replied. "Martin Fitzroy married Annie Murphy, his father's mistress but actually served as stepfather to her existing child, James Murphy. It was believed that James Murphy was James VI's bastard as well as Martin and thus Martin's little brother, but James never recognized him. James Murphy would eventually go out and become a famous sea captain as well as marrying seven times as well as keeping numerous mistresses in the town. Most of the town can trace their lineage back to him these days. His latter descendants were less prolific and the male line died out—"

"In 2020," I replied, repeating what I'd said to the professor. "So it was renamed Bean Manor after the town when it became public property. Got it. It's not named after the Sawney Bean legend at all."

Annie smiled. "Correct. Yes, as you may have guessed, the village is leaning heavily into the old story."

I looked into her eyes. "What's your take on it?"

Annie smiled brightly. "I believe every town is entitled to a one good scary story. Bean just happens to have a bunch."

"So, I take it you don't believe Alexander Bean was married to a witch and in contact with a bunch of underground dwelling monsters," Karl said, clenching his fists. He was reacting intensely to all of this.

Professor Warner glared at Karl as if he'd given away the secret. The Professor may have believed in utter nonsense, but he had the good sense to not advertise it to the world.

Lisa facepalmed.

"Oh, you mean the ghoul legend?" Annie asked, surprising everyone. "How there is a vast city of underground dwelling pre-humans dwelling underneath Bennane Head and that the Bean clan was a bunch of their worshipers, learning the worship of K'Tullu and Yog-Sothith among other fel practices."

Everyone stared at her.

"Yeah, that," I replied.

Karl looked at her if she was suddenly a glass of water and he was a man dying of thirst. "So you have heard the stories?"

"In America, a hundred years is a long time and in Scotland, a hundred miles is a long distance," Annie said, paraphrasing the old joke. Bean is a relatively new community in Scotland, and it predates the age of your country twice over. I looked up you Miskatonic folk when you made the arrangements for your stay and it was quite the read. You can find anything on the internet these days. Aiye, I've heard the stories told about my hometown. However, you'll find that ghouls are just another name for very common legends. Underhill dwelling monsters are just the same fairy stories from all over the island. Redcaps eating the flesh of the living, changelings being substituted for human bairns, and hideous monsters taking the shape of beautiful women to seduce men into siring half-human offspring. Old Francois Balfour just slapped an Arabic name on 'em and gussied it up for his scary book."

Despite her flippant manner, it was strange for a random tour guide to be familiar with a 17th century book of occult mysticism. Even if the Bean clan was mentioned in it. "I suppose the age of the book has lent it a certain credibility."

"Pfft," Annie said, smirking. "The 17th century is yesterday. *Cultes de Goules* is only old to Americans. It's like believing HG Wells got his idea for Morlocks from Bean just because he stayed the weekend here."

"Oh, he did?" I asked, happy to discuss that factoid with her. It was a surprise to find someone who had a knowledge of my area of specialty without getting drawn into the utter quackery that it seemed to induce in just about everyone else.

"An all-too-common perspective among my peers, Ms. Devlin," Professor Warner said, unhappily.

"They're real," Karl muttered under his breath. "They're real."

Damn, he really had drunk the Kool-Aid. I needed to talk to my friend about this but maybe after we were out of Scotland and had a little distance from the subject. Besides, he didn't seem like he wanted to be told that there was no Rapunzel or gingerbread house in the woods.

Instead, I looked at Annie. "Listen, this is going to seem forward, but would you like to discuss this further? Professor, would it be okay to go have lunch with her? It seems like everything is set up here and—"

Professor Warner, sadly, killed my hopes of asking her out. "I'm afraid that's not going to be possible, Mr. Jameson. We must prepare for exploring the caves under Bennane Head."

Gee thanks, Professor. "Ah."

"You won't be getting much luck out of that exploration," Annie said, a pained expression on her face. "The caves are only six hundred feet deep. It was meant to be the base of Alexander "Sawney" Bean but there's no city to be found there. Maybe if it was like Tolkien's *The Hobbit* and the goblins opened the Earth to swallow people but—"

"Don't encourage him," I said aloud, before realizing I had. Shit.

Professor Warner just shook his head. "Ms. Delapore?"

Lisa lowered her arms, apparently having finished whatever psychic woo or magic she was trying to do. "I definitely feel something here, professor. I think we're at the center of it all."

"Excellent," Professor Warner said. "Ms. Devlin, you have been extremely helpful, but I think we'll be working alone from this point onward. If you could leave a number for where we can have our meals delivered from, that will be all."

Annie realized she was being dismissed and a pained expression passed across her face but also something approaching pity. Whether it was for me, or the entire group was impossible to guess, though. Maybe a little bit of both.

"Good luck with your studies then," Annie said, looking at me. "Another time then."

Yeah, that wasn't going to happen.

In the distance, a storm started to pull in from off the coast. It wasn't exactly supernatural, this being Scotland and all, but it reflected my mood perfectly.

Chapter Three

The rest of the day was miserable, and the night wasn't much better. The storm meant we didn't get to explore the Sawney Bean caves but it wasn't like there wasn't a huge chunk of information about the internet. We could have stayed at home in the Miskatonic Library and been able to look at the pictures the local tour guides had taken for us. They were on the town's website for Chrissake.

Professor Warner set up a bunch of kirilian cameras, air pressure monitoring devices, brain wave recorders, and other machines of dubious practicality throughout the house. I didn't bother questioning them even though we were supposed to be hunting a lost civilization versus ghosts. Karl refused to talk to him throughout the encounter and practically bit my head off when I suggested we sneak out for a pint. Lisa was also in full witch mode, seemingly soaking up the weirdness of

Murphy Manor/Bean Manor despite the place having been re-constructed in the frigging *Seventies* according to the brochure left by Annie. Hell, I'd grown up in a house older than that.

About the only thing to recommend the trip was the fact that the Devil's Pit barbecue was a living argument against the stereotype of Scottish people being lousy cooks. If Chef Gordon Ramsey hadn't already destroyed that reputation, the fantastic meat extravaganza I had there would be the final blow to it. Seriously, so good I ended up stuffing myself more than on Thanskgiving both lunch and dinner.

By the time I went to sleep, I was determined to just suffer my way through the rest of the trip and start to figure out other options than the Armitage Award. I was not a good fit for all this weirdness and not even a free trip to Scotland was worth it if I had to spend the entire time debating UFOs and mole people. I just wanted to relax and put out anything spooky from my mind.

So, of course, I had nightmares that would have given Wes Craven pause.

I dreamed of the primordial inhabitants of the island, naked and carrying items of stone, fleeing in terror from the bipedal wolf-faced monsters that poured out of the ground and dragged both men as well as women to their doom.

I saw ancient stone monuments erected throughout the island, marking the spots where the ghouls. The first villages and agriculture were accompanied by tools. Futile attempts to fight back nevertheless emboldened the people that began to worship the wolfmen's gods and call upon things from the sea to fight them.

I saw the relationship between the wolfmen and the humans change as the former set themselves up as gods. They assumed human forms and demanded blood sacrifices willingly offered by the priests to allow the numbers of the surface dwellers to grow.

I saw ghouls begin to claim human brides and husbands, creating strange mutant hybrids that could shapeshift and walk between the worlds. The ghouls, for that was what they were, humans, and their hybrids were at last one people or at least something approaching one people.

That was when the Others emerged from the ground. Hideous, white-skinned blind creatures that had been raised in the darkness from the ancestors of humanity, kept in pens and bred like cattle.

The Others slaughtered ghouls, hybrids, and humans alike before devouring them like their masters had them. Semi-intelligent, cannibalistic, and mutated by the hideous experiments their former owners had done to them. They spread like a virus through the tunnels of the Earth, raping and pillaging until they formed a new species of humanity.

Us.

"Ah," I said, waking up with a ringing in my ears. I was inside one of the upstairs guest bedrooms, still in my boxers and a t-shirt with the storm still raging outside. It was two AM, and I had a massive headache.

I was also hungry.

Really hungry.

Shaking my head, I slid out of the bed and put on a pair of sweatpants before heading out into the rest of the manor. There was a banging noise that only got louder after I went out my room's door and as much as I wanted to see if there was any leftover food from the Devil's Pit, that seemed something worth investigating.

Much to my surprise, I had to head into the mansion's cellar to find the source of the noise that was much louder than I'd expected and sounded like someone chopping wood. Mind you, I'd always had good hearing.

There, among a bunch of empty wine racks, paint cans, and other leftover materials from when Murphy Manor was renovated as an Air B&B, I saw Professor Warner without his shirt on hacking into the side of the wooden wall paneling with an ax. Surprisingly, the professor was pretty ripped for a man his age and looked like an old professional wrestler. That managed to hold my attention long enough to need a second to process that he was *hacking into the wall with an ax*.

"Professor, what the hell are you doing?" I asked, staring at the sight, and wondering if I was still dreaming.

"Come here, boy, give me a hand," Professor Warner said, taking another swing and then pausing for a moment to catch his breath.

"You do realize we don't own this house, right?" I asked, staring.

"I said come here and help!" Professor Warner shouted, staring at me with intense eyes that put Karl's own today to shame.

"Right," I said, walking up to the wooden paneling and pulling it on it. The Professor had made a dent in it, but it wasn't until I put my back into it that I managed to rip several layers of wood free. I wasn't sure what I was even trying to accomplish before the last layer gave way and a staircase was exposed.

It wasn't a normal staircase either, one made of wood or concrete, but something that looked to have been chiseled and carved out of the cavernous walls that surrounded it. It was, by itself, a pretty impressive find as the crudeness of the carvings made me think this had been done centuries ago rather than years. I could see fairly deep down the tunnels, I'd always had good lowlight vision, but there was something about the yawning abyss below that made me sick to contemplate it.

I could feel the wind pouring up from the sea below, no matter how strange the logistics of that would require. I could also hear the crashing waves. This was definitely an entrance down to the Sawney Bean caverns below. It didn't change much but if the professor was willing to pay the price for repairs then he'd actually made a genuine discovery: yes, it turned out, that the locals had once had a passage down to the cave system.

"Behold!" Professor Warner said.

"Congratulations, Professor," I said, trying and failing to contain my sarcasm. "You've discovered a hole in the ground."

"A hole leading to the caverns' true entrance!" Professor Warner said, staring with what I could only describe as madness in his eyes.

"True entrance?" I asked, wondering what the hell he was talking about.

"The one in the front would never serve as true entrance to the ultraterrestial's lair," Professor Warner explained. "The Bean clan would need their own private hidden entrance for communicating with their masters. The front might have contained bodies, an abattoir, or stored victims for King James' goons to find but the actual center of the cult-clan's rituals would have to be behind walls of solid rock. This is just like the Delapore estate! A secret entrance covered up to hide the town's dark forbidden history!"

I pitied Professor Warner in that moment more than I was angry for wasting months on his so-called research. "Except, there's other possibilities here too. It could be a priest hole for Catholics during the time of Protestant repression, it could be a smuggler's den down there, or it could be one of the landowners just wanted to expand his house into the caverns below for storage and did a shit job of it."

Professor Warner wasn't looking at me, though. "Do you know why I selected you for the Armitage Award, son?"

He'd never called me son before, and I wasn't sure I liked it. "Because you respected my academic prowess and skepticism?"

Professor Warner scoffed as if that were a particularly ridiculous answer. "Your mother, my boy."

"My mother?" I asked, really hoping this wasn't going to be about how my mother had traded sex for my scholarship. The fact my mind even went there should tell you about the likelihood of that being the case, which was sadly a non-zero. My mother had always been a wild one and it wouldn't have been the first time she'd cheated on my dad. He tolerated it with good grace and honestly seemed a little afraid of her at times.

"Yes," Professor Warner said, his voice distant and echoing as he kept his gaze focused on the stone steps before us. "Your mother, Mary, saved my career. My sanity even."

That remained to be seen. "What do you mean?"

"Do you remember the Arkham subway collapse of 92'?" Professor Warner said.

"I know *of* it," I said, wondering what he was getting at.

Like Boston' subway system, a lot of state money and government pork had been spent trying to expand the underground railway system. Questions of embezzlement and mismanagement of materials had dogged the effort for decades, though. The project had been started in my dad's era and carried on well into mine. The 92' Collapse had almost, if you pardoned the pun, derailed the whole thing.

I didn't know much more than any other Arkham local but the local mobsters, we still had Irish ones instead of Russia, had apparently been substituting poor quality cement among other materials while pocketing the difference. When they'd opened one of the first functioning subway stations, the entire thing had collapsed and a train full of passengers had been buried alive for a week. Thirteen people had died and twenty-three more people had been hospitalized with permanent injuries ranging from brain damage to lost limbs. Last I checked, the State of Massachusetts was still dealing with lawsuits related to it.

"I was there," Professor Warner said, shaking his head. "I was working on my doctorate at the time and with both my wife and child. Neither of them made it."

I blinked. "Christ, I had no idea."

Professor Warner grimaced at the mention of Christ, which was one of those things that I'd noticed but never asked about. He struck me as one of those people who'd probably been religious at one point in their life before going the opposite direction as only someone really pissed off at God and fate can. Not so much as an atheist as religiously traumatized.

"We were not alone down there," Professor Warner said, shaking his head. "The tunnels had been made as a challenge by the Lodge of

Starry Wisdom and Brotherhood of the Sleeping God, a way to channel the dark powers of the Earth that interfered with the ones who'd dwelled below. They took it personally and made an example of us. They hadn't expected so many of us to survive, though. There was much debate among them about what to do with us. They spoke English among themselves, you see, and we could hear them and their twisted debate as they dragged off the dead or dying. I can still hear the whispers and *crunching*."

What the professor was describing was madness, worse than madness, but I found myself entranced as I absolutely knew he was describing the truth as he remembered it. "There was cannibalism on the train?"

"It's not cannibalism when a ghoul eats a human, any more than when a shark eats a minnow. They can breed with our kind but that is because they can adopt our form and transform our DNA to their needs, but it is no more a mixing of the races than a Cuckoo leaving their egg in another's nest," Professor Warner said, his face wrinkled in disgust. "But yes, the cannibalism came in time. For all their pretensions of being a superior species, they were squeamish at the process of murdering us individually. But we knew too many of their secrets to be allowed to walk away."

I would regret for the rest of my life what I asked next. "What happened?"

"A dark compact was struck forged of shared loathing and shame as well as desperate need for survival," Professor Warner said. "Those who were willing to eat of their fellow human beings would be allowed to live while those who refused would die. I was desperate to save my daughter and willing to do anything. She was only eight and we were already hunger and thirst ravaged."

"You did it," I said.

"Yes," Professor Warner said. "I fed the horrific strips of my fellow passengers to my daughter myself. My wife refused, disgusted, and tried to stop me. It was my fellow passengers who fell upon her and the other dissenters that ended her. In the end, it was resolved in a night and the rescue team found us the next day, lowering cleaner food down to us in baskets afterward. The authorities covered up what happened afterward, and much was attributed to oxygen deprivation and trauma. But I knew the truth."

"What happened to your daughter?" I asked, knowing it couldn't have been my mother.

"She was changed by the experience but not in the way you'd think," Professor Warner said. "The flesh seemed to trigger some sort of metamorphosis or perhaps it was the dark blessings the ghouls worked over the meat. Her skin grew pale as alabaster, her hair white like an old woman's, and she began to fear the light like suffered porphyria. By the time she was fourteen, I knew I'd lost her, and she vanished. The police didn't even bother to investigate me, and I sometimes wish they'd arrested me for killing her. I would feel less guilt."

My conscious mind was already weaving together the deranged story and trying to come up with a rationale alternative to what he was saying: after being traumatized in a cave-in, possible desperate means to survive, he'd woven an elaborate justification about monsters to cope with events. Maybe his daughter had suffered from a condition related to the accident either chemical or mental. Maybe he'd killed her and was covering it up. Maybe she had just run away or died of her condition. Seeking some way to make sense of it all, he'd become obsessed with the occult and pseudo-science with Miskatonic University not wanting to fire him due to his history. No, that didn't make any sense. It was close but wrong.

"How does my mother fit into all this?" I asked, knowing I was just feeding into his delusions but desperate to know.

Professor Warner barely seemed to acknowledge me. "I spent years researching the occult and seeking answers to the kind of horrors below us. I thought I'd find a sympathetic ear with the board of Miskatonic but was rebuffed. They knew of the ghouls, of course. Had known about them for a century, in fact, but considered them better left undisturbed. They only feed on the dead. *They do not hunt our kind.* Bah! Your mother brought me the journal that proved otherwise."

"Journal?" I asked.

"Sawney Bean's journal, dictated by his wife since he was functionally illiterate. It detailed all of the gruesome things that he and his cult did for their evil masters. The pagan murder rites and human sacrifices that accompanied their foul banquets of the dead. They did not wait for the dead to be in the ground to begin their feasts but hunted them. It was proof of the malevolence of the race so much more advanced than our own being every bit the degenerate savages that I thought they were."

That was the missing piece and I felt sick about it. My mother was an artist and a bit of a con woman. She'd obviously forged some kind of artifact for the Professor to find and he'd taken it at face value. He probably knew, at least on some level, it was a phony too or he would have presented it to the world, but it was proof of his fancies having a basis in reality as long as it existed. I had to give it to mom, she'd managed to keep me in college despite everything. Unfortunately, it had been at the cost of manipulating a poor madman.

"What do you hope to find?" I asked, knowing that the only way to break him out of this delusion would be to head down.

Maybe not even then.

"Evidence," Professor Warren said, sadly. "More evidence. Enough to present not just to the Miskatonic Board but their allies that we can't just keep covering this all up. We'd never win against them in a direct conflict, they knew about atomic theory when we were still banging rocks together in the Stone Age, but we can prepare."

I took a deep breath. "I'll get a flashlight. Do you want to get Lisa and Karl?"

"No," Professor Warren said, taking a deep breath. "They've grown too close to this."

I nodded and stared down into the void. I really, really hoped that I was just going to find a flooded cavern down there.

Chapter Four

I had made a horrible mistake.

I'd expected to find the steps leading right down into the caverns and a flooded entrance, which would have cut our trip short and brought an end to the insanity. I didn't know if Professor Warner was genuinely ill or just the victim of a bunch of conspiracy theories that had piled up in what might have once been a brilliant mind, but the result was the same—he was no longer a harmless old kook talking about aliens and mole people but now bringing people deeper into his delusions.

In my case, literally because we were going deeper and what was around me had to be a delusion. The staircase had just kept going and going deeper into the ground with it opening into passages that were far larger as well as twisting than the underground of Bean could have possibly made real.

For the first twenty minutes or so, I came up with excuse after excuse that this was a trick of the light or my mind was just playing tricks on me. The walls had hideous shapes carved into them that I kept insisting was just natural formations that happened to take the appearance of ghastly faces with inhuman qualities. Except geometry and my own senses betrayed me with as I found myself walking over a perfectly smooth stone bridge that crossed a seemingly endlessly deep cavern that was the source of the wind I'd felt before. The walls were also riddled with the carvings, so much so that it would have taken a thriving civilization several decades to carve them along the wall even if they'd had modern technology plus motorized pullies or scaffolding that could be built from the void below.

"This isn't happening," I muttered, shaking my head as I kept the flashlight in my hands pressed forward. "This isn't happening."

"This is just the antechamber," Professor Warner said, his voice disturbingly calm as if seeing all of this was laying his mind's torments to rest rather than enflaming them as they were mine. "We have barely begun to probe the edges of the ghoul's kingdom."

I stopped and turned the flashlight on him. He covered his face. "Professor, this is real!"

"Yes, obviously," Professor Warner said, chuckling as if it was all a sick joke. "If any of this were allowed to come out into the public, we could prove the Hyborian Age and older civilizations still. These rocks are but the newest creations of Earth's oldest inhabitants."

I was close to panic now. "What do you mean if any of this were allowed to come out into the public? You're talking like, what, the Men in Black?"

Professor Warner shook his head. "If only it were merely human conspiracy that held the truth back, Mr. Jameson. No, I fear the issue is a far more elemental one. It is evolution itself that works against us as academics."

"Evolution?" I asked, finally finding myself open to the madness that I'd previously dismissed.

Professor Warner pulled out a pack of cigarettes that looked older than me and lit up. "Five years clean. Disgusting habit but if I'm ever going to go back, it might as well be now. Yes, evolution. The most blessed gift that humanity ever received from the raw forces of nature, though I have some suspicions it was husbanded in, was the inability to collate the truth of the cosmos."

"I don't understand," I said, feeling a chill unrelated to the unconscionably hot hair.

"We are cattle, Mr. Jameson," Professor Warner said, lighting up. "Bred with blinders and ear plugs that prevent us from seeing the truth of the horrors around us. The world is not composed of four dimensions but an ever infinitely expanding deck of layers that each contain their own unique levels of hostility. String Theory, multiverses, aliens, gods, demons, Heaven, and Hell are perhaps the closest the human mind can come to appreciating the various things around us. Evolution benefited us, though, by being only to see in a tiny spectrum and simply ignore the truth around us. The herd of humanity moves forward, losing only a handful of members each year, and we do not panic. This allows us to keep breeding new generations to be prey animals for our masters."

I stared at him. "That's...insane."

"Insane are those handfuls of humans that are born with an extra sense, perhaps because of ancestry not of this Earth, or a mutation that lets them pierce what is around us. They, we, are a threat to the herd. We show them the things that they cannot possibly live with and thus we must be ostracized or destroyed," Professor Warner said, almost sad.

"I don't understand," I said, lying. I could understand what he was saying, and it terrified me. I was scared shitless and all I'd seen so far were some impossible examples of geology and construction.

"If you carved into the side of the cliff face of Bennane Head, dug a mile deep, you would never find this cavern. It exists on another layer of the deck that other races can shuffle as easily as you and I can walk through a door." Professor Warner took a long drag off his cigarette. "I never expected to find an actual entrance to one of the ghoul doors or, if I did, I never expected to be able to go through. From that, I believe we shall not be allowed to leave. I am content with that decision, to be reunited with my family in what worlds beyond may exist or peaceful oblivion, but I regret that you have come with me on this."

I stared at him, letting his words sink in and almost pushed him over into the abyss out of fury. Instead, I decided I would leave immediately and pretend this strange journey had never happened. If he wanted to die in some strange alien cave surrounded by hideous statues, then let him. This would be something I'd dismiss as a dream in the morning and never think of again. I'd buy a fucking ticket outward and get the Hell out of the country, Armitage Award, or not.

Except, that wasn't an option.

There were noises coming from the way we came. Noises that were like the scratching on a blackboard mixed with the skittering of rats. Noises that triggered long repressed and deeply buried instincts that made me think of a deer running from a fire in the woods. It was nothing concrete but every instinct in my body screamed at me to run, so I did. I turned around and started running deeper into the twisted tunnels of the cavern despite it being against all reason. My flashlight fell from my hands as I stumbled yet I kept running, starting to see the passages with a light that came not from the rock itself.

Voices whispered in my ear that did not sound entirely human but a throat approximation of English that could be heard from all directions around me.

RUN.

RUN.

RUN.

COME HOME.

The last set of words caused me to fall over completely as I entered another chamber and fell down a flight of stairs. I felt bones crack and hit my head as I rolled to the base and found myself in some sort of chamber that I would have called a temple if it had been built with human hands. There was a nasty crunching as I rolled around on the ground, trying, and failing to get up as the room started spinning around me. It was a tall cylindrical chamber with more statues filling it. There was no source of light within, but I could see as brightly as in daytime even as my consciousness was fading.

The most telling of the statues, the one that drew my attention most was familiar from my time in Miskatonic University. A bibulous squid-like humanoid thing that had been sketched many times over in various blasphemous texts and things I'd dismissed previously as badly done mythology or monster-drawings: K'Tullu. Its tentacled mouth was open wide as if to swallow me as its four eyes each contained a kind of pulsating gem. I ran my hands through the crunching material I could feel biting into my back and picked up the pieces, cutting my hand as I did so.

I stared at the contents.

Bone fragments.

Skull fragments.

Human teeth.

I remember laughing before screaming until I passed out.

I woke up with blood in my eyes.

I reached up to wipe it away and felt it leaking still from my forehead where I had a huge gash. Cleaning my face with my sleeve, I found myself still in the horrifying temple where the ground was covered in heaps of dried human bones scattered around like it was a waste pit for a barbecue. It was not that sight that horrified me, though. No, my mind had already processed that I was in a whole new terrifying nightmare that I was unable to escape. The smell of fresh meat, blood, and other, nastier fluids wafted over from a stone table where two familiar figures were having a ghastly feast.

Karl and Lisa were standing there, their fingers and mouths covered in viscera as they pawed like wild animals at the corpse of Professor Warner. He'd had his head smashed in and they were using stolen kitchen knives and weird stone tools I could only assume had been stolen from the artifacts at Miskatonic University. The two had deranged expressions on their face, mixtures of joy and rapture crossed with some small pushed down sense of disgust.

The sight sickened me before I began to crawl away or tried to, at least, the crunching noise of my movement against the bones beneath me drawing their attention.

"Hey Rick," Karl said, turning as he continued to chew on his cannibalistic feast. I didn't know how he could stand there not throwing up what was in his mouth but just kept chewing. I wanted to throw up from twenty feet away.

I asked what was, at that time, a very reasonable question. "What the ever-loving *fuck*?"

"It's real," Lisa said, managing to force herself to swallow whatever it was she was eating from our late professor. "All of it. The Ultraterrestials, Great Cthulhu, the gods of our ancestors, and the coming apocalypse. All of it is real."

Karl looked at me like he was trying to explain a new phone app or show off his new car. He gestured up to the statue. "They came with him, don't you see? The K'nyanians! That's what the ghouls call themselves! They weren't human, not at first! But they came down with him and can shift their forms to resemble whatever the reigning species of the time is! They bred our ancestors to be food! Food! Unintelligent cattle and pigs! Meat! But we grew minds! The spark of life!"

"The true gods have blessed us," Lisa said, clasping her hands in prayer. "Yog-Sothoth, Cthulhu, and Shub-Niggurath! All true religion is about the body! The consumption of the blood and flesh! Because it was the gods showing us how to become like them! To be immortal and eternal, free from all the bullshit!"

Karl stared at me as if trying to see something inside me. "My family has worshiped the Old Ones for as long as the white man has been in our country, Rick. But it's all nonsense. Stupid robes and chants when the real magic is here in the Old Country. Down here in the dark places. I saw how you were disgusted by the Professor's idiocy. His stupid theories and speculation like a cow wondering why his friends kept vanishing when they off to slaughter! The books show the rituals, Rick! The rituals to become like ghouls! We can become wild and free and immortal!"

I finally managed to climb to my feet and overcome my terror. This place was the gathering place of the Bean clan, a temple shrine to the Great Old Ones they'd decided to carry out their foul rituals to worship. It wasn't a sacred place to the ghouls, though. This horrible mess was just the product of the Bean clan themselves. I didn't know how I knew it but I knew it. It was a cargo cult like the islanders who had created replicas of airfields and airplanes during World War II because they didn't have the context for understanding what the hell they were seeing. Both my friends were completely off their gourds, trying to comprehend something beyond their understanding and aping the behavior of beings they could never hope to be a part of.

"You killed our teacher and ate him," I said, very slowly. "You two are *goddamn nutjobs.*"

Karl stared at me with the kind of look you'd give someone who'd metamorphized into a bug before your eyes. Lisa just looked disappointed even as she choked, clearly having a bit of difficulty keeping down raw human meat. Because you know, reality.

"You've always had a small mind, Rick," Karl said, shaking his head and walking toward me with one of the stone knives in his right hand. "If you don't understand what worshiping the ghouls could accomplish then you're just meat."

"You are not worshiping the ghouls, Mr. Butcher," An echoing Annie Devlin's voice spoke throughout the chamber. "You are worshiping the *sluagh.*"

"What?" I asked, looking around for the source of it.

"Sluagh, redcaps, troglodytes, Morlocks," Annie said, repeating the various names of underground monsters. "Their names don't matter, and one is as good as any other. But the sluagh are not the ghoul race. We are the People, and they are the Husbanded."

Karl looked up to see our tour guide descending the steps I'd fallen. He had a feral, animalistic expression on his face and lifted his knife as if to threaten her. Unfortunately, for him, she was carrying an old Lee-Enfield rifle left over from the Great Wars. Annie lifted it and fired, striking Karl in the chest with the sound of a thunderclap. Karl dropped his knife on the ground and started bleeding profusely, filling the chamber even more with the scent of blood.

"No, no, no," Lisa said, stepping back. "I'm supposed to be immortal."

Annie reloaded the rifle and aimed it at Lisa. "You're not even one of the Husbanded, dear."

A second thunderclap filled the room and I saw the girl I'd had a crush on for weeks fall to the ground, her face struck by the round and forcing me to look away. In the span of a few minutes, I'd become the sole survivor of this little expedition. One that I'd dismissed as nothing more than a free vacation chasing fairy stories.

"Please don't kill me!" I said, covering my face. "I didn't see anything!"

It was a bold-faced lie and we both knew it. I would have done anything in that moment to take back everything I'd seen. Investigating the ghouls and the Legend of Sawney Bean had resulted in all becoming doomed and I hated it. I just wanted to be back home, safe in my father's garage, working on his old corvette, the Blue Meanie like I'd used to do on weekends before college.

"Why would I want to kill you, Richard?" Annie spoke.

I looked up, confused. She was descending the stairs now and i saw her shimmer and shake as if I was seeing past an illusion now. What I saw underneath the glamour was not a human woman at all but a kind of dog-like humanoid that looked like something out of a horror movies. Yet, I couldn't put into words, she was still beautiful. The rifle was very real, though, and fit perfectly into her all-too-human hands.

"What's going on?" I asked, staring forward.

"Your friend was right, Richard," Annie spoke, her voice soothing. "The People did breed the Husbanded from the primates of this world as food. We cultivated food we could digest from the primordial soup across a hundred million years. The last and most nourishing of our livestock we trained to take care of itself, to build little villages and feed themselves, but that made them too ghoul-like for many of us. So we gave them their freedom and often ate from their dead. Some of us could not tolerate that, though, and dismissed claims they were feeling creatures. They bred particularly nasty and hungry variants that much of the people above are now descended from. Sadly, they have ever tried to rise above their station. To wear clothes and worship our gods in hopes of being like us. To eat the flesh of others like them. They believed they could become like the K'nyanians but they can't be. Only a rare few human bloodlines carry any of our line and we do our best to bring them back to the People."

"The creatures outside looked from pig to man, and from man to pig, and from pig to man again; but already it was impossible to say which was which," I said, reciting the final line of *Animal Farm*. It seemed almost hilarious in retrospect. Or maybe I was laughing so I didn't scream.

"Yes," Annie said. "You are not one of them. Your mother is a lost one of our kind. You know that now, don't you?"

"Yes," I whispered. Somehow, I did. Ever since I'd been here and experienced the dream, I'd felt like I was falling deeper and deeper into a dark new world that I would never escape. Now, I knew there was no escape, and I was destined to spend the rest of my life here in the darkness. As Nietzsche would say, I had stared into the abyss and now it was staring back at me.

"Your mother knew what you were," Annie whispered. "How could she not? She arranged for you to become the Professor's student and come here. A place that would awaken your long-buried side. She knew, just as I did, that you would be able to enter the gateways meant for ghouls and other creatures of our gods. It was important we bring you here now."

"Why now?" I said, my throat dry and my stomach aching.

"It is almost time," Annie said. "The humans have boiled the Earth's oceans and awakened the sleepers. This is not the first time they have stirred but may well be the last. We must recall our children and hide below in our warrens where we will survive the Rising. Only then can we exit out into what brave new world we might find."

I would have cried but I already felt myself changing into something that held no tears. Something *hungry*. Everything around me suddenly smelled so delicious, overwhelming any disgust or lingering humanity I possessed; humanity that I'd never possessed it turned out. "I need to eat. Please."

Annie stroked my face, and I felt the fur on her hand "Then let us eat. It would be wrong to let it go to waste."

And God help me, I did.

"The Urge" is another novelette written for The Book of Ghouls. *In this case because the anthology had come up a bit short. However, necessity is the mother of invention, and I got a chance to write a story about Jackie Howard from* Cthulhu Armageddon. *This takes place sometime before* The Tree of Azathoth *but after the character has moved to the Dreaming City. It's a noir detective story and very strongly inspired by the TV movie Cast a Deadly Spell.*

Despite the Mythos being very common in the Dreaming City, I think this is actually closer to Lovecraft's storytelling than my work usually is. I'm particularly proud of the ending.

THE URGE

A *Cthulhu Armageddon* short story

Chapter One

"So, you want me to kill your son, huh?" I asked, taking my hands out of the pockets of my waist coat to adjust the fedora on my head. A lot of folks didn't much care for a woman wearing man's clothing in the Dreaming City. The Dreamlands liked everything anachronistic, but I was a private dick and I sure as shit wasn't going to be running after targets in high heels or tight dresses.

Across from me in the apothecary shop were my two potential suckers, er, I mean customers, who were bald-headed with large ears as well as visible canines whenever they opened their mouth. Just inhuman enough to let people know they weren't your typical Dreamlander humans. I could see past the glamours they wore to the canine horrors beneath, just like they could see past my visage, but we all preferred to wear masks when living topside.

The shop was a typical one in that it catered to superstitious, dabblers, and alternative medicine types far more than it did the serious professionals. In the Dreaming City, everyone could wield magic if they set their minds to it but most of us preferred to keep it at arm's length. The price for real sorcery was your sanity and most people preferred frog legs tea and fake rhino horn for their remedies over the actual juju powered by the Old Ones.

Walter Crait, the husband, was wearing a pair of black slacks and a plain white t-shirt with an apron over it. "No, we don't want our son killed, Ms. Howard. We want Martin taken back alive if possible."

"Call me Jackie," I said. "It's the at all possible part that I wanted to clarify on. If your son has gone feral then there's not necessarily much that I can do about that."

Feral ghouls were something of an ugly stereotype among our people, but it was something that still had a basis in reality. For all the hate groups' propaganda that every ghoul was a ticking time bomb to cannibalistic berserker rages, it only happened to a few troubled souls. Usually, they were changelings that couldn't handle the transformation from humanity to ghouldom and retreated into a savage animalistic predator state.

Mrs. Linda Crait put on a pair of bifocals as she wore a plain blouse and floor length blue dress. "It's not that he's gone feral. It's more complicated than that."

"Uncomplicate it then," I said, dryly. "Because every minute we talk here is another one I could be looking for him or you could be finding a new shamus because I won't take a case where my clients hold out on me."

"Please you're the only one we can trust," Walter said.

"That remains to be seen," I said, crossing my arms. "I may be furry underneath this red hair and white skin but don't try and pull any of this 'we're all in this together' bull crap. I was raised on the surface of the Earth by humans."

There was a sharp divide in the Dreaming City among the ghouls who could be called "orthodox" and "secular" if you needed to put labels on it. The orthodox ghouls were the ones who had been raised underground or in the Dreaming City's vast warrens. The secular, mostly changelings but some half-breeds like myself, were as often as not people who had been brought up among the people we later learned to eat. I'd been lucky to grow up with parents who didn't care I was a monster, mostly because they were monsters themselves, but that left me distinctly isolated from what was supposed to be a big extended family.

Bullcrap.

"It's the Urge," Linda said, finally admitting what they'd been holding out on.

"Ah," I said, as if that explained everything and it did. The Urge was a primal instinct among the ghouls, as much as our need to eat the flesh of sentient beings. It was the urge to reproduce. Not the urge to have sex, which ghouls roughly had the same level of as humans. No, it was instead a kind of primordial need to either sire an heir or carry one to term that started as an unpleasant itch before gradually dominating your thoughts. The term "biological clock is ticking" didn't work as a metaphor unless the biological clock was a time bomb. "So, he needs to find a mate, put a bun in the oven, and hunt for a few byakhee eggs to impress the lucky lady's parents. What's the problem? Is he gay? Commitment phobic? Bad breath?"

According to legend, it had been placed into the ghoul species by Tsathoggua to guarantee the immortal species kept reproducing. Why he/she/it thought this would be a problem with ghouls unlike virtually every other species in the cosmos was anyone's guess but there it was.

The Urge was nondiscriminatory and a major source of upheaval among the secular ghouls. Couples were routinely broken up, families destroyed, and religious vows violated when the Urge struck an individual that needed to find the most suitable mate possible in short order. Thankfully, it only happened about every hundred years but meant that it could add up when some ghouls I knew were old enough to remember when the oceans drank Atlantis.

"Martin is a self-hating ghoul," Walter said, softly. "He was the product of one of my dalliances in the mortal world during my own Urge period."

"Your wife is very understanding," I said, sarcastically.

"I took him as my own once he became part of our household." Linda shrugged. "I conceived a daughter later during my Urge. These things happen."

"He grew up among human parents until I was able to rescue him from them at age twenty," Walter said, pausing. "It was very traumatic to find out his true nature and took many years for him to adjust."

"Uh huh," I said, getting bored. "Could you jump to the part why he's going insane?"

"He promised he would never pass along his cursed blood," Walter said, gesturing to the apothecary shelves. "So, Martin took the Milk of Ghataskhi and destroyed his ability to sire. The Urge remains, though."

I stared at them. "You're telling me that your son disappeared, has probably lost his mind, may start attacking people soon, and is almost certainly going to contribute to more people in the Dreaming City hating us because he gave himself an alchemical vasectomy?"

"Yes," Walter said, nodding. "He must be brought back so the Ritual of Tayah'nal'oo can be performed."

I nodded. "Which I clearly know."

"It will spawn a child from his blood," Linda said. "A homunculus that will satisfy the Urge for the next century."

I looked between them. "And I take it he didn't like this option when it was explained to him the first time?"

Homunculi were little, tiny wizard and priestly servants that barely had any sentience. They were the kind of thing that got out into the city at large and ended up scurrying in the shadows after their masters died, living off blood and vermin. Knowing they were the product of someone's own blood but denied any chance at a real life made my skin crawl. Why was it there didn't seem to be any magic that wasn't inherently vile?

"He refused," Linda said. "Now he has no choice."

I didn't want to point out he very much had a choice. It was a choice between becoming a monster in mind as well as body, creating a monster, or merciful death as a man.

"Alright, I'll take the case," I said, knowing I was going to regret it. "Now we just have to discuss my fee."

Thankfully, it turned out selling exotic animal parts and powdered flowers to suckers paid well and I had a small black ruby from Leng with the promise of another one should I bring him back alive. Killing Martin was something they absolutely wanted to avoid but I got the impression both parents considered it to be preferable to his succumbing to madness. The rest of the ghoul community would come down on them and the Dreaming City's authorities on ghouldom if he ended up murdering humans in his madness. Feral ghouls threatened the fragile peace between all the peoples in the Dreamlands and the Craits had a few hundred other children from their millennia of life to worry about.

Unfortunately, when I arrived at my office, I found another complication waiting for me. He was trouble, I could tell with his sharp dress sense, nice shoes, black jacket, black tie, blond hair, and pretty boy features. Late twenties to early thirties and from money. Worse, I could tell he was one of the most dangerous things a human could be in the Dreaming City: an academic. The little golden Greek letter pin on his lapel told me he was from the University.

"Ms. Howard?" the man spoke in the kind of generic New England accent the upper crust tended to speak around here despite the fact New England hadn't existed for centuries, at least the one I was from. But I was hardly the one to complain about anachronism.

My office was a study in contrasts and stereotypes both. It had a desk covered in files, a bookshelf of bad detective fiction, a coatrack with a hidden gun in the spare trench coat I kept there, and a window showing the Dreaming City outside. The Dreaming City was a composite of just about everyone's dreams, at least among humans, of what a bustling metropolis should be.

It was a refuge for some people, a prison for others. In an infinite multiverse of worlds all doomed to die at the hands of the Great Old Ones when they rose, it was a waystation for those refusing to die just yet. The way I perceived it was something around the 1940s due to all the old comic books I'd used to read during my mortal years: Batman, Superman, and Dick Tracy. Other people? Well, the city was in the eye of the beholder. I imagined some people saw it as more akin to ancient Sumner or Tenochtitlan.

"That's what it says on my door," I said, walking toward my desk. "I see you just let yourself in?"

"The super says you haven't paid your rent in two months and agreed to show me the place," the man said, calmly.

Being a detective in the Dreaming City should have been easy given all the secrets everyone was hiding but the problem was that most people were more interested in keeping them covered up than paying to discover them. It also didn't help that the demihuman peoples, like ghouls and Deep Ones, preferred to solve things in-house. The fact I'd been hired by the Craits was something of a minor miracle and I had to wonder if that meant the elders of the local clan had advised them on a more extreme solution regarding Martin. But what could be more extreme than killing him? I was missing something.

I frowned before flopping myself down in the swivel chair behind my desk. "Yeah, well, I'll be dealing with that soon. May I ask who the hell you are and what you want with me?"

"My name is Percival Madison," the man said, giving a name that positively oozed class. "I'm a graduate student at the University."

"Nice to meet you, Percy," I said, putting my hands behind my head and leaning back. "How can I help you?"

"I want to help you find Martin," Percy said, looking down at my chest as I stretched before up at my face. Men were men, easily fooled by appearances. I wondered just what he would think if he could see the real me. Then again, many men of my acquaintance didn't care if they didn't have to. That was the key to a successful relationship in my opinion: dishonesty.

"News travels fast," I said, pausing. "No offense, you don't strike me as the kind of person the Craits would tell their business too."

"On the contrary, I'm an old friend of the family," Percy said, adjusting his tie. "My area of special concern is human-ghoul relations. I'm the author of *On the Origins and Culture of Ghouls*. That was my thesis and a project Martin helped on."

"Get out," I said, gesturing to the door. "I'm not a science experiment or something for you to study."

"I know where Martin is and what he's up to," Percy said. "And it could be the answer to something I've been working on for years."

I paused, sighing. "Alright, you have five minutes, Pretty Boy. You realize that your friend did something stupid and is probably going to get so horny now that he gnaws someone's face off, right?"

The Urge was one of two ways that ghouls tended to end up going feral. If you didn't have a child in a century then it would take over. The other was refusing to eat the flesh or brains of sentient people. A ghoul who didn't indulge in cannibalism, if you considered eating humans or other thinking creatures that, was one who would also lose his mind. We had to spread our existence and be the boogeymen or feed on other races' dead if we didn't want to become the monsters that others feared us to be.

"Yes," Percy said, shaking his head. "I encouraged Martin to not feel disgust toward who he was and simply do what was necessary. Instead, he rejected that and now seeks an alternative means to cure himself of what he views as a disease."

I found myself annoyed by Percy almost instantly as there was only one person more annoying than someone who hated ghouls for what they were born as: someone who was intrigued by us as something exotic and alluring. I didn't want to have to deal with any werewolf fanboys or cannibal enthusiasts.

"You said you knew where he is and what he's doing," I said, dryly. "Get to it."

Percy nodded. "Our studies extensively examined the idea that ghouls were the products of the Great Old Ones modifying one of the races they encountered on their long journey to Earth from Vhoorl, in the 23rd Nebula. Possibly Xoth where Cthulhu mated with Idh-yaa. It is there they developed their ability to shapeshift and mate with any—"

"Speak English, Doc," I said, having absolutely no care about the places and planets humans speculated the supernatural came from. Some things were beyond mortal comprehension and nothing good ever came from trying to figure them out. A surprising thing for a private detective to claim but life was just full of little ironies.

"I'm only a Master of Anthropology," Percy said, sheepishly. "He wants to summon Azathoth, Sultan of All Demons, to make him pure."

Chapter Two

The hairs on the back of my neck stood up, which was damn impressive if you knew how many I had underneath my glamour.

"Azathoth?" I asked, staring at him. "Isn't that like summoning God to change a flat tire?"

I wasn't a witch or occult scholar, but I'd heard enough crazy talk from cultists as well as my fellow demihumans to get the basic gist. There were the Great Old Ones, the Other Gods, Yog-Sothoth, and above even that was Azathoth. Azathoth was the supreme being in the multiverse, existing in the heart of creation and destruction as the entity that bound all living things. Unlike most creator deities, though, it was pointless to worship him because he was both blind and dumb. Also insane. Which explained a lot about the universe once you thought about it.

"The madness of Martin's plot is known to me," Percy said, pulling out a pair of spectacles and starting to clean them with an honest-to-God silk handkerchief. Seriously, he was way too posh for my office. "Unfortunately, that doesn't mean he's not capable of doing what he intends to do."

"Explain to me what you mean by that as if you assume my formal education is this much." I lifted two fingers and pressed them together. I'd not even been born in the City but a dead world village where the height of technology had been a windmill-powered generator and a gas guzzling Corvette left over from before the world ended.

Percy put on his pair of glasses and looked damn good in them. "The University has many relics acquired from the waking world, even places that are no longer in existence or away from the various permutations of the Earth. One of these is an alleged relic of the Xothian ancestor race of the ghoul species, the one Martin and I dubbed the Efreet, after the—"

"Yes, genies," I said, knowing that much.

"Err, not quite but close enough for the layman," Percy said, having that kind of 'I want to lecture on this subject but am not going to' that a lot of male intellectuals just loved. I hated that it turned me on. "Either way, the Pipes of the Demon Sultan—"

"Did you name it that?" I asked, raising an eyebrow.

"Maybe," Percy said, abashed. "Either way, the Pipes of the Demon Sultan were said to be something used by the Xothian Efreet to summon manifestations of Azathoth during the cosmic alignments. The Xothian Efreet would then bind the blind idiot god's avatars and force them to grant wishes."

"So, it summons genies who grant wishes," I said, nodding. It wasn't the weirdest shit I'd encountered in my time as a gumshoe, not by far. "Maybe we should let him do it. If he hates being a ghoul that much, becoming a human might not be the worst thing. Mind you, I bet his parents would just consider that a death sentence by other means. What? Thirty or forty more years of life? Barely an eyeblink in a ghoul's life."

Percy's expression told me I was missing something. "I'm afraid it isn't that simple."

"It never is," I said, sighing. "So, pretty boy, what is the downside that I'm missing for him tooting his own horn?"

"Pipes," Percy corrected. "The Xothian Efreet were a space capable people that rode byakhee to uninhabited systems across the galaxy to perform their summonings. That is because each of the systems would subsequently develop a black hole."

I blinked slowly. "That seems bad."

"You could say that," Percy said.

"That sounds city-destroying bad," I repeated.

"Yes," Percy said. "It's difficult to speculate on what exactly a gravity singularity would do in a reality formed from consciousness but the City and all surrounding lands for as far as the mind can conceive."

Something wasn't adding up. "So, why the hell would Martin want to summon the Big Bad Demon God? It doesn't seem like being human would be worth it if it meant dragging the entirety of the world down with him."

Percy frowned. "I don't know. He should know better."

I nodded. "Well, thank you for your tip, Percy. Did you tell the authorities?"

Percy narrowed his eyes. "The only people I trust less with the Pipes of the Demon Sultan than Martin would be the police. If they somehow did manage to stop him, a miracle, then it would end up on sale to some rich dabbler with more money than knowledge. Then the world would certainly be doomed."

It was a surprisingly sensible decision from someone who clearly came from money and didn't have the kind of experience with cops I did. "Smart move. Still, I think this is where we part ways."

"I need to come with you," Percy said, simply. "Only I can possibly talk Martin down and the Pipes must be retrieved for safekeeping. They are vital evidence in proving my thesis on ghoul origins."

He was smart not to trust me even if I didn't want a planet destroying magic wish-granting device. You could never be too careful in the big city. "Sorry, Pretty Boy, I work alone."

"I can tell you where Martin's apartment is."

"His parents already gave me the address," I said.

"His real apartment."

Percy owned a 1930 Rolls Royce Phantom that he gave me a lift in toward the nice part of town. He was packing a Colt Detective Special in a holster under his jacket as well. We were nearby a set of art deco apartments that were in a nearly completed building, all glass, and weird angles. It was not yet for sale but still being shown to the public. Apparently, Martin had been using the basement for his research after bribing the owners.

"Why have a separate apartment?" I asked, sitting across from him as we found a parking place.

"The University is riddled with cultists and wannabe wizards," Percy replied. "When we discovered the nature of the Pipes, we decided to continue our research into the origins of ghouldom and their connection to the Xothian artifacts we'd found in private."

I could have asked him why he thought Martin was any better hands for this weird world-destroying magic. Or him for that matter. Anyone having weird world-destroying magic. Instead, I asked something personal. "So, why are you interested in ghoul history?"

"Why not ghoul history?" Percy asked, surprised.

"Most humans who study us just want to figure out how to kill us easier," I said, shrugging. "It's the immortal shape-changing cannibal werewolf thing. It's a real turn off to most people."

If Percy found my joke funny or even noticed it was a joke, he didn't give any indication. "I believe history is the key to learning how to understand one another. Humans, Deep Ones, Yigians, and perhaps even other more inhuman species. The truth will set us free."

His naiveité was touching. "The only two species that get along in the Dreamlands are humans and cats. That's because humans are enslaved by felines and happily so."

Stepping out of the car, I headed to the bulkhead entrance to the apartments. I had my Colt single action army revolver drawn. The single greatest handgun ever invented. I didn't expect Martin to have succumbed to feraldom yet, but I wasn't discounting the Urge was already affecting his sanity. That might have been the reason for his cockamamie plan to summon Azathoth and become a real boy. The thing was that the Urge usually made you want to gnaw people's faces off rather than practice black magic. I needed more information on what was going on.

Reaching the door, I tested the knob and found it to be unlocked. Which was a good sign as it indicated Martin might have been home. Kicking the door open, I found myself in a place less like a proper bachelor apartment and more like some paranoiac's mind prison. There were papers taped up against the walls, scattered across the floor, a literal drawing board filled with illustrations, and a collection of stone artifacts scattered about that had probably been lifted from the University. On one side of the wall, there was a set of star charts for a corner of the Milky Way I wasn't familiar with, and the word FREEDOM written across it in red paint. It was right next to a map of downtown. Near the open door to the bathroom was a large two-door wardrobe. The place smelled of stale coffee, cigarettes, incense, and blood—which was never a good combination. No sign of Martin himself.

"Your friend needs to hire a cleaning lady," I said, putting away my gun. "Does he normally decorate in crazy?"

Percy followed me in. showing he was at least willing to follow my lead in dangerous situations. Good, doing otherwise would have gotten him killed. "No, I can definitely say this is new. Normally, Martin is extremely tidy."

"Is it possible someone tossed the place?" I asked, looking around.

"Perhaps," Percy said, picking up some of the papers on the ground. "This is definitely our research, though. Except he's gone off on a large number of tangents that seem extremely speculatory."

"Define speculatory," I said, wondering if this was a case of an academic having gone off his gourd because he'd seen things man was not meant to know. I'd never heard of it happening to a ghoul before, but it wasn't *impossible*.

"Martin and I had some luck translating fragments of the Xoth tablets recovered by some Leng traders," Percy replied. "The tablets are older than anything other than Elder Thing writing or the text on the walls of R'lyeh itself. They spoke of the society that existed on Xoth and what may have happened to it. The Efreet's, I mean."

"No offense but that was like a billion years ago," I said, confused. "Who gives a shit?"

Surprisingly, Percy didn't correct my estimate of how long ago it probably was. "The dinosaurs were not yet even evolved, let alone humanity by this time. Still, he was particularly interested in the legends of the Old Ones bringing the ghoul race with them and, more precisely, how they had uplifted them."

"Uplifted?" I asked.

"Granted immortality, shape-changing, and sapience," Percy rattled off those facts. "Supposedly, the Xothians were nothing more than savage animals before they were blessed by the travelers from the stars. The Great Old Ones named their race as the K'nyanians and made them chief among their servitors. Ghoul creation legends are transmitted orally by tradition but enough of them have been written down to give a sense of how their religion functions to even an inquisitive outsider."

"Ah, it's a religion thing," I said, regretting bringing it up. "That explains it. People get really antsy when you start poking holes in their creation myth. I knew one Deep One fisherman who took a harpoon to his brother's head when he suggested that, maybe, Cthulhu didn't consider the fishmen to be his holy heirs but just vermin setting up in his tomb while he slept."

"Hmm," Percy said, clearly not listening as he continued to examine the documents. "He's cross referenced the Elder Things civilization and Great Race as well as lack of fossil record regarding anything other than those two periods before the Hyborian Age. I don't understand what his point is, though."

"Yeah, well a fossil record is hard to verify in the Dreamlands. Maybe we evolved here." I turned to him before realizing I was distracted by his presence. So much so, I'd wanted him to ramble on about this nonsense rather than shut up as I'd normally do so.

Dammit.

Not now.

I had my own problems to deal with.

"Unlikely," Percy replied. "The Dreamlands is immaterial and immortal. Ghouls can leave and enter physically but the life processes of the mortal world don't happen naturally. Traditional bioscience and alchemy show that ghouls had to have evolved in the Waking World originally before migrating here. Same as humans."

"It sounds like you both need a girlfriend," I said, pausing. "Or boyfriend, I'm not judgy."

Percy looked up from the papers, annoyed. I hoped he wasn't one of those weirdos who were fine with ghouls but got bigoted about his own kind. "Martin's issues with sex are part of the reason we're here. As for me, I don't lack for female attention. I was married until recently to a Jewish woman named Sonia. Sadly, it didn't work out. I was too much of a homebody for her."

Good, then I wouldn't have to kill her. Dammit, of all the ironies. Now I was dealing with it. "So, any luck on finding out where he is?"

Percy walked up to the star chart on the wall. "Unfortunately, about the only thing I can confirm is that he's worked on reconstructing the original Efreet ritual to summon Azathoth and definitely plans to perform it somewhere here in the city. Specifically, the downtown area."

"So somewhere among a million or so residents, great," I muttered. "Any idea when this world-destroying ritual is supposed to happen?"

"Tomorrow night," Percy said.

"Of course it is," I muttered. "It's never in three thousand years or last month but you missed it."

"Much experience in world ending disasters?" Percy asked.

"No, but I know every cult in the city looks forward to the end of the world," I replied. "They always think that they'll either be spared or are crazy enough not to care. One thing that puzzles me, though."

"One thing?" Percy asked, sarcastically.

Okay, he had a point there. "One of the things that puzzles me is why Martin is going so hard on all this ghoul stuff if he hates being one."

Percy looked confused. "Martin doesn't hate being a ghoul."

I blinked. "What?"

"He hates being part-human," Percy said. "Being a ghoul is something that makes him feel immensely proud. He despises that his father mated with a woman in the Waking World. All our work together was accompanied by things like, 'you are a credit to your race', and 'if only you'd been born better.'"

I believed him. "The Craits have been lying to me. Either that or they have no idea what their child has been up to."

That was when there was a banging noise in the wardrobe. I wasn't sure what the hell I might find inside. Approaching as I gestured for Percy to stand back, the doors to the wardrobe burst open and a fur-faced ghoul in a cap, linen shirt, and pants burst out. It wasn't attempting to attack, though, but bowl past us. Rather than shoot him in the back, I holstered my weapon before running after him.

"Stop!" I shouted, not exactly having time to be eloquent as I went after the furry bastard.

I managed to catch up quickly while he went up the stairs, tackling him to the ground.

"Don't hurt me!" the ghoul said, sounding all too human. This was probably not one of the older members of our race. They tended to be less of, well, a wimp.

I lifted back my fist. "Who the hell are you and where is Martin?"

"My name is L-Leonard," the ghoul said. "I d-don't know where Martin is."

"What's your relationship to him?" I asked.

"I w-work at the funeral home, Restful Hearts," the ghoul said. "I get him the parts he needed."

"You're his dealer?" I asked, shaking my head.

As mentioned, ghouls needed the flesh of sentient beings to keep our head on straight. For the ghouls who belong to the orthodox sects, they tunneled through the Dreamlands into the various mortal worlds to steal the bodies of the buried dead. Hopefully ones without all the nasty formaldehyde and other chemicals that ruined the taste. For those of us who lived a more secular life, well, we had to find our own bodies to munch on. I'll be honest, you didn't want to know what happened to the bodies of the guys I had to polish off during my private detective work. I mean, I didn't set out to do it. I wasn't a serial killer, just the regular kind. For money and usually in self-defense. The other guys were assholes. Okay, I was making myself sound like a monster even to myself. Oh well, waste not want not.

"Yeah," Leonard said, frowning. "He stiffed me on the last batch too! I can't even afford a good glamour anymore! I can't do my job looking like this! I'm going to have to move back to my clan."

I got up off him. "You poor thing. Well, we need to find him or we're all going to have a helluva lot more problems than unpaid bills."

"I think I may have a way of finding him," Percy said, heading up the stairs. In his hand was a clump of fur, Martin's I presumed.

"Let me guess," I said, sighing. "Magic."

"Magic," Percy said.

Chapter Three

"I hate magic," I muttered, keeping my hands in my pockets as we walked down the streets of Downtown.

"It's just a tool. Neither good nor evil," Percy said, holding up an ornate bronze compass that had an elaborately etched star on the bottom that made me uncomfortable just looking at it. Inside the compass was stuffed bits of Martin's fur, a piece of paper containing his true name, and a punch of doodles that I didn't understand the meaning of.

Percy was apparently an amateur thaumaturge and while a rare skill on Earth among humans, was common as dirt among the educated classes of the city. It was the same as most places in the Dreamlands as every priest, king, and advisor depended on sorcery to survive against the real powers of the universe. At least the ones humans could even conceive of opposing.

Which wasn't many.

I rolled my eyes before pulling out one of my hands and sticking a thumb out that I aimed at my heart. "See, that's what humans say and they're always wrong. My mother was a witch, and my father was a dabbler. Every time they used sorcery, it made them worse people. No matter the reason, good, bad, or indifferent. They both said, come on, Jackie, everyone uses magic. Well, not me. I may need a shoeshine and am back on my rent, but no one has a lien on my soul. I own it free and clear."

I did know a bit of magic myself. My mother had taught me how to edit memories and how to lull most men as well as some women into loving you. Neither of which were things that I particularly wanted to demonstrate. Magic wasn't inherently evil according to the people I knew but it always seemed to end up being used for the basest most selfish reasons.

"Is that from a movie?" Percy asked, still staring at the compass. We'd been walking around downtown for hours, and I was starting to think this had been an enormously bad idea. And by starting, I meant I'd started thinking that and was about ready to hurl the goddamn compass into the bay. Just as soon as I bummed a lift off Percy to the docks.

I grimaced, turning away. "I may be paraphrasing 1991's *Cast a Deadly Spell*. They showed it here at the movie theatre last year, or was it twenty years ago? Eh, time runs weird around here. I remembered the speech, at least."

"Mmm hmm," Percy said, not looking up. "By your parents, I assume you mean your adoptivee parents?"

"Yeah," I muttered. "My birth mother didn't survive birthing me. How did you know?"

"You are very human for a ghoul," Percy said. "Even a hybrid."

"Is that an insult or a compliment?" I asked, curious.

"Yes," Percy said, looking up. "We're here."

"You're kidding," I said, looking up. We were now just outside the Randolph Carter History Museum, devoted to trying to make some sort of narrative from the imagination of Earth's greatest dreamer. It was a big blocky building that dominated a large chunk of the area despite the fact its real estate would have been more valuable given over to a skyscraper or bank. None of the city council would touch the place, though, due to the fear of offending its subject.

At least among humans, Randolph Carter had created the Dreaming City from his longing for New England during his quest to find Unknown Kadath. Apparently, he had done such a good job the gods of Kadath had taken up residency here for a few years and populated the place with their spawn. I didn't take that kind of thinking too seriously since every mythology seemed to want to make its people the children of gods.

"The compass doesn't lie," Percy said. "He's inside."

"Martin? Inside? Right now?" I asked, honestly surprised this had worked.

"That is what I mean," Percy said, frowning. "This is a very good place for him to do the ritual."

"How is that?" I asked, confused. "Seems pretty public."

"Not when it's closed," Percy said. "Which happened a few minutes ago. The best ritual rooms cost upward of $200,000 in Republic dollars or an equivalent in gold. The Carter History Museum has its own on display that could be easily repurposed. It also wouldn't require Martin to involve any of the local lodges or fraternities."

"So, he's doing the End of the World on the cheap," I said, sarcastically.

"World ending magic is expensive. Far more so than a professor can afford, even tenured," Percy said in such a deadpan tone I didn't know if he was joking or not.

"So, we just go in there, beat the living crap out of him, take the Pipes, and the world is saved?" I said, pounding my fist into my palm. "I like this plan."

"That's not a plan," Percy said. "Especially if Martin brought along his henchmen."

"His what now?" I asked, doing a double take. "He has *henchmen* now?"

"Henchpersons. Henchthings. Students," Percy replied, frowning. "Ones taken advantage of by Martin's charisma and belief that he is onto something glorious about the origins of the ghoul race. Ones that believe he might be able to share the immortality of the ghoul race and perhaps induce transformations."

I stared at Percy. "That's not describing students. That's describing a cult. You didn't think a cult was worth mentioning?"

"I'm mentioning it now," Percy said. "Albeit, I probably should have mentioned it earlier."

"You think?" I asked. "Maybe we should have brought that Leonard guy. An extra pair of hands in getting Martin to cough up what he owes might have been helpful."

"Assuming he was telling the truth," Percy said, frowning. "There's something very strange going on here."

"You mean aside from a guy who wants to destroy the world so he can get wishes," I replied. "Which seems to be a dumb action since the world is kind of necessary to enjoy the wishes. Assuming you're wishing for anything normal."

Which was a big if.

"Yes, aside from that," Percy said, frowning.

"You may be right," I said, frowning. "In any case, I can see everyone already leaving through the front door. If we're going to get into this place, I suggest we take the back."

"If we're doing the rush him plan."

"So, yes."

Percy put away his compass and nodded.

Breaking into the museum was easy for someone who had been breaking into buildings for the better part of decades. Private detectives weren't supposed to break the law as part of their job but the laws in the Dreaming City were more suggestions than hard rules. Technically, I was pretty sure liquor was still illegal because it had been when Randolph Carter had dreamed the place into existence. The people who hired me as their private dick did so because they knew I'd be going the extra mile.

Now, I was going the extra mile to save the world or, at least, the city. Allegedly. I was presently hoping Percy was full of crap and he was confusing some conch shell or old ghoul relic as something that could summon the God of Gods. Even in the Dreamlands, the kind of magic that could do that was rare as a night-gaunt's teeth.

The interior of the museum looked pretty much as you'd expect a place like it would: full of trinkets and bones left over from the remains of what people alleged to be Randolph Carter's adventures. He was an interesting character even if you didn't buy into his mythology and one of the few humans that even orthodox ghouls spoke of with reverence. There were relics of Ulthar, a gallery of Pickman originals, historical artifacts from Celephaïs, and rebuilt temples to both Nyarlathotep as well as Nodens.

Unfortunately, what we didn't find was any sign of Martin or his so-called cult. We managed to avoid the underpaid rent-a-cops that oversaw protecting the museum, which frankly was not difficult because they were trying very hard not to see us or anything else that might end up killing them messily and without great difficulty. Eventually Percy's compass led us to an empty exhibit room with no sign of the man. There was just a bare tile floor and white brick walls with a mirror covering one.

"Well, if the world ends because we can't find the guy, I will laugh," I muttered, not actually finding it funny at all.

"I don't understand," Percy said, looking at the compass.

"It doesn't work, what's to understand," I replied. "Maybe Martin has worked up some juju to protect himself from being found."

"If he was that good of a magician then he wouldn't need a stolen artifact to make himself pure," Percy said, walking around in a circle.

"By pure, you mean—" I still wasn't getting this. Being distracted by the beginnings of the Urge wasn't helping matters.

"A ghoul with no human blood," Percy replied.

That was the part I didn't get. "Yeah, but ghouls with human blood and without it are the same, aren't they? They wouldn't be able to mate otherwise."

"That was always a question of our research," Percy replied. "The closest answer we were ever able to get from ghouls or doctors was, 'it's magic. Don't question it.'"

I got the impression that answer didn't fully satisfy Percy even if it worked for me. "Yeah, well, Pretty Boy you..." That was when I smelled something very familiar: blood.

"What?" Percy asked.

"Here," I said, going up the mirror. "It's coming from inside here."

Percy walked up to the mirror that just showed our reflections. The glass was unusually dark, though, and I could feel the smell of blood wafting from within. There were other smells as well, fire and incense.

"I see," Percy said, reaching into the mirror and causing it to ripple like a pool of water.

"This is gonna suck," I muttered.

"Probably," Percy said, pulling out his gun before stepping through the mirror.

I followed him.

The sight that greeted us on the other side of the looking glass was pretty much straight out of one of the Pulps I occasionally indulged in when bored out of my skull. There was a big pentagram made from red paint on the ground, an enormous altar in the center, and torches standing at strategic places throughout the large stone chamber that had ghastly statues spread throughout.

The thing that really gave the place its ambience, though, was the five black robed guys standing at the points of the star and the sixth looming over the altar. The only thing missing was a nubile young sacrifice on the altar, a shame really, and there was instead a weird, twisted horn with three ends. If you were to need an image for 'alien musical instrument', you could probably have done worse taking a picture of this thing.

There was a sky above us that depicted alien constellations that I didn't recognize as well as stars that were different colors from the ones that normally hung over the Dreaming City. Red, yellow, magenta, and colors only ghoul eyes had words for were present. I didn't know if we'd been transported into another dimension or were just in another part of the Dreamlands.

"The Xoth Exhibit," Percy said, instead, with pistol drawn. "It's not supposed to open for another month. You covered it up with a glamour."

Ah, more illusions. I pulled out my pistol as well and took aim.

"Yes," the central robed guy said, which I presumed to be Martin Crait. I couldn't tell at this angle and the fact he was wearing a particularly hideous wax mask of an eight eyed thing. His voice was muffled under the mask but still understandable. "It is a shame that no one will ever be able to see the research we did together, Percival, but a greater calling demands this reproduction of a long dead race's religion. I take it you are the woman that my so-called parents have hired to thwart me?"

"Jackie Howard, PI," I introduced myself. "Thwart is a strong word but they wanted me to bring you back to them before you did something stupid. They think you're going feral because you can't put a bun in some ghoul girl's oven. I'm getting the impression something much bigger is going on."

That was one thing I'd figured out when dealing with wizards, businessmen, and gangsters: they all loved to hear themselves talk. "Yes. You were not hired to retrieve me but to silence me. They hired you because you are an outsider and the truth that I hold in my heart is dangerous to all of those who are of ghoul blood."

I was very stupid with my next question. I should have just shot the guy and his goons then taken the pipes. I would have gotten paid either way. "What truth?"

"Ghouls are human," Martin said, his voice full of absolute loathing and disgust.

"Martin, we've talked about this," said Percy.

"They're human!"

"Okay, and?" I asked.

Martin pulled back as if I'd said something ludicrous. "The teachings of the ghoul race are that we came with the Great Old Ones from Xoth. That we were modified in their image and turned into their chosen servitors. Instead, this is all lies propagated by the priests and elders. The Great Old Ones came with no servitors resembling us! The original Xothian race were the flying polyps! Ghouls are just yet another offshoot of the infantile hominids the Elder Things experimented on. Warped by the dreams of the Sleeping Ones and no more their holy children than any other puerile mammal. The whole history of the ghoul race is falsehood based on superstition!"

"Okay, and?" I asked, not getting it.

"Fascinating," Percy said, clearly more interested in this than I was.

"Silence!" Martin shouted, balling his fists. "You do not understand, Ms. Howard." Men told me that a lot, usually in connection with who else they had been caught sleeping with. This time he might be telling me the truth. "You could not comprehend the burden of knowing that ghouldom is not the center of the universe! That we are but insignificant specks of nothing that have no role in the favored plans of the true masters of the cosmos!"

"No," I replied, honestly. "I can't say that I can. To have that illusion stripped away means I would have had to have believed I was the center of everything to begin with. I don't get why you intend to blow the horn of judgement, though. You going to summon up God just so you can spit in his face? If you are, respect for ambition, but I can't let you do that."

"I am going to make the ghoul race pure," Martin said, coldly. "To destroy this wretched half-existence and every other ghoul in the Dreamlands before rebirthing us as a new species! One that will—"

That was when I shot him. I emptied my revolver into the mad academic in what was probably murder but I considered to be justified because 'plotting to destroy the world and become a god' was basic grounds for execution in my opinion. A couple of his cultists ran to stop me, one of them drawing a sacrificial knife, but both went down in a hail of Percy's bullets. One day those guys are going to learn to carry guns, but this was not that day.

The others ran for the right side of the room where they opened a fire exit that had been covered up by the set design around us. Moonlight streamed in as the door burst open, before closing behind the fleeing grad students.

"Well, that was suspiciously easy," I said, walking over to Martin's body on the ground.

"Don't jinx us," Percy said, lowering his pistol and looking at the bodies of the two cultists he'd killed. "This is going to be hard to explain to the police."

"For twenty bucks each, I know five Micks who will swear you were playing poker with them all night," I said, looking down at Martin's body. He was still, one of the shots having gone through his heart. "Assuming you don't want to say you were with me instead. Which is an option."

"Excuse me?" Percy asked.

I reached down and removed Martin's mask, exposing the human-like furry face of a hybrid who hadn't completed the transformation between ghoul and man. It was less like the canine face of a true ghoul and more like the Wolfman played by Lon Chaney Junior. It was the face of a man who had been confronted with his humanity every time he looked in a mirror and undermined his sense of divine destiny.

"Yeah, I'm not getting paid, am I?" I muttered, wondering how I was going to explain this to his parents.

That was when someone hit me over the back of the head with a pistol grip.

Chapter Four

I admit, I was fully expecting to awaken to Percy standing over me with a smug expression on his face that said, 'Oh, ho, ho, ho, private detective lady, you fell for my trap. I used your attraction to me to manipulate you before betraying you in a way that should have been obvious from the start. Look at me being so rich, pretty, and smug.'

Okay, yeah, I had issues.

Blame the father of my first son, who I haven't mentioned for a reason. Instead, much to my surprise, I saw Percy was battered and blue next to me. He was tied up to one of the torch posts with his hands bound in rope. That wouldn't have kept him tied up, but I suspected he wasn't going anywhere from the beating he'd received. I, by contrast, felt unharmed but was presently tied to the altar where the Pipes of the Demon Sultan had been on display. Oh, and someone had taken my clothes.

Great.

Thanks for that.

I wondered if we'd missed some of Martin's followers but the answer to who was holding us prisoner came moments later when I saw the face of Mrs. Crait, wearing a plain summer dress but staring at me with empty soulless eyes. Mr. Crait was sharpening knives nearby, whistling a little Irish ditty.

Well, that was ominous.

I struggled in the ropes binding me. "I can understand how you might be upset at how my encounter with your son went. Given the unpleasantness involved, I'm willing to waive my fee and—"

"Those aren't the Craits,'" Percy said, looking up with one side of his glasses smashed in.

"Pardon?" I asked, looking down at him then at Linda and Walt.

"They're wearing their skins," Percy replied.

Linda just smiled and I saw her face twist and contort in a way not even a talented shapeshifter could pull off.

I blinked, processing that. "Huh. Just what the hell are you then? No, wait, let me guess. Great Race of Yith?"

"Very clever, Ms. Howard," said not-Walt.

Not that clever. When the perp was displacing someone else's mind so they could occupy the body, the most likely suspect was a race which had that as their standard MO.

"Yith?" said Percy, baffled. "What possible interest could you have in the origin of the ghouls?"

Non-Linda just looked at us with increasingly inhuman eyes.

"They're prospecting," I said. "Looking for new a territory to take over. A new species they can parasitize. The entire Yith population migrates together through time and space, taking over one species after another."

"Your work was very useful," said the fake Mrs Crait. "You discovered the Children of Xoth, whom we have only heard whispered of in legend. And Martin, with his obsession with ghoul lore, was able to find the Pipes which had for so long escaped us."

"And you just don't care about this world being destroyed," I said. "Because you'll all psychically teleport somewhere else before it happens. Leaving some other suckers in your bodies to get disintegrated. Like you always do."

"We will claim the bodies of the Xoth in the Cretaceous Period and move on when we are done with them," said non-Linda with a shrug. "We will survive all things."

Bizarrely, that meant that the Yith that existed sixty-five or sixty-seven million years ago were inhabiting the bodies of the Xoth. Except, this was a group of Yith from before then, who were now going back in time to take the Xoth's bodies, which they already had in my timeline, which would lead to the Xoth's extinction, which would lead to the ghouls claiming their origin story, which would lead to Percy here making a paper on them that the Yith would find, that would encourage them to steal the Xoth's bodies in the past that—Great Tsathoggua, I hated time travel.

"The human will tell us how to bring forth Azathoth and we will sing the song that ends this diseased illusion and get us the information we need to carry out our next Great Migration. We have not yet begun to torment him to bring out his secrets."

"Yeah, well, Percy is not nearly stupid enough—" I started to say, wanting the cops to show up for the first time in my life.

"Please don't hurt her," Percy said, speaking up. "I'll do what you say."

"Pretty boy, what are you doing?" I asked, confused. "If you help these people, then we'll all die."

"I love her," Percy said, speaking up and was either suffering a concussion or had lost all sanity. "If you promise to let her go, I'll tell you how to perform the ritual."

Martin and Linda exchanged a look.

"Agreed," Martin said, before I could point out that this would only get me an extra minute of so of life before the black hole swallowed everything.

Percy began reciting a spell of some kind that was clearly never meant for human tongues and sounded like he was clearing his throat. It would have been humorous if not for the fact I could hear scratching at the air like someone was starting to claw through an invisible wall. *"Ach'tang gh'tagh Azathoth. Ach'tang g'tagh Nyarlathotep. Gul'tum'ack Yog-Sothoth. Shakal'un'zabaalm!"*

The Yithians began repeating his words, speaking it far faster as well as like a choir.

"Maahch'tuul! Maahch'tuul! Naka Azathoth! Naka Azathoth!" Percy continued speaking. "Blow the horn that ends worlds! Release the Lord of All Djinn!"

"Stop this, Percy!" I shouted. "You can't want this to happen! Stop!"

That was when a single frightening note was blown upon the horn, and I would have done anything to make my ears burst at its presence. I could hear it joining a chorus of a hundred other awful instruments. The Yithians let forth a cheer, each speaking joyous praise to gods that felt nothing for them or any other being in the cosmos. Not even themselves.

Then silence.

The silence lasted a minute. "Percy?"

"I'm here," Percy said.

I opened my eyes and saw we were still in the room, but the flying polyps were gone. A trail of blood was coming from each of Percy's closed eyes, and I suspected he would never see again.

"What the hell just happened?" I asked. "The world didn't end. I think."

"The Pipes of the Demon Sultan are not limited to summoning Azathoth," Percy said, coughing. "They can also send you to his court at the center of the universe, or, well, galaxy. The translation is a bit iffy. Either way, I don't think we'll be seeing either of those two individuals again."

"Couldn't have happened to a nicer pair of people." I started gnawing on the ropes binding me with inhuman teeth, disrupting my glamour and revealing the hideous dog-like thing beneath. Once my arms were free, I ripped the ropes binding my legs away and went to Percy's side. I hated what I looked like and knowing that Percy would look upon my animalistic furred form with revulsion, especially since the Urge made it clearer with every moment, he was the one I wanted as my mate.

"I'm sorry. Maybe there's something we can do for your eyes."

"I doubt it," Percy said. "Even closed, my eyes witnessed things that burned away Sodom and Gomorrah."

"And that love stuff?" I asked.

"A trick," He said. "I'm sorry."

"It's fine," I said, feeling the side of his face with the tips of my fingers. "But I need something from you."

Percy didn't respond.

"Step away from the human," another voice spoke behind me.

There, Leonard was standing with a shotgun. Gone was the petrified looking drug dealer and in his place was a cold-blooded lupine with a face human enough to show off his inherent thuggishness.

"Oh, you've got to be kidding me," I said, turning my head. "What the hell do you want?"

"To silence the blasphemer," Leonard said, scowling. "I appreciate you finding Martin and his cult. I managed to get the three students who fled when they practically ran to my car. I'll deliver their bodies to the butcher, and they'll join the ranks of the city's missing soon enough. Martin, being one of us, will be burned."

I noticed his body was still off to one side, slowly rotting from where he'd died earlier. Like most men, he'd emptied his bowels upon death. Which, to ghouls, wasn't inherently disgusting to smell but certainly noticeable. There was no sign of the Pipes of the Demon Sultan and I hoped they'd gone with the Not-Craits to meet their god.

"Yeah, well, he's dead and I'm not getting paid," I said, keeping myself between him and Percy.

"He means me," Percy said, breathing softly but shallowly. "Don't you?"

"Yes," Leonard snarled, a look of disgust in his all-too-human eyes. "The Elders have demanded his death as well."

Great, so Leonard actually working for the orthodox ghouls. "He just helped save the world, jackass."

"He knows too much," Leonard said, growling. "The secrets of Xoth can never be shared."

I stared at him. "Seriously? This is all about the fact ghouls didn't come from another planet? Who cares."

"*I do*," Leonard said, growling. "Our society is kept together by the knowledge we are the Children of the Great Old Ones and that they are our mother, father, and masters. Without their power and judgment looming over us, our society would rip itself apart. People would lose all hope and become wild as the animals we truly descend from. That cannot be allowed."

I had to wonder about anyone who was only kept from going on a killing spree by the idea they'd be smacked down by a bunch of alien gods. "Listen, if it's not true then things like the Urge and feraldom can be treated. They're not some divine curse—"

Leonard lifted his shotgun. "Step aside, Jackie Howard. The only reason I am sparing your life is because you are kin to us. You may not acknowledge the bonds of blood that bind us all together, but I do."

"Let him do it,' Percy said, coughing. "The burden of the knowledge I carry can only cause more misery."

He sounded broken and I couldn't help but wonder if it was because we'd killed his friend, his life's work almost destroyed the world, or he'd gazed into the heart of the cosmos only to see a monster rather than a divinity.

"Alright," I said, slowly getting up. "I guess this has to end only one way."

"Good call," Leonard said, gesturing with his shotgun. "Get out of the way."

I responded by ripping his throat out with my teeth.

No one was going to harm my mate.

The steamer ship leaving the Dreaming City would head to Ulthar next and from there, we would seek out a fairy tunnel to take us to one of the many Earths that lay beyond the Dreamlands. The 1920s, 1940s, or 2000s were all time periods that were appropriate for living and well before the era when the Great Old Ones usually rose.

I stood on the deck, once more covered in a glamour and visibly pregnant with my second child. I was dressed as a proper lady, now, and while I hated it, it was a small sacrifice to make for my family. The Urge was satisfied and there was no need to continue the charade of being Percy's wife, but I'd grown accustomed, addicted you might say, to being his human consort. Like the fairy queens of old, I was playing the role of a housewife until the time that he passed away.

It would not be long.

Seeing the sight of Azathoth and his court, even though closed eyes, had stripped my husband of his health as well as his sight. He had only a few years left in him even with the magics I'd done to remove his memory of everything related to ghouldom, our history, the origins of the species, and the larger reality above us.

Percy had never held being a ghoul against me and I knew that he'd accepted me as I was. Yet, it was easier to believe the lie that I was a human woman once my magics got into his psyche.

Easier for his family, easier for society, and easier to keep him alive when the orthodox ghouls still wanted his head. All of Martin's papers had been burned and the University had repudiated their work once it had become clear they'd stolen artifacts like the Pipes of the Demon

Sultan. I suspected there were also human wizards who despised the notion that the races capable of interbreeding with mankind were closer to cousins than cuckoos.

When we reached Earth, probably New England, I intended to take away the rest of Percy's memories of the Dreaming City so he could enjoy his remaining years in peace. With any luck, he would forget his wife and child were monsters. There was no end of reasons for why a man might have lost his sight and memory after all. It was a violation of his free will and his magic, but I understood, now, why my mother did such things to her lovers. Why my own father had been troubled by his own terrible burden of knowledge that he had struggled with.

Because sometimes ignorance was bliss.

AUTHOR'S NOTE

I'd like to thank you for reading this book. The publishing industry is changing dramatically since the advent of eBooks. It is now very difficult to get any book noticed, regardless of quality. If you enjoyed this book, you could do some very simple things to help me attract attention. Word of mouth is the number one source of success for novels, so simply telling family and friends about the book is a great start.

Here are a few other ways of helping out, if you are so inclined:

* **Post a rating or review where you purchased the eBook**
* **Post a rating or review on Goodreads**
* **Talk about the book or write a review on Facebook**
* **Tell folks about the book in a blog post.**

If you like any of my other books, please feel free to check them out. A lot of my series are interlinked, and you never know when you'll find someone familiar showing up. Obviously, check out *Cthulhu Armageddon* if you'd like more of John's adventures. Also, if you liked the short stories here then know the other stories by other authors in The Books of Cthulhu (*Tales of the Al-Azif, Tales of Yog-Sothoth, Tales of Nyarlathotep, Time Loopers, The Book of Hastur*, and *The Book of Ghouls*) are fantastic.

MEET THE AUTHOR

C. T. Phipps is a lifelong student of horror, science fiction, and fantasy. An avid tabletop gamer, he discovered this passion led him to write and turned him into a lifelong geek. He is a regular blogger and also a reviewer for The Bookie Monster.

Bibliography

<u>Novels</u>

The Rules of Supervillainy (Supervillainy Saga #1)
The Games of Supervillainy (Supervillainy Saga #2)
The Secrets of Supervillainy (Supervillainy Saga #3)
The Kingdom of Supervillainy (Supervillainy Saga #4)
The Tournament of Supervillainy (Supervillainy Saga #5)
The Future of Supervillainy (Supervillainy Saga #6)
The Horror of Supervillainy (Supervillainy Saga #7)
Tales of Supervillainy: Cindy's Seven (Supervillainy Saga #8)
The Fall of Supervillainy (Supervillainy Saga #9)

I Was a Teenage Weredeer (The Bright Falls Mysteries, Book 1)

An American Weredeer in Michigan (The Bright Falls Mysteries, Book 2)
A Nightmare on Elk Street (The Bright Falls Mysteries, Book 3)

Esoterrorism (Red Room, Vol. 1)
Eldritch Ops (Red Room, Vol. 2)
The Fall of the House (Red Room, Vol. 3)

Agent G: Infiltrator (Agent G, Vol. 1)
Agent G: Saboteur (Agent G, Vol. 2)
Agent G: Assassin (Agent G, Vol. 3)

Cthulhu Armageddon (Cthulhu Armageddon, Vol. 1)
The Tower of Zhaal (Cthulhu Armageddon, Vol. 2)
The Tree of Azathoth (Cthulhu Armageddon, Vol. 3)

Lucifer's Star (Lucifer's Star, Vol. 1)
Lucifer's Nebula (Lucifer's Star, Vol. 2)

Straight Outta Fangton (Straight Outta Fangton, Vol. 1)
100 Miles and Vampin' (Straight Outta Fangton, Vol. 2)
Vampiraz4Life (Straight Outta Fangton, Vol. 3)

Wraith Knight (Wraith Knight, Vol. 1)
Wraith Lord (Wraith Knight, Vol. 2)
Wraith King (Wraith Knight, Vol. 3)

Dark Destiny (Dark Destiny, Vol. 1)
Destiny's Paradox (Dark Destiny, Vol. 2)

Brightblade (The Morgan Detective Agency, Book 1)

Daughter of the Cyber Dragons (The Cyber Dragons Series, Book 1)
Revenge of the Cyber Dragons (The Cyber Dragons Series, Book 2)
End of the Cyber Dragons (The Cyber Dragons Series, Book 3)

Space Academy Dropouts (The Space Academy Series, Book 1)
Space Academy Rejects (The Space Academy Series, Book 2)
Space Academy Washouts (The Space Academy Series, Book 3)

Moon Cops on the Moon (Moon Cops, Book 1)
Moon City Vice (Moon Cops, Book 2)

Psycho Killers in Love

Tales of an Eldritch Wasteland

Anthologies (as editor)
Blackest Knights
Blackest Spells
Tales of Capes and Cowls
Tales of the Al-Azif
Tales of Yog-Sothoth

Curious about other Crossroad Press books? Stop by our website:
http://crossroadpress.com
We offer quality writing
in digital, audio, and print formats.

Subscribe to our newsletter on the website homepage and receive a
free eBook.